My Brother, My Friend, My Enemy

Also by George Winston Martin

"I WILL GIVE THEM ONE MORE SHOT:"
Ramsey's 1st Regiment Georgia Volunteers

My Brother, My Friend, My Enemy

A Novel of the American Civil War

George Winston Martin

CreateSpace
2012

Front Cover Photos

Top Right: "Portrait of Pvt. William S. Askew, Company A, (Newnan Guards), 1st Georgia Infantry, C.S.A.," Reproduction # LC-B8184-10604, Library of Congress Prints and Photographs Division, Washington, D.C.

Top Left: Unknown Union artilleryman, 1864, collection of the author.

Bottom: "Antietam, Maryland. A lone grave," Reproduction # LC-DIG-cwpb-01109, Library of Congress Prints and Photographs Division, Washington, D.C.

Cover design by George W. Martin.

To Cathy
Who has always believed in me

This is a work of fiction. All of the characters, organizations and events portrayed in this novel are either the products of the author's imagination or are used fictionally.

We are not enemies, but friends. We must not be enemies. Though passion may have strained it must not break our bonds of affection. The mystic chords of memory, stretching from every battlefield and patriot grave to every living heart and hearthstone all over this broad land, will yet swell the chorus of the Union, when again touched, as surely they will be, by the better angels of our nature.

Abraham Lincoln – March 4, 1861

We feel that our cause is just and holy; we protest solemnly in the face of mankind that we desire peace at any sacrifice save that of honour and independence; we ask no conquest, no aggrandizement, no concession of any kind from the States with which we were lately confederated; all we ask is to be let alone; that those who never held power over us shall not now attempt our subjugation by arms.

Jefferson Davis – April 29, 1861

PART ONE

"Never, never, never believe any war will be smooth and easy, or that anyone who embarks on the strange voyage can measure the tides and hurricanes he will encounter. The statesman who yields to war fever must realize that once the signal is given, he is no longer the master of policy but the slave of unforeseeable and uncontrollable events."
– Winston Churchill

1859

"Willie! Willie, please stop screaming!" Melissa Marsh tugged at her older brother's arm. "Please, Willie, wake up. You're scaring me!"

The sound of his sister's voice jarred William Marsh awake. His eyelids fluttered. The canopy of the ancient oak had earlier shaded him from the sun's rays, but now he was fully exposed. The afternoon heat and humidity could be intense in north Georgia, even in late October, but the sweat on his shirt was not just from the sun's warmth. Rising to his elbows, he blinked to clear his eyes.

The alarm on Melissa's face was unsettling. "You were crying out in your sleep. You okay?"

"I'm all *right*! Go get your shoes on." William's show of exasperation masked his gratitude for her rousing him. He shuddered. The nightmare had invaded his sleep once again.

The sun was dropping lower toward the horizon. Time to get on home where evening chores were waiting. Rising from the grass, he rubbed his face, reacting with irritation to the scratch of sunburned skin.

Plopping down next to her brother, Melissa pulled on her stockings and began lacing up her shoes. Her faded gingham dress was soaked, and water droplets spun from her hair. She must have gone wading in the stream against their mother's direct instructions not to do so again. Now they would catch it. At least this time she had taken off her stockings. "Aw, 'Lissa, did you fall in again?"

Melissa giggled. "Uh, huh. Didn't land in the mud this time, though."

"Okay, let's get on back," said William with resignation. "Mebbe you'll dry off before we get home. If you don't tell Ma you went wading again, I won't. Then we'll both stay out of trouble." Rubbing his eyes to wipe away the drowsiness, he stumbled down the path as Melissa skipped on ahead. Try as he might, he couldn't push the nightmare from his mind.

Lucinda Marsh sat on the front porch busily shucking corn, a bucket between her feet filled with discarded husks. Every few minutes she would glance toward the west to see if William and Melissa were on their way back. It was getting late. She was trying not to be worried; after all, they were good children, if a little scatter-brained. She always found it difficult to be hard with them, though; to apply the discipline that a father would have provided. Laying a partially uncovered ear aside, she leaned back into the rocker, letting her eyelids close. Her chest rose and fell as a sigh escaped her lips. *Oh, Aaron, where did you go?* The rocker glided back and forth as her mind drifted back, back to the early years. Memories of long ago, when she was young. And one horrible day.

The years dropped away as Lucinda's thoughts turned back to the time her father, Thomas Corning, had ventured from South Carolina with the flood of eager fortune hunters looking for gold in North Georgia. Dragging his wife Lucretia and their daughter along, he set up camp in the hills outside the small village of Dahlonega. Panning, sluicing and other means of searching yielded just enough of the yellow metal to whet his appetite for more.

Sickness swept the mining camps; an outbreak of typhoid fever claimed Lucinda's mother. Lucretia's death devastated Corning. In ill health himself, he fretted about his daughter, barely sixteen years of age. What would become of his Lucinda if something should happen to him? A possible answer appeared in the figure of a tall, brawny Yankee, newly arrived in the gold fields.

Aaron Marsh had come to Dahlonega to seek his fortune, traveling from the distant forests of northern New Hampshire. Taking a fancy to Lucinda, he actively courted her, then asked Corning for her hand. She did find the handsome, sandy-haired Northerner attractive, but could not bring herself to love him. Nevertheless, after much prodding from her father, she agreed to Aaron's proposal. Relieved his daughter would be cared for, Corning kissed her goodbye, returning to Columbia where he hoped to recover his health. Barely two months later word reached Lucinda that her father had succumbed to his illness.

Aaron set about building a cabin for his young wife. A modest affair, it was constructed frontier style from hand-hewn squared logs. The corners were notched to lock the timbers together to keep them from shifting. An unconscious smile crept across Lucinda's face; she remembered how they had worked together to knead red Georgia clay into chinking to fill gaps between the logs. Split wooden shingles covered the roof. Centered on one end of the main room, a stone fireplace provided heat and a place for cooking. Overhead was a loft reached by a ladder, which provided storage and sleeping areas for their children. Light was obtained from a single small window on the opposite side. There was a small room in the back for their bedroom. A barn was constructed a short distance from the house, also built from logs.

Lucinda's husband made a valiant effort to eke out a living, dividing his time between scraping in the mines and growing a few crops. Over time, the couple's affection blossomed into an abiding love. Sorrow came with a stillborn child, then joy at the birth of two sons, Thomas in 1839, and William in 1841. As time passed, Aaron and his family lived a simple life, but they were content. By the spring of 1847 Lucinda was expecting again. Two nights after Melissa was born, Aaron kissed his wife and newborn baby, then rode into town to celebrate with his friends.

By late the next morning, Lucinda was frantic. Aaron had not returned. Her infant daughter in her arms and sons by her side, Lucinda drove their buckboard into town. She wandered through the camps, the mines, the saloons. She even visited the brothels, searching in vain. Her husband had vanished without any trace.

Lucinda gripped the arms of the rocker as long repressed emotions surged upward. Questions that had no answers flooded her thoughts. *Where are you, Aaron? Where did you go?*

The sound of small feet pounding across the porch startled Lucinda back into the present. Beads of water sprayed from Melissa's still wet hair as the girl flew through the cabin door. Tossing the half-shucked ear into a bucket, Lucinda reached for a towel to wipe the spatters from her face. She watched intently as William shuffled along the path toward the house, kicking up dust with each step. Except for that thick tousle of sandy hair, the resemblance to Aaron never ceased to amaze her.

"Don't you track dirt into my house," she said, her frown deepening. "I thought I told you to keep your sister out of that creek, especially after she fell in the mud last time. Mercy! It's hard enough keeping clothes on you as it is, what with you young'uns growing so fast. And where are the apples you were supposed to be picking for me?"

An image of a muslin sack, filled with fruit but still lying under the old oak, burst into William's mind. He stared at his shoes. "Sorry, Ma."

Lucinda scrutinized her son for a few moments, maternal instinct telling her that something was bothering. "What's wrong?"

"Nothin'."

The answer failed to satisfy her. Something was definitely not right. "You had another nightmare, didn't you?" she asked.

"Don't want to talk about it."

Kneeling beside the rocker, Lucinda scooped up scattered slivers of cornhusks. "Well, you best get on with your chores. Supper will be ready directly."

William trudged toward the barn. Their solitary cow swung its head to look at him, then gave a low moo. Pulling up a stool, he began to milk. As he worked the udders, squeezing the warm liquid into a tin bucket, he tried to forget the dream by mulling over an earlier discussion with Henry Merrow.

Henry and William were the best of friends, despite their diverse background. Henry's father was Captain Bartholomew Merrow, owner of Greenfield Plantation. The elder Merrow was a veteran of the Mexican War, where he had served with the Georgia volunteer regiment.

This morning Henry was full of the news from Virginia. Some abolitionist fanatic and his gang of cutthroats had attacked the government arsenal at Harper's Ferry, but had been stopped by soldiers sent from Washington. Their scheme had been to arm slaves, provoking an uprising. Henry related how the raiders had been armed with guns and pikes; their plan must have been to turn the slaves loose to murder their masters. Henry's father had declared that this proved the Yankees were out to destroy the Southern way of life, and that secession was the only answer.

Henry said he heard the county officials had proposed a recruiting drive to bring the local militia company, known as the Dahlonega Volunteers, up to full strength. He declared that he and William should join up right away. "It's our duty to defend the South's honor," he had said. Henry followed that with a quip about the gals going crazy over a fellow in uniform. William chuckled. It would take more than a gray suit with brass buttons to attract any girl to Henry. But, oh, how he would like to impress Mary. She would certainly be dazzled to see him in uniform. And who knew where that could lead.

Secession. The best of friends quarreled violently over the word. For him, the idea was thrilling. If secession came to be, there would be a war. Leastwise, that's what everyone was saying. War—now there would be the adventure of a lifetime. When he was younger, he had joined the other boys listening spellbound as Mexican War veterans spun their tales of glory and conquest.

Finishing up the milking, he laid a cloth over the bucket to keep off flies. Standing, he stretched, then leaned against the barn door. As he watched dim lamplight flickering from the cabin, a plan of action began to form in his mind. At supper he'd reveal his intention to enlist. Surely his mother will applaud the decision. Yes, of course, she would. He could see it. After he announced his purpose, she would leap up and hug him tightly, all the while proclaiming what a brave and noble young man he was. *Yes, indeedy. It'll be wonderful.*

The conversation at the dinner table began with another scolding about Melissa getting wet in the creek, followed by a discussion about the next day's chores. William watched his mother carefully, waiting for the right moment.

Lucinda wiped her lips with a napkin. "I've been meaning to ask, have you heard any more about poor Joshua? He's been missing over a month now."

"I think he got away this time." William stabbed at a potato with his fork. "They lost his track up in the mountains. Henry says Mr. Monroe is fit to be tied. If and when he catches Joshua again, there'll be hell to pay."

"William, you watch your tongue." Lucinda frowned. "I never cared for that overseer. He's black-hearted and cruel. It's such a shame. You, Thomas, Henry and Joshua were such good friends when you were little. Couldn't keep the four of you apart. Always getting into trouble."

A laugh. "Yeah, lots of times." William's smile faded. "But when we got older, seems though he got kinda, well, unfriendly, like he didn't want to hang around us anymore."

"You can't blame him for that, William. The grown up slaves aren't supposed to associate with white folks."

"I know, but the last couple of years he's gotten downright uppity. Shouldn't have talked back like he was doing. Got him whipped. Then he tried to run away. Twice. That's what got him branded."

"That's a horrible punishment, to brand a boy just like cattle."

"He shouldn't have run away. Should've known better."

"I almost hope the poor boy never gets found. He'd be better off dead if they catch him again. Pass the butter, please." Lucinda accepted the butter dish from Melissa. "I've never felt rightly comfortable about the whole thing—slavery, that is. There's something about the whole system that just doesn't, well, feel right."

"If the big planters didn't have the slaves, how would they get their crops in? Their fields cleared? All the other work done?"

Feeling left out of the conversation, Melissa chimed in. "You wouldn't want to be a slave, would you?"

William shrugged. "Never thought much about it. After all, it's the darkie's place to be a slave. That's what Henry says."

"Henry says a lot of things," said Lucinda. "Doesn't mean you should listen to him all the time."

"We don't have any slaves, and we do just fine," said Melissa.

"What do you know about it, 'Lissa?" William rolled his eyes. "You're just a little girl."

Melissa stuck out her tongue. "I know a lot more'n you do 'bout lots of things. I can read and write better'n you."

Lucinda waggled her finger. "That's enough, both of you." She turned to William. "Your sister's right about one thing. I can't imagine us owning a servant."

William struggled to hide his frustration. Dinner was almost finished and he hadn't found his opening. It was time to push the issue. "Henry also said that tomorrow in town they're goin' to sign up recruits for the militia. They figure the county needs more protection, what with so much trouble in other states."

"What kind of trouble?"

"Like what happened up at Harper's Ferry. It took soldiers to put down the uprising. If John Brown had succeeded, there would've been blacks with guns running all over the country, killing white folks."

"Gracious. I didn't know it was that serious. Maybe we do need some more soldiers, to keep the peace."

Sensing his opportunity, William's voice filled with resolve. "That's right. That's why Henry and I are goin' to join the militia. We'll show those damned black abolitionists a thing or two." He waited for the pride and delight to shine on his mother's face.

His expectations shattered as Lucinda's expression transformed from smile to shock to anger. Standing, she leaned over the table, shaking her finger in his face. "And just how long have you had that fool notion in your head? No son of mine is going to run around in one of those silly soldier suits getting into Lord knows what kind of trouble! There's plenty of work to do here on the farm without you going off on some fool adventure!" She dropped back in her chair. "And I'll thank you not to use such language in front of your sister!"

William sat paralyzed, his jaw hanging. "B-B-But, Ma! Henry says that it's our *duty* to be in the militia. We were going to town tomorrow to enlist. I told him I would."

"Henry Merrow is a rich good-for-nothing who hasn't done a lick of work his whole life! I certainly am not letting him drag you along on one of his hair-brained schemes! I've no husband, and Thomas has gone north 'til Lord-knows-when." She shook her head. "No, no, no. I need you here."

"But, Ma—."

"I don't want to hear another word about it!"

Lucinda sank into her chair. A gloomy silence hung over the table as they finished their meal.

Following the clearing away of the dishes, Melissa took over the table to do her schoolwork, while William retrieved his clay pipe and tobacco pouch from the mantle. "You just take that outside right now." said Lucinda. "You know I don't like it stinking up my house."

He filled the pipe, lighting it with a small coal from the fireplace. Stepping out onto the porch, he settled down into Lucinda's chair. Rings of whitish-gray smoke curled around his head. The moon, almost full, was rising, casting a silvery glow across the barnyard.

A glimmer of light lit the doorway as Lucinda emerged carrying a small candle lantern. William took a seat on the porch steps so his mother could have the rocker. He continued to puff on his pipe while Lucinda rocked slowly. "Are you all right?" she asked.

William looked away. "Yeah, why?"

"Seems like you've been having an awful lot of nightmares, lately. I hear you cry out just about every night."

No reply. Lucinda noticed an involuntary tremble. "Talk to me," she said. "I can tell when something is working at you. Maybe you'll feel better if you talk about it."

"All right." William rapped his pipe against a post to knock out the ashes. "It's the same thing every time. I'm walking through the woods. The sun's shining, the birds are singing—it's really nice. But after a little bit the sky gets full of dark clouds, then starts to lightning all around. I feel like I'm surrounded by something—I don't know— evil. I try to turn around, to run away, but I can't. Something is making me keep going. The trees and bushes try to grab at me, and it's like the lightning is trying to hit me."

Lucinda had stopped rocking. She leaned forward, her expression deepening with concern.

"It's really dark and hazy," William continued, "like a late night fog. A man dressed all in dark clothes and riding a black horse comes charging at me from the mist. I want to get away, but I can't move. Then I'm looking down on myself, from overhead. There's a rifle lying

11

on the ground next to me. I see myself reach down, grab the gun, and shoot at the man. The shot knocks the rider out of his saddle. I run over to where the man is lying on the ground. He's got a hat covering his face. I reach down and pull off the hat . . . ."

Tears welled in William's eyes. Grasping his arm, Lucinda could feel him shaking. "What was it, son? What did you see?"

Embarrassed, William took several deep breaths to compose himself. "I don't know," he said, his voice barely above a whisper. "Right then there's a bright flash, like lightning. Then I wake up. All I can remember is that it's horrifying—and I don't know why."

He glanced up at his mother. "I've had the same nightmare over and over for the past few months. I wish I knew why."

"It may be you've just gotten yourself all tuckered out, what with all the work to do around the farm." She reached out to stroke his hair. "With your father gone and your brother up north, you're the man around here. That's an awful lot of responsibility to put on a youngster's shoulders. That's probably what's giving you the nightmares."

William shook his head. "I don't know. Can't figure out what's causing it." A glance at his mother. "Didn't you say once that Grandma used to dream about things that hadn't happened yet?"

Lucinda leaned back in the rocker. "People used to say that your grandmother could see the future. She had a gift, they said. Would have dreams about things that hadn't happened yet. Premonitions."

William looked at her. "What about you? You ever had dreams that came true?"

"I don't really know. Sometimes I've dreamt things that seemed to come true later, but I always figured it was just a coincidence."

"I don't want a 'gift' like that. Not if I keep dreaming such terrible things. I wish it would stop."

Lucinda tried unsuccessfully to stifle a yawn. Rising, she said, "It's getting late, dear. Go on to bed. Why don't you sleep a little later tomorrow? I think it might do you some good." She blew him a kiss, then went inside.

William sat alone for several minutes before he rose to follow her. Setting his pipe back on the mantle, he reached out to grasp the ladder. Stepping onto the first rung, he hesitated a moment before starting to climb. *Sleep. The only way it'll do me any good is if I don't dream.*

Chapter 2

Early the next morning, William lay in his bed, staring at the dark, heavy wooden beams above. His mother's reaction the previous night troubled him. *I'm grown up now. Why can't Ma see that?* He was eighteen, old enough to decide what was best for himself. She didn't know what an honor it would be to serve in the Volunteers. After all, there was a war coming. In his mind's eye, he pictured himself as a great warrior, decorated in battle and respected throughout the town. Just like Captain Merrow. Besides, everyone else his age was going to be in it. He didn't want to be left out. And then there was Mary . . . .

Daughter of the local schoolmaster, Mary Stewart seemed to draw every boy in town with her uncommon beauty. William had been smitten from the moment he first caught sight of her coming out of the Mercantile with her father. For the past year he tried to catch her attention. Every now and then she would give him a coy glance, but then would start flirting with some other boy, flinging her long, coal black tresses like a flag signaling her presence.

Here was his chance to impress her, to show her he was worth her attention. Throwing off the covers, he reached for his trousers. His mind was made up. He didn't like to go against his mother's wishes, but it was time for him to make his own decisions. She would see he was right.

Descending the ladder, William carried his shoes as he crept to the door. Once outside, he tugged them on, then dashed to the barn, rushing to finish his chores. Once completed, he threw a saddle on his horse and mounted. Riding up to the porch, he called out, "Got to go to town, Ma."

Tugging on the bridle, he was about to turn down the path when Lucinda stepped outside. "Wait a minute," she said.

A lump rose in William's throat. Was she going to ask him why he was going to town? If she did, he couldn't very well lie to her.

"While you're there, stop in the Mercantile and ask Jedidiah if he's gotten in any new flannel. With winter coming you're going to need some new shirts, and Melissa will have to have a dress or two. Oh, and

13

see if there's any mail. I haven't gotten a letter from that brother of yours in over two months. Don't be gone too long."

"Okay, Ma," Relieved, he galloped off.

Before long William came to the turnoff leading to Greenfield Plantation. Trotting up the path to the great whitewashed brick house, he tethered the horse in front of the wide columned porch. He rapped the brass doorknocker a couple of times, then stepped back as the ornate door swung open. A house servant in dark blue satin livery peered out. "G'mornin', Mister William. Mister Henry's upstairs gettin' himself dressed. Be down in a minute. Come in and set yourself."

"Thanks, Hoppy." Entering the foyer, William glanced around to make sure no one was listening. His voice dropped low. "Say, any news about Joshua?"

Hoppy's eyes darted about. "Ain't caught him yet, far as I know," he said in a whisper. "Monroe, he really mad."

William gave Hoppy a pat on the arm. "Just between you and me, I hope he gets away."

A mischievous grin spread across Hoppy's face. Whistling a low, curious tune, he took another quick glance around, then disappeared through a side door.

William settled into a chair near the bottom of a grand, curving staircase. A gentle tinkling drifted from overhead, produced by a slight breeze passing through the multitude of crystals adorning an enormous chandelier. A sensation of shabbiness enveloped him as he ogled the surrounding splendor.

After a few minutes, William began to feel as if someone was watching him. Looking around, he spied Henry's younger brother, Stephen, peering at him from behind the banister at the bottom of the stairs. Grasping the rail and leaning out over the stairs, the boy grinned and asked excitedly, "You really gonna join up today? Wish I was old enough. I'd be a good soldier!"

Annoyed, William let out an low grunt. He really didn't want to have a discussion with a 14-year old kid. "Where's your brother?"

"Upstairs getting dressed," Stephen replied. "Be down in a minute. Don't ya think I'd be a good soldier?"

Before he could reply, William's attention was drawn to the sound of creaking floorboards overhead. Henry bounded down the stairs. "So, Willie-boy, are we off to join our comrades-in-arms?"

William coughed, glancing around the room without answering.

Irritation at his friend's silence flashed in Henry's eyes. "Well, you ready or not?"

"I guess so."

"What do you mean 'you guess so'? Yesterday you were all-fired set to do it."

"Ma didn't take too kindly to the idea when I brought it up last night. She's got something against soldierin'."

Henry's puzzled expression melted, transforming into a jolly smile. "Well, just wait 'til she sees you in uniform. I'll bet she'll be mighty proud of you then! Come on, let's get going!" Laughing, he bolted out the door.

William hurried after him, and soon the pair was thundering down the road to Dahlonega.

High in the North Georgia mountains, Dahlonega stood on land that had been inhabited by the Cherokee long before white men had ever laid eyes on the region. In 1828 a hunter discovered a rock encrusted with gold; soon hundreds of people were pouring into Cherokee Indian lands in search of fortunes. Lumpkin County was created by the State of Georgia in 1832, and Dahlonega became its county seat a year later. In 1836 a new courthouse rose, flecks of gold sparkling in the red clay of its bricks. By 1838, the United States Government decided the land had become too valuable to leave in Indian hands. The Cherokee must give up their claims. The tribe was rounded up, forced to trek hundreds of miles to the Oklahoma territory. Scores died on what came to be known as the "Trail of Tears."

Even though the California gold rush had drawn away many prospectors and mineworkers, by 1859 Dahlonega was still a bustling and thriving community. The Federal authorities established a mint there to process the gold being mined into coins, which helped fund the growth of the young nation.

Entering town, the two friends slowed their mounts to a trot. William pulled up, pointing toward a building to the right. "Got to run some errands for Ma first."

"Okay, but be sure to be at the courthouse by noon. That's when they start signing up the new recruits."

"I'll be there."

William tethered his horse to one of the rails in front of a large store, whose enormous overhead sign proclaimed "GENERAL

MERCANTILE" in enormous red letters. "Jedidiah McCay, Proprietor" was printed in smaller script underneath. Old floorboards creaked as William entered. A large glass jar filled with peppermint sticks caught his eye as he approached the counter. Saliva began to flow as his taste buds recalled the minty-sweet flavor.

A voice full of mirth boomed out. "Five for a penny, just like always." William spun as Jedidiah McCay stepped from behind a stack of kegs.

Heat spread within William's cheeks. "Those things are just for kids. I'm eighteen."

The grin on McCay's face widened. "Are you now?"

Stifling an urge to run for the door, William pointed to a rack of postal slots. "We got any mail today?"

The merchant chuckled as he stepped behind the counter. "Seems like there was something," Reaching up to the mail cabinet, he plucked out an envelope. "Let's see . . . ah, yes, here's a letter—all the way from up north."

William snatched the letter out of McCay's hand without reply. Recognizing his brother's handwriting, he felt ecstatic. Ma would be real happy to get this. It might just put her in a better mood when he got up the nerve to tell her what he was about to do. This couldn't have been better timed.

Distracted by his thoughts as he walked toward the door, William was almost through it before he remembered his other task. "Oh, yeah, Ma wants to know if you've got any new flannel for shirts and dresses and the like."

"Just got in a new shipment the other day, but if your Ma wants any of it she'd better high tail it over here soon. Mrs. Merrow is buying up all the cloth and sewing notions in town, especially all the wool that's available. Seems like she's fixing to make the new uniforms for the militia; coats, pants, flannel shirts and all." McCay studied William for a moment before asking, "You going to join up? I mean, you being eighteen and all *grown up* now." He burst out laughing at his own joke.

William felt his face getting hot again. "Yes, I am! I'm gonna be right in line with Henry Merrow when the courthouse opens!" Storming from the store, he slid the letter into his saddlebag, then strolled up the street toward the courthouse.

Approaching the square, William listened to the crescendo of voices rising from the crowd gathered around the raised portico. Positioned around the courthouse were members of the Dahlonega Volunteers, the local militia company. The citizen-soldiers stood at

16

attention, their bayoneted muskets shining in the mid-day sun. County Councilman Harrison Dean stood in front of a row of seated men, some resplendent in military uniforms. William recognized white-haired Captain Alfred Harris, commander of the Volunteers. Seated next to Harris was Bartholomew Merrow. Dean was speaking to the crowd. "Furthermore, my friends, it is the duty of *every* young man to serve in his state's defense. Georgia will not allow the northern despots to crush her beneath the heel of tyranny! The time is coming when the shackles that bind us to this unholy union will be thrown off; and when that day is at hand, we will need the strong arms of our brave sons to defend our liberty and our rights!" A roar of agreement went up from the throng.

"Today we gather to augment our own Dahlonega Volunteers, whose purpose will be to safeguard those rights. Shortly we will open the muster rolls for those brave young lads who wish to serve in the defense of their native state." Dean took a breath as he mopped his forehead with his handkerchief. "Now, my friends, I wish to present to you our most illustrious citizen. He is a man who is no stranger to the rigors of military life, and in whom we place our trust in leading our eager volunteers in their role. I give you—First Lieutenant Bartholomew Merrow!"

Thunderous applause erupted as Merrow rose from his chair. An elegant dress sword hung from his side. The saber had been presented to him by the town upon his return from Mexico. William stood transfixed. Merrow was the very picture of a military man, straight as a ramrod in his blue uniform. Suddenly William gulped. *Wait a minute*, he thought, *why would Dean call him "lieutenant?"*

Merrow gazed out from the courthouse portico. Clearing his throat, he began to speak. "My friends, today I look out upon a glorious sight. I see the flower of Georgia's manhood poised to rush forward in answer to her call. I see young men with a passion in their souls for freedom—freedom that the founding fathers guaranteed to us in the Declaration of Independence and the Constitution. Those men of Virginia, North and South Carolina, and yes, *Georgia*, had a vision of the right and just way for this country to be governed. It states in the Constitution that those powers not delegated directly to the Federal Government are given to the states."

"But dark times have come. The Congress of the United States has stripped away more and more of the rightful authority of the states. The Northern brigands in Congress have attacked our very way of life, stifling our trade with oppressive tariffs, passing wicked laws that strip us of our dignity. At each turn our Southern legislators are blocked as they attempt to keep the Yankees from destroying the sovereignty of state governments."

"Now we hear of the murderous acts of John Brown and his army of Kansas ruffians invading our sister state of Virginia, not just intending murder and pillage, but to raise an insurrection of slaves! This horrible act of barbarism was carried out by men—no, not men, but *vermin*, whose purpose was to turn slave against master, servant against provider. Remember well the lessons of Nat Turner and his band of renegades. Remember the horribly mutilated men, women and children he left in his terrible rampage. We cannot allow this calamity to befall us ever again! It is time to invoke our God-given right to defend ourselves."

Merrow had worked himself up to a fever pitch. Pausing, he took several deep breaths before resuming. "Friends, we do not band together in this fashion in order to compel the northern people to bend to our will. We do not ask them to change their way of life for us. We ask only to be left alone to live our lives as we have for more than a century; yes, from even before this republic was founded."

Extending his right arm, he gestured toward the group of eager recruits. "Now we ask these brave young souls to step forward and perform that noble act which will endear them to their friends, their family and their countrymen—now is their time to follow in the footsteps of their illustrious ancestors who defended our rights and liberties in the Great Revolution of 1776. And I will be proud to help lead these courageous sons of Georgia through any struggle which may lie ahead."

Merrow drew his sword, raising it in salute. "Many of you know me by my former rank as captain in the United States Army. Let me assure you that my primary allegiance is to my home, my state—my Georgia. I am now honored and pleased to serve as first lieutenant, under our distinguished Captain Harris. I thank you, one and all!"

The crowd howled with patriotic fire. Councilman Dean strode back to the top of the steps. "Thank you, Lieutenant." Raising his cane, he pointed toward tables at the bottom of the courthouse steps, each manned by a uniformed clerk busily preparing enlistment papers and setting out pens. "Young men of Lumpkin County. It is now time to open the rolls. Those of you who desire to serve your state, come forward. The Dahlonega Volunteers await you!"

Within moments there was a line of noisy, enthusiastic lads. A commotion rose as a tall, muscular man elbowed and shoved his way into the front, glowering at the other men as he pushed them aside. "I intend to be the first to enlist, and no man better get in my way."

It was Jonathon Evans, a scoundrel whose reputation as the town bully was well known throughout the county. Standing over six feet, he towered over the people of the village. This in itself intimidated most townsfolk, and coupled with his raging temper gave reason for most people to avoid him whenever possible. Few people doubted that Evans and the hooligans he associated with were responsible for many unsolved crimes.

The soldier seated behind the table did not appear impressed, nor did he seem to care about Evans's bullying. Holding out a pen, he pointed to a sheet of paper. "Make your mark here."

Watching the disturbance, William found himself glued in place, unable to move. His mind filled with his mother's voice, pleading with him to stop. His head swam as he desperately tried to decide what to do. Here was the moment he had waited for, but now he was afraid to go against his mother's wishes, something he had never done.

"Hey, Willie!" The shout brought him out of his deliberation. Through the chaos he caught a glimpse of Henry gesturing to him. "Get over here! I've got a place in line for you!"

Before he could react, a soft voice came from behind. "Don't you hear Henry calling you?" He spun to behold Mary Stewart gazing at him with a puzzled look. "Surely you're going to enlist, aren't you, Willie? You're not afraid, are you?"

William stared at her for a moment, then straightened, making himself as tall as he could. "Of course I'm goin' to sign up. I'm not afraid of nothin'. I just didn't want to get run over by all those damn fools over there."

He turned smartly on his heels, striding toward the line of eager young men where Henry was waiting. "Here I am, now let's get this done!" He was glancing over his shoulder, making sure Mary was watching, when an abrupt "NEXT!" made him snap his attention forward.

Lifting the pen, he hesitated. His mother's voice resounded in his mind again, begging him to stop. The enlistment officer gave him a withering glare as the pen hovered. He glanced once more toward Mary. Reinvigorated by her smile, he resolutely signed his name in the book, underlining his signature with a flourish. Immediately, he felt as though a great weight had been lifted.

After the last volunteer had signed, a tally was made and handed to Councilman Dean. He held up the paper. "Gentlemen! I am pleased to announce that we have had thirty-six courageous souls sign their names to our muster! They are directed to appear at the Old Mustering Grounds on the first Saturday of next month for their first drill, and to receive their uniforms, which are being graciously donated by Lieutenant Merrow and his lovely wife. We wish them all God-speed as they go forth on their great adventure, and pray for them as they prepare to defend their homes against tyranny!"

Searching through the crowd, William tried to locate Mary. Spying her near the Mercantile, he strutted over. Henry called after him. "Hey, where you goin'? We've got some celebratin' to do!"

Over his shoulder, William replied, "You go ahead. I've got somethin' important to take care of."

"Yeah, I see that." Henry's retort was thick with mock outrage. "Just you be careful that she doesn't try to kiss you. A woman's been the downfall of many a soldier."

Mary's focus was toward Jonathon Evans and his gang as William approached. He cleared his throat to attract her attention. Turning to him, she paused for a moment, then said, "So you did it. Now you're to be a soldier. I believe you'll look handsome in uniform."

William felt warm all over. "Thank you. I'm glad you think so. I think you are the most lovely girl I have ever seen." He blushed, embarrassed at blurting out the words.

"Why, Mr. Marsh, what a nice compliment. I've always thought that you were very attractive, too."

He couldn't help stammering. "Do you—would you—like to go to the Harvest Dance with me next month?"

Glancing once more toward Evans, Mary let out a sigh dripping with disappointment. "All right, I'll go with you. Looks like nobody else is going to ask me." Without another word, she turned and walked away, every few moments looking toward Jonathon.

William remained there, watching until Mary disappeared into her house. He couldn't believe his good fortune. Letting out a bellow, he ran to the Mercantile and leapt on his horse. Townsfolk stared in amazement as he raced out of town at a full gallop, howling like a wolf as he disappeared. Henry yelled out as he whizzed past. "Remember to stop once you get home!"

William was only a short distance from the farm when he reined up his lathered horse. Dismounting, he led the animal up the road to the cabin. With each step, his elation faded, replaced by a growing dread. Guilt began to weigh down on his shoulders. *Lord, how am I going to tell Ma what I've done?*

Chapter 3

Lucinda was excited to receive the letter from Thomas. Once the evening chores were done and dinner was over the family sat around the fireplace eagerly waiting for her to begin reading. Carefully breaking the seal on the homemade envelope, she pulled out the letter.

Lymington, New Hampshire
October 17, 1859

Dearest Mother,

> *I take pen in hand to drop you a few lines. I am well, as are the preacher and Mrs. Marsh. I am sorry I have taken so long to write, but Uncle Benjamin and I have been away up to Canada again. They call for his preaching more and more.*

Lucinda stopped to adjust her spectacles. "My goodness! It seems like he's gone to Canada most of the time now."

William was intrigued. "Uncle Benjamin must preach one hell of a sermon for them folks to want to hear him so much."

Lucinda glared. "I've told you before to watch your language in front of Melissa!" Placing her glasses back on her nose, she continued:

> *The weather has turned cold fast. The notion that winter is on its way makes me wish sometimes that I was back there in Georgia with you, Willie and Lissa.*
> *The snow will be flying soon. The preacher says we will likely have a hard winter this year. The cows and horses are getting more shaggy than I have seen in a long time, and the pine trees are full to busting with cones. We have been real busy with the harvest and wood-cutting.*
> *Mother, the whole country around was just wild with colors this fall. The trees looked like they were on fire on the mountains. It was truly something to see. Someday I would like to come fetch you up here to see*

21

just how pretty this country is. Sometimes I wonder just why Pa left here.

It seemed to William as though his mother sagged slightly in the chair. For a moment William thought she was going to cry. "You okay, Ma?"

Lucinda gazed into the fireplace, flames reflecting in her lenses. "I'm all right. It's just that . . . . Well, I'll finish this later." She folded the letter and slid it back into the envelope. Removing her glasses, she rubbed her eyes for a moment, then turned to William. "What did Jedediah say about the flannel?"

"He said if you want any you had best buy it quick. Mrs. Merrow is buying everything in town to make uniforms for the militia."

Alarm flashed in Lucinda's eyes. "How am I supposed to get clothes on you for this winter if I can't get cloth. If she's planning to have all those soldier suits made up—."

Her face lit up as a wonderful thought crossed her mind. "My heavens! She must be planning a month's work! This could be a wonderful chance to earn extra money! Surely she will want me for sewing. I wonder how many uniforms she needs to have made?"

Without pausing to think, William blurted, "Thirty-six."

Lucinda glanced quizzically at her son. "How do you know that?"

William suddenly felt trapped. He had to tell her what he had done. But how could he? His "noble act" now felt tarnished.

Lucinda continued to stare at him. "What's the matter?"

Fidgeting in his seat, feeling as if he was guilty of all the sins of the world, William was unable to look her in the face. "I—I—I enlisted," he finally muttered.

Lucinda's glasses bounced off the floor. "You did *what?* After I told you how I felt about it?"

Shrinking down in his chair, William tried to make himself as small as he now felt. "But you didn't say I couldn't, just that you didn't want me to. Besides, I'm eighteen now. The law says I'm supposed to be in the militia anyway."

Lucinda stared at him with an expression that shifted between anger and fright. She tried to speak, but could not. William looked at her in alarm. She looked as if she might faint. Without speaking another word, she stood and walked out the door.

Melissa began to sob. "Why did you do that, Willie? You hurt Ma."

Standing, William pointed up to the loft. "Be quiet! You just be quiet! Get yourself upstairs to bed!" Tears streaming from her eyes, Melissa climbed the ladder to the bed loft.

Lucinda sat in her old rocking chair, gliding back and forth, her cheeks glistening with moisture. William walked out onto the porch, kneeling down beside her. "I'm sorry, Ma. I didn't mean to make you mad. It's just that—well, everything just kind of happened at once. There was so much goin' on, and after what Mary said, I just had to sign up."

Lucinda looked down at her son. "Mary Stewart? What did she say to you?"

"She asked me if I was afraid to join up."

"So you enlisted to please her?"

"It wasn't just that. The captain was giving a big speech, getting the crowd all pumped up. Henry's been pestering me for weeks to join. Even Mr. McCay asked me whether I was going to. My head was spinning. Afterwards, I felt really good, like I'd done the right thing."

Lucinda's exasperation was giving way to a grudging admiration for her son. Still so much a boy, but trying so hard to be a man. She had known that it was a matter of time before he would take his first steps away from the farm. Deep down, she realized how proud she was of him for taking on the responsibilities that she knew he would face. "Well, I guess what's done is done. We'll just have to make sure that you get done up proper. Hitch up the wagon for me in the morning. I'll be goin' over to Greenfield to work on those soldier suits."

Rising, William stepped behind the rocker, wrapping his arms around his mother's shoulders. For a several minutes they remained in the embrace, when at length, Lucinda gently pulled William's arms away. Standing, she kissed him on the cheek, then passed through the door.

Relief burst from William's lungs as he sat in the rocker. As he gently swayed back and forth, he reflected on the day's events. So many things had happened that were to affect his future. Most important was Mary expressing affection for him. And bless his mother, she would not stand in the way of his becoming a soldier. A war was coming, and he was sure to be in it. Earlier that day he had thought the prospect of war to be glorious, but now it frightened him a little. Would Mary wait for him? What if he should be badly hurt? Or worse? William shook his head. He was being foolish.

The moonlit farmyard began to dim as wisps of clouds moved across the night sky, concealing the bright crescent. From across the mountains to the west he could make out the muffled echo of far away thunder. A breath of moist coolness brushed his cheeks; a portent of rain soon to come. The rumble increased in volume as the storm drew nearer. In William's imagination the sound was almost like . . . *musketry—no, cannon fire. Yeah, artillery, like a battle far off. Glorious, glorious.*

Chapter 4

Many hundreds of miles from north Georgia, William's older brother Thomas sat on the porch stairs of his uncle's farmhouse. His bones ached from long hours on horseback; and as he breathed in the cold night air, he reflected on how good it felt to finally be home.

He and his uncle had returned earlier that day from "special duties" which had taken them into Canada. Pins seemed to jab his legs as he stretched. How many times had they made the trip? He'd lost count. *Strange how things work out. Here I sit, a poor Southern boy from Georgia. If my mother and brother knew what we were doing, they would have a fit.* Looking up at the almost full moon, he thought back over how his path had led to this place.

Several years had passed since Thomas received the invitation from his uncle, asking him to come up to New England. "It's time for the eldest son to see where his roots are," Pastor Benjamin Marsh had written in his letter. Marsh, who owned a two-hundred acre farm near the northern New Hampshire township of Lymington, also functioned as lay preacher for the residents of the area.

Thomas had barely been able to control his excitement at the prospect. Here was a chance to satisfy his yearning to see places and people that he had read about, and to walk the land his father had known as a boy. He had vehemently argued the practicality of his going with his mother; after all, there would be one less mouth for Lucinda to feed. After much persuading, she reluctantly agreed to let him go.

The preacher paid for Thomas's train passage from Atlanta to Boston, and had also provided funds for food and lodging during the journey. Riding the cars was in itself a great adventure for a lad of sixteen. In several cities it was necessary to change from one train to another due to the lack of a standard gauge for railroad tracks. Arriving in Baltimore, he marveled as huge draft horses pulled the cars of his train from one side of town to the other. New York City's immensity astounded him, with scores of buildings more than five stories tall. While there he indulged by spending 25 cents to see the displays at P.T. Barnum's Museum. It was an enormous amount of money, but well worth it. To see the exhibits of wild animals and strange side-show

...s was thrilling, as was a short stage production starring Barnum's ...mous midget attraction, Colonel Tom Thumb.

Pastor Marsh was waiting for him at the train station in Boston. Before starting for home, Marsh showed Thomas many of the historic sites around the old city, including the Old North Church, from which signal lanterns had alerted Paul Revere to begin his midnight ride to rouse the Minutemen.

Heading west from town, they passed through Lexington, where the opening shots of the Revolutionary War had been fired. Thomas was transfixed as his uncle described how local farmers and townsfolk had banded together to stop the British regulars at a small bridge at Concord, then continued to fire on the redcoats as they retreated back to Boston.

Traveling north into New Hampshire, they passed through Franconia Notch. Carved through the hard granite mountains by ancient glaciers, immense craggy cliffs towered above them. The preacher halted the horse at the base of one prominence and motioned to Thomas. Pointing toward one of the high cliffs, he said, "Look up there."

Thomas gazed upward to behold the perfect likeness of a man's profile, high on the side of the mountain. Astonished, he exclaimed, "Who carved that face on the mountain?"

Whipping the reins, Marsh replied, "The hand of God wielded the chisel. Some call him the Old Man of the Mountains, and some have named him the Great Stone Face. He has gazed out from there for centuries untold, and shall watch man's doings for many, many years to come."

It took several days by buggy to reach Marsh's Hill. A trim, white-washed two-story farmhouse came into view as they climbed the last hundred yards up the rise. Thomas was impressed by the size of the farm, compared with the little plot he had left in Georgia. The house stood near the crest of a hill overlooking several small valleys. Several yards up behind it was a large red barn. Fences made of stacked fieldstone bordered the road leading up the hill. Great woodlots of evergreens, maples, and oaks surrounded the hill, with occasional spaces where forest had been cleared to make room for pastureland and crops. Small creeks seemed to flow in several directions at once. Surrounding them were the peaks making up numerous mountain ranges. Off in the distance was one particularly lofty mountain, which the preacher said was named for George Washington.

As the two weary travelers stepped down from the carriage, Rebecca Marsh emerged from the house, greeting Thomas warmly. Plump but not unattractive, the soft-spoken woman exhibited a gentle nature that immediately put him at ease.

Over the next few months Pastor Marsh and his nephew enjoyed many long discussions. At first they mostly talked about the Marsh family history. Thomas discovered that he was a descendant of several of the Pilgrims who had sailed on the Mayflower to America in search of religious freedom. Various ancestors had fought and perished in Indian conflicts, and he learned that one of his forebears had served in the Continental Army during the Revolution. "He didn't do anything brave or fight in any of the great battles." Thomas detected a slight tone of disappointment in his uncle's voice. "Mainly he was shuffled from place to place and did guard duty. He ended up getting out of the army when his father secured a substitute and took him home."

After a time Marsh began to query Thomas about his sentiments regarding slavery. "I would expect that, being born in the South, that you would lean in favor of the practice."

Thomas shifted uncomfortably in his chair. "Not many people from my region own slaves. Just a few plantation owners like Captain Merrow. Most folks work their farms, or in the mines, or in town. Actually, I agree with many down South who feel that slavery should be allowed to die out as an institution. It stains an otherwise gracious lifestyle. On the surface, everything is grand and graceful, full of 'gentlemen' and their 'ladies'. But when I saw the poor darkies in their old, drafty cabins and cast-off clothes, doing the work so their masters can get rich, it left me with a feeling of shame. This was a shoddy way to treat other human beings. Of course, I knew of slaveholders that treated their nigras decently, but I have seen the ugly side, too."

Thomas's response surprised the preacher. "Your answer gratifies me, though I confess I did not expect it." He studied his nephew for a few moments. "I must explain to you the reason for asking these questions. There are things that happen on this farm which must be kept a guarded secret." The preacher went on to explain that, unbeknownst to most of his friends and neighbors, Marsh's Hill was a "whistle stop" on the Underground Railroad, a clandestine operation aiding runaway slaves as they attempted to escape north to freedom. Using the excuse of going to minister to his Canadian brethren, Marsh actually transported fugitives across the border.

The rugged New England mountain ranges had many passes and glacial notches through which smugglers moved all conceivable kinds of contraband. Pastor Marsh knew them all, and used them to advantage to spirit his human cargo across the national boundary. He had been active for years in the anti-slavery movement; indeed, his trip to Boston to greet Thomas had given him the opportunity to meet with several of the city's leading abolitionists. Amazed to discover what his uncle was doing, Thomas swore never to reveal his secret. And as time passed, he became involved in the preacher's abolitionist work, eventually traveling along as his uncle escorted runaways north to Canada.

Thomas never could quite shake a deep-seated uneasiness about this business, though. Being Southern-born, he had known many people who held slaves. He thought often of the Merrow family at Greenfield Plantation, just over the hill. He remembered how Henry had been such a good friend to him and his brother when they were boys.

And then there was Joshua, the slave boy who accompanied them on many of their misadventures. The South's "peculiar institution" had always troubled Thomas, and it had saddened him to watch Joshua change from a bright, friendly youth to an embittered, rebellious young man. Just before Thomas had left Georgia, Joshua had attempted an escape, but was caught within a few days. Hunted down by dogs, he was barely alive when dragged back to Greenfield. Thomas had been visiting Henry when Joshua was brought back, and was a witness to his punishment. The image of his friend being flogged still haunted him.

Thomas shivered as the frosty October air penetrated his coat. He was about to turn to go in the house when he heard footsteps coming from behind. The preacher stepped up and placed a hand on his shoulder. "You still up? I expected you would have been in bed asleep after our long journey."

"Just wondering how Ma and the kids were doing."

Marsh frowned. "I detect something else, as well. Feeling a little guilty again, I expect."

"Some," answered Thomas, "I still feel a little out of place here, like I should be back in Georgia helping Ma with the farm, and keeping Willie and 'Lissa out of trouble. And with all the bad blood 'twixt North and South, maybe it's time I went back."

Marsh looked at Thomas intently. "Sounds like someone's made a comment about you being a Southerner again. You become homesick every time someone gives you trouble about your birthplace."

"I know he didn't mean anything by it, but Peter kept going on and on about 'those Southern bastards and their damn overseers'." A stern look spread over Marsh's face. "Oh, I'm sorry, Uncle, but that's the way he said it."

"A point can be made without resorting to gutter language," Marsh said. "I shall have to have a word with young Peter at the first opportunity. As for what he said, I know it troubles you, having been raised in a slave state. It is only natural that you would feel some anxiety about what we're doing. But deep down inside your heart, I believe you know that we are doing a just and good task. Aiding these poor creatures as they escape bondage and seek freedom is holy work. The nigras are so much like children, needing our help to show them the way."

The preacher turned toward the door. "Now it is time for sleep. There is much around the farm that has waited during our absence. We will have to be up early on the morrow if we are ever to catch up." With a final pat on Thomas's shoulder, Marsh returned inside.

Marsh's comments continued to echo in Thomas's ears. *Poor creatures. Children.* He shook his head. *Even a man like you feels that the darkies are inferior.*

He took in another long, cold breath. *Oh, well, I really shouldn't criticize. Must've been the Southerner in me.*

The next few weeks were so busy that Thomas had little time to dwell on his internal conflicts. There were fences to mend, stones to pull up, leaking roofs to fix, and firewood to cut. Snowflakes were already noticeable floating in the chilly late autumn air. Much work was needed to prepare for the long winter season.

Chapter 5

William finished his chores early, then rode into town. Mr. McCay let him use the back room of the general store to clean up. Sauntering over to Mary's house, he rapped on the door, then stepped back, slowly rocking on his heels. He was glad the weather had stayed clear. *Nice night for the Harvest Dance.*

It seemed as though an eternity had passed before the door opened, revealing what appeared to William to be an angel from heaven. Enamored by the vision, he failed to notice the slight sneer Mary's face betrayed as she surveyed his dusty, threadbare clothes. "Don't just stare at me," she said, "Let's go. I want to dance."

Hesitating a moment before reaching out to take William's proffered arm, Mary gingerly wrapped her hand around his sleeve. As they walked down the street William regaled Mary with tales of the glories he planned to achieve in the militia. In his deliriously happy state he wasn't noticing the decidedly forced smile on her face.

The festivities were in full swing by the time they arrived. William felt as though they were floating high in the clouds. Even the occasional sour note from the band could not deflate the wonderful feeling. Catching Henry as he waltzed by, William whispered into his ear. "What's that music they're playing?"

Henry laughed. "Oh, that's the new song that's being played all over—they say it's called Dixie."

"Well, whatever it is, they aren't playing it very good."

The band was beginning a Virginia Reel when a commotion rose near the door. Jonathon Evans was pushing his way through the crowd. One couple slow to get out of the way were nearly knocked to the floor. Sauntering up to the pair, he grabbed William by the shoulder. "My turn, Marsh,"

William yanked out of Jonathon's grip. "Wait your turn," he said as he turned to look at Mary. Expecting to see offense at Evan's rudeness in her face, he was shocked to observe her gazing at him as though awestruck. Before William had time to react, he felt a hand clamp around his arm.

Dragging William aside, Evans snarled, "I'd say my turn is right now. The lady wants to dance with a *real* man, not some sniveling little puppy dog like you!"

William again looked at Mary. Glancing coyly back to him, she smiled, then put her arms around Jonathon's neck. He couldn't believe his eyes. How could she do this to him? She was *his* girl . . . .

Stunned, he felt a warm flush crawling up his neck as he watched Jonathon and Mary whirl around the dance floor. When they laughed, he just knew that they were snickering at him.

Edging closer, he waited for the music to end, then deliberately stepped between the two. "All right, Jonathon, you've had your dance. I'm Mary's escort this evening, so you can just find someone else to dance with." Stretching his out hand, he was dumbfounded when Mary retreated.

Evans let out a guffaw. "Hah! I guess we know how that goes. Now get out of the way." He gave William a shove, sending him stumbling backward.

William's eyes blurred. Without thinking, he charged, catching Jonathon around the midsection. The force of the impact knocked Mary to one side as the two men crashed into a table full of refreshments. As they struggled to rise, several men rushed to restrain them before the fight could continue. Jedidiah McCay pushed in between the combatants. "Jonathon, that's enough for you tonight! Boys, make sure he leaves!"

Panting from the exertions, Evans glared at William. "I'm not done with you, Marsh! We'll finish this some other time." He jerked his arms away from his detainers and stormed from the room.

McCay watched Evans leave, then turned to William. "As for you, Willie, I think you should leave, too. You'd best get on home. And watch out you don't come across Evans again tonight. He's a mean one, and is liable to do anything."

William glanced around for Mary. Several ladies had helped her up and were escorting her to a separate room so she could compose herself. In the instant before disappearing through the door, the glare she directed at William felt like a red-hot poker. As he took his hat down from a peg, McCay stopped him with a hand on the shoulder. "I'll say one thing for you, boy. You've got guts trying to take on the likes of that hoodlum. Now get on home—and be careful."

The day soon came to commence drilling of the new militiamen. Planning to be the first ones to the drill field, William and Henry were dismayed to find that over half of the recruits had arrived ahead of them. The men joked and carried on as if present at a social gathering. Two of the young men engaged in mock swordplay using branches snapped from a nearby tree. Off on another side of the field, older members of the Dahlonega Volunteers were practicing their drill.

William and Henry sought out a soft bed of grass under the shade of a tree while they waited for the officers to arrive. Off to one side of the field, William spotted Jonathon Evans leaning against a fence. Catching William's look, Evans glared back with a look full of malice, then turned away. Henry noticed the glance. "Watch out for him, friend. That fellow has it in for you."

The clatter of hooves diverted William's attention from his rival. Captain Harris, Lieutenant Merrow and several others in uniform cantered into the field. "They're here," he said as he shook Henry from his doze. Rising, the two trotted toward the other recruits.

Dismounting slowly and with deliberation, Captain Harris seated himself on a camp stool. Lieutenant Merrow remained on his horse, rising to stand in the stirrups. "Gentlemen, it does my heart proud to see you assembled here this morning. Remember this day well, for now you enter that most glorious of professions—today you begin the process of becoming soldiers! You have much work ahead of you as you commence your training, but I have no fear that you will quickly master the skills required. Before much time passes, I expect to ride at the head of the finest military organization ever fielded!" The men cheered. William felt tremendous pride welling up within him, dispelling all of his doubts and fears.

Merrow raised his hand to quiet the men. "Now we shall begin to turn you from citizens into soldiers. Sergeant Fitzpatrick, front and center!" Marching briskly up from behind the officers came Gerald Fitzpatrick. Well known and liked in the community, Fitzpatrick had come from Ireland some twenty years earlier. He had served in Merrow's regiment during the Mexican-American War, earning his sergeant's stripes for his gallant conduct in action.

"With your permission, sir." Fitzpatrick saluted Captain Harris, who nodded, then Merrow. Turning to face the men, he held up a small book. "All right now, me boys. I have here in my hand a copy of *Hardee's Tactics*. This is the book of instruction used by the Army of the United States to teach ladies like you how to be soldiers. The first thing we've got to do with you is to make you *stand* like a soldier. The first command to learn is 'Fall In.' First we'll watch the veterans show you how it's done. Dahlonega Volunteers, FALL IN!"

GEORGE WINSTON MARTIN

Quickly the uniformed militiamen took their places, coming to attention as they formed two neat ranks. Fitzpatrick smiled. "Now, you see, when I gives the order, you line up in two lines, with the tallest ones on the right, and the shortest ones on the left. Let's give it a try. Now, recruits, FALL IN!" A mad scramble ensued as the men tried to find their places in line. Several men were sent sprawling to the ground, especially those who got into Jonathon Evans' way. Fists began to swing.

Evans's scuffle drew Fitzpatrick's attention. After disentangling the hotheads, he pointed to the monstrous revolving pistol protruding from a holster riding low on Jonathon's hip. "And just what are you doing with that weapon, boy-o? Everyone was told not to bring any firearms with them."

"Feel naked without it, Sarge. Besides, soldiers are supposed to have guns, aren't they?"

"Handguns are for officers, only, bub. Infantry uses muskets."

"So when do we get our guns?"

Fitzpatrick snorted. "Guns, is it! It'll be a long time before I'll entrust you ladies with guns! Before you get guns you've got to learn to march and maneuver! Once you can *march* like a soldier then you'll learn to *shoot* like a soldier. And heaven help us when that day comes!" Striding close up enough to Evans to bump his chest, the sergeant looked straight into the bully's face, set his jaw, and yelled, "Now, get rid of that sidearm!"

Stunned, Evans fell back a step. Unstrapping his belt, he sullenly walked over to his horse, draping the holster over the saddle, then resumed his place in line without a word. Murmurs rose from the incredulous recruits.

Fitzpatrick slapped his trouser leg. "Now that we have dispensed with that little entertainment, let's try it again. FALL IN!"

After the dust cleared, two ragged lines of men stood before the sergeant. Sniggers rose as the veterans could hardly contain their amusement. Fitzpatrick cast his eyes heavenward in disbelief. "All right, boy-o's, what we have here is the saddest excuse for ranks I have ever seen in me life. And I'll have you know, I've seen the worst!"

Lieutenant Merrow had dismounted and was engaged in conversation with Captain Harris. He motioned for Fitzpatrick to come. Shortly thereafter, the sergeant ordered the uniformed Volunteers to break ranks, releasing them from further duty.

Fitzpatrick planted himself in front of the recruits. "All right, ladies, now we get to work." As the afternoon wore on, the sergeant explained, cursed, pushed, prodded, shoved and otherwise manipulated the recruits until he was able to get them to fall in somewhat satisfactorily. The grumbling grew louder as each hour passed. Fitzpatrick was in each recruit's face, yelling and screaming at them. Jonathon's unwillingness to follow orders drew his special ire.

After several hours of drilling, Merrow mounted his horse and rode over to Fitzpatrick. "That's enough for today, sergeant. Let's give the men a rest." He turned his mount toward the recruits to address them. "Well done, soldiers! I can truthfully say I'm proud of you! Now the ladies of our fair town have a reward for you. They have worked diligently to supply you with your uniforms, and now you shall have them issued. Sergeant! March the men over to receive their uniforms!" A wild cheer went up from the throng.

"FALL IN," Fitzpatrick watched with astonishment as the men formed ranks perfectly for the first time that day. Even Jonathon appeared to be caught up in the excitement. "The command is 'Forward, March! On the word march you will step out lively with the left foot, and will keep in step all the way! FOR-WARD, MARCH!" The result was more of an animated shuffle than a march. The disgusted Fitzpatrick gave up, letting them amble along at their own pace. *This will change, by God.*

The column moved slowly toward a large wall tent pitched in one corner of the field. Halting the men, Fitzpatrick directed them to line up in front of several tables stacked high with paper-wrapped bundles.

Henry and William could hardly restrain themselves as they waited in line with the other recruits. This was the moment they had long looked forward to, the chance to don their war garments. William's mother had worked for weeks with several other ladies at Greenfield making the uniforms. She had brought home material to fit William, but he had resisted. "I want to get mine the same time as everyone else," he had said, "The other fella's would get jealous if'n they knew I got to wear one before the rest of them." Lucinda couldn't quite fathom the youthful logic, but went along.

Finally they reached the quartermaster's table. "I want lots of buttons," quipped Henry. The quartermaster sergeant shot him an irritated glance, then tossed a loosely tied bundle at him. Turning to William, he pitched a similar parcel at him.   Frantically   tearing open the wrappings, they gazed with wonder at the contents. The short jackets were cadet-gray wool, single-breasted, with a row of bright brass buttons down the front, and sported a high, stand-up collar. The trousers were of the same material, with black piping running down the seam. To complete the outfit, they each received a flannel shirt, cloth suspenders and a white waist belt. This last was held in place with a brass oval buckle bearing the letters "U S." After he managed to get the coat on, William looked towards his friend, and abruptly burst out laughing. Henry had a quizzical look on his face. "Just what's so blasted funny?"

William was laughing so hard he could barely stammer out his answer. "Well, just look at us. I think we need to do some tradin'!"

Glancing back and forth between his friend and himself, Henry suddenly realized what had so amused William. The pair looked ludicrous—Henry's pants were so long that they bagged around his feet, while William's trousers ended around mid-calf. Quickly they swapped among the other men until all had achieved a reasonably well fitting uniform.

Next they were given their caps. They were small, made of wool matching the coat material, and had a small leather bill and chin strap. Henry was eager to show off his worldliness. "They're called 'kepis', from the French. It's what their soldiers wear."

William held up what appeared to be a large white handkerchief that was stitched round on the end. "Now what the devil is this supposed to be?"

Henry was quick with the explanation. "That's a 'havelock'. It's to keep the sun off your neck." Henry then proceeded to demonstrate how to fit the contraption over his kepi. William was setting the cap on his head when he noticed Captain Harris, Merrow and the other officers mounting their horses. Sergeant Fitzpatrick strolled up to the group. "All right, boys, the captain says that you are all dismissed, but invites you to stay for refreshments." He drew open the flap of the tent to reveal two boxes full of liquor bottles. "Beer and whiskey for those that wants it."

Each grabbing a bottle of beer, William and Henry found a shaded spot to sit and enjoy their drinks. As he took a swig, William noticed Jonathon covertly slide a whiskey bottle into his saddlebag. Catching William's glance, Evans shot him an angry look, then swung up onto the horse and clattered off down the road.

Shadows of late afternoon began to stretch across the field. "Time for me to be gettin' on home," said William. "Got to get started on my chores."

"Well, just remember to take that uniform off before you go to bed. Those buttons will make it kind of hard to get to sleep!"

William laughed as he climbed up into his saddle. "See you later," Snapping the reins, he pointed the horse toward home.

As he slowly rode down the road, William tried to go through the drill in his mind. He was determined to get it right if it was that last thing he did. Lost in thought, William let the horse go along at its own pace. Rounding a bend, his reverie was brought to a jarring end as he found the road blocked by three mounted men. It was Jonathon Evans, along with two of the street bullies he associated with, Hiram Parker and Joseph Collins.

Evans took a swig of whiskey, then sneered at William. "Well, if it ain't the little farm boy what thinks he's a soldier. Don't he look pretty!" Sweat began to pour under William's heavy wool jacket as he glanced about, looking for an escape route. Evans dismounted, handing his reins to one of the other men. "Course this uniform looks too shiny and clean for a rough and ready soldier boy. Mebbe we should dirty it up a little—you know, just so folks will think you've been—."

As Evans reached to grab his coat, William thrust out with his foot, trying to kick free. Evans dodged, then grabbed William's leg. With a shove, he pushed William off the saddle. Flailing wildly, William tried to regain his seat, but found himself falling. He landed with a thud on his back, kicking up a cloud of dust. Evans slapped the rear of the horse, sending it galloping off down the road. The two other men had dismounted by now, and the three ruffians circled William.

Before he could get fully to his feet, Evans lashed a fist at William's jaw, knocking the boy to his knees. Several times he tried to stand, but every time he attempted to get up one of them would knock him back down again. Blow after blow rained down, but still William would not give up trying to rise and fight back.

Suddenly the hoodlums stopped their attack, finally allowing William to rise to his feet. Swaying slightly, with blood oozing from cuts on his face, he turned to face Jonathon. Before he could take a step, though, his arms were grabbed and pinioned behind him. He struggled feebly, unable to break free in his weakened state.

Evans directed an evil leer to the other man. "I declare, Collins, Parker's caught himself a dirty little pig!" He reached down to his boot and drew out a mean-looking knife. "Mebbe we should slice him up for bacon!" Parker and Collins roared with laughter. William felt faint. Evans slid the dirk back into its sheath. Spying the relieved look on

William's face, he chortled. "Oh, we're not done yet, Marsh. We've got something special just for you! Hang onto him, Parker."

While Parker kept William's arms pinned, Evans pulled his heavy dragoon revolver from the rough leather holster slung from his belt. William swallowed hard as Jonathon leveled the gun at him. "Let him down, Hiram," said Evans. William sank back to the ground as Parker released his arms. Evans turned the gun over in his hand, grasping the barrel. "What you just got was for fun. This is for making a fool of me at the dance!"

Evans raised the pistol over his head like a club. William feebly raised his arm to try to fend off the coming blow. Before Evans could strike, though, Collins stopped him. "Hold up! There's a horse comin'!"

At that moment Lieutenant Merrow appeared from around the bend. Caught by surprise, he reined his horse to a stop. "I beg your pardon, but what is going on here?"

Merrow surveyed the scene for a few moments. "Well, now, this hardly seems fair—three against one. May I be permitted to even the odds a bit?" His face betraying just the slightest hint of a smirk, the officer reached down to his waist belt, drawing his saber from its scabbard with an agonizingly slow motion. The sound of steel rasping on steel was electric. Evan's face went white as he rapidly holstered the pistol and ran for his horse. Collins and Parker scrambled to follow.

As the trio galloped away, William looked up at Merrow in gratitude. "Thanks, Captain . . . uh, Lieutenant," he said, "They were about to turn me into mincemeat."

Merrow returned his saber to its scabbard. "Think nothing of it, my lad. That was Jonathon Evans, wasn't it? It seems to me I saw him at the drill earlier, giving the sergeant quite a few problems."

"Yes, sir," said William, "He joined the company with the rest of us."

A scowl crossed Merrow's brow. "We need every man we can muster, but there always seems to be one of his kind in every outfit. We don't need ruffians who could destroy the morale of a good unit. I think we shall find a way to have Mr. Evans dropped from the rolls." The lieutenant looked down at William. "As for you, you handled yourself quite well just now. We need men who aren't afraid to fight, even when the situation seems hopeless. See Fitzpatrick at the next drill session. I think corporal's stripes will look just fine on those sleeves."

William was stunned. He stammered out a "thank you, sir," but couldn't get anything else out.

Merrow grinned. "Now, get on home and clean yourself up." William could do little more than nod and give a weak salute as the lieutenant wheeled his horse and rode away. He stared down the road as Merrow's dust cloud slowly dissipated, then let out a war-whoop. Excitement over the sudden promotion quickly dissipated, though, when he realized that his horse was nowhere to be seen. It took him the better part of an hour to locate the animal.

Arriving home, he strutted through the door as if he were the King of England. Unimpressed, Melissa let out a loud sniff. "Just a lot of stupid boys carryin' on like they was sumthin' special."

All Lucinda noticed was the dirt and bruises. "It warn't nothin', Ma," he blurted as he avoided her eyes. "Just a bunch of the recruits got a little carried away in all the excitement." When she queried about the blood from his nose he mumbled something about falling off the horse, then rapidly changed the subject. He proudly described how he had earned Lieutenant Merrow's appreciation of how good a soldier he was, and how the officer had bestowed upon him the exulted rank of corporal, being extremely careful to avoid any mention of the beating.

Listening patiently, while he went on and on about the day's events, his mother knew he wasn't being truthful about the beating he had obviously taken. Still felt uncomfortable with his military service, deep down within her she also felt a strong sense of pride at her son's accomplishments.

William changed from his uniform to work clothes and headed for the barn to complete his evening chores. In bed after supper, he lay staring at the logs overhead, thoughts whirling with fantasies of the great deeds he planned to accomplish as one of the elite officer corps.

While her son drifted off to sleep, Lucinda gazed up toward his loft, a silent prayer on her lips. *Please take care of him, Lord. Oh, how I wish his father were here to guide him.*

Chapter 6

Snowflakes were flittering around outside the window late one evening when Thomas noticed a glimmer of light in the distance. "Someone's coming," he said, motioning for his uncle.

Marsh peered out into the gloom, watching as the flickering pinprick of light drew nearer. Drawing on his coat, he opened the door and stepped out onto the porch, Thomas following. They began shivering almost instantly as the frigid wind cut through their clothing. Rebecca closed the door, but left just a crack so she could observe. "I think it's friend Russell," said Marsh. "What in Heaven's name would he be doing out on a night like this?"

Before long a carriage pulled up in front of the house. "Hello, Benjamin," Russell could barely get the words out through chattering teeth. "I'd be obliged if I could come in. I have important information for you."

"Of course, of course!" Marsh helped him down from the carriage seat. "Come in before you freeze to death. Thomas, please take friend Russell's horse to the barn." He called to his wife. "Rebecca, pray get something hot for our guest to drink."

While the preacher hastened Mr. Russell into the house, Thomas gathered the reins and led the horse toward the barn. After unhitching and leading the animal into a stall with feed and water, Thomas made his way through the arctic wind back to the house. There he found his uncle and Russell seated next to the fire, a steaming mug of coffee clamped in Russell's hands. Rebecca quickly brought another, which Thomas accepted with gratitude. The warmth of the comforting liquid seemed to flow through his limbs.

Marsh was struggling to contain his indignation. "Go on with your news. You say we must go out again right away? That's insane. It's almost December! Surely they can't mean a delivery with the weather worsening with each passing moment."

Russell took a sip from his cup. "Aye," he said, "It seems that an extra shipment was sent off with no notion of the conditions. Now it's on its way here, and probably will arrive within the next few days. Before I left town to come here I telegraphed Antoine Cusson to expect us. Peter should be on his way here now."

"Can't the shipment be delayed?" Anxiety tinged the preacher's question. "Winter is coming on in earnest—the notches will be impassable!" He pointed toward the window. "Just look at the snow already flying outside!"

Russell leaned forward in his chair. "We dare not stop them at this late date. If we were to turn them back now we would surely lose them to the authorities who enforce that damnable law," he said, referring to the Fugitive Slave Act, which required Federal law enforcers to detain escaped slaves, and aid in returning them to their masters.

Marsh slumped back in his chair, his fingers drumming furiously on the cracked leather armrest. Rising, he began to pace around the room. For long minutes, he walked to and fro, immersed in thought and mumbling to himself as he tried to resolve this quandary. Halting, he looked straight at Russell. "Very well," he said, "But we must make haste in preparing for the journey. Friend Russell, you will stay tonight. In the morning after your return to the village, would you please alert our friends across the border that we shall attempt to proceed north as soon as we receive the delivery. Also, please make it known around town that I have received an urgent summons from Canada, and must depart within the next few days to tend my flock there. Thomas, first thing tomorrow please ready our special room in the barn."

Early the next morning Thomas hitched up the carriage and brought it up to the house. Russell climbed up into the seat, then reached down to shake his hand. "Tell your Benjamin I'll send word as soon as I know when to expect delivery." Watching his uncle's friend drive off, Thomas couldn't resist chuckling, amused at how they kept speaking about 'shipments' and 'deliveries,' as if discussing a cargo of farm equipment. He walked back into the barn, being careful to avoid new mud puddles. The snow had ended during the night, and the temperature was rising. White patches remained on the ground, but they were quickly melting, even in the shadows.

Heading toward a dark corner, Thomas pulled aside a piece of canvas, then brushed back a layer of straw on the floor to reveal a trap door. Opening it, he descended the steps into what had been an old root cellar. Several straw-filled mattresses lay piled in a corner, and along one wall leaned a few knocked down trestle tables. Dank and musty, the odor permeating the cellar caused Thomas to gag. Soon, though, fresh air made its way in through the open trap door, allowing him to breathe a bit easier. He surveyed the scene. *Not much for living. But it does make a decent hideout.* Setting to work, he swept out the room and assembled the tables. Pulling the mattresses outside, he spread them around behind the barn to air.

Four days later Russell sent notice to expect the fugitives' appearance before nightfall. Preparations at the farm were stepped up in anticipation of their arrival. Rebecca spent several hours preparing food for the travelers. Soon all was in readiness. Marsh kept a close watch on the road. As evening shadows began to spread across the valleys, a wagon pulled by two large draft horses approached the farm.

Watching the wagon roll up the hill, Thomas took silent inventory of the occupants. There were four women, six men, and five children of various ages. The clothing they wore were an odd assortment of garments showing many different stages of wear, and had been gathered for them at stops along the route to replace the rags worn since their escape. Thomas viewed them with mixed emotions, as he always did when there were new arrivals. He felt amusement at the outlandish dress, and concern about their physical condition. He also felt disgust with himself for the tinge of revulsion that stirred in the back of his thoughts.

Observing the fugitives intently as they descended from the wagon, Thomas could see both curiosity and fear in their eyes. Until they crossed into Canada there was still the constant threat of recapture, a danger they were all too aware of.

After a few minutes, Thomas raised his hand. "Please, come with me. We have a special room in our barn where you will be safe until the time comes to head north again. There are soft straw beds and food waiting for you." As they followed, he entered the barn, leading them down through the hidden trap door. Seeing the tables groaning with food, the famished travelers rushed to fill their empty bellies.

A few moments later, Thomas became aware of one man holding back, standing in the shadow cast by the flickering lamps. "Come, friend," he said, "come and eat. You will need your strength for the next part of your journey."

Still the man hung back. After a few seconds, he spoke with such a low voice that Thomas could not understand the words. "What's that you say?"

The man spoke again, this time loud enough for Thomas to hear. "I knows you," he drawled, "Does you remember me?" Curiosity suddenly piqued, Thomas lifted his lantern so the light fell over the man's face—then almost dropped it from surprise. "Joshua?"

Thomas stood there, stunned, staring as if he beheld a ghost. Joshua grinned. "You best shut your mouth. You'll catch flies."

Hastily setting down the lantern, Thomas raced to embrace his old friend. "How—when—Lord above, it is good to see you!"

Later, as the others settled themselves for the evening, Thomas and Joshua sat at one of the tables talking. "I just had to 'scape," said Joshua, "Monroe the overseer said he was goin' to use me as an example for what the others would get if they tried to run away. He 'bout beat me to death, and branded me to boot. Look what he done to my back with the cat." He loosened his shirt. Thomas winced as he removed it to display a back tattooed with ugly ridges and scars. A whip-like device made with several knotted leather cords, the cat-o-nine-tails could slice open the skin when in the hands of someone experienced in its use. Thomas remembered Henry Merrow matter-of-factly describing similar lashings dealt to other slaves.

"Last time he catched me, Ol' Monroe did this." Joshua turned his right arm up to show what looked to be the letter "G" scarred into the flesh. "That G is for Greenfield. They branded me just like some old cow." Rage flickered in Joshua's eyes. "I'd like to kill that man someday for what he did to me. I ain't no animal, even if'n my skin is black."

The next few days were busy as the group prepared to head for Canada. Peter Cusson arrived from Quebec Province to join the party as guide. It was to his family's farm just over the border that Marsh transported the runaways. And it had been his comments about southerners that had so irritated Thomas. Almost immediately the preacher took Peter aside and berated him for his foul language. Thomas winced; he had received such a chastising from his uncle once before, and knew why Peter's face was so white afterwards. He would be constantly hearing about this from Peter until they reached his farm.

The band had to be ready to travel quickly. Fortunately, the weather remained mild, but as Marsh warned, winter blizzards would not be long in arriving. It was imperative they leave at once. After allowing only one more day for the fugitives to rest, they made ready to leave.

Long before sunrise, with only torches and the light of the moon for illumination, the party assembled in the barnyard. Thomas and Peter each took their place as cart drivers. Pulling on his coat, Pastor Marsh gently kissed Rebecca good-bye, and mounted his horse. "Let us pray," he said, lifting his eyes heavenward. "Oh, Lord Jehovah, give us thy divine guidance and strength as we endeavor to deliver these of thy oppressed children from bondage to freedom. Blind the eyes of our enemies so they may not see us as we travel through the wilderness.

Hold the wrath of thy winter storms so that we may complete our journey quickly and return safely home. Blessed be the name of our Lord. Amen." He gazed out over the procession. "Let us now go forward, secure in the knowledge that it is the Lord's work we do. Thomas! Peter! Start your teams!" With a snap of reins, they commenced their journey north.

Joshua sat next to Thomas in the front of their wagon. "Your uncle, he sure is a man who knows the Lord."

"That he does." Thomas smiled. *And I hope the good Lord was listening to him.*

Chapter 7

"Come on, you God-damn jackass, MOVE!" Peter swung his whip at the unresponsive mule. Thomas winced as he watched Pastor Marsh turn to give his friend a withering glare. Peter paid no attention. His wagon had become stuck while trying to cross a stream, and now one of the mules had decided he would not pull another step. The blacks that had been riding clambered out into the icy mountain water. Making their way to the bank, they sat down to wait. Nothing that Peter could say or do made any difference—the mule would not proceed.

Joshua scowled "I don't like him whippin' that animal. I knows what it feels like. Mebbe I can help." Getting down from the wagon seat, he splashed out into the brook toward the mule. He caught Peter's arm just as he began to swing the whip again. "Hole up there. Let me try."

Peter lowered the whip. He handed the reins to Joshua. "If you can make this stubborn beast move, I salute you, mon ami."

Joshua moved in front of the mule, gently stroking its face, then its ears. The group watched intently as he whispered softly, all the while rubbing the animal's head. Gathering the reins, he gently but firmly began to pull. The mule resisted for a few moments, then took a step. A cheer rose from the bank as Joshua led the team out of the brook. Speechless, Peter could only stare unbelievingly as Joshua returned the reins. "Mules an' men work a hole lot better when they ain't gettin' beat up on. You should 'member that."

As the group kept traveling further northward, Joshua and Thomas continued reminiscing about their boyhood in Georgia. "Willie is growed to be a fine young man," said Joshua, "You'd be right proud of the way he helps his ma around the farm. Course, he's picked up the same notion's as that Henry Merrow, as far as it comes to where us blacks' place is. Last couple of times I sawed him, he wouldn't even look me in the eye."

Thomas slapped the reins to urge the mule to move faster. "Willie and I used to get into some pretty good fights over that subject. He really has a good heart—and it's hard to be different from all your friends."

Joshua snorted. "Well, I *was* a fren'! 'Jes like a puppy an' a kitten is frens when they's youngstas. I never could figger out why *you* was so diff'rent."

Thomas mused a bit before replying. "I was never sure about that myself. I always saw things contrary to everyone else. I even think Henry was glad that I left when I did. Anyways, I want to hear how you got away from Greenfield. Just how long did it take you to get to uncle's farm?"

Joshua's expression turned reflective. "I'm not sure jest how long it was. But it took 'siderable time to get away. The first couple of nights I hid out in a real swampy place in one of the mountain hollers. I got down and rolled in a mud bog 'til I got all covered up, so to take the scent off me. The dogs got real close to me two or three times but I kept real still layin' down in that mud. After I was real sure they was gone I started moving toward the north. I knew I was goin' the right way cuz my granddaddy showed me how to find the north star, an' I jest kept follerin' that. I moved along mostly at night, pickin' my way 'long the ridge tops. During the day I had to stay hid in the thickets and not show myself."

"Must'a took nigh on five or six days before I got to the big river near Chattanooga. I sneaked up on an ol' packet boat and hid under some crates they had piled up near the back. I thought I was dead for sure when I hear someone start movin' them boxes. But it was a big black fella what worked on the boat. Lor-dy, was he surprised to find me hidin'! He helped me by keepin' anyone from findin' me back there, and bringin' me food. The boat was headed for Knoxville but jest 'fore we got there that big fella brings me some old clothes and says to slide off the boat real quiet like at the next bend in the river. He tells me how to get to this little farm outside of town 'thout anyone seein' me. He says to give the man at that place a special word and he'd take care a me. Well, suh, I was scared to death I'd get caught, but I does jest like he says, and next thing I knows, I'm being moved from this house to that barn to this cave to that boat; an before you knows it, I'se here! Funny thing is, all them people kept talkin' bout railroads, but I never did get on no train."

Thomas laughed at that. "They call what we're doing the 'Underground Railroad'—no trains involved but we move a lot of people. My uncle's farm is a 'whistle stop' on the trail."

The party worked its way steadily northward through the high granite mountains of northern New Hampshire. Good fortune continued to smile on them in the form of mild, late autumn weather. This was doubly fortunate, because Pastor Marsh would not allow fires when they camped at night. To escape detection, they traveled up through the interior of the state, staying away from the main routes. Much of their course followed the rock-strewn Androscoggin River, which wound its way down through dense forests along the western side of the state. Marsh planned to pass along an old stage road through Dixville Notch, then skirt the small township of Colebrook. By the time they reached that point, they would be only a couple of days from the Canadian border.

It was getting very late in the afternoon when they arrived at the base of Dixville Notch. Everyone bent to the task of pushing the wagons up through the narrow pass. The towering cliffs ringing them cast shadows as dark as night within the notch, even though the tops of the granite pinnacles were still bathed in the reddish light of the setting sun. Torches were hastily lit to aid them in finding their way through.

Marsh prodded the exhausted travelers onward. "Keep moving, keep moving! We're almost there." Soon the preacher found the spot he was looking for—a fairly level meadow next to a small pond. "We shall stay here for tonight. The mountain walls around us will shield us from prying eyes. Campfires will be allowed this evening."

Knowing they would not have to pass another cold night with no fire gave heart to the weary travelers. Quickly they set about gathering firewood and stretching their worn pieces of canvas to create shelters. Distant rumblings echoing throughout the gorge announced the coming of a winter storm. The temperature was dropping quickly. Thomas and Joshua laid their bedrolls under one of the wagons. "Probably get some snow," said Thomas. "It's sure cold enough for it."

Joshua grinned. "I'm jes' lookin' forward to some hot food."

Thomas looked upward at the fading light reflecting off the highest peak. He admired the craggy rock formations above. *It's so beautiful here.* One outcropping in particular caught his attention. It seemed to extend out over the valley like a sentinel, guarding all below it. As he gazed at the stone, darkness fell across it as if a curtain had been drawn. The edges of threateningly dark clouds were spreading across the sky. He felt a cold splash of water on his cheek. Soon, a frigid rain began to fall. The exhausted travelers huddled in their blankets beneath the flapping canvas lean-to's and drifted off to sleep.

While the travelers slumbered fitfully below, rainwater collected in multiple cracks within the cliff walls. Though the drizzle had come to an end, liquid continued to collect in numerous cavities and slowly turned to ice, expanding as the temperature dropped below freezing. The giant rock which had earlier caught Thomas's attention was shoved by this faint bit of stress. Small showers of stones and dirt caused by the rock's movement fell into the cracks; this in turn pushed a bit more on the stone. Finally the rock was levered beyond its point of balance—and with a grinding roar, began to fall away from the mountainside.

At first, only the sensitive ears of the pack animals could pick up the sound. The terrified braying of the mules woke the travelers. Thomas sleepily lifted his head. *What the devil . . . ?* Shivering from the cold, he tried to discern what was causing the animals to react so. Suddenly, he heard a dull, cracking sound that seemed to be coming from far above. He glanced upward—and the sight he beheld jolted him instantly awake in horror. Illuminated by the hazy, dim pre-dawn glow, the gigantic stone seemed to be peeling itself from the top of the cliff. Momentarily paralyzed by the awesome sight, he could only stare—then, regaining his wits, he yelled with all the power his lungs could muster. "Avalanche! Get to cover! Move, Move!"

Screams erupted from the women as they awoke to the danger. With precious few seconds left before the stone hurtled down upon them, Thomas desperately scanned the surrounding area for refuge. Catching sight of an outcropping of rock, he screamed to Peter and pointed. "Over there! Get under that!" While dashing toward the opening himself, he frantically looked about, trying to locate his uncle.

Suddenly he heard a wail of terror from one of the women. He stopped and turned to see a small child running toward one of the wagons. The mother began to run to fetch the child. Thomas yelled to Joshua, "Stop her! I'll get the girl!"

Dodging the stones and dirt showering down on him, he scrambled to the child and scooped her up. "My dolly, my dolly!" cried the girl, as she squirmed in Thomas's grip. Out of time and caught in the open, he dove under the wagon, hoping against hope that they would be spared. Rocks and dirt poured down from above, pounding on the fragile bed of the cart.

Several anxious moments later, the cascade began to subside. An eerie quiet settled upon the meadow. The air was thick with rock dust. The battered wagon had protected them, but the slide had covered it with dirt and stones. The little girl whimpered as she trembled in Thomas's arms. Digging at the debris which imprisoned them, he opened a passage through the rubble, working his way out into the open air. The dusty air burned his throat. "Where's my mommy?" sobbed the girl.

Gently lifting the child, Thomas stumbled about trying to get his bearings. After a few moments, he noticed a dull glow a short distance away. Moving carefully through the gloom, Thomas came upon Joshua building a fire. Shortly Pastor Marsh emerged from the darkness, assisting an injured woman toward the warmth of the fire. The little girl let out a squeal of recognition and dashed to her mother's waiting arms. As time passed more of the group found their way toward the light. Torches were lit, and the men set out to locate missing members of the party. Rising like smoke, the dust cloud was illuminated by the light of the rising sun above the cliffs.

As the injured were cared for, the dead were recovered and brought to the gathering place, where they were carefully laid out. Marsh glanced around, looking to see who had survived. "Where's Peter?" Frantically searching by the light of the torches, they fanned out trying to locate him.

Suddenly Joshua called out. "Over here!" Thomas rushed to the waving torch. Peter lay under the rock outcropping that Thomas had pointed out to him. One of the boulders raining down from the mountainside had evidently bounced in, pinning the Canadian. Thomas shuddered convulsively as he stared at Peter's face, wincing at the terror imprinted in his friend's still-open eyes.

Despair and guilt overwhelmed Thomas. Unable to move, he could only stare vacantly as Peter's body was gently carried to where the other victims lay. Pastor Marsh attempted to put his arm around Thomas's shoulders, but his nephew shrugged him off. "My boy, we must look to the Lord's mercy to help us through this tragedy," said Marsh softly.

Thomas whirled. Tears were forming tracks through the dust coating his face. "This makes no sense. Those people lived their whole lives in bondage. And then, just as they are about to taste freedom for the first time, they're killed by a damnable rockslide. Where's the justice in that? And Peter—he was trying to help them!"

Marsh opened his mouth to speak but Thomas cut him off. "Don't you understand? I killed him! I told Peter to get under there. It's my fault he's dead! And please don't tell me that 'God works in mysterious ways.' I see no mercy in all this." With that Thomas turned and stalked away. Marsh gazed after his nephew with quiet sadness. He knew that nothing he could say at this moment would make Thomas understand.

That day was spent tending wounds and burying the dead. Three men, two women, and two of the children had perished in the landslide, as well as three of the mules. Peter's body was carefully wrapped and placed in the bed of a wagon, to be returned to his family. Marsh called the survivors together to give a eulogy for those who had perished and to give thanks for the survival of the others. Thomas toiled feverishly digging graves and mending wagons, but otherwise stayed away from the group. Joshua tried to speak to him but all Thomas would do was shrug and turn away.

Resuming their trek early the next morning, the travelers paused north of Colebrook to rest. Marsh rode into town to purchase food and to ascertain the condition of the roads going north. The way ahead was reported clear, though snow was beginning to accumulate in the mountains. The passage of two more days found them at the Canadian border. The preacher dropped to his knees, bidding the others to do likewise to give thanks for their deliverance. Joshua clapped his hand on Thomas's back. "Ju-bi-lee! We is free!"

Thomas turned slowly and looked at his friend. "Yes, you are free," he said sadly, "And I hope you remember what that freedom has cost."

Joshua recoiled as if struck by a whip. "I knows what it cost. I also knows that your fren' lived all his life a free man, and died a free man. This is the first time in my life I can say I'se free, and if I was struck dead right now, it'd be worth it!"

At last, the tiny farm of the Cusson family came into view. Spying the weary travelers from the window, Augustine Cusson rose from his chair to greet them. Disturbed by the sad expressions on each face as they passed him, he grasped the bridle of Pastor Marsh's horse. "What has happened, friend Benjamin?"

Dismounting, the preacher wrapped his arm around Augustine's shoulder. "Your son is no longer with us," he said softly, "I am so sorry." As Marsh told Cusson about the landslide, the elderly man sank to his knees. He moaned, "Mon dieu, why?"

Marsh knelt beside him, and took his hands. "Come, my friend. Let us pray together, and find solace in His name."

Thomas gaped at them. *Go ahead, pray. See what good prayers will do for your son now.*

Anxious to return home before the weather closed in, Thomas and Pastor Marsh remained just through the next day. Marsh conducted the service as the Cusson's buried their son on a small hill overlooking their farm. Though deeply grief-stricken, Augustine assured the preacher that he would care for the fugitives. Early the next morning they bade farewell, and began the journey back to New Hampshire. Joshua had tried without success to cheer Thomas, but the farewell he received from his friend was lacking in any visible trace of emotion.

Now freed from the necessity of covert movements, the travelers were able to move quickly. This was fortunate, as winter was coming on in force. They were able to secure passage on a wagon heading down alongside the Connecticut River. Strong gale-force winds were whipping the snow as the two weary men finally arrived at Marsh's Hill. Mrs. Marsh embraced her husband as though returned from the dead. As she turned to greet Thomas, however, she was brought up short by the ashen look to his face. He mumbled a curt "hello," then stepped past her into the house. Rebecca started to follow but was gently restrained by her husband. "Thomas has suffered a severe blow to his soul. We shall have to be very patient with him while he heals." Marsh went on to explain about the tragedy in Dixville Notch.

Rebecca lifted her hand to her heart as she listened to the tale of horror. "Oh, my poor, poor dear."

Upon reaching his upstairs room, Thomas stripped off his mud-covered boots and flung them away. Not bothering to disrobe, he threw himself on the bed. He felt a desperate need for sleep, but the more he tried, the more his head swam with the journey's events. His mind's eye kept going back and forth between the gigantic rock beginning its fall from the cliff, and the sight of Peter's shattered, lifeless body.

How can it be, he thought, that a man can be born and grow up with such potential to do so many things—and then have his life snuffed out so quickly and by so senseless an event as a rock falling on him. A man is such a fragile being, he mused. His uncle had said that God has a reason and a purpose for all things. But what possible purpose could there be for Peter's death? He let out a moan. *It's my fault. I killed my friend.*

Chapter 8

A court-martial hastily arranged by Lieutenant Merrow found Jonathon Evans guilty of the assault on William, ordering Evans to be drummed out of the company. He was ceremoniously stripped of his uniform coat and marched under guard from the drill grounds. As Evans passed through the ranks, he couldn't help notice the smirk of pleasure on William Marsh's face. Evans glowered back, taking some satisfaction when the smile quickly vanished, replaced by a look of pale fear.

Over the next few weeks, Evans encountered the results of his being cashiered. Townspeople who had never liked his presence now openly shunned him. He was no longer welcome even by Collins and the other ruffians he had so long associated with. Only that half-wit Hiram Parker would have anything to do with him. His loathing for William grew with each snub he received, for he blamed Marsh for all his bad luck.

The final straw came when the owner of the livery informed him that his services were no longer needed. Business had been bad, explained the liveryman, so he had to let Jonathon go. "You're full of shit!" Evans had cried when told he was to clear his belongings from his small room behind the stables. "You're just like every other asshole in this town." Pulling his knife, he would have assaulted the old man if not brought up short by a shotgun shoved in his face.

Having no place else to go, Jonathon took up residence in an abandoned barn just outside of town. The decision to leave the county was made one night as he tossed and turned on his pallet. Sleep would not come, so he finally lay on his back, staring up at the rafters while weighing his options. *They're all bastards. Every one of 'em. And Willie Marsh is the worst of all. Someday I'm going to make him pay.*

But how? He had hardly any money. Nobody was about to stake him around here.

As he continued to stare upwards at the sagging beams, the realization came that he had no chance if he stayed in Lumpkin County. He couldn't even earn a living as a thief or road agent, for he was too well known in the region, and would certainly be recognized and hunted down. No, he had to get away from here, to go somewhere where he wasn't known.

Reaching up from his cot, he slipped his belt and holster from its peg. Drawing the old dragoon pistol, he spun the cylinder, sighting down the barrel as if aiming. In his mind's eye he imagined William Marsh sitting trussed up, helplessly waiting for the shot that would kill him. *Yep, someday I'm going to do you, Willie-boy.* Lifting the weapon, he studied the scene of battle between soldiers and Indians engraved on the cylinder. The old gun was the only thing left to him by his father, killed in the Mexican War. Couldn't have happened to a nicer fellow, he thought, remembering the beatings his father had inflicted on him as a child.

This wouldn't do, he thought. *Too big and clunky and hard to get ammunition for. Need something easier to load with more power.*

A mental image of the liveryman's shotgun aimed at his face popped into his thoughts, causing him to shiver. *A shotgun.* He grinned. *Hey, that's it. A scattergun is scarier. Can load that with just about anything.*

Now, where was he going to get a shotgun? Steal one, maybe? *Wonder if storekeeper McCay has one—maybe do a trade.*

As morning broke, Jonathon saddled his mare and rode into town. Tying up in front of the Mercantile, he glanced about as he strode up the steps to the door. Looking toward Isaac Stewart's house, he caught a glimpse of movement in one of the upstairs windows. He was sure that someone was peering at him through a slit in the curtains, but they closed when he tried to get a better view by shielding his eyes with his hand. *Mary Stewart. Busybody slut.*

Sorting mail behind the counter, Jedidiah McCay barely paid any attention when Evans came through the door. Dropping the revolver on the counter, he waited several moments for McCay to acknowledge his presence. His anger growing as Jedidiah continued to ignore him, Evans finally exploded. Picking up the pistol, he slammed it back down on the counter, yelling "Hey, storekeep! How 'bout some service!"

McCay slipped one more letter into a slot, then slowly turned. "Oh, hello, Jonathon. Didn't notice you come in. What can I do for you?"

Evans pushed the pistol across the counter toward Jedidiah. "I'm looking for a shotgun. You be willing to do a swap for this?"

Jedidiah picked up the massive revolver and cocked the hammer. "I don't know. This old thing is in pretty rough shape."

"But it shoots good. With all the goin's on, somebody will probably want a good handgun to take to war."

"Hopefully it won't come to that. Why do you want to trade this, anyway?"

"I'm leaving town. Pistol's no good for hunting."

"What kind of hunting you planning to do?"

"Whatever kind's needed. You going to trade or not?"

"Well . . . let me see what I've got." McCay pulled an old double-barreled shotgun from a rack behind the counter. "This one's not much to look at, but it's a solid shooter. I've shot it myself." He handed the gun to Jonathon.

Evans examined the piece closely, snapping the hammers to check the action. "Kind of old, but looks to be in good shape." He swung the gun around, taking aim in several directions. "Feels good. Yep, this one will do, if you'll trade me even for the pistol."

Jedidiah nodded. "All right, it's a deal. The powder and shot will be extra, though."

"Suit's me. I'll need a pound of each. Got my own flask for the powder."

McCay wrapped up the supplies. "That'll be a dollar."

"Here," replied Jonathon, pulling out a silver coin. "And do me a favor. See that Willie Marsh gets this." He handed McCay a folded piece of paper.

A frown crossed Jedidiah's face. "What's this?"

Jonathon gathered up his packages and the shotgun. "Just see that Marsh gets it," he growled as he headed for the door. Stuffing the packages into a canvas bag strung from the pommel, he swung up into his saddle. Glancing around as he yanked the reins, he caught a fleeting glimpse of someone looking down again from that window in Old Man Stewart's house.

Arriving back at the barn, he tossed the shotgun and bag onto a table, then proceeded to uncinch his horse's saddle. As he pulled the reins from over the horse's head, he was suddenly acutely aware of a presence behind him. Slowly, cautiously, his fingers moved toward the hilt of his knife.

"Jonathon?"

Whirling at the sound of his name, he yanked the blade from its sheath. Squinting in the dim light, he almost dropped the knife when he realized who was there. Standing in the barn's doorway, outlined in the darkness by the light of the fading sunset, stood Mary Stewart.

GEORGE WINSTON MARTIN

Evans slammed the knife back into its scabbard. "What the hell do you want?"

Mary entered, moving slowly toward him. "I heard that you're leaving town."

"Word gets around fast. What's it to you?"

Mary kept on until she was standing before him. "I want you to take me with you."

The words stunned him. For a moment he could not speak, finally mumbling, "Yeh, sure."

"I mean it. I love you, and I want to go wherever you go."

Jonathon turned to hang the reins on a peg. "And just what gave you that fool idea?"

Mary reached out, laying her palm on Jonathon's cheek. "You can't live without me."

"And just what makes you think that?"

She stroked Jonathon's face. "Let me show you." Her hand shot up behind Evan's head, pulling it toward her.

As they kissed, Mary's other fingers worked to undo the buttons on Jonathon's shirt. Drawing back, she began to giggle as she pulled the cloth from his shoulders, exposing his bare chest.

Spinning about, she darted into an empty stall. Stepping into the middle of a pile of hay, she glanced enigmatically back at him over her shoulder, then slowly turned to face him. Evans watched with mounting excitement as her hand rose to finger the top hook of her blouse. Slowly each clasp was released, and the garment dropped away, revealing her white corset. Raising her arms, she beckoned him to come.

Morning sunlight filtered through boards of the barn's walls as Mary awoke to the sound of creaking leather. Looking around, she reached for her dress, pulling it to her as she sat up. Jonathon was pulling the cinch strap tight around his horse. Picking up her chemise, she rose and drew on the garment.

Slipping up behind Evans as he strapped a blanket to the back of the saddle, she wrapped her arms around him, and nuzzled her cheek into his back. "I want to go with you," she said softly.

Grasping her arms, Jonathon pried them from around his chest. "Can't."

Mary drew back, suddenly anxious. "Why not?"

58

Evans stepped over to a table, gathering up his shotgun and canvas sack. "Cause you'd just slow me down. I want to get as far as possible from this piss-ass town as I can."

"But what about last night?"

"Last night was last night. Nothing more, nothing less."

"But I love you . . . and you love me, too. You said so."

Jonathon looped the drawstring of the sack on the saddle's pommel. "A man'll say lots of things when he's 'involved.' Don't mean it's true."

"I don't care what you're saying now. I know you love me, and I'll wait for you to come back."

Swinging into the saddle, Jonathon leaned down to pat Mary's head. "Mean's no never mind to me. You'll be waiting a mighty long time." With that, Evans sat up and spurred his horse.

A single tear, more from rage than sadness, trickled down Mary's cheek as she watched Evans gallop away. *Oh, no, darlin.' That's not the end. You'll be hearing from me again.*

Chapter 9

As the months of 1860 passed, secession fever swept across the South. Many of the inhabitants of Dahlonega embraced the notion, but there were also many who opposed separation as a great evil.

William poured all his energies into the militia, often to the detriment of his farm chores. Sergeant Fitzpatrick had loaned him a copy of *Hardee's Tactics* to study. As the new first corporal of the company, he was expected to assist in the training of the new recruits. Most nights would find him bent over the pages, trying to make sense of the many difficult words. He cursed himself many times for not staying with his schoolwork. Several times he was forced to ask an amused Melissa to sound out a particularly difficult word.

Between chores, he would try to put theory into practice, attempting with great difficulty to figure out the difference between "rank" and "file". Using his old flintlock squirrel rifle, he tried to master the manual of arms. "Shoulder, Arms! Right Shoulder Shift, Arms!" He bellowed out the commands while trying to follow the illustrations in the book. The cow started at each shout, once even kicking over a pail full of milk. Bayonet drill was accomplished by jamming a sharpened stick into the muzzle.

At least one problem had seemingly resolved itself. William had taken great pleasure watching Evans being dismissed from the company, though the look his foe gave as he left caused a chill to go down William's spine.

The relief William felt when Evans left town was short lived, however. Shortly after his adversary's departure, William was picking up supplies at the Mercantile. Jedidiah McCay handed him a folded slip of paper. "I was told to make sure you got this."

William's face went ashen when he read:

You did this to me. Some day you will pay. I won't forget.

William showed McCay the note. "If he ever comes back, I'm in trouble."

The shopkeeper frowned. "Look's like you need to watch your back. No tellin' what he's likely to do. Looks as though he's left these parts, but you'd probably better keep your squirrel gun loaded and handy."

William's pursuit of Mary Stewart had not slowed, though her actions at the dance still bewildered him. She would not even look in his direction for some time following the event. Something had caused her to pass him up for Jonathon that night, he thought. Surely, he must have done something wrong, something that had made her angry with him. Trying a new avenue toward winning her forgiveness, he decided to call on her father.

Even though he had detested school, William had always respected Isaac Stewart as an intelligent and fair man. He knew that the school teacher was one of the many townspeople strongly against secession, so he tried to avoid mentioning it. Unfortunately, it was next to impossible to keep the subject out of a conversation these days. "I like you, my boy," Stewart said, "though I do not approve of your association with the militia. The fire-eaters in South Carolina and here are determined to break up our glorious Union. Even so, I respect you as a hard worker and provider for your family. Your mother has always been a good friend. And Jedidiah McCay always speaks highly of you." Then he frowned. "However, I think you had best give up trying to impress my daughter. I do not think that you would be happy with her."

William was stunned. "B—B—But, sir! I would do anything to make her happy! Anything!"

Stewart's broad shoulders sagged. "I believe you, son. But my daughter has a strong will, and definitely a mind of her own. She will never be satisfied with just one man's attentions. She is much like her mother in that respect." He stared at a woman's portrait on the wall.

William had seen the painting of Mary's mother several times, and he had always marveled at the strong resemblance between mother and daughter. He knew what the schoolmaster was referring to. Everyone in town knew of the scandalous affair involving Julia Stewart.

Several years previous an adventurous young man had come to Dahlonega to take his share of the gold strike. Going by the name Drake, his method for acquiring the yellow metal was not to sweat in the mines; rather, he took up residence in the local tavern and proceeded to deprive the miners of their diggings with the deft use of cards. He was a handsome scoundrel, and one day happened to cross paths with the Stewart family. Isaac paid little attention to him other than a polite "good day."

Julia, however, was instantly smitten by Drake's good looks and swaggering manner. Determined to learn more about this mysterious stranger, she arranged it so that she "accidentally" bumped into him while coming out from McCay's store. After a few minutes of light banter, he took his leave—but not before Julia slipped him a note proposing that they meet with "less formality" in a location that would assure them more privacy. Intrigued by this dark beauty, Drake kept the rendezvous, and before long tongues were wagging throughout town about the affair. A quiet, soft-spoken man, Stewart tried to ignore the gossip, not wanting to believe what was being said.

After closing the schoolhouse one afternoon, he had come home to find that she had fled, along with her clothes and all the money they had carefully saved. Their daughter Mary had been deposited with the lady next door.

Jedidiah McCay had urged him to chase them down, but Stewart simply turned away and went back to his house, there to try to raise Mary as best he could, alone.

Stewart turned back towards William. "I will not try to discourage you further if you wish to see my daughter. But I believe you will be destined for great disappointment. Mary will never be able to give her affections to a single person, and I fear that her wild spirit will bring much unhappiness to anyone who attempts to tame her, yourself included. However, if you still wish to try, I will speak to her on your behalf."

Joy welled up within William's breast. Stewart's warning was immediately forgotten. He pumped the schoolmaster's hand. "Thank you, sir, thank you!"

Chapter 10

Far away up north Thomas ignored the political turmoil enveloping the country. Ever since his return from Canada, he had become progressively more withdrawn, descending with each passing day into a dark melancholy. Strong liquor became his constant companion—he increasingly frequented the taverns in town, and Pastor Marsh found many bottles secreted around the farm. Marsh warned Thomas that he would not hold with strong spirits being consumed on his property and that he would destroy any liquor that he discovered. Shortly thereafter, coming upon his uncle in the process of smashing one of his precious stashes, Thomas flew into a rage, barely restraining himself from assaulting the old man.

Impassioned rhetoric intensified throughout North and South as the presidential campaign of 1860 moved toward its climax. Moderates were drowned out by extremists from either side of the Mason-Dixon Line. With the approach of Election Day, the southern fire-eaters proclaimed that the election of Abraham Lincoln would give the Southern states no choice but to secede from the Union. And if the Federal government tried to force them to stay, there would be war.

Thomas continued to sink farther into depression as the year passed. No longer did he accompany his uncle north into Canada. He cared little about the excitement and anxiety of the 1860 presidential campaign. Marsh was squarely behind a little known candidate from Illinois, Abraham Lincoln, though many of his acquaintances backed Senator Stephen Douglas. Many evenings the Marsh front porch reverberated with loud political arguments.

Much as he wanted to ignore the growing sectional split, however, he could not avoid it. Even though he had lived in New Hampshire for many years, Thomas found himself becoming more ostracized with each passing day. People with whom he had enjoyed only a cursory acquaintance now would not speak to him, and he even found close friends sometimes avoiding his company. More than once the words "damn southerner" floated past his ear. His frequent bouts of drunkeness did little to improve his popularity.

Election night 1860 found the Marsh porch the scene of a furious political discussion. The preacher was arguing passionately in favor of Lincoln's election. Marsh's friend Russell shouted back that Lincoln didn't stand a chance against Douglas, the "Little Giant."

The conversation was of no interest to Thomas. With no comment as to where he was headed, he saddled his horse and rode into Lymington. Election celebrations were going on all over the village. Entering the tavern, he ordered a bottle, tossed a couple of coins on the bar and took his accustomed place at a rear corner table. He preferred to stay as far in the background as possible while he drank, to avoid possible confrontations.

While Thomas downed one shot glass after another, the crowd in the tavern was growing increasingly boisterous. Even though it would take a day or two before the results of the voting were known, most in the saloon were Lincoln men, and they were already celebrating his victory. Anyone proclaiming allegiance to any of the other candidates was likely to find himself tossed out onto the street.

It was near midnight when one of the rowdies staggered his way toward Thomas's table. "Well, if it ain't our own local secesh."

Thomas peered up from under the brim of his hat toward the drunk. "Friend, I have no quarrel with you. All I wish is to be left alone."

The inebriated trouble-maker spat on the table. "Damn southron slave-holder! This time we'll get someone for pres'dent that won't take no guff off'n the likes of you!"

Thomas's eyes narrowed to slits, but he remained still. "I have no interest in this election. Furthermore, I own no slaves and never have. I am against slavery as much as you. Now please just leave me to myself."

Too drunk for more than selective hearing, the lout was working himself into a blind rage. Grabbing the edge of the table, he tossed it aside, then stood over Thomas, both hands balled into fists. "Stinkin' slaver, I'll take care of you right now!" He lunged, but was so wobbly it was easy for Thomas to leap aside. Stumbling over the now-vacant chair, the bully crashed headlong into the wall.

Staggering to his feet, he prepared to charge again, but was brought up short by the black void of a derringer muzzle aimed directly at his nose. Instantly, his enraged expression melted into shocked fright. "I told you I want no trouble," said Thomas, a slight tremor in his voice. "Now I'll thank you to kindly stay right there while I leave."

Everyone in the tavern was staring at him, and it was evident that more than a few of them would like to finish what the drunk had attempted. Glancing about, he observed that the way to the door was blocked.

The whiskey circulating in Thomas's bloodstream was causing his head to swim. Cornered, he was trying desperately to come up with a plan of escape when a voice came from behind. "Hey, friend." Thomas whirled and aimed his pistol.

The man in the shadows raised his hand. "Whoa, boy, don't shoot me! Looks like you need a little help gettin' away from this crowd." He motioned toward a door half hidden behind a curtain. "Come on with me, quick!"

Thomas waved the derringer toward the crowd. "I intend to leave quietly. It would be very unhealthy for anyone who tried to keep me from doing so." With that, he and the stranger darted out the back door. They kept running, first up one alley, then down another until they were certain that there was no pursuit.

The two finally stopped, leaning against a wall as they gasped for breath. Thomas felt extremely lightheaded from both the exertion and the whiskey. "My thanks to you," he said to the stranger, the words emerging more as a wheeze. "I was in a bit of a spot back there."

"Glad t'do it. Didn't seem like you could get a fair shake in with that bunch. Name's James Stark."

"Thomas Marsh."

"Seem's like you're not too popular in this town, least not in that tavern. Those folks ain't too keen on southerners right now. Where you hail from?"

Thomas winced. He wasn't sure he should say, not knowing this fellow's politics. "Is that really important?"

Stark laughed. "Don't worry. North Carolina's where I hail from. But I've been here long enough to call myself a Yankee. Trouble is, a lot of people right now figger that where yer born makes more difference than what ya believe. Lot of folks in my neck of the woods don't hold with slavery. Hell, most of 'em are too *poor* to own slaves."

"Well, well. I'm from Georgia. Born in Dahlonega, northeast of Atlanta. I've know slaveholders there who are good people, but I always felt uncomfortable with it."

Stark let out a sigh. "Looks like we're jes a couple of lost southrens."

Thomas grinned. "Fish out of water both places." He liked this fellow. Maybe he had finally found a friend.

Chapter 11

"William, be careful!" Concentrating on the task of sewing up a rip in one of Melissa's dresses, Lucinda was startled by the clang of a pewter plate on the wooden floor.

Gobbling down his breakfast, William had knocked the dish from the table while stretching for a biscuit. "Sorry, Ma," he muttered, trying not to spit out food while stuffing more bread into his mouth.

Lucinda wagged her finger at her son. "Slow down. You'll make yourself sick."

William reached down to retrieve the plate, then snatched another biscuit as he sprang from the table. "Can't slow down. Can't be late for drill today." He disappeared into the bedroom.

"What's so important about today?"

William was tugging on his uniform coat as he reemerged. "You'll see. I'll have something special with me when I get back."

Excited chatter filling the air greeted William at the drill field. Several wagons were drawn up at one end. Standing next to the tongue of one was Sergeant Fitzpatrick, rapidly making notations in a small book, while Lieutenant Merrow and the other officers gathered in conversation off to one side. Dozing in a camp chair was Captain Harris, silvery hair revealed when his hat tumbled unnoticed to the ground.

Samuel Craig, a gangly young fellow who liked to know everything that went on, ran up to William, his face aglow with youthful anticipation. He pointed toward the wagons. "We really gonna get 'em today?"

William grinned. "Today's the day! They're in those crates."

Sergeant Fitzpatrick shouted at the company to fall in. Lieutenant Merrow mounted his horse and rode to the front of the ranks. Standing in the stirrups, he addressed the men. "Soldiers! The shipment from the Augusta Arsenal has arrived! Today our new members will receive proper arms! Sergeant—distribute the muskets!"

Kepis flew into the air as the men raised a cheer. As the recruits marched to the wagons, William could see the long, rough wooden crates. His eyes gleamed as Fitzpatrick pried open the topmost box.

Pulling out the uppermost gun, the sergeant handed it down. The 1822 Springfield musket was enormous in William's grip. Close to five feet long, its polished barrel glinted in the sun. The lock mechanism, converted from flintlock to the newer percussion ignition, looked enormous; much larger than the delicate cock and pan on his squirrel rifle. The .69 caliber bore yawned open like the barrel of a cannon.

From another container came a large leather cartridge box, slung on a white cross belt. Next was a white waist belt with a brass oval buckle, the letters "U.S." stamped on it. Hung from the belt was a black scabbard sheathing a long, deadly-looking bayonet. Quickly William donned the accouterments and hefted the musket onto his shoulder. He felt as if he could take on any manner of enemy.

Once the last man received his arms, the order to fall in was given. The men moved into their ranks with a great clatter, unused as they were to moving with the extra bulk and weight of the muskets and accouterments. The rest of the afternoon was taken up by drill in the manual of arms. One soldier asked impatiently when they were going to get to shoot them.

"Just as soon as I know for sartin that you won't kill each other on the first volley!" retorted Sergeant Fitzpatrick, who then dismissed the troops.

William spent the next week diligently cleaning and oiling his musket. By the day of the next drill session, he had worked himself into a fever pitch in anticipation of firing the weapon.

As they lined up to receive their ammunition, each man was issued several cylindrical paper cartridges containing a measured charge of black powder. What amused them most about the rounds were the projectiles concealed inside. James Hunt yelled out to Fitzpatrick. "Hey, Sarge! What's with all the little shot in with the ball?"

The sergeant held up one cartridge. "These are buck-and-ball. One large round ball and three buckshot will make the other darlin' dance quite a jig when it comes at him." William gulped. The mental image of a man's flesh being ripped apart by such lethal blast somehow didn't quite fit in with his ideal of "honorable wounds" described by the veterans of the Mexican War.

Following several practice tries, the soldiers were finally allowed to ram powder and ball down the bore of their weapons, after which they shouldered their arms in preparation for firing. "Ready!" bellowed Fitzpatrick, taking place behind the ranks. The long firearms all swung up to the proper position. "Point!" Stocks rose to shoulders, muzzles pointed downrange toward a row of bottles. Soldiers in the rear leaned forward between their front rank comrades.

"FIRE!"

Flame belched forth as the ragged volley tore the air. As the cloud of white smoke cleared, Fitzpatrick surveyed a chaotic scene. Several soldiers were flat on their backs, knocked backward by the force of the recoil. One man was hollering in pain as blood dribbled down his face—the man behind him had held the musket lock too close, and a small shard of the copper percussion cap had lodged in his cheek. Fitzpatrick peered toward the targets. One bottle was missing; the rest stood untouched. Fitzpatrick covered his eyes as he slowly shook his head. *Lord give me strength.*

With the coolness of spring giving way to the heat and humidity of summer, Lucinda's anxieties multiplied. She had heard almost nothing from Thomas, and the few letters she received from Pastor Marsh were notable by how little he mentioned of her older son. It was almost as though her brother-in-law was trying to avoid talking about Thomas. And with war fever raging all across the region, she knew it was just a matter of time before William might be called to march away.

Her son's infatuation with Mary Stewart made her fret, too. That girl was wild, and seemed to be cut out of the same cloth as her mother. Lucinda was so afraid that her son would be hurt. William had managed to talk Mary into letting him take her for a buggy ride one evening, and he hadn't come home at all. The next day he came dragging in to do his chores, but didn't seem to care that he was totally exhausted. At dinner Lucinda asked how the evening went. William's face went red. "Just fine," he replied with an odd smile, but said nothing more.

Since the events at the dance, William had tried many times to persuade Mary to let him escort her again. On several occasions he saw her in the company of Hiram Parker, one of the hoodlums that had beaten him. Most times when he tried to speak to her, she would just stick her nose up into the air and walk away. With the passing of several months, though, her anger toward him seemed to dissipate. Maybe she was finally tired of associating with those ruffians, he hoped. Or maybe her father had managed to have that promised little talk with her.

Then one day, he chanced to encounter her near the schoolhouse. Stammering out a hello, he managed to ask if she would be interested in taking a buggy ride that evening. After a moment's hesitation, Mary said yes. William was jubilant. He couldn't believe his good fortune. He raced home to get his uniform clean so as to impress her. Driving Mr. McCay's borrowed rig, he arrived at the Stewart house after dinner. As he helped Mary into the seat, he missed the somber look on Mr. Stewart's face.

No words were spoken between them during the ride into the countryside. Finally William pulled up at a lovely spot next to the river. Turning to Mary, he said awkwardly, "This is my favorite place. I come here a lot to fish, and sometimes just to think. Nobody bothers me here." Mary glanced around, obviously unimpressed. He went on. "I need to ask you something. What happened at the dance? Why did you go to dancin' with Evans after you had said you were my girl? And why did you take more'n a year to talk to me again?"

Mary looked away for several moments, then turned to William. "I was so mad at you," she said, her voice tinged with prickliness.

William was amazed. "Why?"

"All you ever talked about was the militia. And you were wearing such horribly dirty clothes when you came to my house. I was so embarrassed to be seen with you."

William was mortified. "But, they were the best I had. Least wise, 'til I got this uniform. And I wanted to be the best soldier possible, so's you'd be proud of me."

"A girl wants a certain amount of attention from a man, just to let her know he hasn't lost interest in her." Mary slid closer to William's side. "After all, you don't want me to be bored, do you?"

Warmth rose around William's neck as he felt aware of Mary's body cozying up to his. He desperately tried to think of anything smart and proper to say as he gazed into her face. She looked at him for a few moments, then spoke softly. "Well, are you going to kiss me or not?"

William felt as though he was about to pass out. Nervously wrapping his arm around her shoulder, he hesitantly placed his lips to hers; then was startled when she wrapped her hand behind his head, aggressively drawing him tightly to her mouth.

Long minutes passed as the two kissed. Suddenly, Mary pushed him away. Unable to suppress a titter at his look of bewilderment, she put her fingers on his lips. "Not now, my love. The time will come for us. Now I think you should take me home."

"Uh . . . okay," he stammered. Trying to collect himself, William picked up the reins and urged the horse back down the road to town. Pulling up in front of Mary's house, he lifted her from the seat and escorted her to the door. Giving in to an impulse to attempt another kiss, he leaned forward. Mary pulled back, shaking her head. "For goodness sake, not *now*. My father may be watching." She gave him a little peck on the cheek, and with a quick "Good night," disappeared inside. William remained standing for a few moments, gently rubbing the spot on his cheek. Climbing back into the buggy, he drove back out to the place by the river. Tying the horse to a tree, he lay down in the grass, gazing up at the star-filled sky, a million thoughts swirling in his brain.

Chapter 12

Autumn once more descended across the mountains of North Georgia. Forests transformed from green to brilliant reds and gold, then to gray as leaves gently fluttered to earth. Other changes, political ones, loomed over the country. Farmers harvesting their crops, miners slaving in their holes in the earth and tradesmen carrying on their business watched and waited as Election Day came and passed.

With Lincoln's election, the southern states acted quickly on their threats. South Carolina took the lead, adopting an ordinance of secession on December 20 in a frenzied convention in Columbia. With the coming of the new year of 1861, the other states of the Deep South followed in rapid succession; Mississippi on January 9, Florida, January 10, Alabama, January 11. William and the other Dahlonega Volunteers cheered when Georgia seceded on January 19. Musket fire echoed across the town, and anvils rang as blacksmiths pounded them in celebration. Louisiana joined the other states on January 26, and on February 1, Texas left the Union.

Quickly the seceding states sent delegates to Montgomery, Alabama, to begin the process of setting up a new nation and government, to be known as the Confederate States of America. Jefferson Davis was sworn in as the Confederacy's first president on George Washington's birthday, February 22. The Southern legislature set about to raise an army and to acquire all posts occupied by the United States within the boundaries of the Confederacy.

Lumpkin County was aflutter with the news from Charleston, South Carolina. The Federal fort in the harbor known as Sumter was surrounded by artillery batteries. General Beauregard, the local commander, had demanded the forts' evacuation. A ship attempting to deliver provisions to the garrison had been fired upon and turned back. It was just a matter of time before the fragile truce between the garrison and the eager gunners on land would fall apart. The residents of Dahlonega anticipated that war was imminent.

The Dahlonega Volunteers were kept busy preparing, drilling at every opportunity. Considering themselves no longer part of the United States, the men all turned their belt buckles upside down. The "U S" now became "S N", for "Southern Nation". The boys were eager and ready to go to war. All they needed now was a flag.

A suitable banner was soon theirs. Several of the town's ladies, including Mrs. Merrow and Lucinda Marsh, formed a sewing society to create a flag to be presented to the company.

The Volunteers fell in at the Old Mustering Grounds, then marched to the courthouse square, Captain Harris and his officers riding in front of the column. Arriving at the square, the company was formed back into ranks and given the order for parade rest. Harris and his officers climbed the stairs up to the courthouse platform. Waiting there were the mayor and his wife, along with several other town officials. Harris saluted, then shook the mayor's hand.

Motioning for the gathering to hold its applause, the mayor spoke. "Captain Harris, the young ladies of Dahlonega would now like to present you and your men with your battle colors." The mayor motioned to his wife, who came forward and handed a carefully wrapped parcel to the captain. Harris slowly untied the package and withdrew the folded cloth. With Lieutenant Merrow's help he spread out the flag for his men and the crowd to see. Made of silk bordered with a gold fringe, the banner was designed after the "Stars and Bars," the new national flag of the Confederacy. The flag had a large blue square in one corner holding a constellation of seven white stars in a circle, with a field made of three wide stripes—red on top, white in the center, and red on the bottom.

Sergeant Fitzpatrick barked out new orders. "Color Guard, front and center to receive colors!" Sergeant Samuel Hoskins stepped forward to take possession of the flag, and carefully attached it to its staff.

"Ladies and good people of Dahlonega," said Harris, "These soldiers give their pledge that this flag shall never be stained with dishonor—that they would die to a man rather than see it fall before the enemy!"

Each passing day brought more apprehension to Lucinda. With war descending upon the country, she knew that William would soon be leaving with his company. She could not drive away the mental image of her son being maimed or even killed on some far away battlefield. Of even greater terror for her was the possibility of him disappearing without a trace, as had happened to Aaron. Another source of distress was how she would get all the farm chores finished, especially the heavy work that always needed doing. William had given her Henry's assurance of the loan of one or more of Greenfield's slaves any time she might need them. Lucinda's father had never owned any slaves, and the thought of them working in her garden and barn made her uneasy.

New enlistees poured in to fill the rolls of the Dahlonega Volunteers. The company rapidly filled to a full strength of one hundred men plus officers, and was forced to turn away many disappointed recruits. For the time being, it seemed that the Confederacy had more volunteers for service than it could equip.

Dividing time between all his activities was becoming quite a challenge for William. Captain Harris had offered the services of the company to Governor Joseph E. Brown, so the Volunteers might be called away at any time. He worked feverishly trying to complete the many farm projects such as fence mending, plowing and patching the cabin's roof. Most of these chores had been left undone while he spent his days with the militia. Now they had to be finished before his departure. Fortunately Lieutenant Merrow had sharply reduced the number of drills so the men could spend as much time as possible getting their affairs in order.

Of course, time could always be found for courting Mary. Most evenings after chores were finished, William would clean himself up and set off for town to see her. He took great pains to make sure that he was clothed suitably, not wanting to embarrass her again with his appearance. He seldom wore his uniform on these outings in deference to her father, who was becoming increasingly vocal against the secessionists. Many times Stewart would argue his case for the Union with such eloquence that William would begin to doubt his own convictions. Mary, on the other hand, had little interest in the breakup of the states. She was constantly complaining how the war would make it more difficult for her to get the latest fashion information, or how it was already becoming hard to find her favorite lotions and scents at the Mercantile.

Later they would go for walks around town. William yearned for another kiss, but somehow the opportunity never quite seemed to present itself. Her distance frustrated him, but like the temptation of forbidden fruit, caused him to desire her all the more.

"Hey, Willie!" William jumped, dropping his pipe, his daydream of Mary shattered by Henry's shout. Retrieving the corncob, he glared while knocking out the ashes. "What's the big idea?"

Henry laughed. "I just thought you might like to know some awfully important news. Last night I overheard Father and Lieutenant Rhodes talking. Seems that Governor Brown has sent Captain Harris a letter ordering the company to Macon . . . right away!"

William's jaw dropped. "You mean . . . ?"

"Yep. We're about to head off to war!"

"Oh—my—God! When?"

Henry shrugged. "Not sure. Didn't hear the whole conversation. But soon for certain!" He and William cavorted around the yard, whooping like Indians.

Suddenly William stopped dead in his tracks. He ran toward the barn. Henry yelled after him. "Hey, where you going?"

"Got to get to town! I want to tell Mary before she hears it from someone else." William frantically saddled his horse. *She just has to give me a kiss when she finds this out!* Leaping into the saddle, he rode out of the barn shouting, "Thanks, Henry!" as he passed his befuddled friend.

Henry scratched his head as he stared at the dissipating dust cloud. *Well, friend, I hope you get what you're wishing for.* He frowned as he mounted his own horse. *Watch out for her, Willie. She's no good for you.*

Galloping up to the Stewart house, William jumped from the saddle, taking the steps two at a time. He rapped impatiently. Opening the door, Mr. Stewart informed him that Mary was not inside, having gone down to the store to pick up a few notions. William thanked Stewart hastily and dashed off toward the Mercantile. "She was here a few minutes ago," said Jedidiah McCay, "Hiram Parker came in, and she left with him."

William was stunned. Why would Mary want to be seen with that hooligan? "Any idea where they went?"

"Don't know for sure, but looked like they were goin' down toward the schoolhouse."

Muttering a quick thanks, William trotted off down the street. Approaching the school, he could hear faint laughter issuing from within. It sounded a lot like Mary's voice. Carefully he circled the building, seeking a place to get a look inside without being seen. Finding a broken chair, he propped it against the wall, then gingerly climbed up to peer in a window. Dust on the glass, along with the darkness inside, made it difficult to see. Catching a glimpse of movement, he stretched up to see better, wobbling uncertainly on his perch. What he saw next made his eyes fly wide open with disbelief.

Mary and Parker lay together on the teacher's table, partially disrobed and locked in a passionate embrace.

The shock of the scene caused William to lose his balance on the sagging chair. Down he went with a loud crash.

William desperately wanted to run, but, dazed by the fall, took several moments before he could scramble to his feet. The schoolhouse door burst open. Mary came rushing out, her clothes in disarray from being thrown on in haste. William heard a bang and figured that Parker must have run out the door on the far side, slamming it as he exited.

Mary glared at William with a mixture of fury and embarrassment as he slowly brushed dirt from his clothes. "Just what were you doing, William Marsh? What gives you the right to spy on me?"

Absolutely speechless, all William could do was gape at her with disbelieving eyes. Furious, she continued to berate. "Don't look at me that way! You don't own me. It's my business who I associate with!"

"But I thought—I thought that you were my girl again." The words almost choked in William's throat.

"*Your* girl! I don't belong to anybody! You're just somebody I could have a little fun with, that's all. I told you I was 'your girl' just to make sure you'd keep coming back. But you're not fun anymore, you little pest! And it's because of you that the only *real* man in this town had to leave! But just you wait. Jonathon is going to make it big, and when he does, he'll be back for me!"

Mary finished fastening her blouse, then turned and stormed away. William felt as if his whole world had just crashed. Almost stumbling as he climbed the steps, he entered the schoolhouse. For several minutes he stared at the teacher's table. Pulling up a chair, he sat, laying his head on the table. He felt worn-out and crushed as tears welling from his eyes wet the pine boards.

William awoke to find himself in total darkness. He lurched around the unlit schoolroom as he made his way to the door. Stepping outside, he took a long breath of the cool, early spring night air. He was done with her, he declared to himself. She was the one who had lost out, not him. If she wanted to hang around losers and good-for-nothings like Evans and Parker, well, he didn't want to have anything more to do with her.

He slowly ambled up the street to the Stewart's house to retrieve his horse. Once again, tears began to roll down his cheeks as he looked at the lamp lit windows of her house. *No! I'll not cry for her. Ever again!* Mounting, he turned up the road toward home.

Chapter 13

The news that Henry had overheard turned out to be true. The day had finally come for the Dahlonega Volunteers to depart. Lieutenant Merrow sent word to everyone in the unit about the orders from Governor Brown. Once the Volunteers reached Macon they were to be combined with other companies from different parts of the state into a full infantry regiment.

Lucinda prepared an especially large breakfast for William that first day of April. "There's no tellin' when you'll get a decent meal again," she said, as he protested at the heaping plate of food placed before him.

After he finished eating, they walked out onto the porch together. From across the mountains came the echo of a distant rumble of thunder. "Sounds like a storm might be coming," said William. He grasped his mother's hands. "Wish you'd come to town to see me off."

Lucinda pulled her son's hand to her cheek. "No, I want to say good-bye here in the quiet of our home, not with all the hullabaloo at the courthouse." Moisture welled in her eyes as she reached out to fasten his top coat button. "Now you do good and take care of yourself."

Gently grasping her hands, William said, "Don't cry, Ma. I'll be back home in no time after we whip them Yankees. One good look at our muskets and they'll skedaddle. I 'spect that I'll be back in time to bring in the hay this summer."

Just then, a wagon bearing Henry and several other men careened into the yard, driven by one of Greenfield's slaves. Henry was waving and hollering. "C'mon, Willie!" William glared at him. Catching the look, Henry grinned. "I beg your pardon, sir! I mean *First Corporal William Marsh,* sir! Get your stripes over here! We got to get to the courthouse before we get left behind!"

Turning back to Lucinda, William wiped a tear from her cheek. "Good-bye, Ma—Mother." They looked at each other for a moment, then embraced. William reached for his musket, and then turned to Melissa, rubbing his hand on her head, ruffling her hair. "So long, squirt. Take care of Ma 'til I get back. And stay out of the creek!"

Giving her a quick hug, he dashed to the wagon, leaping aboard to the cheers and backslaps of the men.

Lucinda continued to watch long after they disappeared down the road. Feeling suddenly weak, she sat down in her rocker. Melissa knelt beside Lucinda and laid her head in her mother's lap. "Willie'll be back soon, won't he?" she asked.

Drawing a handkerchief from her apron pocket, Lucinda dabbed at her eyes. "I hope so, darling, I truly hope so."

As the wagon tore down the road toward town, William felt exhilarated—and just a little scared. Partly anxious at the prospect of war and battle, but mostly afraid that he would do something that would make him look foolish to the other men. He also thought about being away from home for so long—and so far. He was barely away, and already was missing the comfort of home and family.

Rain was falling as the Volunteers gathered at the Lumpkin County Courthouse. The downpour made it nearly impossible to load the company wagons, so for the time being, the soldiers crowded into the courthouse to stay dry. Inside, Lieutenant Rhodes was showing off his new sidearm to anyone who displayed the slightest interest. "Yessir," he crowed, "just got this from the Mercantile. This Colt Dragoon will blow away any Yankee that gets too close!"

A festive air pervaded Dahlonega as the soldiers gathered for their departure, even with the rain. The loyal Unionists remained behind the locked doors of their homes for their own safety, though William noticed a small U.S. flag draped defiantly in one window. The local musical group had been mustered in as the company band, and now they were playing with boisterous enthusiasm, with strong emphasis on "The Bonnie Blue Flag." William could not help wincing at several off-key notes. They sure haven't gotten any better with practice, he thought.

Climbing to the courthouse balcony, Captain Harris doffed his hat to acknowledge the assembled crowd. His voice trembling with emotion, the old soldier began to speak. "My friends, I am extremely grateful for this wonderful display of pride for the Volunteers. As we journey off to war in defense of our homes and loved ones, we shall always remember your kind support. I pledge to you now that I shall do everything in my power to safeguard these courageous soldiers through whatever travails we may encounter. We now take our leave of you, but be assured that you all shall be in our minds and our hearts." Returning his hat to his head, he gave the crowd a smart salute.

Shortly before noon the storm clouds abated, and sunshine flooded the square. Sweating soldiers rushed to fill their wagons with supplies.

A cheer went up from the throng as Lieutenant Merrow, resplendent on a coal black charger, threaded his way through the crowd. Leaning down from his saddle, he gave Sgt. Fitzpatrick the order. "Assemble the men, Sergeant."

Fitzpatrick bellowed at the soldiers. "All right you ladies! FALL IN!" The men sprinted for their now-familiar places in line, two ranks deep. "From the right, by two's, COUNT!" was the next command, and a chorus of "ONE! TWO! ONE! TWO!" echoed down the line. The next step was to insert the corporals into the line, and William took his assigned place on the far right of the front rank.

After several more commands, the company maneuvered into its marching formation of a column four men wide, holding their muskets at the shoulder arms. "Colors to the front!" came the next order. William and the others around him watched with pride as the color guard moved up to the front of the troops. Captain Harris and his lieutenants now took station at the head of the column. Turning in his saddle toward the soldiers, he surveyed them for a moment, pride beaming from his face. He raised his sword. "Company, forward, MARCH!" Instantly the drummers began to beat out a cadence, and the Dahlonega Volunteers started forward.

As the company headed down the road which led south, the soldiers could see flags waving and hear the people cheering for them. Just as on the day Georgia seceded, the ringing of hammers on anvils filled the air as blacksmiths saluted the troops. William could feel the overwhelming wave of pride sweeping through the ranks. The men tightened up their marching, each foot hitting the ground at exactly the same instant. He wanted to see into the awe-struck spectators' faces, but kept his discipline and directed his gaze straight ahead. Bayoneted muskets glinted in the sun as the crowd roared its pleasure with the martial display. Lieutenant Merrow doffed his hat left and right in salute to the townspeople.

Try as he might, William could not resist the urge to sneak a quick look about. Scanning the crowd in hopes of a last glimpse of his friends, he suddenly caught sight of Mary peering from around the corner of the courthouse. For a moment their eyes locked, and it seemed as though he could see a look of longing on her face. After the briefest of moments, however, the expression changed to one of haughtiness and disgust. His last image of her was with her nose in the air as she scornfully turned away. What he could not see were the tears that were trickling down her cheeks.

Winding its way down through the mountains enroute to the Georgia piedmont, the column toiled along. The troops had barely made a mile before they began to feel as though the weight of their knapsacks, accouterments and muskets were growing exponentially. The command "route step, arms at will," was received with relief. Now the men could walk at their own pace, and shift their muskets to more comfortable positions.

It was slow progress. Grumbling soon began to rise from the ranks. "Seems like somebody should have built a railroad through here," moaned Henry Merrow.

"Would have been nice," replied William. "We'll just have to wait 'til we get to Atlanta. We can ride to Macon from there."

Henry snorted. "Hell, the damn war will be over before we get there. We're going to be so late getting to Macon that the regiment will leave without us."

"Don't you worry your pretty little head, me boy," called out Sergeant Fitzpatrick. "You'll get your share of fightin'."

By early afternoon of the fourth day, the Volunteers were marching through downtown Atlanta, much to the surprise of the city's leaders. Caught unprepared, the mayor offered to let the company rest in the armory of one of the local companies, the Gate City Guard. Captain Harris was advised that the Guard had departed Atlanta several days earlier for Macon, and would be part of the same regiment that would include the Dahlonega troops. Grateful for the respite, William and the other soldiers unrolled their blankets on the armory floor and tried to get some sleep. The elderly Harris, looking pale and exhausted from the march, was shown to a cot in the officers' quarters.

Shortly before midnight the soldiers were roused, formed into ranks, and marched to the depot, where a train waited to transport them to Macon. Equipment was transferred into boxcars while the soldiers clambered aboard.

The sun was rising in the eastern sky as the locomotive pulled into Macon. Sergeant Fitzpatrick hollered for the men to collect their knapsacks and accouterments, and form into ranks. Lieutenant Merrow made arrangements with the stationmaster for transporting the company's baggage and equipment to Camp Oglethorpe, where they would meet the rest of their new regiment. Within a short time the column was on the march. Arriving at the camp's gate, the captain halted the company and instructed them fall out to rest. Lieutenant Merrow rode up to the guard, who directed him to the adjutant's tent. While the men waited, they listened to the chorus of yelled commands, bugle calls and drums. "They sure do keep them drilling a lot," said Henry.

"Sure sounds that way," said William. "Bet we'll show them new recruits a thing or two 'bout how to drill, I 'spect. Look, here comes the lieutenant."

Merrow cantered up to the waiting group, ordering Sergeant Fitzpatrick to fall them in again. Soon they were marching through the neat rows of white tents in search of their own site. Reaching the far side, Merrow halted the company, ordering them to fall out and prepare encampment. Before long the men had their own A-shaped tents set up, forming two long rows facing each other. At the head of the company street were the sergeants' tents, and behind them two larger wall tents were raised for the officers. The men were given their freedom to relax for the rest of that day. Some wandered around the camps, looking for friends, or in some cases, a good card game.

It wasn't long after their arrival that a trio of soldiers approached the Volunteers' campsite. They were nattily attired in dark blue frock coats fronted with red breast panels, held in place by three rows of shiny brass buttons. William and Henry rose from their cards to greet the strangers. "Hello, there," said William as he stuck out his hand.

The lead man, wearing three stripes on his sleeve, grasped William's hand firmly. "Welcome to Camp Oglethorpe. I'm Tom Jackson, first sergeant of the Gate City Guard." He pointed toward his companions. "This here's Third Sergeant Gaines Chisholm, and that's First Corporal Orme. We call him "Quill" cause we can't pronounce his first name."

"It's Aquilla, but that's okay," said the corporal, "Glad to see you all finally made it."

A hand clapped on William's shoulder. "Nice to see some real soldiers, for a change," said Sergeant Fitzpatrick as he offered his hand. "Gate City Guards, is it? We had the pleasure of stopping for awhile in your armory."

Jackson laughed as he shook hands with Fitzpatrick. "Thanks for the compliment. Hope the good citizens of Atlanta treated you well. Oh, almost forgot." He pulled an envelope from behind his breast panel. "This is for your captain."

Fitzpatrick stuck the envelope in his pocket. "I'll see he gets it. Any idea what's in it?"

"All I know is your company was late arriving. The regiment is already formed, and we leave for Florida starting tomorrow." Seeing the shocked look on William, Henry and Sergeant Fitzpatrick's faces, Jackson quickly continued. "Don't worry, gents, you're coming, too. Your company has been designated Company H of the First Georgia Volunteer Infantry, commanded by Colonel James Ramsey."

Relief flooded over the three Volunteers. "Boy-O, I thought for certain you were going to say we were too late," said Fitzpatrick.

Sergeant Chisholm grinned. "Somebody important wants you along, for some reason. Heard tell it was Governor Brown. Too bad you missed his speech yesterday. Real humdinger."

"Yeah," said Corporal Orme, "How'd that last line go?"

Jackson thought for a moment. "Went something like, 'Go then, and may the God of battles go with you, and lead, protect and defend you, till the last footprint of the invader shall be obliterated from the soil of our common country'."

"That's impressive," said Henry.

"Brown's an impressive fellow," replied Jackson. "So's Ramsey, even if he was just a lieutenant before getting himself elected colonel. Anyway, you boys better get some rest. You're not going to get much after this, especially after we get to Pensacola."

Chapter 14

The news flashed across the country like a shock wave. On April 12, 1861, the batteries surrounding Fort Sumter had erupted like a ring of fire. Shot and shell cascaded into the brick fort centered in Charleston Harbor. Beginning at 4:30 in the early morning, the barrage continued through the day and on into the following afternoon. The fort returned fire slowly but caused little damage on shore, other than a few holes in some houses. Sumter, on the other hand, suffered greatly, with fires breaking out constantly. Finally, post commander Major Robert Anderson agreed to surrender the fort.

Events rapidly accelerated with Sumter's capitulation. President Lincoln issued a call for 75,000 volunteers to put down the rebellion. Considering this an act of aggression, the state of Virginia, which up to then had resisted the call for separation, elected to cast its lot with the seceding states. The Old Dominion left the Union on April 17. Within another month, North Carolina, Tennessee and Arkansas had joined the Confederacy. Quickly the Confederate government put out its own call for volunteers to serve in the various armed services.

In New Hampshire, volunteers also flocked to the recruiting offices. The state's quota for enlistees was quickly met and exceeded. Most young men looked forward to a glorious adventure. Many wanted to get into a regiment and march off to battle before it was all over. It was taken for granted that the war would be finished in just a few months, so they wanted to get into it before they were left out. The enthusiastic recruits figured that it would only take a good show of force against those southern backwoodsmen to make them see the error of their ways. To most volunteers, the issue was simply the restoration of the Union. Those who saw this conflict as a holy war against slavery were decidedly in the minority.

Thomas and his new-found friend James Stark did their best to maintain a low profile during the uproar. Being southern-born, they were looked upon with suspicion. They were thankful that this kept them from being caught up in the rush to arms. Many of the town's young men were scorned by their sweethearts if they did not immediately enlist. Several actually received packages containing petticoats, a mockery against their seeming lack of courage.

Pastor Marsh was one of those who prayed that the conflict now upon the nation would rid it of slavery. He had long abhorred the thought of a clash of arms between North and South, but now that it had come, he hoped fervently that the conflict would bring about the abolition of that institution.

Of more immediate concern, however, was what to do with his nephew. Thomas' thirst for hard liquor grew unabated. He rarely helped with the farm chores anymore, and even when sober, his increasingly vulgar manner shocked and worried Benjamin and Rebecca.

Setting the family table one evening, Rebecca took note that Thomas had not returned to the house as usual after chores. Benjamin had been out in the fields all day, so was not expected back for some time yet. But Thomas should have been in by now. Stepping out onto the back porch, she called his name, but received no answer.

Lighting an oil lamp, Rebecca walked through the deepening gloom up to the barn. The lack of any light from within increased her anxiety. Where could he be? She called out for him again through the large doors, but again all was quiet. She became aware of a faint sliver of light emanating from an inside corner. Stepping closer, she could make out a dull glow coming from the hidden room.

Raising the door, Rebecca peered in. "Thomas, are you down there?" A low moan issued from within. Pulling the door fully open, she carefully made her way down the steps. The light she had seen was from a tallow candle set on an overturned bucket. Thomas was seated on the floor leaning against one wall, a whisky bottle cradled like a baby in his arms. Another bottle, empty of its contents, lay by his side. Alarmed, Rebecca rushed to him. "Dear Lord, Thomas, are you all right? Speak to me!"

His eyes fluttered, then opened slightly. He glanced blearily up toward his aunt, then turned his head away. "Leave me be. Don't want you here to see me like this. Just go away!" With that, he grabbed the empty bottle and flung it toward her, just missing her head.

Frightened by this unexpected and radical change of personality, Rebecca nonetheless knelt next to him, putting her hand on his arm. "Please let me help you to the house and your bed. You're in no condition to be left alone."

Thomas jerked his arm away. "Go away!" He put his hands up to his temples, stroking furiously as if to rub the pain from his head.

Rising shakily to his feet, he stood looking around for a few moments. The room began to spin. He slammed against the wall, the whiskey bottle spinning out of his hands. Before he could catch it, it smashed onto the floor, alcohol spraying in all directions. Rebecca recoiled at his expression of savage fury.

"God-damn it!" he cried, "I told you to leave me be!" Caught up in a drunken rage, he swung with his open hand, catching her across the face. Rebecca staggered back, losing her grip on the lamp. It crashed to the floor, exploding in flames. The burning lamp oil flared as it mixed with the alcohol soaked sawdust. Rebecca screamed as tongues of fire leapt up, catching her dress.

His senses dulled from the whiskey, Thomas was frozen in place, unable to make his arms and legs move. He could only stare numbly at the inferno growing around him. A glowing bit of straw floating in the heated air landed on his forehead. He batted at it, as if stung by a bee.

The slight bit of pain seemed to awaken him. Finally conscious of Rebecca's cries, he burst through the flames, ripping away the burning fabric of her dress. Wrapping his arms around her, he dragged her toward the door. They stumbled together out of the barn, collapsing on the ground outside. Gulping in lungfuls of cool night air, the pair lay gasping for breath.

Pastor Marsh was galloping into the barnyard. "God in Heaven! Rebecca, Thomas, are you all right?" Leaping from his horse, Marsh dashed to his wife's side. Her face contorted from the pain from her burns.

Marsh looked over to Thomas, who lay gasping on the ground, then turned to stare at the barn. Straw, hay and the dry timbers within fueled the growing inferno. Realizing there was nothing he could do, he turned back to his wife. Lifting her as gently as possible, he carried her to the house.

Thomas remained prostrate on the ground until heat and flying sparks forced him to move. Stumbling toward the house, he collapsed on the wide porch steps. Rising to a seated position, he stared at the fire. Burying his face in his hands, he began to cry. "My God, my God, what have I done?"

He heard the door open and close, and footsteps on the porch, but could not bring himself to move. Marsh sat down beside him on the step, reaching out with his hand to Thomas's shoulder. "She will be all right, though it will take some time for the burns to heal." Thomas turned his tear-stained head away. "Don't you understand? She could be dead! And your barn . . . I—It's all my fault!"

Marsh patted Thomas's shoulder. "Your aunt told me what happened, that you fell against her and she dropped the lamp. It was simply an accident. We are fortunate that the animals had been turned out to pasture. We only lost a few chickens. God has blessed us in that regard."

Thomas stared at his uncle in amazement as realization dawned. Rebecca had not revealed that he had struck her.

Pastor Marsh left early the next morning to consult with a banker in town. He hoped to arrange for a loan to pay for rebuilding the barn. Thomas sat at the table, carefully going over in his mind what he wanted to say to Rebecca. Marshaling his courage, he began to climb the stairs to her room. Lifting his hand to her door, he froze before knocking, unsure whether he should proceed.

"Is that you, Thomas? Please come in." The words coming from within shocked him back to reality.

Slowly opening the door, he stepped into the room. Rebecca lay in the middle of her great featherbed, covered with a large hand-made quilt. Tears began to well in Thomas's eyes at the sight of bandages covering her hands and arms. She smiled. "I am all right. Please don't be upset. I was waiting for you to come."

"I am so very, very sorry. You must hate me."

"Of course I don't hate you. You were not in control of yourself," she said softly, "It was the liquor's fault, not yours."

"But Uncle Benjamin . . . you didn't tell him what really happened."

"What I told him was true. You stumbled and I dropped the lantern. That was a sufficient explanation. There was no reason to create hard feelings. Your uncle has enough to worry about right now."

"Yeah, mostly because of me." Thomas exhaled noisily. "Well, he won't have that worry much longer. I've decided that it's time for me to leave."

Stunned, Rebecca reached out her bandaged hand toward him. "There's no reason to leave! You belong here with your family."

"I've thought it over, and it would be better for all concerned if I left."

"Please, Thomas, don't make a rash decision. If you're afraid I would tell Benjamin—."

"No, this is something that I've been thinking about for some time. What happened last night only served to make me realize that I must leave here . . . before something even more terrible happens."

Rebecca fought to hold back her tears. "You're not going to leave right away, are you? And where would you go? Back to Georgia?"

Crossing the room to a window, Thomas raised the shades, staring out at the smoking rubble where the barn once stood. "No, it wouldn't be safe for me to travel south right now. And I don't know if I could look people in the eye there knowing what I've been involved with. I'll stay to help Uncle Benjamin rebuild the barn. I owe him that much. Then I figure I'll move into town. I have a friend there I can stay with."

"Just remember that you will always be welcome here." Rebecca dabbed her eyes with a handkerchief. "And know that you will stay in our prayers."

Thomas leaned over and kissed his aunt on the forehead. "I will. Thank you for all you've meant to me. You have helped me more than you will ever know."

Barely three weeks had passed when Marsh's neighbors and friends came together for a barn raising. Some of the men hewed and chiseled at great beams that would form the bones of the structure. Others sawed planks to be used for floors and siding. Wives and sweethearts kept the tables full of food and drink for the hungry workers. Teams of horses pulled while men lifted and pushed the frame pieces into place, locking them together with large pegs pounded through carefully drilled holes.

Pastor Marsh was delighted with the progress. Even Thomas was in much higher spirits. He seemed to be everywhere, involved in all aspects of the construction. Marsh kept a close eye on him through the activity, pleasantly surprised that he was abstaining from touching even a drop of liquor.

Thomas noticed several blue uniforms among the workers, but politics were forgotten in the midst of the frantic activity. He heard no disparaging remarks about being a southerner that day.

With the arrival of dusk, the newly constructed barn frame was lit with lanterns, coming alive with merriment and dancing as all celebrated the raising. The smell of freshly cut wood mingled with the scents of cakes and pies. Lively music kept the floor bouncing from the exuberant dancers. Pastor and Mrs. Marsh stood together, swelling with happiness at the gaiety surrounding them. As Thomas joined them, Marsh slapped him on the back. "I'm proud of you, my boy. You've done a wonderful job overseeing the building. This barn will stand for a hundred years!"

Though gratified, Thomas could only produce a weak smile. "Thank you. I really do appreciate it. I'm glad I was able to make some amends for what I did. Once we get the siding and roof on, I'll get my things together and move into town."

Rebecca grimaced. Marsh's pipe fell from his mouth. "What do you mean, move into town? What's this all about?"

Thomas looked at Rebecca, confused. "I'm sorry, I thought you knew. I thought surely that Aunt Rebecca would have told you."

"Told me what? What's going on here?" The preacher turned to his wife, his face now stern.

"Forgive me, Benjamin. I did mean to tell you. Thomas feels strongly that he should move out on his own. He told me the night of the fire that he plans to take up rooms with a friend in town. I've been hoping to find a way to dissuade him, but I've not been successful."

Marsh remained silent for several moments as he digested this unexpected news. Finally he spoke. "My boy, there is no need for this. Yes, we have had our differences, but there has never been a time that you were not welcome here. Please reconsider."

"I do thank you for all you've done for me," said Thomas, "But I really feel this is the best thing for all. James Stark has already agreed to let me stay with him."

"I believe you are making a mistake, nephew, but . . . ," Marsh extended his hand. "I can see on your face that your mind is made up. Our door will always be open to you, no matter what may come."

Thomas took his uncle's hand. "Thank you. I need to sort things out, to find out who I am. When I do, I'll be back."

PART TWO

"War means fighting. The business of the soldier is to fight. Armies are not called out to dig trenches, to throw up breastworks, to live in camps, but to find the enemy and strike him; to invade his country, and do him all possible damage in the shortest possible time. This will involve great destruction of life and property while it lasts; but such a war will of necessity be of brief continuance, and so would be an economy of life and property in the end." – General Thomas J. "Stonewall" Jackson

Chapter 15

camp georgia florida
may 14 1861

dearest mother

I take pen in hand to let you know I am well I am real sorry I have not writ to you before this but we have been pretty busy after we got mustered into the army all the companys was given a different letter to go by we are company H we got ordered to go to florida to join up with genril braggs army there we rode the cars down to montgomery then down to a little town they call garland the tracks were out after that so we had to march a long ways to get to another place to get on a train you would have slapped your ears to hear all the cussin in that march our packs got so heavy that some of the men started tossin stuff out along the road

we are camped right next to a beach on the gulf of mexico it is an awful place the sand fleas eat us up a night and the sun beats down on us during the daytime henry gets red as a beet in the face sometimes we go swimmin in the ocean genril bragg keeps us drillin all the time youd think by now we'd know what we was doin but the genril don't seem to think so henry and me went to town and had our image struck I had 2 pictures made and am sending one home for you to have

the yankees still have soldiers out in fort pickens and sometimes we can hear their band playing I will stop writing now so I can get this off to you say hello to everyone for me and tell them we are ready to defend our homes from anything the yankees try to do

your son,
william

N. B. we have got a new captain captain harris has resigned on account he is said to be too old to stay in the army our new captain is captain cabiness from another company he knew some of the dahlonega boys so got voted in henry was real mad he figgerd that his pa would be the new captain

The First Georgia's stay on the Florida coast would not last long, for near the end of May the regiment received orders to proceed north. Cheers rose from the ranks when the troops discovered their destination—Richmond, Virginia, the new capital of the Confederacy. The men were certain that this meant they would soon be in the thick of the fighting. Camp was struck with amazing speed by the eager soldiers.

The Dahlonega Volunteers' new captain, Thomas Cabiness, motioned to Lieutenant Merrow. "Fall the men out and proceed to the cars, Lieutenant." Loud "moo's" rose up as the soldiers clambered on board the cattle cars of a waiting train, while Cabiness and the other officers proceeded to the relative comfort of two passenger cars hitched behind the tender. "Look's like the 'ossifers' get all the good seats," grumbled Henry, "While we lowly privates get treated like fat beef being sent off to market. This is no way to treat a gentleman!"

Samuel Craig laughed. "That's what we are, cattle for the slaughterhouse!" Almost as soon as the comment escaped his lips, he realized it wasn't so funny. The expressions of those who had heard told him they didn't think so either.

A loud, long blast from the locomotive's whistle signaled time to start. The behemoth's enormous driver wheels slowly began to turn, showering sparks to both sides as they slipped on the iron rails. As the wheels began to grip, the cars of the train lurched, then began to move slowly forward. Cheer after cheer went up as the train pulled away from the station. Sergeant Fitzpatrick was not amused by the crack of muskets being fired skyward in excitement. *God-damned, bloody idiots, wastin' rounds like that.*

It wasn't long before the air inside the cattle cars began to thicken, and the heat soon became unbearable. Musket butts were employed with vigor to knock holes in the side of the cars, and many of the men clambered up on top.

Rounding a particularly sharp bend, the cars rocked precariously. Suddenly a shout went up as one man lost his hold and tumbled off the roof. Frantic signals were sent to the engineer to stop the train, but the engine traveled almost a mile before it could be halted. Fitzpatrick, William and several other men raced back down the tracks to find the soldier. When they reached him, they discovered it was Samuel Craig, the kid who had uttered the tactless comment. He lay with his head bent back at an odd angle, having slammed into a rock outcropping. Craig had died instantly of a broken neck.

William was stunned and sickened by the sight. He hadn't known Craig all that well, mostly as a nuisance. Overwhelmed by the senselessness of this death, he also felt guilt for the times he had tried to avoid the boy's incessant queries. The company's first casualty, Craig wasn't even accorded the honor of dying in battle.

The men fashioned a makeshift stretcher using muskets and blankets to carry Craig back to the train. The body was laid out across the seats in back of one of the passenger cars. "We'll ship him home at the first whistle stop we come to," said Lieutenant Merrow., "Can't do anything more than that right now. The captain will telegraph his family when we get there." William could only imagine the grief and dismay the dead man's family might experience when they learned what had happened.

During the rest of the trip to Richmond, the men were subdued as each contemplated the death of their comrade in arms. Many of them had never seen a dead man before. This war wasn't as much fun as it used to be.

The regiment's camp outside of the Confederacy's new capital city was soon crawling with visitors wanting to get a look at the sunburned Georgians. Most prominent among the guests were President Jefferson Davis and Virginia Governor John Letcher, for whom Colonel Ramsey ordered three cheers.

Richmond was aflutter with news of a small engagement nearby at a place known as Big Bethel. Little more than a skirmish between two organized mobs, it ended with Union troops being driven from the field. Celebrations erupted all over the city and in the camps for the 'decisive' victory.

Just days later the regiment was once again ordered into ranks. Colonel Ramsey appeared, followed by the other field officers, Lieutenant Colonel James O. Clarke and Major George H. Thompson. Stepping onto a cracker box so as to be seen by all, Ramsey began to address the troops. "Soldiers! I know you are anxious to show your steel to the northern invaders who dare to pollute the soil of the Old Dominion. Now you shall have your chance." Ramsey held aloft a piece of paper. "Here are orders for this regiment to proceed west, to join our brothers-in-arms who are even now facing Yankee hordes massing in Ohio. We are to join the newly formed Army of the Northwest, to help our comrades wash out the invaders' footprints in his heart's blood!"

Ramsey raised his hand, still dark from the Florida sun, and pointed westward. "There is the road that leads to the enemy. Tomorrow, we march!" he declared.

A pre-dawn mist enveloped the encampment as drums began their staccato clamor. Bleary-eyed soldiers, weary from lack of sleep due to a night of celebration and revelry, sluggishly boarded the cars of a waiting train. William found himself dozing almost before he reached his seat.

The troops were revived by an unbelievable sight greeting them when the train chugged into the next station. The amazed Georgians beheld tables with bright white cloths, piled high with food and surrounded by a multitude of pretty girls. From the rafters of the station house hung banners proclaiming "Welcome to the Brave Defenders of Southern Rights" and "God Bless The Confederate States." Filing off the train, each man was taken in arm by one of the ladies and led to a table.

After too short a stay the men were ordered back into the cars. The train pulled out as the crowd cheered, while jeers and catcalls were hurled at two soldiers sprinting down the track trying to catch up. Dallying too long with a couple of the young ladies, they were nearly left behind.

Reaching Staunton, the regiment was ordered off the train and into camp, to rest up for the next part of their journey, a march of over one hundred miles into the Allegheny Mountains. The stark, rugged peaks loomed high in the western sky. Henry pointed toward one particularly imposing height. "Is that snow?"

"In June?" William strained to see. "Can't be. But it sure looks like it."

Listening to William and Henry's exchange, a farmer forking straw from his wagon stopped to rest. "That's snow, all right," he said. "Worst weather anywhere up in those mountains. Rains all the time. Many a time I've seen rain turn into a blizzard up there, even in the middle of summer." He shook his head. "Don't envy you boys, none, not where you're headed."

William shivered. "Thanks a lot."

The farmer grinned. "One more thing. Bad area for snakes."

Henry looked aghast. "Snakes?"

"Yep. Rattlesnakes. All over round the valleys and along the rivers. Best watch out where you pitch your tent."

Chapter 16

Pain lanced through Jonathon Evans's gum as he bit into his last piece of cornbread. Muttering a curse, he spat out the moldy mass. *So much for breakfast.* Working with his finger, he was finally able to extricate a sharp bit of husk lodged between two teeth. Retrieving a tin cup, he filled it with coffee, then took a sip. The warm liquid swishing in his mouth soothed the ache.

Damn it to hell. The curse was directed more toward himself than the ache in his mouth. Evans had precious little to show for his efforts in the year or so since leaving Dahlonega. It seemed that his luck couldn't get much worse. The few jobs he had been able to acquire hadn't lasted long, largely due to his violent temper.

His attempts at thievery had likewise been failures. Rubbing the spot on his leg where a guard's shotgun pellets had lodged, Evans grimaced. He had barely escaped during that botched robbery attempt.

Angrily, he threw the cup at the fire, sending up a shower of sparks. *I'm going nowhere fast. Got to think of something.* Lifting his pack, he pulled out a greasy piece of newsprint previously used to wrap the cornbread. *The Knoxville Daily Register,* blared the masthead. Jonathon began to read. An editorial, written by one J. Austin Sperry, demanded that local Union men be required to take an oath of allegiance to the Confederate States, or else be thrown in jail. Jonathon grinned. *Good man.*

An advertisement caught his eye:

DEFEND YOUR COUNTRY

I Desire to Raise a Company of Cavalry for State Service. All wishing to join will meet at the Knox County Courthouse on WEDNESDAY EVENING, at 5 o'clock.

LAWRENCE J. HAMILTON, CAPT.

Hey, maybe this is it. Jonathon glanced at the date on the page. *Dammit. Printed two weeks ago. But maybe . . . , well, Knoxville's only ten miles from here.*

Gathering up his gear, Jonathon hurriedly saddled his horse. It was worth a try, he thought. Maybe they still need men.

An hour later, Evans pulled up before the Knox County Courthouse. Tethering his horse, he climbed the steps toward two soldiers seated at the top. "Hey, boys, you know where I can find Captain Lawrence Hamilton?"

One of the pair, a stocky man with greasy hair, nonchalantly let loose a stream of tobacco juice, then squinted at Jonathon. "Who wants to know?"

"I do." Evans proffered the piece of newspaper. "Saw he's looking for good men. I'd like to join up."

Oily Hair laughed. "Do tell? Will ya looky here, B. F., we got a volunteer."

The other soldier stood. Tall and thin, he seemed to unwind as he rose. "You ever do any soldierin'?"

"Spent a little time in the militia."

The thin soldier tilted his head as he scrutinized Jonathon. "Why ain't you with 'em now?"

"They was foot soldiers," replied Evans, annoyed at the questions. "I'd rather ride."

"Hamilton's company pulled out a couple of days ago," said Oily Hair, "but we might be able to help you out. We're with Captain Andrew Knight's company. We still have room for a good man."

Jonathon rubbed his chin, then shrugged, trying not to demonstrate too much interest. "Long as I can kill Yanks, one unit's good as another."

"Good, good." The greasy-haired soldier stuck out his hand. "Bill Ryles, at your service. This here's B. F. Dumas."

"B. F.?"

"That's for Benjamin Franklin. My pa thought Franklin was the smartest man that ever lived. Just call me Ben."

"C'mon with me," said Ryles, slapping Jonathon on the shoulder. "I'll take you over to the lieutenant to get you signed up, and get your gear issued. You got a gun?"

Jonathon pointed toward his horse. "Shotgun."

"A revolver would be better," said Dumas. "Too bad you don't have a pistol. We don't have enough guns, so that shotgun you're totin'

102

will have to do you for now. What's available around here is in short supply."

"I might know where to get one," said Evans, remembering his old dragoon revolver. *I'll write to Parker. He can get it back from McCay, even if he has to steal it.*

After signing enlistment papers, Ryles and Dumas escorted Jonathon to the camp of Captain Knight's company. Once his horse was picketed with the rest of the troop's animals, they strolled over to the quartermaster's tent to draw a uniform and equipment.

Coming around the corner of a tent, Ryles stopped dead in his tracks. "Aw, shit, it would have to be him."

Evans looked around. "Who?"

Ryles pointed toward a diminutive, sallow-faced soldier seated behind a table in front of a large wall tent. "That's Sergeant Blackburn. You best watch out for that one. I think he's a little bit . . . strange."

Evans studied the corporal. "Just what do you mean, 'strange?'"

Dumas guffawed. "Me, I figger he's tetched in the head—thinks those stripes mean he's a general or somthin'."

Ryles shook his head. "You best not let him touch your mail, if you don't want it read. Some says he keeps letters, especially from girl-folk. Probably cuz' he never got any mail hisself."

Dumas snickered. "Ha! He most likely never 'got any,' period." He gave a sly wink. "If you know what I mean."

The smile faded from Ryles's face. "Uh, oh, look out, here he comes." Blackburn had risen from his chair and was coming toward them.

Sauntering up to the trio, Sergeant Blackburn snarled, "What're you men talking 'bout? I bet you're talking 'bout *me* again, aren't ya? You know I don't like being talked about behind my back." He glared at the soldiers. "I'll fix you, Ryles. You've got twelve extra hours of picket duty!"

"Aw, c'mon, Sarge, we wasn't talking about you. Why, we were just giving Evans here the low-down on the troop."

Blackburn spun to face Jonathon. The pint-sized sergeant's eyes barely reached Evan's chest. His fist shot up, finger wiggling just off the tip of Evan's nose. "You best not let these shirkers talk you into any trouble, Evans. *I'm* in charge of this here squad, and don't you ever forget it, bub."

"Hell, Sarge, I ain't trying to make trouble. I just want to kill Yanks."

The pitch of Blackburn's voice rose an octave. "That's *Sergeant* Blackburn to you," he screeched as he jabbed Jonathon in the chest. "Don't you *ever* call me "sarge" again—*you got that?*"

Jonathon grabbed Blackburn's finger, twisting it around as the sergeant let out a howl of pain. "Looky here, you little toad-faced maggot, I don't like being pushed."

Releasing Blackburn's digit, Evans shoved past him toward the quartermaster's tent. "C'mon, fellas," he said, motioning to Ryles and Dumas. "Let's get my traps."

Shivering in his rage, Blackburn massaged his rapidly swelling finger. "You broke it," he wailed. "I'll have you up on charges for this, you just wait!"

True to his word, Blackburn preferred charges against Evans for assault, but as the trial began, it soon became apparent just how detested the sergeant was in the troop. Company Surgeon Merrill, who splinted Blackburn's injured finger, testified that the sergeant, not Evans, instigated the incident, and that Evans was simply trying to defend himself "from completely unprovoked harassment." The court-martial quickly devolved into an indictment of Blackburn as others came forward to testify about his cruelty and malicious behavior. As a result, Evans was freed with a simple reprimand. Blackburn, on the other hand, received notice from Captain Knight that he was being reduced from sergeant to corporal. Stunned into silence, Blackburn boiled with rage.

Drill was the order of the next few weeks as the new soldiers learned cavalry formations. Much time was spent getting the horses used to the sound of firearms. Many a trooper landed in the dirt following the blast of a fieldpiece.

Jonathon and his new acquaintances tried to keep as much distance as possible between themselves and Corporal Blackburn, who conspicuously rubbed his hand every time they encountered him. "That man's gonna make life difficult," said Ryles.

"I can handle him," replied Evans, trying not to show his uneasiness.

"Mail's here," said Dumas as he came around the corner of the tent. Seated on a camp stool cleaning his shotgun, Evans paid no notice.

Dumas leaned down, waving two envelopes in front of Jonathon's face. "You actually got a couple," he said, lifting one to his nose. "Smells sweet as a rose. You didn't tell us you had a girl back home."

Laying the shotgun aside, Jonathon reached out, snatching the letters from Dumas's hand. "What the hell are you talking about?" He sniffed. One envelope did exude a flowery scent.

Still leaning forward with an eager expression on his face, Dumas asked, "Well, you going to read them?"

Jonathon lifted the flap on the tent. "Yeah—in private." He disappeared inside.

Dumas called after him, "Hey, not fair. I didn't get anything, and you got *two*!" He shuffled away, hand in pockets, kicking at dry clods of dirt. "Not fair at all," he muttered.

Evans inspected the envelopes. The scented one was addressed with a flowing cursive style. The other was written with coarse, block style letters. Guessing that one was from Hiram Parker, he opened it first.

To Johnathan

> *I am writing in answer to your letter asking about the gun you traded to storekeeper McCay. He does not have it anymore. He said he sold it to an lootenant in cap harris company before they went to florida. That's the same company that willie marsh is in.*

"Damn!" Without reading another word, Jonathon crumpled the paper, dropping it to the floor of the tent. *Damn it to hell. Now where am I going to get a pistol?* He swung with his fist, knocking a tin cup and candle from the box he used as a table. *Everything that goes wrong has something to do with Willie Marsh.*

Jonathon picked up the scented letter and took another sniff. Tearing open the envelope, he glanced at the signature line first, and was shocked to discover that the writer was Mary Stewart. *Now how the hell did she know where I was?* Then realization dawned. *Must've been that stupid Parker. I'll bet he told her.* He began to read:

My darling Jonathon,

> *I put pen to paper with excitement, now that I finally know where you have disappeared to. My feelings for you are as strong as ever. I long to be with you, to know you again as we did that night before you left. I dream of the day when you will come back to take me*

> *away from this horrible place. Please write to me soon.*
> *Please tell me that you love me as much as I do you. I*
> *will write to you as often as I can.*

"Well, now, ain't that lovely," Jonathon muttered to himself. "Just what I need. Some little love-lorn bitch sending me scented letters. Makes me sick." Scooping up Parker's wadded letter, he exited the tent. Tossing the two missives into the campfire, he watched as the paper flamed, curled and turned to ash. Resuming his seat on the campstool, he returned to the task of cleaning his shotgun. He'd just as soon not get any more mail, he thought as he jammed a cleaning rod down the bore.

In an odd sort of way, Jonathon would get his wish. Two weeks later, a wagon pulled up in the camp. The driver called out to a trooper passing by, "Hey, soldier, I've got mail here. Where do you want it?"

"Corporal Blackburn's in charge of sorting mail."

The wagon master pulled a sack bulging with letters from behind his seat. "Here, you see that he gets it. I've got to head out."

Blackburn was at his customary place at the quartermaster's tent, when the soldier plopped the bag down in front of him. "Hey Corp, mail just came in. Hurry up and sort it, okay, Corp? I ain't got a letter from my Ophelia in over a month. I'm sure there's a letter from her in that bag. You'll hurry up and pass them letters out quick, won't you, Corp?"

Blackburn scowled. "Don't get your drawers in a knot, Haskell. I'll have the mail ready after a bit. You go on back and report to the captain."

Haskell's shoulders sagged. Turning to leave, he glanced back at Blackburn. "You'll let me know right away if I got a letter, won't ya, Corp?"

"I said I would," screeched the corporal. "Now get back to the captain and leave me be."

Dumping the bag's contents onto the ground, he set to work sorting through the envelopes and packages. One letter, obviously written by a woman's hand, caught his attention. Lifting it from the stack, he read the address. "Well, well, here's a pretty letter for Mister Evans." Blackburn glanced around. No one was watching, but just to be safe, he slipped into the big wall tent. Tearing open the envelope, he began to read. The missive was full of flowery phrases of love and devotion. Blackburn could barely contain his excitement as he continued reading explicit descriptions of the writer's intentions once Evans returned. *Whoever this woman is,* he thought as the words roused him, *she is* no lady. Caught up in the intensity of his reaction, he was oblivious to the blare of a bugle call.

A loud rapping on the tent pole startled him, almost causing him to rip the letter. "Hey, Corp, that's assembly," called out Haskell.

Red-faced, Blackburn quickly inspected himself, making sure nothing embarrassing was visible. "Keep your shirt on," he hollered as he snatched up his sword belt. "I'll be right there. He slipped the letter into his inside jacket pocket. *Fancy words from a pretty girl aren't for the likes of you, Evans.*

Chapter 17

camp laurel hill, virginia
june 27, 1861

dearest mother

I take pen in hand to write you a few more lines to let you know I am well we are now camped in the mountains in the western part of virginia these mountains are higher than any we have back in georgia and a lot colder too even though it is summer we have to keep a fire going all the time to keep warm

we are now commanded by general garnett who is a virginian but he likes us georgians right well we marched all the way from stawnton to here which some says was over a hundred miles one feller said he was going to kill a yank for every mile they made him walk at first lots of folks gave us food and drink but when we got closer to here the people are more for the union and don't like us much a funny thing happened when we camped one night some fellers set their tent up but then came running out fast they had put it up over a snake there are lots of rattlesnakes here

something sad happened too during the march a soldier from another company got drunk and shot and killed another soldier in a different company its too bad when our own soldiers shoot each other before we get a chance to shoot yankees

it is said that the yankees are over in ohio getting ready to come after us but I don't think they will be able to get us out of here the general has been having us dig really good forts here so don't you worry we will be safe behind our logs and dirt

your loving son
william

Laying aside his pen, William scanned the paper. It did seem as though all they ever did was dig and cut down trees as they built earthworks. As usual, Henry seemed to grumble the most. "I came to fight, not to dig holes. It ain't proper for gentlemen to hide behind piled up dirt when the fighting starts. I just want to kill some Yanks."

June passed into July as the men settled into the dull routine of camp. Any type of diversion became welcome. Letters from home were prized, and couriers were practically mobbed when mail was received. Lucinda wrote that all was well at home, though it was hard keeping the farm up without him. She would always end by saying how proud she was of him. William would read each letter over and over again. He would feel guilty for leaving her and Melissa alone, but Lucinda's closing would always boost his spirits.

The calm was not to endure, however. From over the hills floated the clank and clatter of troops on the move. Yankee soldiers were approaching, said the scouts, coming in from across the Ohio River. Thousands of Union troops were soon taking up positions just a few miles from the Rebel camp at Laurel Hill. Untold numbers more were converging on General Garnett's other position to the south at Rich Mountain. Anxious eyes scanned the western hills for glimpses of the invaders, and ears listened for the sounds of troops moving to attack.

Restless and unable to sleep in the early July heat and humidity, William lay in his tent early one morning, reading his mother's latest missive for the umpteenth time. Suddenly the silence was ruptured by the crack of a musket being fired. Sticking his head out of the tent, he could see Sergeant Fitzpatrick staring off toward the picket lines. "What goes?" he asked. Before the sergeant could reply, there was a burst of firing.

Fitzpatrick grabbed his belt and cartridge box. "FALL IN! Get your lousy butts into line!" The company street came alive with men scrambling to fasten their accouterments and find their places.

Lieutenants Merrow and Rhodes came rushing up, buttoning their tunics and fastening their sword belts. "Good, good," muttered Captain Cabiness when he saw the troops were already assembled. Merrow motioned Fitzpatrick to him. After a few moments of conversation, the sergeant saluted, then whirled and ran back toward the ranks.

"LOAD!" Hurriedly William reached down to his cartridge box and withdrew one of the paper-wrapped bullets. Ripping off the end of the tube with his teeth, he poured the powder down the barrel, then dropped the ball and buckshot into the muzzle, followed by the paper.

As he nervously withdrew the ramrod from its rings, he glanced around rapidly to see how the other men were doing. Henry was fumbling with another cartridge—he had torn his first one with so much force that the powder and ball had spewed out onto the ground. Returning his attention to his own musket, William rammed the load down the barrel, giving it a couple of good thumps to seat it well. He then quickly moved to the shoulder arms position, holding the musket by its trigger guard upright against his right shoulder, and waited for the next command. Finally all the men reached the same position, at which point the captain gave the command to order arms.

Clouds were gathering overhead, and before long a misty rain began to fall. As the men waited, they listened with growing unease to the crackle of musketry filtering through the trees. Occasionally, a ragged volley was heard, but mostly the sounds of individual fire would rise and fall. "Almost sounds like someone's stackin' boards," said Color Sergeant Hoskins. The soldiers chattered nervously as they waited, some going on about how brave they would be, some about how the Yanks were sure to turn and skedaddle once Company H appeared on the battle line.

Suddenly a rider was seen approaching through the woods that screened the regiment from the fighting. Clattering up to Colonel Ramsey, he saluted, handing the colonel a slip of paper. The soldiers watched intently as Ramsey quickly read the note. He saluted the courier and spoke a few words. The courier returned the salute, then wheeled his horse and raced back through the trees. The men knew instinctively that action must be at hand as they observed the colonel bark orders to his captains and send them scurrying off to their companies.

Silence descended over the ranks as the chattering gave way to anxious anticipation. Many of the men were thinking of their loved ones at home, wondering if they would ever see them again. Some, including William, prayed that they would show themselves to be good soldiers, and not disgrace themselves by showing fear. Henry was thinking about living up to his boasts. A few were eager for the chance to kill Yankees. The shuffling of feet and repeated dry coughs revealed the nervousness that prevailed in the line.

Captain Cabiness quickly bawled out orders. "Atten-SHUN! Shoulder, ARMS! Right shoulder shift, ARMS!" The hundred-odd muskets of Company H rotated quickly from their resting position up to the men's shoulders. "Right, FACE! Forward at the quick-step, MARCH!" With a lurch the column started forward. Moving nearly at the run, the men had great difficulty keeping muskets on their shoulders while holding place in line.

Turning to observe the regiment's progress, William caught a glimpse of other companies disappearing in the opposite direction. Motioning to Fitzpatrick, he pointed and asked, "What goes, Sarge?"

"There might be Yanks out on the left side of the camp, too," replied the sergeant, "so the colonel is taking half the regiment that way. The Gate City Guards are under attack out on the right. Lieutenant Colonel Clarke is taking us that way to give them a hand."

Clarke's troops had gone barely a quarter mile when they were abruptly brought to a halt. Two companies were ordered further down the road while the Dahlonega Volunteers and one other company were instructed to right face. William and his comrades found themselves staring up the slope of a small hill. Stepping out in front of the soldiers, Clarke pointed toward the crest. "There are Yankees up there," he yelled, "trying to flank our soldiers on the next rise. We're going to drive them off."

Clarke drew his sword, raising it over his head. "Up the hill, men," he cried, "and remember you are *Georgians!* Now, *Charge!*" William and his comrades let out a whoop, and the line rushed up the slope. The formation quickly lost cohesion as it bent and broke around trees and bushes, but the soldiers swept around the obstructions as they continued up the rise toward the top. Musket balls began crashing through the tree limbs above their heads.

Just below the crest, the two companies were ordered to halt and reform their line. Fitzpatrick roared out. "All right, you ladies! Now you gets your chance to shoot at real live Yanks! Company, Atten-SHUN! Come to the ready! Cap your weapons!" Quickly William withdrew a small brass cap from his belt pouch and fitted it over the musket nipple. "Ready! Aim!" Up came the muskets. "FIRE!!!" A sheet of flame blazed from a hundred muzzles. Grayish-white smoke blanketed the slope.

William could not see a thing as he peered ahead, curious what effect the volley had. "Reload and fire at will!" yelled Captain Cabiness. Frantically, William pulled out another cartridge and rammed it down the barrel, then capped and fired again.

Even with the rain William's mouth felt as though it were full of dry sand. So this was how it felt to be under fire. Images of his body being torn apart by bullets flashed through his mind's eye. Terror rose up from within. He wanted to run, to get away, to be anywhere but here. He glanced around to the other men hunkered down behind trees and rocks. Fear was on the face of many. Some looked almost serene, and a few had an expression of curiosity. He glanced at Henry. His friend's face was screwed up in fright, and it looked as if he was trying to dig himself under a boulder.

Lieutenant Merrow stood a short distance to the rear pointing with his saber. William marveled at how unruffled he looked—not flinching a bit as bullets whizzed by. Catching sight of William looking at him, Merrow grinned. Instantly, William felt his fear slide away.

Reaching down, he took Henry by the arm, shaking him slightly. "It's okay, Henry. We're going to be all right. Look up at your father. He's not afraid." Trembling, Henry turned to look. Merrow smiled again, then snapped a quick salute. William felt his friend relax.

Musket discharges echoed across the hill as the two sides blasted away at each other with seemingly little effect. A constant shower of leaves and pine needles flittered down on the troops as minie balls zipped overhead through the trees. Overheated from the repeated discharges, William's musket barrel felt red-hot in his hand.

Another whoop abruptly rose from off to one side. Clarke's two other companies had charged up the hill and were joining the fighting. With the increase in fire from the Confederate ranks came a corresponding slackening of gunfire from the Union side of the hill. "They're retreating," called out Lieutenant Merrow. "Now's the time, boys! Drive them! Drive them!"

Leaving the shelter of the trees, the Georgians started forward. Coming up beside a tree trunk pocked with gashes, William could see the Yankees retreating pell-mell down the opposite slope of the hill. Caught up in the exhilaration of battle, he wanted to rush after them, to push them all the way back over the Ohio River.

"Reform!" The shout filtered down through the trees. "First Georgia, reform and fall in!" Reluctantly William broke off from the chase, working his way back up to the hilltop where the four companies of the First Georgia were collecting. Officers checking for casualties were amazed to discover that the only wound suffered was by one man hit in the leg by a ball that ricocheted off an oak tree. The body of a northern soldier was found sprawled out behind another tree, his face destroyed by the effects of a buck-and-ball blast. William touched Henry's sleeve. "Well, you wanted to see a dead Yankee, pard." Henry shuddered, but remained silent. For a moment William thought his friend was going to be sick.

Chapter 18

Over the next few days, the First Georgia rotated with the several Virginia regiments in and out of the forward ditches, exchanging fire with Federal troops and remaining alert for signs of an assault. Rain was constant; the soldiers could never seem to get completely dry.

Late one evening, William and his company were posted in the ditches, watching the flare of the Union artillery. Someone had calculated that it took twelve seconds from the time they saw the muzzle flash until the shell hurtled by, giving them that much time to duck down into the trench.

"This is getting boring," grumbled Henry. "I wish they'd go ahead and attack."

William nodded. "Is kind of hard on the nerves, just waiting for 'em to come." He started at the touch of a hand on his shoulder.

"Okay, Corporal," said Sergeant Fitzpatrick, "get your boys ready to move. We've got to retreat."

Dumbfounded, William stammered, "But we're holding them here just fine. Why should we leave?"

"Colonel Pegram got hisself beat south of here at Rich Mountain, and if we don't skedaddle out of here the Yanks can get into our rear. Now get them up!"

Still confused by the sudden turn of events, William turned and hollered for his squad to fall in. The soldiers quickly found their places in ranks, and once the regiment was formed, Colonel Ramsey gave the order to move out.

The rain grew heavier as the army plodded southward. Streaks of lightning forked across the sky, followed by ever louder rumbles of thunder. William could not remember when he had endured a more miserable night. His sodden uniform seemed to gain weight with each raindrop.

Morning light was beginning to filter through the rainclouds when the column suddenly shuddered to a halt. Captain Cabiness sent Lieutenant Rhodes galloping up ahead to find out what was happening. Rhodes came splashing back through the mud to report. "The road ahead is blocked—the Yankees dropped trees to stop us. The general is trying to figure out what to do."

Orders soon arrived to about face. With escape blocked to the south, the Army of the Northwest would head north instead. By mid-day, as the rain continued to fall in torrents, the troops were climbing through the mountains, following the narrowest of paths. Wagons and troops moving ahead of the First Georgia had churned the trace into a quagmire. Sinking knee-deep into the mud, William struggled to keep his shoes from being literally sucked from his feet.

Lightning created strange shadows all around the column. Apprehension rose as the men imagined a bushwhacker behind every tree. Crashes echoing through the forest spoke of wagons sliding from the roadway into deep ravines. Not only the mud, but also piles of jettisoned equipment served to impede the soldiers' progress.

Henry's grumbling intensified with each sloppy step. "What a waste! Will you look at all this gear? Just thrown out!"

"Either that or they get stuck and block the road, boy-o," growled Sergeant Fitzpatrick. "Now shut your trap. We can do without all the lamentations."

The weary column finally emerged from the mountain pathway into a narrow valley. Reaching a shallow river crossing, General Garnett ordered a halt. Exhausted and soaking wet soldiers sank to the ground, many falling instantly asleep where they lay in soggy grass.

Still overcast skies and drizzle welcomed the troops as they were roused early the next morning to continue the retreat. Swollen by the rains, the river tore at the men's legs as they splashed across. Turning northward, the column snaked along the river valley. The rain that continued to fall further blackened the men's spirits.

Bringing up the rear of the army, the First Georgia was moving up the valley toward the next stream crossing when a distant boom came echoing across the mountains. Almost immediately thereafter, several cavalry scouts came pounding up to Colonel Ramsey, their horses coated in lather. *Going to be some action*, thought William. Ramsey hastily summoned his captains for a quick consultation. Rushing back to his command, Captain Cabiness yelled, "All officers and non-commissioned here, right now!"

Cabiness knelt down as the men circled him. "The Yanks are close up behind us," he began. "Colonel Ramsey has a plan to ambush them when they come across the river. Major Thompson has been ordered to hide six companies over there, including us." Cabiness pointed to a small cornfield several yards away. "Ramsey's going to take position at the north end of the valley, just behind the wagons, to draw the Yanks toward him. They'll probably form line of battle, and when they pass us, we'll all rise and fire a volley into their flank. That'll break up the attack."

The officers all nodded in approval. "It'll be a rout," said Lieutenant Merrow.

Cabiness stood. "All right then. Get the men under cover quickly. No telling how long until the Yanks come across the river."

William and the other corporals and sergeants spread the word among the Volunteers, and soon they were kneeling down, out of sight deep within the cornfield. They could hear Colonel Ramsey barking orders as he positioned the remainder of the regiment.

It was only a matter of minutes before the sound of other troops began filtering through the stalks. "Stay down and keep quiet," hissed Major Thompson. Taking off his hat, the major lifted his head to try to see what was happening. Anxious minutes passed while he surveyed the approaching Federals.

Suddenly Thompson let loose a whispered curse. "God-dammit!" He turned to Cabiness. "They're staying in column of fours! Out of range!"

A thunder of hooves and the rumble of heavy wheels could be heard. Henry cocked his musket. "They're bringing up artillery! We've got to fire on them!"

Thompson whirled, hissing at Henry. "You fire that piece and I'll shoot you myself, you idiot! I said they're out of range. Now stay down!"

Carefully lowering the hammer, Henry looked bewildered. "I don't understand. Why can't we shoot?"

The sound of scattered musket fire began to rise while Sergeant Fitzpatrick worked his way over to Henry's side. "Because, my young innocent, these muskets we carry only have a range of about forty yards, if that. The boys in blue are over a hundred yards away, and have long range guns. You remember that zipping sound we heard when they were shooting at us? They can hit what they please at two hundred yards. So if we were to shoot and give away our position, all they'd have to do is stand off and murder us."

Henry's face went white. "O—kay, I get it now."

Fitzpatrick patted Henry's head. "That's a good boy. Now just keep down and stay quiet."

The battle at the head of the valley was on in earnest. Though taking few casualties, Colonel Ramsey could see that he was hopelessly outnumbered and outgunned. Realizing that he would receive no help from Major Thompson's detachment, he decided enough was enough, ordering his troops to retreat. Scrambling across the river to their rear, the Georgians hurried after the army. The jubilant Federal troops rushed to pursue.

An eerie silence settled over the valley. Peering from the corn, Major Thompson surveyed the area. As far as he could tell, no troops from either side remained, so he stepped out into the open.

A pall of grayish-white smoke hung low in the moist air as the soldiers emerged from the cornfield. "They're all gone," said William.

"All officers to me," called out the major. Before long he and his captains and lieutenants were embroiled in a heated debate.

"You boys uncap your muskets," said Sergeant Fitzpatrick. "Don't want to risk a shot now. There will be more Yanks coming up soon."

Henry pulled the small brass cap from his weapon's nipple. "So what do we do now?"

"I expect that's what the fellows with the braid are all arguing about," replied the sergeant. "I sees it this way: we can't go north—the Yanks are between us and the rest of the army, and we'd have to fight our way through them. We can't go west—that's the way we came, and like I said, there'll be more Yanks coming from there. And we can't go south. That will take us away from our army."

William looked up at the mountains. "So we have to go east."

"Yep. Maybe once we're over that peak we'll find a road or something to follow."

Fitzpatrick's insight proved sound, for shortly the officers were ordering the men to begin climbing the mountain. Reaching the summit, William was shocked by what he saw. As far as the eye could see was a total wilderness. He and Henry looked at each other and then to Fitzpatrick, who only shrugged. "Just a few trees and bushes. Shouldn't take us long to cut through that. Can't go on forever."

By the morning of the fourth day, Thompson's men were in despair. Picking up a stone, Henry threw it as far as he could into the brush. "Can't go on forever, huh? No food since we left Laurel Hill, rain every single day, no game to hunt, and we're totally lost. My clothes are nothing but rags, and I've been eating grass and tree bark."

William slashed at a branch with his knife. "We've got to keep going," he said. "Surely it's not too much farther."

"We're going to all die up here in these God-forsaken mountains. You might as well face it."

William continued to hack at the brush, unable to come up with a reply. *Maybe Henry's right. If we don't find some food soon, we are going to die.*

On into the gloom and unfamiliar country trudged the soldiers. William was so tired and despondent that it took great effort to keep going. Several men dropped out along the road, saying they could go no farther. It was all Sergeant Fitzpatrick could do to keep the column together. "Close up! Keep moving!"

Slipping on a wet rock, Henry crashed to the ground. Rushing to his friend's side, William reached down to help him up. "No," he groaned, "I can't go any farther. Not without something to eat."

"Me, neither," said another soldier.

"I've had it," whispered another.

"I'm not moving from this spot," said a third as he sank to the ground.

All around, the starving and exhausted soldiers sat or lay down, sprawling on the rocks and grass, not caring that the rain continued to pour down upon them. William surveyed the scene with a mixture of dismay and resignation. *I guess this is it.*

A commotion arose in the underbrush. Two soldiers emerged from the forest edge leading a ragged-looking figure. He was escorted to Major Thompson, who was conferring with some of his officers. A sergeant saluted. "Caught this fella' skulkin' around out in the woods. Said he wants to talk to whoever's in charge."

Thompson studied the man, a look of disgust on his face. "And just who are you, old man?"

The apparition smiled, his mouth full of gaps where once were teeth. "Parsons's the name. They call me Tanner Jim. Heard a bunch of you sol'jers was lost up here. Looks like you-all got a peck of trouble here. I can help you out. Show you another way back to your army."

Thompson glared at the codger. "How do I know you won't just lead us into a northern ambush?"

The old man snarled. "I ain't no Yankee lover! And I'll tell you true, the country through which you are headin' is not habitable. I've been raised in these regions, and there is not a living soul within forty miles in the direction you're going, and at the rate you are travelin', you would all perish to death, and your carcasses left for food to the wild beasts of the forest."

A spreading grin replaced the scowl. "I know these hills like no one else. I can get your sol'jers where you want 'em."

Another lively discussion erupted between Thompson and his aides. Few were willing to trust Parsons. The sergeant stepped forward. "Beggin' the Major's pardon." Thompson turned to the soldier. "I'll stay with the old coot. If he tries to pull anything, well, I'll just shoot him."

Staring at the old man for several moments, the major scratched his chin, then nodded. "That's what we'll do. The sergeant here will go with you. If you can get us out of this, you will be well rewarded. But if it appears that you're trying to mislead us, or signal the Yanks, I will blow your head off myself. Agreed?"

"I told ya, I ain't spying for no Yankees. If'n this fella wants to come along, fine. Now y'all need to turn these sol'jers around and head back down the road aways. C'mon, sergeant. I'll show you where we got to turn off."

As Parsons and the sergeant headed back down the road, William roused his men. "All right, then," said Captain Cabiness. "Sergeant Fitzpatrick, have the men about face and stand ready to move."

After much confusion, the column finally got itself turned around and began to retrace its route. They came upon Parsons about a mile back. He motioned them to turn off onto a barely visible trail. "This path is a little tricky, but it'll get ya where yer goin'."

The troops nervously picked their way along the trail as it wound up and down through the mountains. In many places it was barely wide enough for the single file to pass through. Flashes of lightning revealed steep cliffs rising on one side of the pathway along with deep ravines on the other.

Henry ranted on in a continuous stream of complaints. "We're lost. We're never going to get out of these mountains."

"Oh, shut up," snorted William.

Nerve-wracking hours went by as the column worked its way along rocky streams and through dense forest. Darkness was again enveloping the hills as the soldiers reached a clearing, where they were ordered to stop and rest. Leg muscles racked with pain, William found a tree to lay under. He watched as a soldier loaded his musket with wadding, then fired it into a stump. The paper ignited dry branches deep under the log, and soon the roaring fire was surrounded by frigid men.

"Willie, look!" William opened his eyes to see Henry scurrying toward him. "I've got food! Look!" In Henry's hand William spied a tiny piece of cornbread. Barely an inch square, the morsel looked like a feast to the famished boy. Without a thought, William seized the bread from Henry's palm and shoved it into his mouth.

Swallowing, he looked up at his friend. "Sorry, Henry, I didn't mean to snatch that from you."

"It's okay, pard," Henry replied. "Old man Parsons went to his cabin and brought this back. And guess what? Tomorrow he says he's gonna bring us *beef!*"

Parsons was true to his word, driving three fat cows into the clearing the next morning. The cattle were quickly shot and dressed. Some of the men, so famished they could not wait, began devouring raw meat without pausing to cook it.

For the rest of the day, the Georgians ate and rested, regaining their strength. Next morning, with full bellies and bulging haversacks, the soldiers formed up once again. It would take several more days to reach safety, but now the men had food, and with it, hope. Following rivers and finally roads, the troops made their way toward the small town of Monterey.

Suddenly a cheer went up from up front of the column. Word spread quickly back through the ranks. They could see the campfires of the main army camp ahead. Officers tried angrily to quiet the men, but their jubilation was too great to silence.

Colonel Ramsey rode out from the encampment to greet them. He saluted, then reached out his hand to Major Thompson. "By God, sir, I am glad to see you! We thought you were taken!"

Thompson took Ramsey's hand. "It has been a rough go, Colonel. Several groups got separated from us in the mountains, but hopefully they will come in soon. We are happy to be back with the army. I should report to General Garnett."

Gloom clouded Ramsey's face. "You will report to me, Major. I am in command. Garnett was killed back at Corricks Ford. Got hit by a Yank sharpshooter just after we pulled out."

Thompson's face betrayed his shock. Recovering, he said slowly, "Very well, Colonel. With your permission I'll have the men encamp."

"Yes, Major, give them a rest. They've earned it." Thompson passed the word down the line to bivouac as soon as they passed the picket line. The exhausted men simply dropped where they were, falling sound asleep in the wet grass.

William's eyes fluttered. Rain was still coming down and distant thunder rumbled against the mountains. Shaking his head, he slowly opened his eyes and peered around. Henry lay next to him sawing logs. Sitting up, he looked skyward to watch the flashes of lightning. Odd, he thought, that thunder has a pattern to it, like . . . artillery! Suddenly the ground shook as shells began to find the range, hitting all around the camp. William yelled at Henry to head for cover, then turned to see a smoking crater where his friend had been laying. William grabbed his musket and accouterments and ran for his life, heading for the nearby woods. As he entered the trees it seemed as if they reached out for him, trying to impede his flight. Suddenly, he heard a different sound from behind. Turning, he glimpsed a horseman plunging through the underbrush, charging directly toward him. Without conscious thought, William swung his musket up and fired. Man and beast crashed to earth, tumbling over and over, sliding to rest before him. William reached down to remove the man's hat, but he found himself unable to do so. Recoiling, William moved backwards as quickly as he could, wanting desperately to get away from the horrible scene. He looked at his hands, and saw them covered with blood. He screamed—. Screamed—.

"What the bloody hell is wrong with you!" Henry frantically shook William awake.

William blinked, then stared at his comrade. "It was . . . uh, Henry! You're dead!"

Henry gave William another shake. "What do you mean, I'm dead? You 'bout scared the shit out of me!"

The two stared at each other, shudders of fright convulsing through their bodies. "Sorry, Henry," said William, "I didn't mean to scare you. I have this nightmare that keeps coming back every so often. It's been a while since the last one, but it seems like it gets worse each time."

Henry snorted. "Well, don't dream any more around me. Leastwise, don't be so loud about it."

Chapter 19

William and Henry had finally fallen asleep once more when drums began beating out the call for assembly. "Oh, God, not again," groaned Henry as he pulled his blanket over his face.

William yawned and scratched his head. "C'mon, pard," he said, poking his friend. "Got to get up."

The two sleepy comrades donned their accouterments and straggled to the company formation. Wearily the soldiers formed their lines. "I figgered we'd get a chance to stop and rest for just a little bit," said James Hunt, "My legs are just about marched out."

Sergeant Fitzpatrick waited, hands on hips, shaking his head. "What a lovely group of sleepin' beauties. Get your arses into line."

Private Hunt piped up. "What's up, Sarge?"

Fitzpatrick scowled. "Just as soon as the gentleman with the stars on his collar tells me, I'll be sure to enlighten you ladies."

Colonel Ramsey and his officers, including the various company captains and lieutenants, came riding up to the front of the line. For several minutes Ramsey scanned the regiment from the vantage point of his saddle. Finally, he began to speak. "Gentlemen, you have done me proud. You have met the enemy and have kept him back. The army and the nation appreciates your service."

A racking cough interrupted Ramsey's speech. After several minutes, he composed himself to continue. "I know how weary you men must be. Now it is time for rest and to mend. I have directed your captains to designate an officer and one enlisted man to travel to Richmond, for the purpose of securing much needed supplies to replace what was lost during our retreat."

Another long coughing spell. "The remainder of you are released from service for a period of ten days," Ramsey continued. "You are directed to find accommodations among the locals so to regain your strength in preparation for greater exertions to come."

A great shout of approval exploded from the ranks. "Three cheers for the colonel," yelled one soldier.

As William threw his kepi into the air in joy, he noticed Ramsey and Lieutenant Colonel Clarke engaged in a heated argument. "You can't furlough the whole regiment!" said Clarke.

The colonel's eyes flashed as he responded with fury. "Damn you, sir! These men have served gallantly and need rest, and I intend to see that they get it!"

"But, Colonel, we need to consolidate in case the Yankees try to hit us again. This is no time to be dispersing!"

Ramsey exploded. "*I* am in command here, sir, and my decision is final! You are dismissed!" Clarke's face was livid as he snapped a salute and jerked the reins to turn his horse away.

After the company was dismissed, Henry and William made a fire to cook up their meager rations while they pondered where to go on their furlough. Henry stabbed his musket ramrod through a piece of salt pork. "Could go back to Richmond," he said "Didn't have much time to look around while we were there."

William frowned as he mixed flour and water. "I'd really like to try to get home."

Henry held the meat out over the fire. "You know how long it'd take us to get back? We'd spend all our time getting' there and back again."

Wrapping his dough around his own ramrod, William swung it out over the hot coals. "I know," he said, "but it'd be worth it just to have a few days home again."

Henry looked thoughtful. "Would be nice to see Ma again. I s'pose we could find a depot and catch a ride on the cars." He grinned. "Course you just want to see your ma and M'lissa again, right? Or is it possible you want another try with Mary Stewart?" Henry's laugh was cut short as he dodged a thrown stick.

The next morning the two friends prepared to leave camp. Passing Lieutenant Merrow's tent, they hailed Sergeant Fitzpatrick, who was busy filling out morning reports. "You goin', Sarge?"

Glancing up from his paperwork, Fitzpatrick scowled. "You best not be in such an all-fired hurry to leave. The colonel has made a grand mistake and Lieutenant Colonel Clarke has gone to headquarters to report it."

William glanced at Henry. "You think we should wait?"

Lifting his kepi, Henry scratched his head. "Nah, let's go. We've got a legal furlough, and until they change their minds let's make the best of it."

Within twenty-four hours, the two found themselves with empty haversacks and grumbling stomachs. Henry, as usual, was constantly complaining about how hungry he was. William wished he would be quiet—talking about it just made it worse. Their luck seemed to change as they rounded a bend in the road and a ramshackle cabin came into view. A wisp of smoke curled upward from an old stone chimney. William was elated. "Mebbe the folks in that cabin would sell us some food."

Stepping carefully to avoid missing boards on the porch, he rapped on the door. There was no answer, so after knocking a few more times, he slowly cracked open the door and peeked in. "Anybody here?"

"Looks like someone left in an awful hurry," said Henry as he warily entered. The room was in total disarray, furniture thrown everywhere. Their attention was immediately drawn to the half-eaten meal on the table. Glancing at each other, the two famished travelers dove at the food. "Mighty generous of these folks to leave us somethin' to eat."

William gulped down a mouthful, then frowned. "Why you s'pose they left stuff jes' sittin' here like this?"

Henry grinned, his full cheeks puffed out like a chipmunk. "Don't know and don't care."

William took a swig from his canteen. "Been a lot of fightin' around. "Bet they saw us comin' and thought we were flankers for a column. Probably figgered there'd be a lot more comin' down the road after us and skedaddled."

Henry yawned. "Could be. Their bad luck and our good fortune. Guess we might as well settle down here for the night. Be nice to have a roof over our heads for once."

William was drifting in a twilight world, not asleep but also not quite awake, when a distinctive click brought him back to consciousness. Opening his eyes slowly for fear of what he would see, he found himself staring into the cavernous paired muzzles of a shotgun. "Thievin' renegades!" rasped a blurry figure.

Henry rolled over on his blanket and yawned. "What goes?" he muttered. Then his eyes opened to see the shotgun. He screeched, "My, God! Don't shoot!"

"You don't move and I won't shoot! Rose! Get me some light!" The flickering glow of a candle illuminated the scene. Two small girls were peeking around the door into the cabin. A stout, unkempt woman stood beside the man, holding the candle. "Scarin' the hell out of a man's wife and kids and stealin' his food. Give me one good reason why I shouldn't blow you to hell right now!" The man's rage caused the barrel of the gun to shake violently.

William gulped. "Please, sir. We didn't mean to scare you. We haven't eaten for a long time, and we was tired. We knocked on the door but no one was here. We'll gladly pay for the food."

The old man squinted in the candlelight, studying William and Henry. "You Confederate soldiers?"

"Yes sir, First Georgia."

"Well, now." The shotgun barrel dropped. "Couldn't tell in the dark that you were two of our boys. Y'all never can tell these days who's goin' to show up on your doorstep. Name's Chandler. This here's my wife Rose."

Relieved, William stood and offered Chandler his hand. "My name's Marsh. My friend and I are on furlough from the army."

"Good thing you fella's weren't a couple minutes earlier," said Kate, "Some Yankee cavalry went tearing by. We run off when we heard their swords clankin'—it was a Gawd-awful noise. Scared us to death."

Another glance passed between the two comrades. Henry scratched his head. "Don't know how we missed 'em."

"Or how *they* missed *us!*" said William.

Chandler set the shotgun in a corner. "You boys were with Garnett's army? I heard what happened over at Corricks Ford. Too bad y'all got whipped. Leastwise the army over by Richmond done real good."

The last comment puzzled William. "What happened at Richmond?"

"You didn't hear? Why, Gen'ril Beauregard's army whipped the Yanks bad near Manassas. They skedaddled all the way back to Washington."

William and Henry looked at each other dejectedly. "Well, at least some of our boys are doin' good," said William.

"Anyhow, y'all are welcome to stay as long as you'd like. We don't have a lot, but we can sure find somethin' to fill your packs."

The next morning Henry and William were lounging on the cabin steps when a rider came pounding up the road. They were amazed to see Sergeant Fitzpatrick. Henry stood, waving. "What're you doing here, Sarge?"

The sergeant shouted. "All right, you two, pick up your gear and get back to camp!"

Henry was indignant. "But we got a furlough!"

William chimed in. "Yeah, and signed by the colonel hisself!"

"The colonel is under arrest, and those passes are no good," growled the sergeant. "I warned you not to leave. Gen'ril Loring is having everyone rounded up and sent back to camp! Now, get up before I butt-kick you both into the Yankee lines!"

As Fitzpatrick clattered off down the road, the two friends gloomily set about collecting their gear. Rose brought out their haversacks, now bulging with food. William handed her a Confederate five-dollar bill. At first she objected, but finally accepted the money after he insisted. After shaking Chandler's hand, and with a wave goodbye, Henry and William started the long trek back to the army.

Chapter 20

"All right, get in there." The sergeant shoved Jonathon Evans roughly through the door of the old shed. The push caused him to lose his footing, and he crashed to the floor. Slowly rising, he heard a chuckle. Turning, he saw another soldier grin, then roll over on his pallet.

Gazing about, Evans inspected his prison. The shack serving as a guardhouse had a rank, musty smell, and the beams and floorboards were spattered with chicken droppings. Frustrated and angry, Evans picked up a stool and threw it against the bolted door. Startled by the clatter, the other captive turned over and glared. "Whoa, boy, you best settle down and let folks sleep. Won't do you no good to stay het up, anyhow. You keep raisin' a ruckus and them guards'll just throw a bucket of water on you. Now stop making a racket and let me go back to sleep."

Finding a corner with a minimum of fouling, Jonathon slid down to the floor, propping himself against the wall. *Sleep. That's all it was this time. Just snoozing for a few moments. And a stupid watch. Damn that Blackburn. He's always been out to get me. Just like Marsh back in Georgia.* Seemed like he'd been butting heads with most of the two- and three-stripers since he joined up, with Corporal Blackburn in particular. It felt as though Blackburn was trying to stick Jonathon with all the worst duties in camp. Now he was in real trouble. *And it's all that damn corporal's fault.*

Returning from a late trip to the sinks two nights previous, he'd come across a couple of soldiers cutting their way through the back of Surgeon Merrill's tent. Startled, one raised a long bladed knife, the other a bayonet. Jonathon backed away. *I'm done now.*

The half-light of the waning moon revealed the hard faces of B. F. Dumas and Bill Ryles. Relaxing as they recognized Jonathon, Ryles lowered his knife. "Evans, you liked to get yourself skewered, scaring the shit out of us like that."

A wave of relief spilled over Jonathon as the blades dropped. "Just what the hell you fellows up to?"

"Doc's got stuff in here better than that old 'bust-head' we've been brewing. C'mon, he's probably got plenty."

"Where is Merrill?"

"He's off with the other officers. We saw him taking a bottle of 'medicine' with him—that's what gave us the idea. Figger he'll be gone for a while. You want some or not? We got to hurry and get out of here before he decides to come back." Ryles finished slicing open the tent panel. With a quick look around, he disappeared inside. Dumas dove through the opening behind him.

Licking his lips, Evans crept into the tent. Rifling through the doctor's equipment, the trio soon came upon a wooden crate bearing bottles of whiskey. "We'll just 'liberate' a few of these," said Ryles while handing a bottle to Dumas.

A bottle in each hand, Jonathon was making his way back to the cut in the tent canvas when a dim flash of reflected light caught his eye. A fancy pocket watch lay on a small table next to a cot. Setting one of the whiskey bottles on the bed, Jonathon lifted the timepiece. *Aren't you the pretty thing.* Stuffing the watch into his pocket, he grabbed the bottle and hastened to make his exit.

Jonathon emerged through the slit canvas to see the other two thieves creeping off through the trees. Quickly following, he caught up with them as they slipped into a dense thicket. Safely concealed from prying eyes, they proceeded to empty the bottles of their contents.

Woozy from the effects of the liquor, Evans made his way on wobbly legs back to his tent. Crawling into his blanket, he was asleep in an instant. Less than an hour later, the drums rolled for reveille. The beating drums matched, then emphasized the pounding in Jonathon's head. With a string of curses, he dragged himself out of the tent. Struggling to pull his shell jacket on, he stumbled to formation.

"Ah, Mr. Evans, you have chosen to grace us with your presence finally." A sneering Corporal Blackburn stood toe-to-toe with Jonathon. "Seeing as how you've been able to find more time to nap than the rest of the company, you should be pleased to know I've put you at the top of my list for picket duty today."

Jonathon gulped. "I just pulled picket two days ago. It's someone else's turn. You can't change the rotation like that."

"Is that so?" Blackburn turned as the first sergeant came walking up. "Sargeant, this man says I can't put him on picket. Says it's not fair to move him up in the rotation. Course, he doesn't have any problem being late for assembly."

The sergeant pressed his face up to Jonathon's. "Private Evans, you will report for picket duty when the corporal tells you to, or I'll have you bucked and gagged."

Arriving at the picket line, Corporal Blackburn set about to relieve the previous guard. "Evans! You take the first watch on post number one!"

Jonathon couldn't believe it. Still exhausted from the previous night's activities along with lack of sleep, he was reduced to begging, much as it stuck in his throat. "Damn it, Blackburn, please! Let me go on the line next. I didn't get hardly any sleep at all last night."

"Likely up to no good again, that's why you didn't sleep. Well, that's your problem. Take your position!"

Jonathon glared at Blackburn. Raising his shotgun, he swung the barrels slowly until they pointed at the corporal's chest. Blackburn drew back. Jonathon could not suppress a snicker at the look of alarm crossing the corporal's face.

Blackburn's panicked expression quickly changed to wrath. "Get going, Evans, before I have you hauled up on charges!"

God-damn that son of a bitch. Someday he'll pay. Just like I'm gonna take care of Marsh sometime. Jonathon made his way to the designated post, relieving the soldier on duty.

Waves of exhaustion rolled over Jonathon as the day wore on. As each hour passed, he fought the sleepiness every way he could think of. Walking up and down, doing the manual of arms, even reciting what little poetry he knew over and over again.

Jonathon pulled out the pocket watch. Relief flooded over him as he saw that it was just about time for the change of guard. He had made it through. *All right, Blackburn, send the next man.*

Ten minutes went by. Another ten. Now half an hour. Jonathon's anger intensified with the ticking of each minute. The realization began to dawn that Corporal Blackburn intended to leave him out on the picket line until he fell asleep. That would give him the excuse he'd been looking for to prefer charges. He was being set up. Well, Jonathon wasn't going to let him get away with it. He'd outlast him, one way or the other.

One hour passed, followed by another. Jonathon was struggling to stay awake, but he was steadily losing ground. *Got to keep moving. Can't give in.* His legs ached from the constant back and forth. *Can't sit down. Got to stay on my feet. God, my legs hurt. Damn that bastard.*

More time went by. The sun was beginning to set. *Maybe if I sat down for just a minute. Just a minute. Then I'll get back up. Got to rest my legs.*

Jonathon found a boulder that looked like a good seat. *Don't want to get too comfortable.* Sitting, he removed his jacket and laid it over the rock. *Ah, that felt good.* His eyelids fluttered. He thought about his tent. *Be glad when we get relieved. Be great to crawl into my tent and get some sleep.* Eyes snapped open. *No! Don't think about sleep!* His eyes closed. *But . . . I'm so tired . . . tired . . . .*

"Private Evans!" Jonathon blinked to see the blurry image of Blackburn and an officer standing over him. Struggling to clear the cobwebs, he couldn't help noticing the corporal trying to suppress a grin, with little success. The lieutenant was scowling. "On your feet, Private!"

Jonathon struggled to rise. "Sorry, sir, I didn't mean to doze. It was just a few moments. I've been out here so long."

"Quiet, soldier! Sleeping on guard is a serious offense. There is no good reason." The officer pointed toward the rock. "Put on your uniform coat, sir!"

Jonathon reached down to grasp his jacket. As he lifted it off the stone, the pocket watch clattered to the ground.

"What's this?" The lieutenant stooped down to retrieve the watch. "Well, well, look what we've found." He turned it over several times. "Looks a lot like a timepiece reported stolen this morning by the surgeon. Now just how would you happen to have it in your pocket, Evans?

"Found it. Lying on the ground by the sinks."

The lieutenant looked at Blackburn, who was obviously enjoying the sequence of events. "Corporal, Private Evans is under arrest. The charges are theft and sleeping on guard. Have him taken to the guardhouse while I return this and advise the captain."

"Yes, sir!" Blackburn could barely hide his exhultation. "All right, Evans, you heard the lieutenant. March!"

Morning sunlight streaming through cracks in the shed wall awakened Jonathon. He had fallen asleep sitting hunched in the corner. Thousands of red-hot needles were stabbing at his leg. Trying to stand, he looked up to see the other prisoner watching him. "Rub them legs smart like 'til you get the feeling back in them," he said.

Evans felt like telling him to shut up and mind his own business, but the advice seemed sensible. He sat back down and began to massage his leg muscles.

"So what'd you do that landed you this lovely sinkhole?"

Jonathon kept rubbing. "Stole a watch. And took a quick nap on the picket line. Who the hell are you?"

A laugh. "Name's Grainger. B Troop. Got caught having fun with some farmer's daughter. Little bitch wanted it bad, but when her daddy found us in the barn she started screaming rape. He tried to get me with a shotgun but I got it away from him and busted it up. Should'a shot the old bastard. Come morning he shows up at camp complaining to the captain. Next thing I knows I'm under arrest and stuck in here."

Grainger studied his fellow prisoner for a few moments. "Your name Evans?"

Startled, Jonathon stammered, "And just how did you know that?"

"The guard was talkin' 'bout a stolen watch earlier. Said he'd been gabbin' with some corporal from D Troop. Blacky, Blackman, some name like that."

Jonathon glowered. "Blackburn."

"Must be. Anyhow, he says that this Blackburn was tellin' him about how he finally got rid of a real problem case. Set him up real sweet by making him snooze on the picket line. Said they got a bonus when they found a stolen watch from the surgeon. Said his name was Evans and to watch real close, cause he was a dangerous fella."

"I'm going to kill that son of a bitch."

"Not likely. We'll probably get drummed out of the regiment." Grainger scratched his scraggly beard thoughtfully. "I know about some boys that have been doin' right well for themselves. Think we'd both fit right in. You interested?"

"So what does this bunch do?"

"Let's just say they're in business for themselves. They call themselves guerrillas, but between you and me, they're more interested in lining their pockets. Run by a fella calls himself 'Major Baxter.' Don't think he's ever been a real officer, just likes the sound of it. They wear Reb uniforms but don't answer to either side."

"What about killin' Yanks?

"They like to shoot up Feds, but they'll take out anyone that gets in the way."

Jonathon mused on that for a few moments. "Sounds like my kind of folks."

Grainger slapped his knee. "Good! I think I know where to find them. Once we get done with that court-martial, we'll head out. Course they could acquit us."

Jonathon chuckled. "If by some miracle they do let us off, we'll just desert. I'm done with this outfit." His eyes narrowed to slits. "But before we go, I'm going to take care of Blackburn."

As anticipated, both men were convicted by the court-martial of their respective charges, and ordered to be drummed out of the regiment. Their heads were shaved and they were made to wear placards with the roughly painted words "Thief" and "Rapist." Escorted under guard past the picket line, they were ordered to leave and never show themselves near the army again, under penalty of execution. As they were about to walk away, Corporal Blackburn tossed a packet at Evans. "Might as well have your mail. Now, get! If I see you around here again, I'll put a pistol ball in you myself!"

Jonathon caught the package. Jamming it down into his haversack, he gave the corporal an evil smirk. "Don't worry. You won't see me first, I guarantee it."

The pair walked in silence for awhile. Reaching a small stream, they knelt down, scooping the cool water into their mouths. Grainger motioned upstream. "We follow this creek that way, we should come to a town. Then we can steal some horses and supplies."

Jonathon remained on his knees. He took another drink before rising. "Not yet," he said. "I've got some unfinished business back at the camp."

"You're crazy. We'll get shot, we go back there!"

"I'm going. You can stay here if you want or take off. They won't be expecting us to come around. I made a promise to myself and I'm going to keep it. Besides, I made a deal with one of the fella's in my old troop. He should be on picket right about now."

Grainger snorted. "I ain't all that eager to get shot right now. I'll wait here for you. If you ain't back by nightfall, I'm going on."

Jonathon carefully threaded his way through the forest back toward the camp. Working his way along a ravine, he spotted the man he was looking for. Climbing out of the ditch, he walked toward the soldier. Bill Ryles whirled and leveled his carbine. Recognizing Jonathon, he dropped the muzzle. "Damn it, Evans, that's the second time you came sneaking up on me. You're going to get shot that way."

Jonathon smiled. "Don't worry, I won't be around anymore after this. Where's Blackburn?"

Ryles pointed to a stand of trees. "He's off skirmishing with his graybacks over in those woods. Don't take too long. The relief guard is due here pretty soon."

Starting off at a trot, Evans quickly reached the edge of the woods. Making his way through the underbrush, he spied his quarry a short distance ahead.

Blackburn sat on a log, intently picking lice from the seams of his trousers, his saber and carbine leaning against a nearby pine tree. Evans maneuvered so as to come up behind the corporal. Reaching Blackburn's weapons, he grasped the carbine, but quickly changed his mind. Setting the gun on the ground, he quietly picked up the sword belt. A malicious grin spread across his face as he silently drew the saber.

Engrossed in his chore, Blackburn was oblivious to the approaching danger. Evans stealthily closed the gap, his hand gripping the sword hilt like a vise. Suddenly, the snap of a twig caught Blackburn's attention. Standing and swiveling, he saw a flash as the tip of the saber blade drove toward him. Before he could dodge, the sword entered just below the rib cage, the point exiting next to his spine. Unable to move, Blackburn could do little more than gurgle as he stared at his murderer. "Well, now, Corporal, I guess we're square," Jonathon said with a cackle.

Evans yanked back on the saber. Blood poured from the wound, soaking Blackburn and the grass around him as he sank to the ground, a look of stunned surprise still on his face. Evans reached down and took hold of his jacket, feeling inside the pockets. Blackburn raised his hand to stop Jonathon but had no strength left. Evans pulled a watch from the pocket. "Guess this will do me more good than you. Always wanted a good timepiece."

Rising, Evans picked up the corporal's trousers, using them to clean off the saber's blade. Sliding it into the scabbard, he turned to retrieve the carbine. Glancing over his shoulder at the dying Blackburn, he quipped, "So long, Corp. You won't be needing these, so I'll just take them with me."

Leaving Blackburn writhing in the final throes of death, Evans hastened back to the picket line. Ryles had a horse saddled and waiting for him. "Did you take care that little shit?"

Evans swung up into the saddle. "Spit him like a pig. One less corporal for you to worry about." Reaching down, he shook Ryles's hand, then spurred the horse.

135

Chapter 21

camp bartow
september 29, 1861

dearest mother

I take pen in hand to send you a few more lines to let you know I am still well the boys ar in pretty low spirits cause we lost another battle old genril lee was supposed to be all great shakes because he is regular army but we all call him granny now because the Yanks beat him bad over by cheat mountain he had us marching back and forth on muddy roads gettin no where fast colonel rust of arkansas was supposed to attack a fort but lost his nerve he skedaddled back to camp genril lee has gone back to richmond and now we are commanded by genril loring again

it is getting pretty cold here and even tho its only late september we have already seen some snow flyin round some soljers have no shoes and rap their feet with rags I am lucky I still have shoes even tho I do have to tie them up to keep them from fallin apart

you didn't say anything about mary in your last letter I hope she is well please send some new stokins in your next box the butter and coffey you sent in the last box got stole so please send some more

your son
william

For what was likely the tenth time, Lucinda read through her son's letter. Reaching up to the log mantelpiece, she took down a small leather-bound case containing the daguerreotype of William. Brushing her fingers across the glass plate protecting the image, she could not help smiling at the stern expression.

Returning the image to its place on the mantel, Lucinda's thoughts turned to her other son. There had been little by way of news of Thomas. In his most recent correspondence, Pastor Marsh made mention of his nephew having moved into town with a friend, but gave few details. Thomas himself had not written for almost two years. Lucinda was unable to shake an uneasy sense of something wrong.

A sudden draft of cold air caused her to shiver. It seemed as though the frigid wind kept finding new holes in the cabin wall. Placing another log on the fire, she sat on the hearth, staring into the flames. *Oh, when would this horrible war be over.*

Since William's departure last spring, Lucinda and her daughter had done their best to keep up the farm. Henry Merrow's younger brother, Stephen, had been a blessing, stopping by the farm often to see Melissa, always offering Lucinda a helping hand with many of the farm chores. The day before he had helped repair their badly maintained fence. It hadn't taken much for their unruly cow to knock it down. Arriving just as Lucinda and Melissa were chasing the animal around the icy barnyard, Stephen was able to head off the cow and drive it back into the barn.

Invited to stay to dinner, he kept going on about how he was missing out on the war, and how he couldn't wait until he reached eighteen so he could enlist.

Such talk disturbed Lucinda, but she made no comment. After the meal he and Melissa sat in the corner giggling as they shared some secret. It was amusing, and also somewhat unnerving, to witness his awkward attempts at courtship. It was gratifying for her to watch Melissa blossom into an attractive and intelligent young woman.

Rising early, Lucinda surveyed her stock of supplies and decided it was time to head to the Mercantile to pick up a few necessities. The diversion of these infrequent trips to town gave her much enjoyment. She looked forward to seeing Jedidiah McCay again. He always kept her up to date on the war news and the doings around town. And she found herself taking increasing pleasure from his company. "Come on, Melissa," she called out. "We need to hitch up the wagon."

Pulling up in front of the store, Lucinda climbed down from the wagon seat and tied off the horse. Taking Melissa by the hand, she stepped up onto the planking—and was almost knocked over as Mary Stewart came rushing out the door. Mary stared at them for a moment with a contemptuous look, then flew off down the street.

McCay was out the door in an instant. "Lucinda! Are you all right?"

"I'm fine." His use of her first name caused an unexpected thrill. She brushed her dress to straighten it. "Mary seems to be in quite a hurry today."

McCay made no attempt to hide his disgust. "She bursts in here every time the mail rider comes by. She's still pining for that no-account Jonathon Evans."

Jedidiah continued as they entered the store: "She mails a letter to him out in the western army every few days. Then she's always coming by pestering me to see if there's a letter from him. Course he never writes back—don't think she's ever gotten a letter from him since he left town. Probably won't, either."

Lucinda saw an opportunity to change the subject. "Speaking of letters, you wouldn't by chance have any mail for me?"

McCay shook his head. "Sorry, nothing for the last few days. Course it's probably hard for Willie to write, what with that battle and all."

Lucinda's hand rushed to her mouth. "What battle?"

Jedidiah quickly put his hand on her shoulder. "Now don't you go worrying yourself. Willie's fine. I'm sure of it. Camp Bartow was attacked by the Yankees two weeks ago, and our boys gave them a good licking. It was in the newspaper. Old man Beck's boy David got hit in the leg but is doing all right. He was the only casualty from the Volunteers. I 'spect you'll be hearing from Willie about it soon."

Lucinda's hand dropped to her breast. "Oh, thank heavens."

She felt a tug on her dress as she pulled a list out of her pocketbook. Melissa looked up at her with pleading eyes. "Mama, can I look at the bonnets, please?"

Smiling, Lucinda handed her list to McCay, then patted Melissa on the shoulder. "Yes, dear, but don't pull them all off the rack at once."

Squealing with delight, Melissa ran off to the clothing shelves. Jedidiah set to work collecting the items from the list, setting them on the counter. "I'm afraid there aren't any new bonnets on the rack. With the war, I'm not getting in many luxuries." He pointed to Melissa. "She's sure growin' up fast."

Lucinda sighed. "Too fast. She's becoming a lovely young woman. And Stephen Merrow certainly has taken a fancy to her. He's over at the farm constantly. I don't mind, really. He's a nice boy and has helped me so much with the farm work."

"Maybe I could come out sometime to give you a hand."

Lucinda took note of the eagerness in Jedidiah's expression. She could tell he wanted more than just to be helpful, but was either too polite to say it, or too embarrassed. "Why don't you come to dinner Sunday evening? Melissa and I would love to have you stop by."

Jedidiah's face lit up. "I would like that very much. Here, let me help you get your supplies into the wagon."

A familiar voice came from behind as Lucinda helped Melissa up onto the wagon seat. "Oh, Mrs. Marsh!" Lucinda turned to see Mary running up toward her. "I am so very, very sorry about bumping into you earlier. I was in such a hurry that I didn't see you."

Lucinda wasn't sure she believed Mary's sincerity, but answered politely. "That's quite all right, Mary. How are you and your father doing?"

The expression on the young woman's face instantly changed to annoyance. "Father is still going on and on about how the whole town's gone crazy and that the Confederacy will bring us all to ruin! Honestly, I don't know what to do about him! He's becoming a complete and utter embarrassment to me!"

Mary's heartlessness toward her own father stunned Lucinda, who struggled to keep from revealing her surprise. Oblivious to Lucinda's discomfort, Mary continued, "Anyway, *I* am doing quite nicely, thank you. I was just wondering if you had heard anything from Willie. I do hope he's well, I mean, he's such a good boy and I know how much he means to you."

Startled by the remark, Lucinda replied, "I got a letter from him just the other day. He seemed to be in good spirits. Of course, it's hard on the soldiers up in the Virginia mountains." She paused for a moment, then said, "He does always ask about you."

The beginnings of a smile spread across Mary's face, but she stifled it quickly. "Well, you be sure to tell him I'm thinking about him, too, and that I can't wait to see him again. Would you jot down where to send a letter that will reach him? I think I'll write a letter to him right away. Yes, I will."

Skeptical of Mary's earnestness, Lucinda replied, "I don't have anything to write the address down with, but Mr. McCay has it. I'm sure he'll give it to you."

Mary clapped her hands with excitement. "Oh, thank you, thank you, Mrs. Marsh! I'm just so sure Willie will be thrilled to get a letter from me!" Without another word, Mary turned and rushed into the store.

Lucinda unconsciously rolled her eyes. *I hope I've done the right thing,*

"Mama, why are you rushing around so much?" Melissa's comment brought Lucinda up short. She had been racing through the housework trying to get ready for Jedidiah's visit that evening. *Why am I so nervous? After all, he's just a good friend.*

When the anticipated knock came on the door, she found herself almost afraid to answer it. McCay stood in the doorway for a moment, then stammered, "This is for you." He shoved a five-pound bag of coffee into her hands.

"Why, thank you, Jedidiah, this is lovely. Please, please come in. I'll make us a pot right now."

As they sat down to dinner, Lucinda could not help feeling slightly ashamed at the small portions the table held. Jedidiah, on the other hand, made several remarks praising her wonderful cooking. After dinner, Melissa was given a kiss goodnight and whisked up the ladder to bed. Lucinda prepared another pot. "It's wonderful to have coffee again," she said, "I've missed it."

McCay strolled over to the fireplace, picking up William's picture. "Make's a good lookin' soldier. You must be proud of him."

Lucinda handed him a steaming cup. "Very much so. I just wish he could come home. He didn't come out and say it in his last letter, but I think he's gotten a little fed up with soldiering."

"He still pining for Mary Stewart?"

The frown came back to Lucinda's face at the question. "He asks about her in every letter. I'm so afraid she would hurt him again. She seems to think of him more like a toy to play with. And her father doesn't try to control her at all anymore."

Lucinda and Jedidiah moved their chairs toward the fireplace. Taking a sip of coffee, McCay leaned back. "Been hard on old Stewart the last few months, what with all the folks around taking their children out of his school. Can't say as I blame them much, though, what with him spouting off about how the Confederacy is illegal and those that created it being evil. I know he was against secession, but if he's going to live around these parts he needs to tone down that unionist talk. Hell, he's still flying that God-damn Union flag at his house—."

He stopped talking at the sight of Lucinda's reddening cheeks. Taking a moment to clear his throat, he said, "Sorry, ma'am, it kind of slipped out. Anyways, I think Isaac would leave and join up with the

Yankee Army if he could. The only reason he stays here is that no-good daughter of his. Half the time she's screaming at him for doing something wrong. I honestly think she hates him. Willie was smart for getting away from her. She's going to be nothing but trouble. Today she asked me where to mail a letter to him. I gave her the listing, but I couldn't help thinking that I shouldn't have."

An icy jet of air brushed the back of his neck. Standing, he examined a crack in the chinking. "I'll come back out tomorrow with some tools and stop those holes up for you."

Lucinda did not notice the cold air as she gazed directly into Jedidiah's face. "Thank you. That would be sweet of you," Before realizing it, she reached out and put her hand on his arm. Embarrassed, she began to pull it back, but McCay quickly placed his hand over hers, holding it gently in place. For an eternally long minute, the two stared into each other's eyes. Lucinda's heart was racing.

A loud giggle from above interrupted the moment. Lucinda quickly pulled her hand back as both she and Jedidiah looked up to see Melissa, impish grin on her face, peeking down on them from the bed loft. Lucinda waved her finger angrily. "Melissa! You get back into your bed this instant! And stay there!" Her daughter's head immediately disappeared from view.

Jedidiah and Lucinda looked at each other once more, then he stepped toward the door. "I guess I should be getting back to town," he said, his voice betraying more than a twinge of disappointment. "But I will be back in the morning to fix those cracks."

Lucinda followed him out onto the porch. Taking her hand, McCay leaned down and kissed it, then turned hurriedly and mounted his horse. "Goodnight, my dear," he called as he reined the horse toward the road.

Watching him gallop away, Lucinda hoped that in the darkness he had not seen her blush once more. She shivered in the frigid air. Retreating into the cabin, she pulled her old rocker close to the fireplace, wrapping herself tightly in her shawl. A wave of guilt swept over her as she stared deeply into the leaping flames. An image of Jedidiah materialized in her thoughts, but soon was replaced by the dream-like face of Aaron Marsh. *Oh, Aaron, you've been gone so very long. I still don't know whether I am a widow or not. Am I wrong for enjoying Jedidiah's company so much?* The wind whistled through the cracks in the wall. *Am I wrong for wanting just a little happiness?*

Chapter 22

Thomas and his new friend James Stark did their best to keep a low profile around town. The degree of animosity toward them rose and fell with the Union Army's success and failure. It was quite a while after the debacle at Bull Run before they dared make regular appearances in public. The tolerance level got much better after the capture of two Confederate commissioners from the British mail steamer *Trent*.

The two had little trouble finding jobs, with so many men off to war. Currently they were working at the railroad station handling baggage and cargo. Desperate for help, the stationmaster deemed himself lucky to have two healthy laborers, regardless of their origin. On their first day on the job, though, he gave them a stern warning. "Don't make any comments to the passengers. The people around here aren't very eager to associate with southerners right now."

The last train of the day had arrived, and Thomas looked forward to finishing the unloading so he could head down to the tavern for a cold beer. Since the barn fire he had valiantly avoided hard liquor.

He mentally counted the passengers as they stepped down. *Not too many folks on this one. Shouldn't take long at all to finish up tonight.*

He felt a tap on the shoulder. James was pointing toward the last car, a devilish grin on his face. "Hey, look at that dandy."

Down from the car stepped a portly little man dressed in such finery as they had rarely seen. He spoke briefly to the conductor, then handed him a coin. "Yes, sir, Mr. Carroll. Thank you, Mr. Carroll," said the conductor, who then turned and quickly strode over to where James and Thomas were working. "Get this gentleman's bags out. And be quick about it!"

Thomas grumbled as he climbed into the baggage car. *We do the work and he gets tipped.*

Several minutes were required to locate the man's trunks, and then even more time was expended because they were on the bottom of a large stack. Finally they were extricated and moved to the door. The stout dandy was waiting, twirling his mustache and rapping his cane on the platform boards with great impatience. "Well, it certainly took you long enough to find four small cases. Now, load these bags onto my rig, and stop dawdling." Whipping out an embroidered handkerchief, he furiously mopped the sweat from his forehead.

Thomas struggled to contain his irritation. *Pompous windbag.*

Muscling the cases onto a cart, James and Thomas wheeled them over to a buggy waiting at the end of the platform. From inside, a young lady greeted Carroll enthusiastically. "It's so good to see you, Uncle!"

Carroll beamed. "My dear, I am delighted to see how you have blossomed. You look absolutely radiant. The very image of your mother."

Thomas could not help staring. The girl in the buggy was entrancing.

"Hey, watch it! You're going to drop that!" James's shout was too late. Distracted by the sight of Carroll's niece, Thomas released hold of the trunk too soon. It crashed to the ground.

Carroll whirled round. "Be careful with that! Don't you oafs know how to do your job?!" He turned back to the girl. "You see, Stephanie? All the good workers have gone to war. All that remain are lay-abouts like these two."

James could see the flush of anger rising on Thomas' face. He leaned over and whispered to his friend. "Calm down. He's not worth getting in trouble over."

The trunks now safely loaded, Carroll stepped into the buggy, all the while continuing to berate James and Thomas. "It is a sad time for the Union when even a few able-bodied men feel it unnecessary to answer their country's call to arms. One wonders why fine strapping lads like yourself aren't in the army." His tone dripped with sarcasm. "Of, course, army life isn't for everyone. I myself was deemed unfit for the rigors of war, though Lord knows I desired the chance to earn my moment of glory. Bad feet. A pity. I should have enjoyed laying waste to the rebel's homes—teach them a good lesson!"

Thomas shook with rage, desperately wanting to take a swing at the arrogant ass. James clamped a hand on his friend's shoulder and winked. Turning to Carroll, he dropped into the most outrageous southern accent he could muster. "Why, suh, we would be right proud to join the boys in blue. But, there's some here who don't trust us for some reason. Could be because I'm from Nawth Cah-lina and my friend here's from Jo-juh. Course, I can see why you wouldn't want to go down there. I got a friend that could skin a hog like you in no time flat!" Thomas began to laugh, then noticed the annoyed look on the girl's face.

Carroll's face grew scarlet. "Come, Stephanie, let us leave this riff-raff to accost some other poor traveler." He glared at James. "You, sir, are the perfect example for why *we* will triumph in this struggle. A few Southern heathens are no match for our glorious Federal army!" He snapped the reins. As the carriage pulled away, James shouted after them, "More than a few heathens at Manassas!"

Thomas roared with laughter—until he turned to see the stationmaster glowering at them. "You boys seem to forget where you are. I've ignored the fact you're southerners. I've paid you decent wages. And you repay me by humiliating one of the state's most honored citizens!"

"The man was being insulting, and we were defending ourselves." replied James.

The stationmaster obviously did not see it that way. "I warned you to keep your comments to yourself. You and your friend are discharged. Collect your wages and get off my platform."

James cocked his arm as if to hit the man, but Thomas stepped in front of him. "Come on, let's get out of here. There's plenty of other jobs open around town."

The pair headed back to their rooms, James grumbling all the way about pig-headed Yankees. Thomas was not paying attention, however. His mind swam with thoughts of Stephanie Carroll. The image of her face seemed to hang in front of him. He fantasized about the two of them strolling arm in arm. *Damn. There was little chance of that happening. She'll never want to have anything to do with me.*

As Thomas had predicted, it took little time to find alternate employment, though a job as stable boys for the blacksmith was not to James's taste. "There must be *something* better than mucking out stalls," he whined.

"We'll find something," Thomas tossed a shovelful of manure. "But at least we can pay the rent and keep eating."

"I sure don't feel much like eating after working in this stink all day."

"Don't worry. After a few days you won't be able to smell it anymore." Thomas stepped aside just in time to avoid the thrown horse collar.

Strolling downtown a few days later, Thomas had just turned the corner by the general store when a mangy, one-eyed dog charged at him. Snatching up a handful of dirt, Thomas threw it at the animal. The cur yowled, spun and ran away.

Turning to resume his walk, he spied Stephanie Carroll coming out of the post office across the street. She seemed to be having difficulty balancing a stack of packages. He watched with amusement as she struggled to keep the pile from shifting.

From the corner of his eye he caught a sudden movement. The dog he had just chased came streaking up the plank sidewalk toward Miss Carroll. Clearly excited by the swishing of her dress, the scruffy animal leapt at her skirt, sinking its teeth into the fabric. Miss Carroll shrieked. Packages flew everywhere.

Snatching up an axe handle from a barrel, Thomas charged the dog. Letting out a loud yelp, the animal fled with its tail between its legs.

Thomas began gathering up the scattered packages. Balancing them carefully in one arm, he doffed his hat. "Good morning, Miss Carroll."

It was a moment before she recognized him. For an instant her face began to twist into a scowl, but then immediately softened. "Thank you for rescuing me. That little monster came out of nowhere."

"It was entirely my pleasure, ma'am." He felt that he should say something else, but no appropriate words would come.

Her next words caught him by surprise. "I want to apologize for my uncle's rudeness the other day. He can be a bit overbearing at times. But he had no right to speak to you that way."

Taken aback, Thomas blurted, "That's quite all right. No harm done."

"Of course, you were a bit coarse yourself. And your friend's comments were really nasty."

But well deserved. The retort almost slipped out, but Thomas swallowed it down. His mind strained to think of what to say next. He didn't want to spoil this opportunity.

"Well, are you going to stop staring at me and say something?" Her tart remark snapped him back to reality.

"I'm sorry," he said, "I was just thinking to myself how beautiful you are."

"We hardly know each other well enough for a remark like that, sir." Her response was pointed, but the glint in her eyes betrayed delight from his comment.

Thomas's instincts told him that she wanted the conversation to continue, so he took a chance. "I would like to remedy that. May I have permission to call upon you some evening?"

She hesitated for just a moment. "That would be agreeable to me. However, my uncle may have a different opinion. He continued ranting about southern trash all the next day."

Thomas grimaced, then smiled. "Maybe you could soften him up a little bit, and then let me know when it would be safe to come by."

Stephanie's eyes flew open wide. "My goodness, sir, you are the most forward person I have ever met. If I were to do the proper thing, I would be walking away from you right now." The corners of her mouth curled with just the hint of a smile. "I must confess, though, that you do intrigue me. I will see what I can do to smooth the way. But don't expect too much too soon. Uncle Charles has a very hot temper."

The next day a note was delivered to Thomas's rooming house:

> *If you wish to call, please come to 14 Bunker Hill Street at 7:00 p.m. on Thursday. I have given Uncle a bit of a contrived excuse for you being a Southerner. Please be on time. Uncle comes home promptly at 7:30. I need to talk to you before he arrives.*
>
> *Stephanie Carroll*

Contrived excuse? What's that supposed to mean? Puzzled, Thomas could only speculate that Stephanie must have had to do some fast talking to convince Carroll to allow him into their home.

Donning his best outfit, Thomas started off that evening toward his rendezvous. Nervous, he stopped at the tavern for a beer. Thus fortified, he headed off again to Bunker Hill Street. The neighborhood was located on a ridge overlooking town, and the climb winded him. Arriving at Number 14, he paused for a moment to survey the house. All the buildings on the block were embellished with gingerbread trim, but this one was almost overwhelmed by the tremendous amount of decoration. Checking his pocket watch, he could see it was just before 7:00, so he stepped up on the porch and rapped the ornate clapper.

Opening the door, Stephanie asked him to come in. "I am so glad you are on time. We have to make sure your story is straight before Uncle comes home."

Thomas grinned. "I love a good conspiracy."

"Be serious! Uncle is likely to throw you out if you say the wrong thing."

Thomas swallowed a chuckle. "He can't be that sensitive. Doesn't he permit opinions other than his own?

"Not in his house, he doesn't. I have very strong ideas of my own about certain issues, but he wants Auntie and me to be proper ladies of the house—seen but not heard from. Now let's go over your story. I have told Uncle that you came north because you can't abide slavery and you think that secession was wrong."

"Well, you're right on one point. I am against slavery. But as to secession—."

Stephanie cut him off. "It doesn't matter about what you really think. If you want to continue seeing me, then you're going to have to make some compromises." Her eyes pleaded with him. "And I really do want us to have a chance to know each other better."

It felt slightly galling to Thomas to go through this charade. As he gazed into Stephanie's eyes, though, he knew he would do it. He would do anything to be near her. "All right, we'll try it your way."

Squealing with delight, she threw her arms around him in a quick hug. Just as quickly, she pushed him away, saying, "Now, you have to leave."

"What?"

"You have to go out and wait for Uncle to return. Then you can come back and he will never know that we've schemed together. Now please go quickly before he comes!"

Taking position a few yards down the street behind a large maple tree, Thomas waited for Stephanie's uncle to arrive home. His mind raced, full of visions of being arrested for loitering. *I can't believe I'm doing this.*

After what seemed like an eternity Carroll finally appeared, whistling and twirling his cane as he strode up to the house. *Well, at least he's in a good mood.* Stephanie greeted him at the door with a peck on the cheek. Waiting for what seemed like the proper interval, Thomas stepped up to the door and knocked. "Good evening, Mr. Marsh," Stephanie said, "I am so glad you came. I want to thank you again for rescuing me. Won't you please come in."

Emerging from a side room, Carroll stepped forward, offering his hand. "Good evening, my boy. My niece has informed me how you protected her the other day. I would like to thank you most whole-heartedly for that."

Thomas took the hand. "Thank you, Mr. Carroll. It was entirely my honor to be of assistance to your niece."

"Well, young man, you certainly do look more respectable than the last time I laid eyes on you. Let me take this opportunity to apologize for my remarks at the station. Had I known that you were such a staunch unionist I would have been more restrained. Stephanie has explained about your situation. Come, have a seat in the parlor."

Thomas glanced at Stephanie, whose smile appeared nervous and forced. *Just what did she say to him?*

"I'm sure it must be very difficult for you," Carroll continued, "having had to leave your family because of your different beliefs. I must say, though, I applaud your choice. There are not many men who would go against their family, even when they are so obviously wrong."

Wrong? Alarm bells were ringing in Thomas's head. He swallowed hard, trying to arrest the anger rising within. Stephanie was staring at him now, her expression suddenly anxious. Shaking her head, she mouthed a silent *don't*. Nervously turning to Carroll, she said, "Uncle, don't you think we should offer Mr. Marsh some refreshment?"

"Why, of course. Where are my manners. Mr. Marsh, may I pour you a brandy?"

Thomas began to say no, but Stephanie's frantic motions from behind Carroll's back prompted him to accept. Still, he felt uneasy about taking a drink.

"I shall return in a moment. My dear, please keep our guest entertained."

After Carroll left the room, Thomas spun toward Stephanie. "Exactly what did you tell him about me?"

"Just what I told you before, that you had left Georgia because you were against slavery and couldn't abide the thought of secession.

"You sure that's all you said?"

"Well, I did mention that you had a falling out with your family, and that you left because of your convictions."

"But that's not true! I love my family, and have never quarreled with them about anything. Certainly not politics! I came here because my uncle asked me to come."

Stephanie's face radiated annoyance. "Do you want to see me or not? If Uncle even suspects that you have Southern sympathies he will absolutely forbid you to come even close to me. I don't think you want that." Her expression again changed to one of pleading. "I know I don't."

Before he could reply, Carroll returned to the room bearing two laden brandy snifters. "Here you are, my boy," he said, handing one glass to Thomas before taking a seat in an enormous stuffed chair. "Now, I would very much like to learn more about that abominable institution. It would be most enlightening hearing about it from one who has lived among the heathens."

Thomas felt a prickly sensation rising up the back of his neck. He took the glass and sipped. The brandy was delicious. "Actually Mr. Carroll, the people that I knew in Georgia were pretty much ordinary folks, for the most part. Some good, some not so good. But few I would call 'heathens'."

Carroll gave a patronizing smirk. "Oh, come now, my boy. From what Stephanie has told me, you aren't on very friendly terms with the people down south. It seems odd that you would defend them."

Thomas choked down a retort with another sip of brandy. "All I'm saying, Mr. Carroll, is that there are good and bad people everywhere. I knew some mighty nice people around Dahlonega, like the Merrow family. They were always good to us."

"Who are they?"

"They own Greenfield Plantation just outside of town. Mrs. Merrow employed my mother as a seamstress, and my brother and I spent a lot of time there." Feeling increasingly warm, he loosened his tie. The brandy was settling into his system, and he was beginning to regret stopping for that beer.

An intent look crossed Carroll's face. "Did they have slaves?"

"They had about twenty when I left town to come north."

"Did you have any contact with the nigras?"

"I knew several of the people there. One, Joshua, was a very close friend when we were children."

"Then you have witnessed first-hand that wicked institution—the whippings, the separation of families, and other atrocities."

Thomas was taken aback. "Not all slave-owners are monsters. The Merrow's treated their people well, at least for the most part."

"So you contend that they never beat their slaves?"

"There were a few occasions. Mostly when one ran off—to dissuade others from trying it."

"Are you defending the practice?"

"No! I am against slavery, and I believe that secession is a great mistake. It's just not as cut-and-dried an issue as some would believe."

Carroll shot to his feet. "I disagree, sir! There is no middle ground. This is a struggle between right and wrong, and anyone who thinks otherwise is deluded, sir, deluded!"

Thomas' head was swimming. He could stand it no longer. "There are all kinds of good people down south who don't give a whit about slavery one way or the other. They are not deluded. They're just tired of Yankees telling them what to do. The great majority of Southerners have never owned a slave nor have any inclination to do so. My family certainly never did, and never would."

"Just a moment. Are you saying that your family does not hold with slaveholding? I thought you left for that very reason."

"I'm sorry that you were misinformed. I love my family very much. I was invited north by my uncle several years ago."

"Then you are here under false pretenses." Carroll turned to Stephanie. "I am disappointed in you, young lady. You lied to me. Go to your room. I'll decide the proper punishment for you later."

"But Uncle!"

Carroll looked as though he might explode. "Not another word, young lady. Go to your room right now!" Stephanie glanced sorrowfully toward Thomas, then dashed up the stairs.

Carroll turned back to Thomas. "And as for you, sir, get out of my house! Immediately! And stay away from my niece!"

Speechless with anger, Thomas almost threw the snifter at Carroll. With great deliberation, he set the glass on a side table, then turned and slammed out the door.

From the second floor, Stephanie peered out her window, watching with sadness as Thomas stormed away down the hill.

Chapter 23

Thomas fumed as he stomped back toward his rooming house. He felt like hitting someone. Passing the tavern, he decided he needed another beer.

Inside, a rowdy celebration was in progress. Wanting no part of it, Thomas made his way to the bar, planning to buy a bottle, then leave quickly. As he tossed a coin onto the counter, someone grabbed his sleeve, spinning him around.

"I'm buyin' all the rounds tonight, fren'!" The man looked as if he could fall down at any moment. "My son is in the Fourth New Hampshire, in General Tom Sherman's army down in North Carolina. General Sherman beat the Rebs at Port Royal. My boy was there. He's a real hero, is my Horace."

"That's fine," mumbled Thomas, "Real fine. But I only want a beer to drink at home. I'll just pay for it and go."

"Not no way!" insisted the man. "No one else's money is any good tonight. You need more than a puny beer. Joe! Set my friend up here with a whiskey!"

The bartender poured a shot glass full and placed it on the bar in front of Thomas. He stared at the glass for a long moment.

The man seemed insulted at Thomas's hesitation. "Sir, will you not help me toast my brave boy, and our glorious Union? Pick up that glass, sir!"

Thomas could see he was not going to get away from there without placating the proud father. He picked up the glass and raised it. "To Horace." Throwing back his head, he gulped the whiskey down. It felt warm and comforting dribbling down his throat. He beamed as the glass was filled again. Picking it up, he raised it to his lips. At that instant, a wave of dizziness passed over him. He hesitated, the shot glass hovering just an inch from his mouth. *No! I can't do this to myself. I'll not fall down again.* His hand shook slightly as he lowered the still full glass to the bar.

The bartender was staring at him. "You okay?"

"Just dandy," he replied, his voice slurred. "Thanks for the drink, but I must be going." He turned . . . and beheld Pastor Marsh staring at him from the tavern door.

153

Entering, Marsh stepped to a table, pulled out a chair, and motioned for Thomas to join him. Woozy and still angry from the argument with Carroll, Thomas's inclination was to walk out, but he took a seat across from his uncle. Marsh stared at his nephew for several minutes. "I thought you had given up on hard liquor. It seems that you have let temptation get the better of you once again."

Thomas was in no mood for a sermon. "I needed this. And it's really no business of yours what I do as long as I'm not under your roof."

Shocked, Marsh hesitated, then said, "I came to town to invite you to come back to the farm. Your aunt has been after me constantly to come fetch you back. She misses you terribly."

"I'm surprised, given what happened."

"I've told you before. You shouldn't hold yourself responsible for the fire. It was an accident. It could have happened to anyone. Rebecca simply dropped the lamp when you stumbled against her."

Thomas felt awash with anger, frustration and guilt. "But that's not what happened!" he blurted.

"What do you mean by that?"

"She didn't tell you everything. She didn't tell you that I hit her." The words tumbled out unconsciously.

Marsh's jaw dropped. "You *what?*"

Thomas suddenly realized what he was saying, but it was too late. He wanted to disappear, but felt compelled to continue: "Back when the barn burned down. She was trying to help me but I was so liquored up that I didn't know what I was doing. A bottle fell and broke and I was so mad that I slapped her. She dropped the lamp and that's what started the fire."

The preacher rose from his chair, staring at his nephew in disbelief. His face contorted as he tried to control the rage that was building inside. "How *dare* you! How dare you strike Rebecca! She was so good to you! I ought to—!" Clenched fists rose. Thomas had never seen such fury in his uncle.

"There is evil growing in you, boy. The devil of strong drink sits on your shoulder and is taking you down." The words stung like a whip. Marsh's hands unconsciously raised and lowered, obviously barely able to keep from striking out. He shook with the anger convulsing through him.

"Get out of my sight, before I do something I would regret! You are no nephew of mine!"

Thomas recoiled as if shot. He wanted to crawl away and hide. Marsh continued to glare for several seconds, then noticed how quiet the tavern had become. His anger cooling, he became conscious of the shock and sadness on Thomas's face. Shame replaced the anger as he realized how much his harsh words had wounded his nephew.

Thomas began to retreat. Marsh stood still for a moment, then stepped toward him. Tears flowed down Thomas's cheeks as he stumbled backwards. "You won't have to worry about me anymore," he said, "You or Aunt Rebecca. I'll never bother you again." Bolting for the door, he ran out into the night.

"Thomas, wait! I'm sorry!" Marsh called out for him, but it was too late. His nephew was gone.

"All right, all right, hold your horses!" Stark growled sleepily. A frantic pounding had roused him from sound sleep. Opening the door a crack, he was startled to see Pastor Marsh standing outside. Unlatching the chain, he yanked the door open. "Good Lord, Pastor, what are you doing here?"

"I need your help. It's Thomas. We had . . . words. Now I can't find him. I fear he may do something foolish."

Stark rubbed his eyes. "What happened?"

Marsh summarized the encounter. "Please, James, you're the only friend he has in this town. Please help me find him before something happens to him. Do you have any idea where he might be?"

James scratched his chin. "Well, there's another saloon outside of town that he's gone to sometimes. I'll try there."

Throwing on some clothes, James headed to the outskirts of town. The smell of dampness in the air indicated that rain was probably not long in coming. The "saloon" he had mentioned was little more than a shack. Entering, he made his way to the bar, which was just a wide board spread across two barrels. "Have you seen Thomas Marsh?" The bartender laughed as he wiped out a glass with a greasy rag. "Last time I noticed 'im, he was falling out the back door. He owes me two dollars for drinks. You want to take care of that?" James fumbled in his pocket, tossing a couple of coins on the bar. "That's all I've got right now. I'll bring you the rest later."

Stepping through the door, James glanced up and down the alleyway. A heavy rain had begun falling while he was inside, turning the dirt into glue-like mud. The air was thick with the smell of urine and other offensive odors. A low moan caught his attention. Through the rain he could see a figure lying in the slime.

Recognizing his friend, James took hold of his arm, trying to pull him upright. "God-damn it, Thomas, we've got to go to work."

"Leave me alone, Jimmy. I just need another drink!" Thomas snatched his arm out of his friend's grasp, sinking back down into the ooze.

Stark let out a snort of disgust. "That's the last thing you need right now. C'mon, get up and let me get you cleaned off. Your uncle sent me to find you."

"Don't care." Thomas moaned again. "Just leave me be. I'm cursed—I hurt everyone I'm near. Uncle Benjamin and Aunt Rebecca are just about the most decent people I've ever met and all I've done is bring them pain."

"No such luck. You're coming with me right now." James reached down to grasp Thomas' coat. It took great effort but he managed to pull Thomas to his feet. Supporting him as best he could, Stark made their way back to the rooming house.

Peeling off Thomas' mud-drenched clothing, James pushed him onto his bed. "Sleep it off, friend. I'll tell the foreman you're sick."

Thomas awoke with the sensation of a dozen drummers banging away inside his head. The bright light of the sun shining through the window caused his head to hurt all the more. In the fuzzy images before him, he imagined he could see Stephanie's face. He closed his eyes, pulling the covers up over his head. The blankets felt warm and clean. His hands moved down over his chest. *Hold on, now. How did I get out of those clothes? What happened to the mud?*

"Well, it's about time. I thought you were never going to wake up."

His eyes burst open at the sound of her voice. Blinded by the sunlight, he raised his hand to shade his eyes. Stephanie was sitting in a chair next to the bed. Suddenly self-conscious about his nakedness under the blankets, he yanked the covers up to his chin. "What the hell are you doing here?"

"There's no need to use that tone with me, Mr. Thomas Marsh! After Uncle went to bed last night I slipped out to find you. I wanted to tell you how very sorry I was for the way he treated you. But I couldn't find you anywhere. This morning, I went to the stables. James told me what happened. We came right over to see if you were all right. You were lying on the floor in those filthy clothes, so I cleaned you up and put you to bed."

Thomas pulled the covers up even further. "You mean, you . . . undressed me? B-but . . . ."

"Oh, be quiet. I just took enough of your clothes off so I could bathe you. James finished the job and got you into the bed. I didn't see any more than I needed to."

Her bemused expression hinted that she had seen more than she was letting on. Embarrassed, he fought the urge to burst out crying. "I don't understand why you would want to help me. I'm a drunk and a failure. I'll never be welcome in my uncle's home again."

"It was your uncle who sent James out looking for you. He was very upset at what happened. James says he wants to ask your forgiveness for what he said."

Thomas was stunned. "Maybe . . . I guess I'd better go out to the farm to talk sometime. But what about you? You're going to get into trouble coming here. Your uncle was pretty mad at both of us."

Stephanie moved to sit beside him on the bed. "I decided last night that what Uncle doesn't know won't hurt me. He thinks that I'm still just a child that he has to make decisions for. Well, I've been out in the real world and I can think for myself." She reached out with her hand, caressing his cheek. "And I think I want to kiss you."

Their eyes locked together. After a moment, Stephanie slowly began to lean forward. As their lips met, Thomas put his arms around her, drawing her toward him.

After a few moments, Stephanie pulled back from the embrace. Thomas tried to draw her back, but she resisted. "I have to go now."

"I don't want you to," said Thomas softly.

She took his hands gently and placed them on his chest. "I have to. But I'll be back this evening to see how you're doing. You just rest today."

She stood, picked up her coat, and walked to the door. Opening it, she turned back to Thomas. "Don't look so hurt. I promise I'll come back. Don't worry about Uncle. You just get some sleep."

As the door closed, Thomas settled back down under the covers. He looked out the window at the silvery clouds drifting far above, and reflected on the improvement in his fortunes.

Chapter 24

Shivering in the frigid air, William adjusted the tattered quilt around his shoulders. He just couldn't seem to shake the depression and loneliness that weighed heavily upon him. It was New Year's Eve, but he hardly felt like celebrating.

William's sadness was shared by most of the First Georgia. They, along with most of the Army of the Northwest, had joined with General Thomas J. Jackson's Army of the Valley a week earlier. The army was dispirited over its lack of success against the Federals, and Christmas Day only served to add to the melancholy. Being away from family on the holidays was disheartening, especially for those who had never been this far from home before.

Henry coughed. "Dammit, every time I move the smoke blows toward me." He changed position to the other side of the fire. The cold breeze shifted, sending rising smoke in his direction once again. He began coughing violently.

William managed a weak smile. "Just keep it away from me." Turning, he tried to position himself to warm as much of his body as possible. Raising the letter he had already read several times, he began again:

Dahlonega, Georgia
December 7, 1861

Dearest William,

I am so excited that I am finally able to write to you. You have probably thought that I was absolutely horrible for not writing before this. It was not my fault because no one would tell me where to send your letters to. At least not until I bumped into your dear mother at the general store. She told me about some of your adventures in the army, and I was absolutely thrilled to hear that you had been asking about me. Oh, Willie, you don't know how much I have missed you. You were so awful leaving town that day without so much as a goodbye. I was so very angry. But I

159

forgave you, and kept hoping I would get a letter from you. I want you to know what happened with Hiram Parker meant absolutely nothing. I was so upset with my father and he said he just wanted to console me. You weren't there and I needed someone to talk to. He took advantage of my weak moment. I acted like I was angry when you saw us because I was so embarrassed. I have never so much as spoken with him since then.

I want you to write to me and tell me all about your army friends and all the exciting times you are having. I am so proud of you. I want to hear about your glorious battles and the nasty yankees you are sending to perdition.

Yours in affection,
Mary

Lowering the paper, William stared into the flames, his emotions in turmoil. He had long dreamed of receiving a letter from Mary, but now, with that wish fulfilled, he wasn't certain how to proceed. He wanted so much to believe her, but something inside said she was not to be trusted.

He shivered, pulling the quilt tighter around his body. Winter winds in north Georgia were cold, but he could not remember having endured as frigid a winter as here in Virginia.

Looking up, he spied Sergeant Fitzpatrick rushing out from Captain Cabiness's tent. *Shit. Every time he charges around like that we've got orders to move.*

William had guessed correctly. Old "Stonewall" wanted to get at the enemy, and bad weather was of little concern to him. Many in the army considered him a crazy fool.

The tents were struck; and as the earliest rays of sun broke the horizon on the first day of the New Year, the First Georgia took its place in column. Speculation was rampant as to the army's objective, but no one really knew where they were heading. Jackson rarely divulged his battle plans to anyone.

The march began with little incident—in fact, warm temperatures brightened the troops' morale as they filed out of camp. Overheated in their heavy woolen overcoats, many soldiers began to discard the weighty apparel along the side of the road. By early afternoon, however, the weather had begun to rapidly deteriorate. From the darkening sky a light sleet began to fall. Onward the shivering column trudged, making slow headway. The sleet changed over into a freezing rain, making the already slippery road nearly impossible to walk on. Finally going into bivouac late that afternoon, the army had only been able to travel about eight miles from its starting point.

Waking to find their camps coated with a crusty layer of snow, the soldiers formed up once more to resume the march. The volume of grumbling in the ranks grew with each agonizing mile. As usual, Henry was among the most vocal. "Jackson's got to be out of his mind, moving in weather like this."

The column slogged onward along the frozen road, their progress a series of starts and stops. The weight of thousands of feet and dozens of wheels compressed the snow on the road to a rutted sheet of ice, making for treacherous footing. Time after time the army would come to an abrupt halt as horse teams slipped and fell, or as wagons slid on the road. On more than one occasion a man would lose his footing, taking the soldier next to him down also. Sometimes entire companies would collapse in a tangled heap.

Captain Cabiness was thoroughly disgusted by the lack of progress. During one particularly long halt, he ordered Company H to fall out to make fires for boiling coffee. Sergeant Fitzpatrick spoke up. "Sir, the only wood for fires are the fences on the side of the road. You know the orders against burning fence rails."

Cabiness stroked his beard thoughtfully, then said, "Sergeant, tell your men they can take only the top rail from the fence. That should satisfy the orders." Then he looked straight at Fitzpatrick—and winked.

Grinning, Fitzpatrick addressed the company. "Men, you can take the top rail from the fence for your cook fires. Be sure to take *only* the top rail." Fitzpatrick then lowered his voice: "Of course, after the top rail is taken, the next one is on top."

Laughter erupted from the troops as the sergeant's inference became clear. In short order the fence rails completely disappeared. Soon fires were roaring up and down the line.

For William, the next several days were a blur. The winter storm showed little signs of abating anytime soon. The column struggled on through the snow, while confusion as to their destination pervaded the ranks and officer corps. General Jackson still would not divulge his plans, leading to sharp disagreements between the general and his second in command, General Loring. Coming up on the small town of Bath, the First Georgia was sent charging into town, causing the small Union garrison to flee northward toward the Potomac River. Giving chase, Jackson's troops were unable to catch up with the Yankees before they crossed. Jackson, apparently satisfied that he had cleared his flank of enemy forces, now decided to withdraw back toward Bath, from whence to continue his advance on Romney.

Winter descended on the struggling column with a vengeance as the troops worked their way toward Bath. Temperatures hovered well below freezing, and the feet of thousands of men trampled the snow into sheets of ice. Men and horses were exhausted simply trying to stay upright on the slippery landscape.

"Sergeant!" Fitzpatrick and William turned to see Lieutenant Rhodes carefully picking his way over the frozen ground. He motioned to Fitzpatrick. "Sergeant, I've got a job for you. There's an artillery battery just on the other side of that hill. One of their guns slid into the ditch, and they can't get it out by themselves. We'll need about a dozen men to move it."

"Yes, sir." Fitzpatrick turned to William. "Marsh, you and the first three files fall out and follow the lieutenant."

William and his men carefully made their way along the ice-covered road to the artillery piece. The howitzer lay on its side, its limber still attached but jackknifed beside it. Rhodes conferred with the battery commander, then surveyed the gun's position. After a few moments, he motioned to his waiting soldiers. "Come on, boys, stack arms and lend a hand."

William's squad fixed bayonets, then linked their muskets together to form two teepee-like structures, over which they laid their cartridge boxes and belts. Lieutenant Rhodes directed them into position as they gingerly felt their way down into the ditch. "Corporal Marsh, you and Braddock unhitch the limber, then stand by the trail. Gregory and Moore, you take position at the muzzle. The rest of you take hold of the wheel. Once the limber's moved, we'll try to get this thing upright."

While Braddock steadied the trail, William pulled the pin holding the metal ring latching the cannon to the limber. When it came free, several of the waiting artillerymen pulled the limber away from the gun, slowly manhandling it back up onto the road.

"All right, men, let's show these gunners how the infantry sets things right. Everyone grab hold. On the count of three, we'll roll it upright." Rhodes took hold of the wheel, glanced left and right at his men, then exclaimed, "Now! Lift!"

Straining and groaning, the soldiers heaved on the enormous mass of metal and wood. With a groan, the heavy spoked wheel began to rise out of the muddy snow. Ever so slowly, the great gun came upright. Their faces red and contorted with exertion, the men struggled to keep it from falling back.

"C'mon, one more good shove and we've got it! Heave!"

With a final push, the cannon rolled over onto its trail and other wheel. William and the others sank to the ground, exhausted from the effort. Lieutenant Rhodes pulled out a kerchief and wiped his brow. "All right, boys, well done. Move over to the side and rest for a minute."

Gasping for breath, the soldiers half crawled, half walked over to the side of the ditch and collapsed in the snow. On the road a team of mules had been brought up. A heavy rope was run from the traces and attached to the howitzer's trail. The rope pulled taut instantly as the mules were lashed. Slowly the fieldpiece swiveled, then moved up the side of the ditch.

Rhodes called out to William. "Corporal Marsh, have your men collect their weapons. Looks like the artillery boys have this job under control."

"Yes, sir." Wearily, William and the detachment retrieved their muskets from the stack. They were in the act of shoving bayonets back into their scabbards when a cry was heard.

"The rope's breaking! Get some help to the gun!"

Rhodes was still in the ditch, deep in conversation with the battery commander. Hearing the shout, he yelled to his men. "C'mon, boys, grab that thing before it gets away from them!"

William and the soldiers dropped their muskets and rushed to the cannon's wheels, taking hold of the spokes. Keeping a foothold on the slushy ice was near impossible. The mules were braying fearfully as they strained on their harness. Horrified, William watched the rope continue to fray, its strands stretched beyond their limits. The cords broke one by one until only a single strand held. The fieldpiece was almost to the road. "Push harder!" yelled William. "Just a little more!"

The last strand snapped.

Instantly released from the great weight, the mule team was thrown violently forward. Several of the animals tumbled to the ground, thrashing about in their traces. The gun shivered, seeming to take on a life of its own, fighting all efforts to control it. Creaking, it began to roll back.

"We're losing it! Look out!"

The soldiers furiously worked to keep the massive gun from breaking free, but numb fingers and muscles strained beyond their limits could no longer hold back the brass monster. With a rumble and the sound of cracking ice, the howitzer pulled away, half-rolling, half-skidding back down into the ditch. William and the other soldiers slid as they frantically tried to get out of its way. Braddock's feet went out from under him. Flailing as he tried to get out of the behemoth's way, an iron-rimmed wheel rolled over his right ankle, pulverizing the bone. The cannon picked up speed as it seemed to charge at Lieutenant Rhodes and the other officer. The artilleryman was able to jump out of the way, but Rhodes slipped and fell. He screamed as the mass of metal and wood crushed him underneath.

Stunned, William was unable to move. Shocked completely senseless by the tragedy, he could only stare at the scene. Braddock's screams finally brought him out of his stupor. He turned to the other soldiers scattered down the slope of the ditch. "Moore! You see to Braddock! The rest of you, come on! We've got to get that thing off the lieutenant!"

He bent down to the moaning Rhodes. "Don't worry, sir, we'll get you free." Desperately, they took hold of the cannon's wheels, straining mightily to roll it off from the lieutenant's body.

William knelt down next to the stricken officer. The front of his tunic was red-soaked, and blood dribbling from his mouth was freezing into scarlet icicles. He opened his eyes, looked at William, and tried to speak. The only sound that came forth was a sickly gurgle. A few moments later, his eyes closed. One final moan, then his heaving chest went still.

Reaching down with his hand, William felt for any sign of breath from the lieutenant's nose or mouth. There was nothing. William stood slowly. "He's gone." The words were barely audible.

The men stood silently for several minutes with bowed heads. Four soldiers gently moved the lieutenant's body onto a blanket. Rolling up the edges, they gently lifted it. Careful of their footing, they carried Rhodes up the slope of the ditch.

William went over to check on Private Braddock. He lay on the slope, sobbing with pain. Moore had fashioned a tourniquet just above his ankle to stem the flow of blood. Raising Braddock between them, William and Moore helped him up to the road where an ambulance wagon had just arrived. With the help of a couple other men, William and Moore lifted Braddock up into the wagon. Lieutenant Rhodes's body was laid out on the floorboards.

As the ambulance moved off, William turned to his men. "All right, let's get back to the company." No more was said as they picked up their muskets and accouterments, and slowly made their way back to the regiment.

The march went on as the cruel weather continued to sap the troops' strength. Each day fewer miles were completed. The order finally came down from Jackson for the column to go into bivouac. The army's horses were ordered to be roughshod to help them hold their footing, and kettles of water for washing were set to boil.

Six days later the storm finally abated. Under clearing skies and a bright sun the expedition struck out again. Before long Jackson's objective, the town of Romney, was sighted. The army was drawn up into line of battle as skirmishers went forward to reconnoiter the village. Soon word was sent back that Union forces had retired from this position just the day before. Jackson was furious that the enemy had slipped away from him, but most of the troops were relieved. Orders came down for the army to move into the town.

The stench that greeted the troops was overwhelming. Garbage and filth were everywhere, and to add to the misery, it was discovered that the Federals had piled mounds of rotten meat in the courthouse.

Through some stroke of good luck, William's company was billeted in an old schoolhouse. It felt good to be under cover with a chance to finally dry out. A fire was lit in a tiny pot-bellied stove. The tiny bit of heat it gave out was welcome to the freezing, exhausted men.

The next morning, Fitzpatrick sent Henry off to find Braddock. Meanwhile, the sergeant put the company to work cleaning their weapons and accouterments. About an hour later Henry returned to the school. He spoke briefly to Fitzpatrick, then sat down next to William in front of the stove, his face drawn with sorrow.

William looked at Henry for a few moments, not sure whether to question him about their comrade. Finally he decided to ask. "How's Braddock doing?"

Henry stared at William, his lower lip quivering. "He's dead. The steward said he was doing fine after the surgeon amputated his foot. But he caught some kind of galloping pneumonia and just up and died. Sudden like."

The two friends sat without further conversation, staring at the stove. William's thoughts turned between Braddock and Rhodes. He thought of Samuel Craig, the boy killed falling from the train. *How many have to die senseless deaths before this war is over? I was so stupid, thinking that war would be a glorious adventure.*

Chapter 25

The door of the schoolhouse swung open, allowing a freezing blast of wind to burst through. A shower of curses peppered the private sticking his head in. "Close that damn door! You're lettin' the cold in!"

"Corporal Marsh, the lieutenant wants to see you and Sergeant Fitzpatrick. On the double!" The private shouted the instructions, then slammed the door shut just in time to avoid the tin cup thrown at him.

Now what? William was busy trying to free a stuck cleaning wad from the barrel of his musket. Henry chuckled. "What'd you do now, Willie boy?"

"Nothin' that I know of. Here, do me a favor. See if you can clear this barrel. I can't shoot it with that plug in there."

William began shivering the instant he stepped outside. He pulled his quilt tightly around himself, but it was scant protection from the frigid wind. Making his way through the slush to a small hotel where the officers were billeted, William approached a first sergeant working at a desk just inside the lobby. "Corporal Marsh reporting to Lieutenant Merrow, as ordered."

The sergeant glanced up, studying William for a moment. "Lieutenant's gone out for a minute. Set yourself over there 'til he gets back." He pointed to some chairs in a corner, then returned to his paperwork. William draped his quilt across a chair back and sat down.

Sergeant Fitzpatrick came in a few minutes later. He announced himself to the first sergeant, receiving the same instructions to wait. Sitting down next to William, he rubbed his hands together furiously. "Cold as a whore's heart out there. Freeze and thaw, freeze and thaw. I can't get used to this Virginia weather."

William laughed. "Any idea what the lieutenant wants with us?"

"Most likely about the ruckus the other day when Jackson ordered the brigade out to burn railroad bridges. Thought sure enough that some of the officers was going to get themselves shot."

"The boys were pretty mad. I mean, we finally get a chance to get warm, then the general goes and orders us out on another march through frozen hell just to wreck some bridges twenty miles away that the Yanks probably wouldn't be using anyway!"

Fitzpatrick leaned back in his chair. Sticking his foot out, he examined his crumbling footwear. Several layers of burlap were wrapped around each shoe in a forlorn attempt at weatherproofing. "Orders is orders, and I was weaned on following orders, but I wasn't too all fired crazy about tramping across the snow in these poor excuses for bootees."

William gazed about the lobby, amused at the chaos. Soldiers and officers came and went at a dizzying pace. Another sergeant was standing at the desk. The seated first sergeant pointed in William's direction.

Fitzpatrick and William stood as the newcomer walked toward them. After a flamboyant bow, he offered his hand. "Sergeant Jacob Franklin of Company A, Twelfth Georgia, at your service. Let's see, you would be one First Sergeant Gerald Fitzpatrick." He turned to William. "Don't know you, corporal. How'dya do!"

William winced from the pressure of Franklin's grip. "William . . . Marsh . . . . Pleased . . . to meet you."

"And pleased to meet such fine men from Company H. Got a cousin in your company—Ezekiel Franklin. You know him?"

"He's billeted over in one of the houses," Fitzpatrick replied. "So what brings you down here? You here to visit your cousin?"

Franklin shook his head. "Your Lieutenant Merrow sent for me. Any guess what's up?"

Fitzpatrick sat down. "We were just debating that ourselves. Think it might have something to do with the regiment almost mutinying when Stonewall tried to send us out to burn those bridges. Could be trouble from headquarters."

Franklin unwrapped the bright red shawl surrounding his neck. "Well, hope you keep your stripes. I've gone up and down so much that I should just keep mine on with pins—so much the easier to take them off again."

Just then, Lieutenant Merrow came striding into the lobby. Glancing briefly at the trio, he spoke to the desk sergeant, then trotted up the stairs. The sergeant waved for William and the others. "The lieutenant will see you now. Up the stairs, third door on the right. Be sure you knock before going in."

The door was open. William could see Merrow busy with papers at a field desk inside. Fitzpatrick knocked on the doorframe. Merrow looked up. "Come in, gentlemen. Take a seat on the bed." He shuffled a few papers around the desk, then stood, extending his hand to

Sergeant Franklin. "Good to meet you, Franklin. Your Captain Hawkins is an acquaintance of mine, and he speaks very highly of you."

"My thanks, Lieutenant," replied Franklin.

Merrow turned to William and Sergeant Fitzpatrick. "I sent for you because Captain Cabiness wants to make some changes in the command structure of the company. This has been made necessary by the death of Lieutenant Rhodes. Rhodes was not only a valued aide, but his passing away has left me with the loss of a personal friend."

"Will you be needing me to send the lieutenant's belongings home to his wife?" asked Fitzpatrick.

"Thank you, no," replied Merrow. "I posted his effects to his wife yesterday. Sold that big dragoon pistol of his to a Lieutenant Olmstead of the Twelfth Georgia, and sent the money along to her, also. I hope it will help."

"Would that be Lieutenant Geoffrey Olmstead?" asked Franklin.

Merrow nodded. "Ah," said Franklin, "he's a fine fellow."

"Gentlemen," continued Merrow, "Rhodes's death has created a vacancy in our military organization which must be filled. We need men we can count on in these positions. Sergeant Fitzpatrick."

Fitzpatrick stood. "Yes, sir."

Merrow drew a piece of paper from the desk drawer. "Sergeant, I have known you for many years. You have served me faithfully from the Mexican War until now. I was honored to present your name to the captain for promotion, and I am pleased that he agrees with me. He has given me the honor of presenting you with your commission as second lieutenant. Congratulations, Gerald."

He held out the document. Fitzpatrick stood, a look of total surprise on his face. Taking the paper, he stepped back, saluting. "I thank the Lieutenant. I will do my best to justify your faith in me."

Merrow nodded. "Next, we need a new first sergeant to take Fitzpatrick's place. Sergeant Franklin, Captain Hawkins has informed me of the excellent way you have fulfilled your duties with that company, and that he has endorsed you for promotion. As there are no openings in Hawkins's company at the present time, and knowing that you have a relative in the Volunteers, he has recommended you to Captain Cabiness in order that you may have this opportunity for advancement. Of course, if you wish to remain with your old company, I will understand."

Franklin stood and saluted. "Sir, it would be very hard to leave my comrades in Company A. But, for the good of the service, I would be honored to accept the position."

Merrow returned the salute. "Excellent, Franklin, excellent. I will inform Captain Hawkins of your decision. And now for you, Corporal Marsh."

William slowly rose from his chair, hoping but not sure what to expect. He almost forgot to salute.

"Marsh, you have shown great leadership ability, and the men respect you. When Lieutenant Rhodes was killed, you took charge of the situation in a way that did you credit. Therefore, we are promoting you to the position of third sergeant. Congratulations, Sergeant Marsh."

Thunderstruck, William managed a weak salute, then grasped the lieutenant's outstretched hand.

Merrow grinned. "Congratulations to all of you. The captain and I know we can count on each of you through the difficult days ahead. Sergeant Franklin, I want you to return to the Twelfth to pack your kit and await your transfer orders. That will give you some time to say your good-byes. Sergeant Marsh, see the first sergeant at the desk in the lobby. He has your stripes. Lieutenant Fitzpatrick, please remain. I have many things to discuss with you."

Sergeant Franklin and William turned to leave. As they started through the door, Merrow called after them. "Marsh, wait a moment."

William stopped as Merrow came around the desk. "I intended to take care of this myself, but I have to attend an urgent officer's meeting. I think that it will be appreciated coming from you." The lieutenant handed William an envelope. "This is an order raising one Private Henry Merrow to the rank of corporal."

William looked at Lieutenant Merrow in astonishment. Merrow smiled broadly. "Tell Henry that I am very proud of him."

Coming down the stairs, William noticed the activity around the headquarters was increasing. It appeared that every officer of the Army of the Northwest had arrived. He stopped at the desk. "Sergeant Marsh. You have something for me?"

The soldier glanced up, looking hard at William's sleeve. "Sergeant, huh? I only count two stripes." He reached into a drawer and pulled out a small package.

Quickly tearing open the paper, William pulled out two pieces of gray wool cloth, each adorned with three sky-blue cloth stripes. "Just got promoted. Say, what's with all the gold lace around? We getting ready to move again?"

"Not for me to tell. If we are, you'll find out. You want anything else? I'm busy."

170

Heavy, cold rain was turning the village streets to thick muck as William made his way back to the schoolhouse. The air inside was alive with shouts and loud cursing. William spied Henry sitting next to the stove, cleaning his musket and involved in an obviously heated discussion with Randall Gregory.

"What's going on?"

Henry slammed the musket down. "The Virginia regiments are heading back to Winchester to winter quarters. Likely be nice and warm while we're stuck in this God-forsaken, stinking village out in the middle of nowhere."

"Where'd you hear that"

Gregory spoke up. "I was over at the quartermaster's drawing some salt pork. A couple of the Virginia boys were there talking about how Jackson was going to move his headquarters back to Winchester, and that he'd be sure to take his old brigade along with him. Then they looked at me and laughed. Said that the new fish got to stay here. I sure wanted to pop them one."

Henry scowled. "Now I know why the boys are calling them 'Jackson's Lambs'."

Sitting down on his blanket, William reached for his knapsack. "I wonder if that's got something to do with all the hubbub at headquarters. Just about every officer in the army is over there for some big meeting."

"Probably planning another march for us," said Henry. "All them officers are as tetched in the head as Jackson. "Everyone knows you don't go on long marches or fight battles in the middle of winter. Makes me sick to think about it."

"Well, I have something here that might make you feel just a little better." William pulled the envelope from his jacket pocket, handing it to his friend.

"What's that?" Henry asked as he reached for it.

"Read it and find out."

Henry opened the envelope, pulled out the paper, then flopped down on his blanket. Skimming the contents of the document for a moment, he abruptly grasped it tightly with both hands. Sitting bolt upright, his eyes grew wider as he read. William grinned as his friend looked up at him. "You kiddin' me? Corporal? Pa signed this, along with Captain Cabiness."

"It's no joke. Look what I got." William pulled out his brand-new stripes.

"You, a sergeant? Well, well, well. This army is getting crazier by the day. Congratulations, Willie boy!"

"There's more. Fitzpatrick has been promoted to lieutenant, and we're to get a new first sergeant. They're transferring in a fellow from the Twelfth Georgia."

Henry looked dubious. "I'm glad for old Fitz, but I'm not too thrilled with the idea of breaking in a new first sergeant. Who're we getting?"

William was looking through his pack. "Met him over at the hotel. Name's Jacob Franklin. His cousin's in the outfit—Ezekiel Franklin. Seem's a decent sort. You seen my housewife? I need to sew on these stripes."

"Oops, sorry, I borrowed it to fix my trousers while you were gone." Henry reached under his blanket, pulling out a small cloth pouch full of buttons, needles and thread. He tossed it to William.

The rumors of Jackson moving back to Winchester and taking his old "Stonewall" Brigade with him proved true. The soldiers of the Army of the Northwest were near revolt when just about a week later orders came for them to pack up for the return march to Winchester. New rumors flew through the ranks that "Old Fool Tom" was so mad about the orders that he had resigned from command.

First Sergeant Franklin joined Company H as they prepared for the march. There was some grumbling among the other sergeants and some of the men about an outsider taking over Fitzpatrick's position. Franklin quickly won most of them over with his broad smile and even-handed treatment.

Even though they struggled through the deep winter mud, spirits in the First Georgia were high. They had finally gotten out that stinkhole Romney. Many in the ranks planned to take revenge on 'Jackson's Lambs' once they got to Winchester, but the column was halted on the outskirts. Sergeant Franklin came up to William. "We'll go into bivouac outside of town tonight."

William was incredulous. "What for? Why the hell do we have to stay in tents tonight?"

"General Loring has been brought up on charges by General Jackson. They want to keep us away from Stonewall's boys—afraid there'll be trouble."

"If that don't beat all. I thought Jackson had resigned."

"I'm told he got talked out of it by Governor Letcher. Virginia stands by its own. The governor must have pulled some powerful strings in Richmond. Anyway, let's get the men bedded down."

Sitting next to a fire later that evening, William pulled out the letter from Mary. He imagined he could see her face in the flames. *I guess I should write back.* Pulling out the stub of a pencil and a slip of stained paper from his haversack, he tried to compose a letter to her. But no words would come. After staring at the blank sheet for awhile, he finally gave up.

Trying to get warm under his blanket, he dropped off to a restless sleep. In his dream he was chasing Mary, who flitted away from him, just out of reach. Intent on catching her, he failed to notice that she had led him into a deep, dark forest. Suddenly she was gone. From where she disappeared came the dark horseman of his nightmare. The shot, the falling man, the lightning flashed before him again as he awoke bathed in sweat. Afraid that it might happen again, William forced himself to stay awake for several hours before sleep finally overcame him once more, this time mercifully dreamless.

Chapter 26

Lucinda gently shook her daughter. "Melissa. Melissa, darling, wake up. It's time for your medicine."

The bed had been moved down from the loft to the main room so that she could better take care of the sick girl. She felt Melissa's forehead. *Good, the fever's down.*

Melissa groaned softly. She raised her arm to shield her eyes from the sunlight streaming through the small window. "Mama, what's that noise?"

Lucinda smiled. "That's Mr. McCay and Stephen chopping some firewood for us."

Melissa coughed as she sat up. "Stephen's here?"

"Yes, dear. He's been here for a couple of hours, but you were asleep."

A look of annoyance. "Well, why didn't you wake me up?"

"Watch your tone. Right now you need all the sleep you can get. If you're going to get over the influenza, you need your rest. Don't worry, I've invited him and Mr. McCay to stay for supper."

Rising, Lucinda went to the door and peered out. She watched Jedidiah and Stephen as they furiously attacked the stack of wood. She could not help looking on with admiration at McCay as he worked, lifting the twin edged axe high over his head before driving it down to cleanly split a piece of seasoned oak. Stephen dashed in after each cut, scooping up the chunk to deliver to the growing woodpile.

"Mama, why do you look at Mr. McCay like that all the time?" Melissa grinned, then coughed again.

"Now just what is that supposed to mean, young lady?"

"It's just that, well, you always have that funny look on your face every time he's around."

An unexpected warmth rose in Lucinda's cheeks. Embarrassed at her reaction, she turned so as to hide the blush from her daughter. Reaching for two tin cups, she filled them from a bucket of drinking water, then carried them out onto the porch.

The cold outside air caused her to shiver. *Should've put on my shawl.* A late February snowfall had left a dusting of white on the fields and buildings. She called out to the two men. "I think you boys have cut enough wood to last us through the next five winters. Stop and take a drink before you wear yourselves out."

Jedidiah wiped his forehead with his shirtsleeve, then drove the axe into the chopping block. "Obliged, Lucinda." Accepting one of the cups, he sat on the porch step.

"Thanks, Mrs. Marsh," said Stephen, reaching for the second cup. "Is Melissa awake yet?"

Stephen's query brought a smile to Lucinda's face. "Yes. She was asking about you. Said I should've woken her up when you got here."

"She said that? Really? Maybe I should go see how she's doin'."

Stephen was already reaching for the door as Lucinda replied. "Go on in, she's waiting for you."

"They're sure sweet on each other," said Jedidiah as Stephen disappeared into the house. "He's a good boy."

"Yes, he is." Lucinda sat down next to McCay. "They're still so young, though. I don't want them to grow up too fast."

McCay nodded. "There's a lot of children that are having to grow up too soon. I get the casualty lists from the army about once a month now. People crowd around every time I post one, and there always seems to be someone who's lost a son to disease or wounds. It's hard to watch the men trying to comfort their wives."

A look of dismay and alarm flashed in Lucinda's eyes. Reaching out, Jedidah laid his hand on hers. "From everything I hear," he said, "William's unit hasn't seen much fighting. Last I heard, they were in winter quarters somewhere up in Virginia. And they're due to muster out in a month or two. I'm sure he's fine."

"I hope so. I lay awake at night worrying about him." Lucinda shivered again. "Come on inside where it's warmer. It's time to get cleaned up for supper. Afterwards I'll read William's latest letter."

After the meal the chairs were arranged around the fireplace. Lucinda broke the seal on the envelope McCay had brought. "Come, let's see what William has to tell us." Unfolding the rough paper, she began to read:

rominy, virginia
January 24, 1862

dear mother

I take my seat to pen you some lines I am sorry to not have written before but we have had a lot of marching to and fro we are now joined with genril jacksons command in virginia he is a queer one some of the men call him old jack and some call him old fool tom he is always eatin on a lemon and sometimes I have seen him holdin his arm up in the air some says he thinks it balances him we climbed over the mountains to get to the shanandoa valley and come together with jacksons army on christmas day I wished I could have been home christmas it would have been real nice.

Lucinda wiped a small tear from her eye. "It just didn't feel right for him not to be home on Christmas Day. It was the first holiday he's been away."

I have been raised to sargent now and henry is now a corporal sargent fitzpatrick has been promoted to lutenant on account that lutenant rhodes got himself killed by getting run over by a cannon

Lucinda's fingers rose involuntarily to her cheek. "That was so horrible!"

Jedidiah looked down at the floor. "He was a damn good man. His widow's having a hard time of it. Wish there was something we could do for her."

"I'll go see Mrs. Merrow sometime this week," said Lucinda, "Maybe we can organize something to raise some money for Mrs. Rhodes."

Melissa sat up in her bed. "What else does Willie say? I want to hear more."

"All right, all right. Just settle down, young lady. And pull your covers back up." Raising the paper, Lucinda continued:

lots of the men dont like old stonewall much because he is very hard on the army he marches us all over creation and we don't know where we are going to until we get there our year of enlistment in the old first geo. is just about up and a lot of the men don't want to get shot in a battle this close to going home lutenant merrow has already made one speech to the boys about reenlisting for the war because we are needed by the confederacy the govment says that we can change to another part of the army if we reenlist some want to be

177

in the artillery I have been thinking real hard on what I should do

Melissa's face betrayed displeasure. "Why should Willie have to stay in the army? He should come home just as soon as he can!"

McCay shook his head. "I don't agree. His duty is to his country." He turned to Lucinda. "You certainly know I don't want anything to happen to him, but if they all go home, we'll lose the war."

Lucinda looked thoughtful. "I have faith in William. I'm sure he will make the right decision."

we have a new first sargent jacob franklin he likes to talk a lot more than fitzpatrick did but he is an all right fellow we have had lots of long talks about whether to reenlist or not he says that the patriotic thing to do is reup for the war I got a letter from Mary. She says she is sorry for what happened and wants to be my girl again I don't know if I want to believe her or not if you see her tell her I will write her a letter soon I want to make sure I say the right things please write more a letter from home is good for the spirit

your affectionate son
william

Jedediah scowled. "You should write him back and tell him to get that girl out of his head. I still say she's nothing but trouble. All the young men in town are gone off to war, so she doesn't have anyone to fool around with."

Lucinda's cheeks again erupted in scarlet. "Mr. McCay! Please don't talk about such things in front of the children!"

Melissa threw off her blanket and sat up on the edge of the bed. "Oh, mother, I am not a child! I'm almost sixteen!"

Lucinda refolded the letter. "For the moment, you are still *my* child! You get right back under your covers!" Sliding under the blankets, Melissa rolled over to face the wall in an exaggerated show of irritation.

McCay yawned. "Heard anything about that other boy of yours? Seems like I remember you getting a letter from your brother-in-law up north."

"Benjamin wrote to say that Thomas is doing well, and may come to live on the farm again. He's been seeing a girl up there. I feel that there's more going on than he's telling me, just from the way he writes. I wish Thomas himself would write sometime."

Rising, Lucinda reached for her shawl. "Guess I'd better close the barn door and see to it that the cow has enough feed."

Stephen leapt to his feet. "I'll do it for you, Mis' Marsh."

Jedidiah put his hand on Stephen's shoulder. "Why don't you stay here with Melissa for a little while. I'll go out with Mrs. Marsh."

Startled, Melissa and Stephen looked at each other. "Uh, sure. I'll keep an eye on Melissa for you." Stephen dragged a chair over to the side of the bed. Melissa giggled.

McCay reached out to help Lucinda with her shawl. "Shall we go?"

Carrying a pewter candlestick, Lucinda and Jedidiah walked slowly together toward the barn. As they entered, Lucinda turned to him with a smile. "You trying to start a romance between those two?"

McCay picked up a pitchfork. "Well, young Merrow didn't protest much when I suggested he stay." He tossed a forkful of hay into the stall. "Besides, I really wanted to have a little time alone with you."

"Why, Mr. McCay, aren't you being a little forward?"

Leaning the pitchfork against the wall, Jedidiah reached out, taking her hand in his. She felt that she should resist, but did not. Several moments passed while they studied each other's face.

Finally McCay spoke, his voice softened. "Lucinda, I have something I want to say. During the day, at the store . . . well . . . I just can't stop thinking about you." He swallowed hard. "Damn, I've been rehearsing this for the last couple of days, and I'm screwing it up. You have a powerful effect on me, Mrs. Marsh."

Lucinda put her hand to his cheek. "I think I know what you're trying to say. You flatter me, Mr. McCay. I've grown quite fond of you, too."

McCay felt about to explode. "You really mean that? You don't know how happy that makes me." He grasped her arms, pulling her gently toward him. "I want to ask you . . . that is, will you . . . ."

Lucinda placed her fingers gently over his lips, interrupting his question. "I can't, Jedidiah, not yet."

McCay was stunned. "You don't even know what I was going to say."

"Yes, I do. You were going to ask me to marry you. Please don't ask me that, not now."

"But, Lucinda, why not? It's not right, you being out in this cabin, just you and Melissa. I can take care of you."

"I know you can." Tears were forming in Lucinda's eyes. "When the right time comes, then . . . maybe . . . I'll be ready. Please don't ask me just now."

Jedidiah seemed to shrink slightly. The disappointment etching his face pained her. She wrapped her arms around his neck. "Please believe me when I tell you how flattered I am by your attentions. Don't stop caring for me, Jedidiah. I just need some time."

"How much time?"

"I can't tell you that. I don't know myself."

McCay rolled his eyes upward. "Mrs. Marsh, you do know how to bedevil a man, I must say."

With her hand, Lucinda gently drew his head toward hers. "Well, Mr. McCay, maybe this will help." Their lips closed.

Chapter 27

Mary was livid. She felt like breaking every piece of china in the house, and she was well on her way to doing it. Isaac Stewart came running into the parlor just as she smashed another plate. "My god, daughter, what are you doing?"

Wiping at the tears flowing down her face, Mary blurted, "I just found out that Mrs. Merrow is having a ball to raise funds for Lieutenant Rhodes's widow, but I wasn't invited. It's not fair, it's just not fair!"

Stepping carefully over the broken pottery, Isaac walked over to her, placing his hand gently on her back. "There, there, child, I'm sure it was just a mistake. I'll speak to Mrs. Merrow tomorrow."

Mary angrily twisted away from her father's hand. "It's no mistake. I wasn't invited on purpose. And it's all your fault!"

Astonished at her outburst, Stewart asked, "Why do you say that?"

"Everyone avoids me like I have leprosy. Whenever I come up to people talking they see me and abruptly change the subject. But I know what they're saying. 'There is that daughter of Isaac Stewart, the Yankee bastard'."

"You watch your filthy tongue, young lady!" Anger welled up as Isaac struggled vainly to keep his voice calm. "I'll tell you why they talk about you. All the tongues in town are wagging about your dalliances with Hiram Parker and the others. You've inherited your mother's evil streak!"

"My mother has nothing to do with this. You've never been able to live with the fact that she left you for another man!"

Lines of rage began to distort Stewart's face. "Your mother was a no good whore!"

Gasping in disbelief, Mary stared at her father. She had never heard him speak ill about her mother before.

Isaac leaned against the fireplace mantle. Looking up at Julia's portrait, his expression changed to one of intense sorrow. "I was a naive young man when I met her. She was so beautiful she took my breath away. She seduced me, and you were the result. I married Julia so you would have a good name. I thought that being married and with a child, she would curb her passions. But I was wrong. It didn't take long for her to return to her sluttish ways."

Anger again showed on Isaac's face as he turned back to his daughter. "I have tried to bring you up to be a proper young lady, but I see now that I have failed. That is the curse I must live with. But as long as you remain in this house you will do as I say. I will not have you keeping company with a coward and a slacker!"

"What gives you the right to call him a coward!"

Isaac waved his hand with a slicing motion. "Everyone knows Parker cut his own toes off with an axe to avoid going into the army."

"I would think you would be grateful for having one less soldier in the Confederate army."

"With Hiram Parker in the army, the Union might win the war all that much sooner."

"That's just what I might expect from a Yankee-loving traitor!"

Stewart slammed his fist down on a table. "You call *me* traitor! All around us are the traitors! Every one of those fire-eating secessionists that got us into this bloody war should be hung, and the misguided fools that followed them should all be clapped in irons! Mark my words, judgment day will be terrible once the Northern armies prevail, as I am confident they will!" With that, Stewart turned his back to his daughter and climbed the stairs to his room.

Slamming out the front door, Mary stormed up the street. No particular destination in mind, she just wanted to get away from the house and her father. In her fury, she didn't see Parker coming around a corner. Colliding, the impact knocking them both to the ground.

Parker shook his head. "Whoa, missy, you best watch where you're going. No tellin' who you might run into." Standing, he reached down to help Mary to her feet.

As she brushed herself off, Mary looked at Parker with annoyance. *Brute.* Suddenly she felt a familiar longing. *He'd do for now.* Her expression became all sweetness. "Maybe it's you I wanted to run into."

"That so? Now why would you be looking for me?"

"I need someone to . . . talk to. I've just had a horrible argument with my father, and I need some comforting. Do you know someplace where we could go to be . . . alone?" Mary looked straight at Parker, her tongue slowly moving across her lips.

Parker's neck suddenly felt warm. He gulped. "Well, you can come up to my place, if you want."

Mary forcibly took his arm. "Well then, come on. Let's go."

Early next morning Mary awoke to the sound of Parker's heavy snoring. Through the curtain less window she could see first rays of sunlight peeking over the ridge tops. She glanced around the barely furnished room. Moving carefully so as not to wake Parker, she rose, crossing silently to a dresser which held a pitcher and basin. Pouring some water, she washed her face, using her skirt to dry herself as there was no towel handy. Dressing quickly, she opened the door, glancing each way to make sure there was no one around. Mary looked back at sleeping Parker. *Such a disgusting beast.* Slipping down the stairs, she made her way out a back door, satisfied that she had not been seen.

The cold morning air of late March felt refreshing as Mary walked down the street. Passing the Mercantile, she paused, then decided to enter. Jedidiah McCay was busy at his desk writing in a ledger book.

"Good morning, Mr. McCay."

Jedidiah looked up. "You're up a might early, Miss Stewart," he said, observing her wrinkled dress and unbrushed hair

"I had some things to take care of that had to be done first thing. Did any mail come in for me or my father?"

McCay went around the counter to the mail slots. "Just one for you. Looks like it's from William Marsh."

Mary's eyes flew wide open. "From Willie? Oh, please, let me have it!"

Snatching the envelope from his hand, Mary dashed out the door without another word.

Jedidiah shook his head, muttering, "You're welcome."

Mary warily glanced around for her father as she slipped through the door of her house. Isaac was asleep, sitting in a large upholstered rocker next to the fireplace, a shawl wrapped around his shoulders. She crept up the stairs to her room, quietly shutting the door. Throwing herself across the bed, she tore open the envelope.

> *camp near winchester virginia*
> *march 10, 1862*

> *dear mary*

> *I take my seat to pen these lines to say I was so glad to get your letter I was very happy to hear that you are really not mad with me I have thought about you just about every day I am well though it has been a real*

cold winter the snow is beginning to melt and there is mud everywhere

I am now a sergent in old company H henry is corporal and sergent fitzpatrick is now a lutenent our year is just about up lutenant merrow made a big speech asking us to reenlist in the first georgia many in the first georgia have decided to go to other units like the artillery or cavalry I was thinking about joining the cavalry but lutenant merrow says he needs me so I have reenlisted in the first for the war the general said that any one who reenlists will get a 30 day furlough so that means I will be coming home while it will be awhile yet before they let me go but I should get there in a few weeks if I can get to a railhead I want to see you very much I will try to telegraph mister mckay when I know when I am coming it would be so wonderful to see you waiting at the station.

yours in affection
william

Mary rolled onto her back. Holding the letter aloft, she reread the last few lines. He was coming home!

Pressing the letter to her breast, she closed her eyes, trying to imagine what changes she would see in him. She was amazed at her intense physical reaction. *Yes, my dear Willie, I will be there when you return. And this time, my darling, I will have you, body and soul.*

Chapter 28

"Well, you going to see who it is?" James yanked the blanket over his head as he rolled over. The knocking at the door got louder.

Thomas pulled his pillow over his face. "Why the hell can't you?" James grunted what sounded like an obscenity, but otherwise didn't move. The knocking continued. "All right, all right, hold your horses, I'm coming." Wrapping his blanket around himself, Thomas stumbled to the door, throwing it open. "What the hell is it—Oh!"

Pastor Marsh stopped in mid-knock. "I'm sorry to disturb you, Thomas, but I needed to talk to you. May I come in?"

"Uh . . . sure." Thomas stepped back to let his uncle enter.

Sitting up, James reached for his trousers. "You want me to leave?"

Marsh waved his hand. "Hello, James. No, please stay. I will have a question for you." He turned to Thomas, now seated on his bed. "First, I want to offer you my sincere apology for the harsh words I used. I'm sure you know how much I love your Aunt Rebecca. I was overwhelmed with self-righteous anger when you confessed how she was injured."

Thomas fidgeted as he gazed down at the floor, but said nothing.

Taking a seat in a shabby old chair, Marsh continued: "Rebecca and I have done a lot of talking about what occurred that night. She is a good woman, your aunt. She reminded me of something very important. 'To err is human, to forgive, divine.' She forgave you for what happened that very day. She wants you to forgive yourself, and so do I. I also hope that you can find it in your heart to forgive me for the un-Christian way I treated you."

Thomas looked up. "I guess we both got a little hot under the collar."

Pastor Marsh nodded. "True. But now I think it's time to look toward the future. I also wanted to talk with you about your coming home." Thomas opened his mouth, but Marsh cut him off. "Now let me speak my peace. Rebecca and I both feel that the proper place for you is back at the farm. Besides, I need you. It's hard for me to admit this, but I'm not young anymore, and I just can't keep up with the farm work by myself. Please, Thomas, will you come back?" Pastor Marsh extended his hand. "The only request I must make of you is that you promise not to bring any liquor."

Hesitating a moment, Thomas reached out, grasping his uncle's hand. "All right, I'll give it a try. I can't promise I won't take a drink, but I will promise not to do so while on your property."

Marsh beamed. "I guess that's fair. Perhaps, in time, we can help you overcome that particular demon."

"For now, Uncle, I think it would be best to avoid that subject."

"Very well." Marsh turned to James. "My boy, I can't thank you enough for all you've done for Thomas. I can use a good man on the farm. I would like to offer you a job. What do you say?"

James swallowed. "Guess it would beat all hell out of shoveling shit in the stable." Seeing the frown sliding across the preacher's brow, James said, "Oops, sorry, Mr. Marsh. That kind of just slipped out. Yessir, I'll accept your offer, and thank you."

"Good, good." Marsh slapped his hand on his knee, then stood. "When do you think you'll be ready to come out?"

Thomas and James exchanged glances. "I 'spect we can be done here in town in a couple of days," said Thomas.

Pastor Marsh opened the door to leave. "Very good. Rebecca and I look forward to having you back as soon as you can."

The next morning, James went down to the livery to turn in their notice, while Thomas stayed behind to begin packing up their belongings. He was busy going through a drawer when a voice from behind startled him.

"Hello, handsome."

Thomas whirled. Stephanie Carroll was leaning against the doorframe, a wide smile on her face. "Hello, yourself," he replied, grinning. "Come on in."

Stephanie glanced about the room as she entered. "Looks like you've got just about everything stowed already. Of course, you didn't have a lot to begin with. Can I help?"

"Certainly. Why don't you pack up my shaving kit?" He gestured to the dresser. "It's over there by the basin."

Stephanie gathered up Thomas's straight razor, shaving brush and comb. After depositing the items in a leather case she found in the top drawer, she lifted the pitcher from the basin.

Just then, she felt a hand on her waist. Startled, she spun around. Water sloshed from the pitcher onto the front of Thomas's trousers. She put a hand to her mouth, trying desperately to suppress a laugh.

"Oh, Thomas, I am so sorry!" Unable to stifle the urge, she began to giggle, then laughed out loud.

Thomas examined his soaked pants, then looked up at Stephanie with a mischievous smile. Suddenly he reached out, snatching the pitcher from her hand. "I think maybe it's time for *your* baptism."

"You stop that right now!" Stephanie's eyes opened wide in mock horror as Thomas advanced on her with the pitcher. Backing into a corner, she laughed as she tried to avoid being splashed. Thomas raised the pitcher. "Thomas Marsh, you wouldn't dare!" she said in feigned alarm.

"Oh, you think not, do you?" With that, Thomas poured the contents over her head.

"Ooh!" Stephanie sputtered "You are absolutely the most despicable man I have ever met!" She pushed him away. "Get me something to dry off with!"

Tossing the pitcher onto the bed, Thomas found a towel. After dabbing her face and neck, Stephanie reached up, removing the snood which held her hair in the back. Long, brown tresses draped her shoulders. Thomas watched with mounting interest. He reached out to touch her damp ringlets. "You have beautiful hair."

Stephanie took his hand. "Why, thank you, even though you've ruined my hairdo."

Thomas moved closer, putting his other hand on her waist. "Wet or dry, you look lovely." Pulling her close to him, he leaned down to kiss her.

They gazed into each other's eyes for a few moments, then kissed again. Locked in their embrace, they didn't notice that someone was pushing the door open.

"Stephanie!"

Caught by surprise, the two broke their embrace, spinning around to see Charles Carroll standing in the doorway. Thomas's gaze riveted on the small pocket pistol in Carroll's hand.

"I warned you, sir, to stay away from my niece." Carroll motioned with the gun. "Stephanie, come over here."

Frightened, Stephanie looked up at Thomas once more, then slowly crossed over to her uncle. He seized her arm, roughly pulling her to the door. She winced in pain. Angered, Thomas started to move toward them, but stopped when Carroll cocked the revolver. "You stay right where you are, Mister Marsh. I am not a violent man, but I will do whatever is necessary to protect my family's reputation. I've been hearing rumors about how the two of you have been carrying on." He turned to his niece. "And as for you, young lady, I can't believe you would continue to associate with this southern trash."

Tears welled up in Stephanie's eyes. "But Uncle, I . . . I love him."

Carroll's look of shock quickly changed to wrath. He slapped her across the face.

Infuriated, Thomas rushed forward. Before Carroll could raise the pistol again, Thomas grabbed for it. The two men struggled for possession of the gun. Stephanie began to cry, her hands on her cheeks. "Oh, please, stop it, Thomas," she pleaded. "Stop it!"

A sharp crack echoed through the room as a bullet plowed into Carroll's thigh. Thomas suddenly found himself supporting Stephanie's uncle as he went limp. Unable to hold the weight, he could not stop Carroll from sagging to the floor, moaning in pain. In shock, Thomas reached down to pick up the revolver, then turned toward Stephanie.

Stephanie knelt at her uncle's side. Ripping off a piece of her skirt, she quickly wrapped it around the bleeding limb. After satisfying herself that his injury was not life-threatening, she tried to get him to stand. "Come on, Uncle, we need to get you to the doctor."

Thomas reached out his hand. "Let me help you." Stephanie turned her head toward him. The fury contorting her face brought him up short.

"Don't you touch him! Just don't touch him!"

Thomas stood rigid, stunned and bewildered by the sudden turn of events. Suddenly, James appeared at the door. "What the hell is going on here?"

Stephanie put her hand out toward Stark. "Please, James, help me get my uncle to the doctor. He's been hurt."

James looked at Thomas for an explanation, but his friend could only nod. "All right. Hold him for a moment while I get a grip." Hauling Carroll to his feet, Stark wrapped his arm as far as he could around the older man's waist. Draping Carroll's arm over his neck, James carefully maneuvered him out into the hallway.

"Stephanie, I'm sorry. Please . . . ." Thomas put out both hands toward her. After glancing back with an expression of both anger and sadness, she followed Stark through the door. Thomas gaped at the empty space for a few moments. Lying down on the bed, he put his hands under his head and stared at the ceiling.

Night had fallen by the time James returned. In the darkened room he found Thomas still lying on the bed, mumbling incoherently.

James took hold of Thomas's shoulders, shaking him roughly. "C'mon, boy, snap out of it."

Thomas blinked. James gave his friend another shake. Thomas looked around for a moment, then swung his legs over the edge of the bed. The pocket pistol clattered to the floor. As he sat up, James lit a candle. Thomas rubbed his eyes, trying to adjust to the increase in light. Reaching down, he picked up the revolver. He inspected the small firearm for a few moments, spinning the cylinder. Finally he spoke. "Mr. Carroll . . . is he . . . ?"

"He's all right," said James. The ball missed the bone. He'll be pretty sore for awhile, but there's no permanent damage. I think his sensibilities were hurt worse than his leg."

"Stephanie, what about her?"

"She's calmed down quite a bit, but she's still pretty angry with both of you. She was giving her uncle what-for when I left. I think you'd be wise to stay clear of her for awhile."

"She probably won't ever want to see me again." Thomas let out a long, mournful groan.

James picked up his dilapidated canvas carpetbag, rummaging through it to make sure his few possessions were intact. "Don't be stupid, friend. If I've ever seen a girl in love, it's her. She was just upset that her uncle got himself hurt. She'll probably scream at you a little to make herself feel better and to let you know that you got her mad. Then she'll want to start kissin' and carryin' on again."

"You think so?" Thomas perked up a little. What James was saying made sense. Least wise he hoped it did.

"Course I do. In a few days you send her a dozen roses, say you're sorry, and everything will be just dandy again. Now come on, we'd best get going. Your uncle will be wondering what's happened to us."

"Yeah, you're right, we better get a move on." Thomas stood, sliding the revolver into his belt. Stretching, he took one last look around the room to make sure he hadn't forgotten anything. Lifting his pack, he was just reaching for the doorknob when there was a knock.

The slight man standing outside the door reminded Thomas of a scarecrow. Dressed head to toe in black, his clothes hung so loosely they gave him the appearance of wearing a tent. Nevertheless, the set of his jaw told Thomas he was one not to be trifled with.

The man tediously sucked on a cigar as he looked Thomas over intently. "You Thomas Marsh?"

"Yes, and you would be . . . ?"

"Town Constable Mattson. Looks like you were just leaving. Glad I caught you before you did. Understand there was a little trouble here earlier."

Thomas and James exchanged worried glances. The constable reached out, plucking the pistol from Thomas's belt. "This your piece, Mr. Marsh?"

"No, sir, it belongs to the relative of a friend. I was just on my way to return it. Why do you want to know?"

Mattson pulled the hammer to half cock and spun the cylinder. "Looks like one shot's been fired." He sniffed the barrel. "And recently." The constable squinted at Thomas as he uncocked the pistol, placing it in the pocket of his long coat. "Well, Mr. Marsh, I think you'd better come with me. I have a warrant for your arrest, on the charge of assault with intent to commit murder."

Chapter 29

Grainger peered through the branches, carefully studying the farmhouse. Jonathon crept up behind him. "See anyone?"

"Nope, but there's someone there. Smoke's comin' from the chimney."

Evans scratched his beard. "We'd best stay clear, not knowing who's there. Maybe we can find a better place to get supplies."

Grainger looked at Jonathon for a moment, then back at the house. Pulling a bandana from his pocket, he took off his hat and wiped his forehead. Sunlight glinted from the small derringer Grainger kept secreted inside the hat's crown. "We've come a long ways, and we've got a long trail ahead to find Baxter. Too far to go with just one horse. We need another one."

"Why the hell are we going such a long distance to locate this fellow? We're far enough from the army now that they won't find us. I say we just stay where we are."

Grainger grabbed Jonathon by the top of his open jacket. "Because I say so. My brother's with Baxter's outfit. I aim to hook up with him again." He glared at Evans. "You don't like it, you can leave right now." He released Jonathon's jacket with a shove.

"Nobody said anything about leaving. I'll stick with you for now."

Replacing his hat, Grainger looked back at the house for a few moments, then shook his head. "We got to chance it. We'll say we're a couple of scouts. I'll keep a hand on my pistol. If they give us any trouble, we'll just shoot 'em."

The two made their way back to where the horse was tied. Jonathon mounted, then pulled Grainger up behind. As they reined up in front of the house, the door opened a crack. The twin barrels of a shotgun poked through. A voice inside demanded, "Who the hell are you and what do you want?"

Out of sight behind Jonathon, Grainger drew his revolver. Keeping a tight grip on the reins with one hand, Evans raised his other. "No need to be peevish, mister. We're scouts with Forrest's command. Got separated from the army."

Using the shotgun to push the door completely open, the man stepped out. "You just stay right where you are," he said. "Why two on one horse?"

Evans pointed back at Grainger with his thumb. "His horse went lame a ways back. Had to leave it. You seen any soldiers pass this way?"

"Ain't seen no one from either side for a couple of weeks." The farmer studied the pair. "You say you're with Forrest? Thought he was way out west of here."

Jonathon grinned. "Guess that goes to show we're doing our job right, if no one knows he's close by. You got a horse and some supplies we can buy? We'll pay top dollar."

"Only got one horse but she's not for sale. I need her for the farm work." The man lowered the shotgun. "Can sell you some supplies to tide you over, though. Stable your horse over in the barn. You can take supper with us, if you want."

Grainger returned the pistol to its holster, then swung off. Jonathon trotted the horse over to the barn, dismounted, and led it inside. To the right were two stalls, one occupied by a sandy colored mare. Leading his horse into the other, he set to work uncinching the saddle.

As he began to remove the reins, he suddenly felt an awareness of being watched. He finished pulling the reins from the horse's head, then warily turned. A young girl holding a basket full of eggs was watching him intently from the doorway. His eyes moved up and down, taking in her youthful figure. The look on her face gave him the strong impression that she was enjoying his inspection. Wrapping the reins on a hook, he touched his hat. "How do, ma'am."

The girl giggled, then dashed out the door. Chuckling, Jonathon returned to the task of bedding down the horse. Finding a bag of grain, he filled a pail for the animal to feed from.

Coming up onto the house porch, Jonathon was met by the girl. "Come on in," she said, "Supper's on the table." She led through a bare entry hall into a sparsely furnished side room. Grainger was already seated at a well-worn trestle table, busily shoveling stew into his mouth. Taking a seat, Jonathon reached for a biscuit, while the girl spooned stew onto a pewter plate. Her eyes never strayed far from him as she moved around the table. He turned to the farmer. "You've got a pretty daughter, Mister . . . ."

"Name's Snyder." The man looked around at the girl. "Pretty? Hmm. Hadn't thought much about it. Guess you could say so. Hannah takes after her ma."

Evans looked around. "Where is her mother?"

Snyder didn't look up from the bread he was slicing. "Wife died a couple of years ago from the misery."

Jonathon smiled at Hannah. "Well, missy, it's sure nice to eat home cooking again. 'Specially made by a pretty thing like you."

Hannah beamed. "Why, thank you, mister." She spent most of the rest of supper staring at him.

The meal finished, the men crossed from the dining room to a parlor while Hannah cleaned off the table. Sitting down in a well-worn stuffed chair, Snyder pulled out a pipe. Jonathon and Grainger sat in other chairs. "Look, Snyder, we really need that horse of yours," said Grainger. "We've got to get back to the army with our report."

Lighting his pipe, the farmer took a couple of puffs, then replied, "Told you boys before, the horse ain't for sale. Need her for the plowin'."

Jonathon started to speak, but Grainger cut him off. "Well, sir, I guess we'll have to make do. Anyhow, we'd appreciate it if you'd let us bed down here for the night. We'll collect our supplies and be on our way in the morning."

"Haven't got enough room in the house. You can sleep in the barn."

Evans began to retort, but again Grainger stopped him. "Sounds all right." Standing, he started for the door. "You comin', Evans?"

Confused, Jonathon followed his companion in befuddled silence, but once they got to the barn, he could stay quiet no longer. "What the hell was that all about?"

Grainger didn't reply. Piling up some hay, he spread out his blanket.

Jonathon was frustrated by the lack of an answer. "I asked you a question! Why'd you give up on the mare so easy?"

Grainger scowled at Jonathon. "Hell, we're going to steal her anyway. I figgered the old fart would'a ordered us off if we argued too much. We'll just catch a couple hours sleep, then take off early in the morning. We'll be long gone before he figgers out we done stole her."

Jonathon had barely dozed off when the sound of rusty hinges creaking brought him fully awake. From the corner of his eye he could make out a faint glimmer of candlelight. Pretending to be asleep, his hand moved deliberately to the revolver concealed next to his head. The stranger was coming closer. Abruptly, Jonathon sat upright, leveling the pistol at the intruder. The visitor halted, letting out a small, fearful gasp. "Oh, please, don't. It's me, Hannah."

"What the hell are you doin', sneaking up on me?" Jonathon lowered the revolver. "Folks get shot for less than that."

"I'm sorry. I just wanted to talk to you."

Evans laid the pistol on his blanket. Standing, he took the candle from Hannah's hand. Dripping a little wax, he anchored it to the top of a stall post. He turned back to see her looking at him intently, her tongue sliding slowly back and forth on her lower lip. He felt instantly warm. She reached out, fingering the buttons on his jacket. "You have such a nice smile. Ain't had a man smile at me like that. You said inside I was pretty. You really think I'm pretty?"

Jonathon reached out, touching her hair. "Pretty enough to make a man want to take liberties."

Hannah started to draw back, then stopped, allowing Evans to stroke her hair. Suddenly, his hands dropped to her arms. Drawing her close, he leaned down to kiss her. She returned the kiss eagerly. Drawing apart, she smiled. "I liked that."

"So did I. Let's do it again." He drew her roughly to him. Grasping her chin, he kissed her again.

At length, Hannah tried to pull back, but he would not let her. Alarmed by the intensity of Jonathon's kiss, Hannah tried again to push away from him, but he only held her more firmly. She felt as though she could no longer breathe. Shoving harder, she finally freed herself, turning her head to avoid his mouth. "Not so hard. You're hurting me."

Ignoring her plea, Evans wrapped his arms around her, pulling her body tight against his. "Now don't try to make out so innocent. I saw the look you kept giving me during supper. You want this more than I do." Seizing her hair behind her neck, he pinned her arms, then pressed his mouth onto hers once more.

Frightened now, Hannah struggled to free herself. Twisting in Jonathon's clutch, she managed to get one hand loose. Swinging, she slapped him across the face. Surprised by the blow, he lost his grip. Seeing a chance to escape, she spun around to run, only to be blocked by Grainger.

"Hey, now, don't run away." Grainger grabbed her arms. "I don't think the boy's done with you. He just wants a little pleasurin'." He grinned at Jonathon. "You let her get away too easy." Forcing her to the ground, he pulled her arms above her head.

Jonathon looked from him to Hannah. Grabbing her legs to keep from being kicked, he got down on his knees, straddling her. Reaching for her bodice, he ripped it away, exposing her breasts.

A look of horror passed over Hannah's face as she fought to free herself. "No, please, don't! Don't hurt me!"

Grainger kept her arms pinned while Jonathon struggled to undo the buttons of his pants. "C'mon, boy, hurry up and get it done so's I can get my turn."

An angry voice boomed from behind them. "Get off her, you bastards! Get off her, or so help me—!"

Jonathon whirled. Snyder stood in the barn door, shotgun leveled. "God-damn you, I said get off her!"

Holding his trousers with one hand, Jonathon slowly rose to his feet. Grainger released Hannah's wrists. Stumbling to her feet, she pulled up her torn dress, frantically trying to cover her breasts. Backing away from Evans, she scurried to her father, who grabbed her by the arm, yanking her behind him. She sobbed. "Oh, Papa, I'm so sorry."

Snyder pushed her toward the barn door. "You never mind that now, girl. Get yourself into the house. I don't want you here to see what happens to these two."

Grainger stood, then slowly reached up to take off his hat. Keeping it positioned so that Snyder couldn't see his hands, he palmed the derringer.

Clutching her torn clothes to her breasts, Hannah moved toward the door. In the dark shadows she didn't see the sack of grain in her path. Stumbling, she fell to the floor with a shriek.

Distracted by his daughter's cry, Snyder turned his head. Seeing his chance, Grainger brought up the derringer and fired, the ball striking Snyder in the chest. Swinging the shotgun as he reeled, he yanked on the trigger. Grainger dove into the stall, splinters raining down on him as the spray of buckshot tore through the stall boards. Snyder fell forward. As he hit the ground, the second barrel went off. The blast caught Hannah full in the back, knocking her several feet. Landing on her belly, she lay writhing in pain, whimpering. After several moments, she stopped moving.

Grainger stood, brushing the shards of wood from his jacket. "You all right?"

Evans rebuttoned his trousers. "Yeah." He walked over to where Hannah lay. Lifting with the toe of his boot, he rolled her body over. Lifeless eyes gazed up at him. He shivered.

195

Grainger walked over, looked down at her, then back at Evans. "I'll get the mare out while you check around in the house for anything we can use."

Jonathon continued to stare at Hannah's face. "What about them?"

Grainger scowled. "What about 'em? Leave 'em for the wolves."

"But what if someone finds them?"

"So what? There's no one for miles around. And there's nothing to pin it on us. Now get in that house and find us some grub."

Rummaging through the kitchen cupboards, Jonathon quickly filled two sacks with food. As he returned to the barn, he couldn't help looking at Hannah again. Her dead eyes remained wide open, seeming to stare accusingly right at him. Unable to stand the sight, he reached down to close her eyes. Rising again, he glanced over to where Snyder lay, then back to Hannah. *Shit. I just can't leave them like this.*

Grainger was busy cinching a saddle on the mare. Jonathon tied the food sacks together, then tossed them across the saddlebags. Searching for several minutes, he found a pick and shovel. Carrying them out to the side of the barn, he peeled off his jacket. Swinging the pick, he began to dig.

Grainger hollered from inside the barn. "Just what the hell are you doin' out there?" Jonathon kept digging, paying no attention.

Grainger emerged from the barn leading the horses. He stared at Jonathon for a moment. "I said to leave them be. We ain't got time to bury them. Now get your butt out of that hole and let's get going."

Jonathon stood still, his hands gripping the pick handle.

"God dammit, come on!" Grainger picked up the shovel.

Jonathon dropped the pick, then reached down to unsnap his holster. Pulling his revolver, he leveled it at Grainger. "Put that down."

Grainger backed up a step. "Now, simmer down, boy, there's no call to draw down on me."

"I said put the shovel down."

Grainger slowly lowered the shovel to the ground. "You're crazy, boy. All right, you go right ahead. Dig your grave. I'll just take another look through the house." He trudged off toward the farmhouse, muttering.

Jonathon watched Grainger walk away, then holstered the pistol. Picking up the spade, he returned to his task. Satisfied the hole was deep enough, he climbed out, then returned to the barn. Finding several old grain sacks, he used them to wrap the bodies. Dragging them out of the barn, he rolled them into the pit, then proceeded to fill the hole.

His chore finished, Jonathon cleaned himself with water from a rain barrel. He brushed dirt off his trousers as he walked up to the porch where Grainger sat, waiting.

"All right, I'm done now. Let's go."

Grainger glared at Jonathon for a moment. "I can't figger you out, boy. You kill that corporal and don't give it a second thought. You was ready to rape that little girl. But then she goes and gets killed and you get all moral. You best get over that before we meet up with Major Baxter. He don't like fellows with scruples."

Chapter 30

Constable Mattson slid open the viewing port in the heavy cellblock door. "Got a visitor, Marsh." Opening the door, he tapped the bill of his cap as Stephanie Carroll stepped through. "Ten minutes, missy, that's all." He pulled the door closed behind her, throwing the iron bolt.

Thomas rolled off the wooden cot to his feet. He couldn't quite believe she had actually come. In the week since the shooting, he had not had any contact with her, though he had sent several notes begging for forgiveness.

Stephanie stood several feet from the cell, clutching a small basket covered with a blue checked handkerchief. Her eyes roamed around the room, occasionally catching his for a moment, but then quickly moving away. Thomas stared at her, afraid to speak.

Several awkward moments passed. Suddenly, Stephanie thrust the basket toward him. "I . . . brought you some things you might need. Your shaving kit, a book to read . . . ."

Thomas kept looking straight into her eyes as he slowly extended his arms through the bars. "Thank you," he said as he gripped the basket handle with one hand. She kept her hold on the basket as he gently pulled it. Stretching out with his other hand, he grasped her arm softly. Glancing down at his hand, she did not resist, allowing herself to be pulled toward him.

"Oh, Thomas," she said, "I am so very, very sorry that all this happened. I was so unfair to you."

Pulling the basket through the bars, Thomas set it on his cot, then turned back to Stephanie. He reached out, laying one hand on her waist, the other taking her hands. The touch of her body felt wonderful. "I'm sorry, too. I really didn't want that to happen. I was trying to get the gun out of his hands. I never meant to hurt your uncle."

"I know that. I know it was an accident. You were just trying to defend yourself."

He felt as though a weight had been lifted. "I'm glad you understand. I'm so happy you came." His eyes cast downward. "I wasn't sure that you would ever want to see me again."

"At that moment, I was so angry at both of you. Then, all I could think about was getting him to the doctor. Once I knew he would be all right, then I was finally able to start thinking clearly again."

"What happened after you left?"

"James helped me get Uncle down the stairs and across the street to the doctor's office. It's a wonder the whole town didn't come out to see what was going on, the way he was howling. While we were at the doctor's office, he sent a messenger for Judge Hale. The judge and Uncle are old political cronies, and will do just about anything for each other. Uncle demanded Hale issue the arrest warrant for you. Said it was 'time to root out the traitorous rebel scum living among us.' I thought he was going to have James arrested, too, but he took off in a hurry."

"Where'd he go?"

"As far as I know, he went to Pastor Marsh's farm. I don't think the judge had any papers against James, so I think he's all right."

Thomas felt a wave of relief. "That's good. I was worried about him." He held Stephanie's hand tighter. "Why didn't you answer my notes? Didn't you get them?"

"Yes, I did. I didn't come for a few days because if Uncle knew I was here, he'd be furious. I wanted him to have some time to cool down before I spoke to him about you."

"What do you mean?"

"I think I may be able to talk him into dropping the charges."

Thomas's eyes rolled with disbelief. "Don't see how that's possible. He'd sooner see me dead then out on the street again."

Stephanie smiled. "Have a little faith, my darling. I have a few ideas about how to persuade him."

Puzzled, Thomas started to ask how, but the sound of the bolt on the cellblock door stopped him. Stephanie released his hands as Mattson stuck his head in. "Times up, missy."

Stephanie let out a sigh. "I'll see you again soon, I promise." Stopping just before the door, she blew Thomas a kiss, then whisked past Mattson. The constable frowned, then disappeared through the door as it closed with a clang.

The next morning, Pastor Marsh and James came in to visit. Marsh handed Thomas a stack of newspapers. "Thought you might like to see what's been going on while you've been unjustly incarcerated." He sat on a small stool next to the bars. "I saw Mr. Carroll coming down the street yesterday in his carriage. When he stopped in front of the bank, I thought it might be a good opportunity to speak to him regarding your situation. I told him that I have been praying for his speedy recovery. I also begged him to see the error of his actions, but he just 'harrumphed' and ordered the coachman to drive on. I'm afraid there is little Christian charity in his heart toward you."

James reached through the bars, picking up one of the newspapers. "The old coot! I didn't like him the moment I first saw him at the train station." He leafed through the paper, then held it up for Thomas to see. "Look at this headline. 'Latest From Virginia—Rebel Gen'l Jackson Running Wild.' Hear tell they call him 'Stonewall' Jackson—something to do with the battle at Bull Run."

Marsh slapped his knee in disgust. "Three armies in the Shenandoah Valley, and not one can bring him to bay!" He turned to Thomas. "Last letter I got from your mother said that William's regiment is with Jackson."

Thomas was dumbfounded. "William's in the Confederate Army? How long?"

"Pretty close to a year. You've been so caught up with your own troubles over the past few months that you've missed much of what your own family has been doing."

Stung, Thomas covered his face with his hands, his elbows resting on his knees. After a few moments, he looked up. "Willie was always one for going where there was trouble. I guess I shouldn't be surprised that he's serving in the Southern army. Did mother say how he's doing?"

"Said he's as well as could be expected. His letters to his mother always tell about worn clothing and shortages of food, but he seems to be in good spirits."

Thomas leaned back on the cot. "How's Mother doing?"

"She's carrying on as best she can. Once in a while she mentions some storekeeper who comes out to the farm to help out."

Thomas thought for a moment. "That's probably Mr. McCay. He runs the general store."

"Sounds like the name. If I read between the lines correctly, it sounds like she's become quite fond of him."

"When you've written to her, have you told her much . . . about me?"

"I've not told her anything about your troubles. I've generally said you were well and busy, but not much more than that." Marsh looked directly at Thomas. "She misses you, my boy. She doesn't understand why you haven't written. I think it's high time that you sent her a letter."

Thomas threw up his hands. "And say what? That her eldest son burned down his uncle's barn while in a drunken stupor, and then got clapped in jail on a trumped up charge of attempted murder? I can just imagine how that would make her feel!"

"She's your mother, Thomas. She deserves to hear from you."

He thought about it for a few moments. *He's right. It's been too long.* "All right," he said, "I'll write a letter to her. But not right now. Better to wait a little to see what happens. Stephanie told me yesterday that she might be able to do something."

"What can she do?"

"Don't know, but she sounded pretty certain."

James chuckled. "Told you she'd come around."

Thomas smiled. "Yeah, you pegged us both pretty good. I feel like dirt for causing her so much unhappiness. Hopefully I'll be able to make it up to her."

Marsh stood, donning his hat. "I'm certain that you will do so, my boy. Come, James, it's time we should be leaving." He reached through the bars to take Thomas's hand. "You know that I will keep you both in my prayers. It would do you good to take some time to talk to God, also. He will give you comfort during your imprisonment."

Thomas turned his head slightly so his uncle wouldn't see him rolling his eyes. "I'll think about it, sir."

Several hours later, Mattson came in to the cellblock, slamming the door as he entered. Storming over to Thomas's cell, he inserted and turned the key. Swinging the door open, he waved at Thomas. "All right, Marsh, you're free to go."

Incredulous, Thomas asked, "What do you mean?"

Mattson practically snarled. "You deaf or something? I said you can leave."

Warily, Thomas stood, then began to pick up his things. "But what happened to the charges?"

"Carroll dropped the charges, so Judge Hale withdrew the warrant. So I've got nothing to hold you for." Mattson glowered. "Big mistake as far as I'm concerned, but there's nothing I can do about it, at least not now." He wagged his finger inches from Thomas's nose. "You just keep in mind that I'll be watching you and the other Rebs in town. You step out of line again, even to spit on a sidewalk, and I'll haul you back in here faster'n lightning."

Thomas glanced around as he emerged from the jailhouse. Stephanie was seated on a nearby bench. He walked over, sitting down next to her. "Hello," he said.

She looked at him for a moment. "Hello, yourself."

"I didn't really believe you when you said you could get me out of here."

Stephanie smiled. "Now maybe you'll have more faith in me. Let's just say Uncle Charles and I came to an understanding. I told him that I would leave if he continued to be insufferable. I also reminded him about some, shall we say, skeletons in his closet that certain politicians would be very interested in."

Thomas grinned. "Like what?"

"Nothing that I'm about to divulge to you. All I'll tell you is that Uncle has great dreams of becoming a senator. He was involved in a few transgressions as a young man that probably wouldn't set well with voters."

"Sounds like blackmail to me."

"Yes. I should be ashamed, but it was so wickedly delicious. I was so proud of myself, standing up to him. He was so angry he turned a peculiar shade of purple."

A wagon drew up in front of them. Pastor Marsh looked down from the seat. "Well, my boy, are you quite ready to come home where you belong?"

A forced cough caused Thomas to turn. Constable Mattson was leaning just inside the jailhouse door, watching him intently. He glanced up at his uncle, then back to Stephanie. "I think I'd best be going." Nodding toward Mattson, he said, "My continued presence in town is not too welcome right now." He took Stephanie's hand, leaned forward to kiss her. "I'll see you again sometime soon. Thank you for standing by me."

Still holding hands, Thomas and Stephanie rose. "Don't make it too long," she said. "My life has gotten much more interesting since I met you. I don't think I could stand going back to my old dull ways. And another thing . . . ." She moved closer to whisper in his ear. "I love you."

Thomas raised her hand to his lips. "I love you, too. Always remember that." He climbed up to the wagon seat next to the preacher. Marsh smiled at Stephanie. "You are welcome at our house any time you wish to come." He snapped the reins. Thomas turned to wave goodbye as the wagon pulled away.

Stephanie waved back. Turning to leave, she nearly slammed into Mattson, who had silently stepped up behind her. The look on his face as he slowly chewed his wad of tobacco made her feel decidedly uncomfortable.

After staring at her for several moments, he turned his head, spitting a dirty brown glob into the street. "You'd be well advised to stay clear of that fellow, Missy. Him and his southron friend don't belong here among decent folk. They're going to end up bad, you mark me." The loathing in his expression caused her to shudder.

Chapter 31

William eagerly kept watch for familiar landmarks as the train passed the Georgia state line. His excitement grew as the final few miles slipped behind, and the outskirts of Atlanta at last came into sight. Henry slapped him on the back. "Almost home, Willie!" The weight of the returning soldiers tipped the railcar slightly as the train pulled in, every man moving to the platform side, anxiously looking for loved ones. Before the locomotive could come to a complete stop a flood of impatient men boiled out each end of the car.

Trying to keep his footing amidst the chaos, William scanned the crowd for his family. He hoped they would be there. It took the better part of a day to make the ride from Dahlonega to Atlanta.

A shout from a familiar voice caught his attention. Lucinda, Melissa and Jedidiah McCay were standing by the end of the platform. Dodging and weaving his way around the other joyous reunions, he made his way toward them. "Ma!" Just before he reached them, he caught sight of someone else. Mary stood off to one side, her head slightly tilted, a demure smile on her lips. Distracted, he almost collided with his mother. "Oops, sorry about that, Ma." He was speaking to Lucinda but still gazing at Mary. The sight of her entranced him. It was as though nothing else existed.

"William, are you all right?"

His mother's earnest question snapped William back to his senses. He quickly embraced her, then reached to pat Melissa on the head. "Hey, 'Lissa, how'd you get to be such a young lady?"

Jedidiah reached out to grasp William's hand. "Good to have you back, boy. We got into town just before you arrived. Got rooms at the Atlanta Hotel for tonight."

"Oh, William, it's so good to have you home again." Lucinda gazed at her son, not believing the changes she saw. Leaner but more muscular, somewhat more careworn. There was a maturity in his carriage that hadn't been there before. Suddenly there was a tap on her shoulder and the abrupt sound of a throat clearing.

Mary had moved up close behind Lucinda. She stood with hands on hips, tapping her foot with impatience. Seeing her opening, she pushed in between William and his mother. "You're not going to ignore me, are you Willie?" Mary started to wrap her arms around him, but suddenly hesitated. Her nose wrinkled with distaste. "Oh, Willie, you smell disgusting. And your uniform is filthy. The first thing you need to do is take a bath."

William stepped back slightly, stung a little by her criticism. "I guess I do stink a bit. Haven't had a chance at a bath for quite a while. You get so you don't notice."

Mary pinched her nose. "Well, I noticed. Why don't we all head right over to the hotel so you can get cleaned up?"

"That's actually not a bad idea," said McCay. "I'll get the carriage."

Soon they were clattering down the street away from the station. "Say, there, William," said Jedidiah, "what's this I hear about Lieutenant Merrow being promoted?"

William leaned forward in his seat. "Well, the regiment is reorganizing, but Colonel Ramsey won't be commanding. He's been pretty sick ever since that winter march to Romney. So we all had an election and picked new officers. Lieutenant Merrow was elected to be colonel."

"I'll wager Henry is proud as a peacock," said McCay as they pulled up in front of the Atlanta Hotel.

Bathed and wearing clean clothes, William spent most of that evening sitting in the hotel lobby chatting with Mary. It was almost midnight before he returned to his family's room. Stepping carefully lest he wake up his mother, he leaned over the bed to give her a kiss, then slipped under the covers of a pallet laid out on the floor. In the darkness, he didn't see the tear slowly rolling down her cheek.

During the ride from Atlanta back to Dahlonega next day, Mary kept up a lively chatter, constantly interrupting any conversation between William and Lucinda. William's mother was exceedingly thankful when the carriage pulled up in front of her cabin late that afternoon. While Jedidiah and William unloaded their baggage, Lucinda went inside to light a fire.

"All right, Miss Stewart," said Jedidiah. "We're ready to head back to town."

"Just a minute, Mr. McCay," Mary replied. Giving William a quick peck on the cheek, she said, "Now you remember. You promised to come see me tomorrow night."

William grinned sheepishly. "I'll be there for certain."

"You'd better. I won't forgive you if you don't." Mary turned to address Lucinda, who had emerged from the cabin and was standing on the porch. "Thank you so much for allowing me to come along, Mrs. Marsh."

"You're welcome, Mary," said Lucinda, trying not to let her annoyance with the girl show.

Mary began to climb into the carriage, then stepped back down. "Mr. McCay, do you mind if I sit up front with you on the way back to town? I really don't want to sit in the back all by myself."

Jedidiah shrugged. "Suit yourself." Mounting the steps, he grasped Lucinda's hand. "As always, a pleasure, ma'am. May I call on you again soon?"

Lucinda smiled. "Certainly, sir. I would like that."

Jedidiah reached out to shake William's hand once more. "Glad to have you back in one piece, son. We're all proud of you."

William watched the carriage head down the road, returning waves from McCay and Mary. As it disappeared around a corner, he squinted, then shook his head. *Must be seeing things. Looked for a moment like Mary and Mr. McCay were sitting awfully close.*

That night at supper, Lucinda watched with humor and satisfaction as her son wolfed down his food. Thanks to Jedidiah's generosity, she had scraped together enough to ensure that William would be well fed while he was home. He looked up from his plate to see her smiling at him. "What's so funny?" he asked, mouth still half full.

"Oh, nothing, I was just enjoying watching you. Been quite a while since you last sat at this table."

"Seems like a lifetime. I wish I didn't have to go back so soon."

Lucinda sighed. "Don't talk about that. It'll come soon enough. I'm just glad you'll be able to relax here for the next week or so."

"Probably won't hang around the farm too much. Want to see a few people. Starting tomorrow night with Mary."

"I thought you might want to stay home for at least a few days after you got back. I'd like to spend some time hearing about all your travels. And I could use a little help getting some things fixed up. Jedidiah and Stephen have done quite a bit but there's still a lot. "

"I planned on helping out some, but I've only got a week before I have to head back. It took so long to get here I don't have a whole lot of time. I want to see Mary as much as I can."

"I know you want to see her, but you should be careful. Her father's been out of town for a week. She's staying by herself in that house, and it might not look proper."

"Ma, I'm a grown man now. Been out in the world. I reckon I don't really care if it 'looks proper' or not. Nobody's business but mine, as I see it."

"There's been a lot of talk about her over in town. I just want you to be careful."

Eyebrows rising, William asked, "What do you mean, 'a lot of talk'?"

Lucinda realized she had said too much. "Nothing. Mary is simply a high-spirited girl, and I don't want you hurt."

William jumped to his feet, sending his chair flying backward. "I'm not going to get hurt. Sounds like you've been listening to a bunch of old ladies' gossip. Well, I don't want to hear it. Not from anyone, even you!" With that, William stormed out. Lucinda stared at the door, shocked at her son's sudden display of anger.

Stalking out to the barn, William climbed up into the loft, throwing himself down in the loosely packed hay. Feelings of guilt washed over him. First night home after a year and already quarreling. *I shouldn't have gotten all bent out of shape. She was just being a mother.* He lay staring at the barn roof, chewing on a blade of dried grass. *I'll apologize in the morning.*

Late that night, Lucinda heard rustling out by the fireplace. Rising, she drew on her robe. Peeking through her bedroom door, she saw her son laying blankets on the floor next to the hearth. "Why, William, whatever are you doing?"

He looked up at her with a lame grin. "Can't sleep, Ma. Never used to think that old straw mattress was very soft, but I just can't get comfortable on it. Gotten too used to sleeping on the ground."

Lucinda sat down in her rocker. "I'm sorry I got you so upset earlier. I guess I wanted to keep you to myself, you not being here very long. It's hard to realize that you're not my little boy anymore."

William stood, walked over behind her, and wrapped his arms around her. "You were just being a protectful mother. I shouldn't have blown my stack. I know you didn't mean anything by what you said."

Lucinda put her hands on her son's arms. He rocked her gently. "Don't fret about me, Ma. I can take care of myself. After all, I've just gotten through a whole year in the army."

Lucinda patted William's hand. "I know you can. But it's hard for me to stop worrying about you."

William was up early the next day, heading out to the barn. The cow greeted him with a low moo. "Hello, bossy, remember me?" He laughed. He spent the morning busily milking, chopping wood and other tasks. Before, the chores had been such drudgery. But now, the familiarity of the work was a delight.

After a quick midday meal, he asked Lucinda for some soap and a towel. Heading for the creek, he disrobed and plunged in. His skin tingled from the icy water as he lathered. Back at the cabin, he used his father's old straight razor to shave, managing to nick himself several times in the process. Rummaging through his clothing that Lucinda had stored, he pulled out what looked to be the most presentable outfit. "Ma, I think these clothes have shrunk some."

Lucinda smiled. "No, you've filled out more, though on what you've been eating in the army, I'm not sure how." She motioned toward the bedroom door. "Come in here. Let's see if some of your father's clothes would fit better."

Clean and freshly attired, William set out for town. Heading straight for Isaac Stewart's house, he tied his horse up to the rail. Stepping up onto the porch, he hesitated long enough to straighten his jacket, then knocked. After a moment, the door opened. "Hello, Willie," said Mary, "I was beginning to wonder if you were ever going to come."

"Am I a little more presentable now?"

"Willie, you're absolutely handsome. Please come in and take off your coat." She hung his jacket on a hook beside the door, then took his hand, leading him into the parlor. He glanced up at the painting of Julia Stewart. "Your mother was real pretty. You favor her."

"Why, thank you, sir. What a nice compliment. Come, let's sit together."

"Where's Mr. Stewart?

Mary's expression darkened. "Father has gone up somewhere in East Tennessee to see some people. Probably to plot some kind of treachery against the Confederacy with his Yankee friends there."

William was surprised by the wrath in her voice. "Your father? I can't picture him doing something like that."

"He's been an embarrassment to me, the way he carries on against the South. Mrs. Merrow didn't invite me to one of her balls because of it. Sometimes I just hate him." She shook her head. "I don't want to talk about him anymore. The whole subject is repugnant." She let out a loud sniff that signaled an end to the discussion.

They sat in silence for several minutes. Then Mary smiled. "It was so sweet of you, asking about me in all your letters to your mother."

"How'd you know about that?"

"Why, she told me, silly. I just wish you had written to me, at least once."

"I wanted to, but after what happened at the schoolhouse, I didn't think you'd want to hear from me."

"Didn't my letter explain that? I hoped you understood."

"Of course I did."

"Good!" Suddenly she stood up. Taking his hand, she pulled him out of the chair. "Come with me, I've got something to show you."

"What?"

"You'll see." She led him through the parlor and up the stairs. "This is father's room," she said as they passed a door. "I never go in there. Here, this is my room."

William was amazed at the size of the canopy covered four-poster bed centered in the room. Mary pointed to it. "Sit there while I find them." Pulling open the top drawer of a large dresser, she rummaged around inside for several moments before pulling out a packet of envelopes wrapped with a pink ribbon. "Oh, here they are." Sitting next to William, she undid the ribbon. "I just wanted you to see these. These are letters I wrote to you." She handed them to him.

He turned the packet over several times. "Why didn't you send these?"

"Oh, I couldn't send them. Someone else might have seen them." She opened one envelope, pulling out the letter. "I spent lots of evenings writing these to tell you how I felt about you, how much I missed you. It made me feel . . . well, closer." She looked at him for a moment, then reached up, brushing her hand lightly across his cheek. "Do you love me, Willie?"

Caught completely off guard, William stammered, "Yes . . . yes, I think I do." He took her hand. "Do you . . . love me?"

"Yes, William, I do. I always have. And I want you, so much. Please kiss me."

She leaned toward him. Putting his arm around her, he bent down to her waiting lips. They came together, hesitantly at first, then with increasing ardor.

Suddenly Mary pushed him back. Pulling herself to the center of the bed, she began to unbutton her blouse. "I need you, Willie. Take me. Please. Take me now."

William was dumbstruck, his mind whirling. Almost without realization, he climbed onto the bed, kneeling over her. His entire body ached with desire. She was so beautiful. Mary smiled, reaching up to unbutton his shirt.

He couldn't. Goddamn it, *he couldn't!* Lurching backward, he rolled awkwardly away from her, almost falling off the bed.

Mary stared at him, astonished. "What's wrong?"

"I can't."

"What do you mean, you can't?"

Embarrassment rose up around his neck like scalding steam. He wanted to be gone, to be anywhere but here watching the storm erupting on her face.

"Damn it, Willie, what is the matter with you? Why won't you love me?"

"I . . . respect you too much?"

"What?"

"It's just not right. I mean . . . I mean . . . ." He tried frantically to come up with the right words. "We shouldn't do this . . . at least not until after we're married."

"Married! Just what gave you the idea I have any intention of getting married?"

"But I thought you . . . loved me."

"My God, Willie, you are so old-fashioned! Of course I love you. But right now, I'm not sure I like you very much. How could you lead me on, getting me up here, ready to make love, and you just all of a sudden go cold?"

"Wait a minute, this was your idea."

"Oh, now it's all *my* fault. You're not going to deny that you wanted me—you as much as said so."

William's head was spinning. He felt like crying. She had him all mixed up.

"If you don't stop this nonsense right now and make love to me, I'll never speak to you, ever, ever again." She rolled over, her back to him. She lay sobbing with feigned crying.

"I'm—sorry." William felt like trash. He rose, slowly rebuttoning his shirt. Shuffling toward the door, he stood there for a moment, gazing at Mary's heaving figure. "I . . . really am sorry. I won't bother you anymore."

Shocked that her tactic had not succeeded, and amazed that he would actually leave, Mary instantly stopped weeping. Whirling, she sat up, reaching her hand out toward him. "Wait, Willie, please wait. I'm the one who's sorry. You caught me off guard. I just wanted you so much. Please don't go. Stay with me for a little while. We won't do anything but just hold each other."

Pausing for another moment at the door, William slowly turned, then came back to the bed. Still dreadfully embarrassed, sat on the edge of the mattress, his back to her, staring at the wall. Reaching out, Mary gently began to rub his shoulders. After a few moments, William turned to lie down next to her. Gradually working her hand behind his neck, she drew his head forward. They began to kiss. He was amazed how experienced she seemed to be. Her hands moved over his body, massaging him, lifting him to a point beyond control.

Waking the next morning, William drowsily reached across the bed for Mary, but she was gone. Throwing off the covers, he hurriedly pulled on his trousers and shirt as he stumbled toward the door. A wonderful smell rose up the stairwell. By the time he reached the parlor he had managed to button his shirt. Mary was in the kitchen in the back of the house, busily working at the stove. Coming up behind her, he put his hands on her waist. "Well, sleepyhead," she said without turning, "I thought you were never going to wake up."

"I don't think I've slept so well in a long time."

"You certainly snored enough. Kept me awake most of the night."

"Was it just my snoring? Or something else?"

Mary scraped the sizzling ham and eggs onto a plate and set it on the table. "Sit down and eat your breakfast." A movement caught her attention out of the corner of her eye. She looked up to see Parker staring through the window. Startled, she dropped the spoon. "Ooh!"

William glanced up, then spun to see what she was looking at. He saw nothing. Picking up the spoon, he handed it back to her. She was still staring at the window, her hand on her chest. "What's the matter?"

Mary blinked, let out a short, sharp breath, then looked back at him. "Nothing. Nothing but a bit of lightheadedness." The expression of concern on his face amused her. "Don't look at me like that. I'm fine, really. You finish eating. I've got to get dressed."

She rushed out of the room before William could say another word. Once certain she was out of his sight, she peered out a side window. Spying Parker standing next to one of the side buildings, she drew the cords on her robe tight, then quietly opened the front door. Making certain there was no one around to see her, she slipped out onto the porch. She hissed to get Parker's attention. "Just what the hell are you doing here, peeking into my window?"

Parker leered at her. "Just wanted to see what was going on. You've been avoiding me the last few days. Now I see why."

"Don't fret yourself. Willie's only going to be in town another couple of weeks. Be patient." She patted his cheek. "I like patient men. Now you get away from here before someone sees you."

Reentering the house, she peered into the kitchen. William was still eating, showing no evidence of having heard anything. Darting up the stairs to her room, she pulled on a day dress. Returning to the kitchen, she picked up William's empty plate. "Did you have enough?"

"Yes, ma'am, that was good. I was beginning to wonder where you went."

"You should know it takes a lady longer to make herself presentable than a man." She sidled up to him, pressing against his side. "Of course, it might be fun to get unpresentable again."

Suddenly uncomfortable, William stood. "I really need to get on home. Ma will be wondering where I've been."

Her face lit with wicked pleasure. "I'm certain you'll come up with a really good reason." She took his hand, pulling him toward her. "But you're not leaving until you kiss me once more."

Lucinda rushed out the cabin door the moment she saw William approaching. She paced back and forth on the porch while waiting for him to put up his horse. He could see her anxiety on her face as he walked up to the cabin. "What's wrong, Ma?"

"Why didn't you come home last night? I've been beside myself with worry."

"Sorry. Didn't plan to do that. Mary and I talked 'til it was real late. She said she didn't feel right, me riding home so long after dark that she wanted me to sleep in her father's bed." The lie made him uncomfortable, but he certainly wasn't about to tell her the truth.

Lucinda's upraised eyebrow signaled disbelief, but she did not question him further. "Just send me word somehow next time you do that."

Over the next week, William spent every second he could with Mary. Occasionally, her behavior puzzled him. Once while walking together down the sidewalk, she suddenly changed direction, practically dragging him across the street to the Mercantile. William caught sight of Hiram Parker watching them intently as they went inside.

In between visits, William tried to catch up on the war news. Discouraging reports seemed to fill the newspapers. Out in western Tennessee, a terrible two-day battle near a small chapel called Shiloh had killed and wounded thousands on both sides. In Virginia, General Joseph E. Johnston was keeping a close eye on Federal General

McClellan as the Union Army worked its way up the Virginia Peninsula from Fortress Monroe toward Richmond.

The days passed all too quickly. It was time for the furloughed soldiers to return. William was hitching up the wagon when Jedidiah drove up in the carriage. "No need for that, William," he said. "I'm taking you and your family down to Atlanta."

William gave the carriage a quick inspection. "Where's Mary?"

Jedidiah frowned. "She said she wasn't coming to see you off. Something about she didn't want you to see her crying and carrying on."

Crestfallen, William pulled his pack from the wagon and threw it into the carriage. Soon, he and his family started down the road to Atlanta. The next morning, they checked out of the Atlanta Hotel and drove to the train station.

Henry, Stephen and Mrs. Merrow were waiting when they arrived. "Hey, Willie! Didn't see much of you the last week. I guess you were busy. And I'll bet I know who with."

William's cheeks turned scarlet. Up the platform, the conductor was looking at his pocket watch. He signaled the engineer, who then gave a blast on the locomotive's whistle. Turning back to the waiting passengers, he waved. "All aboard!"

Lucinda looked as though she would burst into tears at any second. William hugged her. "Please don't cry, Ma. I'll be okay, I promise."

"You'd best be," she said. "If I see your name on one of those lists at the Mercantile, I'll . . . I'll . . . well, I'll never forgive you."

Henry and his mother embraced. He shook Stephen's hand, then jumped up onto the railcar's steps. "C'mon, Willie, time to get back to the war!"

"Hold your shorts, I'm coming!" William gazed into his mother's eyes one last time, then ran for the train. Leaping up onto the steps, he turned to wave. "I'll get back home when I can, Ma! Hopefully won't be too long! Write lots of letters!"

Lucinda and Melissa waved their handkerchiefs as the train pulled away from the station. Walking as far as they could go to the end of the platform, they watched the cars until they disappeared from sight. They stood for a few moments looking at the empty track, then turned to go. Before reaching the carriage, Lucinda felt a chill pass over her. She took Melissa's hand. "I need to sit down."

Melissa was alarmed. "What's wrong, Mother? Are you getting sick?"

Lucinda sat on a bench next to the station house. "I just had the horrible thought that William might never come home again." She trembled. "I just don't know what I'd do if he was hurt or killed."

Mary flipped the covers from over her head. Stretching her arms above her head, she lazily glanced about the room. Soon her gaze settled on the packet of envelopes tied with pink ribbon. She giggled. *Well, he's gone. But he belongs to me, now.*

A muffled voice emerged from under the bed covers. "What's so funny?"

"Nothing, darling." Pulling back the blankets, she snuggled up next to Parker, wrapping her arms around his chest. "Nothing to worry your little mind about. Now come and make love to me again."

PART THREE

"Hoarse, booming drums of the regiment,
Little souls who thirst for fight,
These men were born to drill and die.
The unexplained glory flies above them,
Great is the battle-god, great, and his kingdom—
A field where a thousand corpses lie." – Stephen Crane.

Chapter 32

Jonathon and Grainger reined up in the center of a creek, permitting their horses to take a long drink. They had crossed Swift Run Gap early that morning after spending the past few days cautiously traversing the Shenandoah Valley. Every few miles they came across signs of war—abandoned equipment, rotting dead horses, signs of skirmishes with blasted trees and torn up ground. A newspaper picked up earlier supplied them with enough information to pass themselves off as scouts for General Turner Ashby's cavalry

Jonathon filled his canteen from the stream. "Gettin' too close to the armies. We're likely to get shot by some nervous picket."

"Not too much further. Last I heard, Baxter's been hiding out in the Wilderness."

"What's that?"

"A patch of good for nothing ground. All growed up with tangles and brush. Those that try to make a go in there just quit after a while. My pa tried for two years to get something to grow, but the ground's poisoned. Some folks says it's evil. Just the place for Baxter and his guerillas to hide out in."

"Where's your folks now?"

Grainger's expression turned melancholy. "They was over near New Market."

Jonathon climbed up into his saddle. "Hell, we was just a few hours ride from there the other day. Would've been easy to swing north—could've gotten some supplies."

"Can't go back there."

Jonathon had never seen his companion look so troubled. "Why not?"

"Killed a fellow in a knife fight. Bill Sorensen thought he was the bull of the woods around the county and didn't cotton to someone even lookin' at his gal. One night he caught her and me kissing. He pulled his knife, I pulled mine. I got cut pretty good but managed to get him right in the heart."

"Sounds like self-defense to me."

"Maybe so, but his family was pretty big and his pa wasn't the forgiving sort. Figgered my life wasn't worth spit if'n I'd stuck around, so I lit out without going back to the farm. Headed west and joined the army." Grainger sniffed. "I wrote to Ma to let her know where I was. Got a letter back from the local parson—said that not long after I left the Sorensens attacked the farm. Killed Ma and Pa and burned the house. Jake got hurt but he was okay. The parson said a couple of men from Baxter's guerrillas found him. Baxter musta felt sorry for him, cause after Jake got better, the major's bunch hit the Sorensen place. Wiped 'em out. That's why I figger he'll let me join up."

Several days later, after stopping for refreshment at a tavern known locally as Chancellorsville, the pair entered an ominous looking forest. The stunted underbrush and bent trees appeared to Jonathon like something from a nightmare. "Welcome to the Wilderness," said Grainger.

Uneasiness rose in Jonathon's chest as they trotted down the road. The further they penetrated the forest, the more the dense foliage screened out the sunlight, increasing the sinister feel. A sense that they were being watched left Jonathon full of apprehension. "You was right about one thing. This place just feels bad."

Grainger said nothing. He was intently peering through the underbrush. "We gotta be getting close now. Need to watch for any signs of them."

"What the hell kind of 'signs' are we looking for?"

"How the hell should I know? Just anything that would point to Baxter's group."

Suddenly Grainger reined the horse to a stop. "Hold up." His hand moved to his holster as he glanced around. "Thought I heard something. Sounded like a gun being cocked."

"You've got good ears, friend." The voice came from behind them. Jonathon and Grainger spun in their saddles. A man stood in the middle of the road behind them, a heavy single-shot pistol in each hand. His tattered gray shell jacket hung open, exposing a large sheathed bowie knife. "Now if you gents would kindly drop your guns on the ground."

Grainger and Jonathon glanced at each other. The man in the road scratched his temple with the muzzle of one pistol. "I know what you're thinking, gents. You're thinking that it's two to one." He let out a whistle. A dozen armed horsemen burst from the underbrush, surrounding them. "I think you can see now that that's not too smart."

Grainger rubbed his chin. "Looks like you've got the drop on us. You by any chance wouldn't be part of Major Baxter's bunch, now would you?"

"Well now, friend, just why would you be asking that?"

"Cause we've ridden a far piece to join up with the major. My brother's riding with him."

"And just who would that darlin' brother be?"

"Jake Grainger."

A murmur rose from the encircling riders. The man with the pistols studied the two intently for a few moments. "You're Jake's brother, you say?"

A grin crossed Grainger's face. "Yep, sure am."

His smile disappeared at the sound of carbines being cocked. Two of the riders leveled their weapons directly at Grainger's head. "Let's drop 'em right now, Curly," said one.

Grainger held up his hands. "Whoa, now, fellas! What gives? Don't Jake ride with you?"

Ignoring the question, Curly shoved one of the big pistols into a holster on his belt, but kept the other aimed at the duo. "Hang on, boys. I know what we'll do with them. We'll just take them to the major. He'll probably have Jake decide whether to string 'em up or join up." He waved the pistol. "Okay, gents, hand your pieces over. We'll take a little ride to camp."

Two horsemen reined up next to Jonathon and Grainger, reaching out to pluck their pistols from their holsters. One waved the muzzle of his revolver within an inch of Jonathon's nose. "Now the carbines," he said, "and that shotgun."

Moving very slowly, the companions handed their short rifles to their captors. "Very good, fellas," said Curly. Holstering the other pistol, he turned, heading off into the underbrush. He reemerged mounted a few moments later. "Okay, gents, let's go. I'm kinda looking forward to see what happens. We ain't had a good hemp party for some time now. 'Course, if you really are Jake's brother, he may just shoot you and be done with it."

"So he is riding with you?" Grainger asked as they turned their horses down the path.

Curly let out a low chortle. "Oh, he's with us, all right. And he's told us all 'bout you running out on your Ma and Pa, and letting 'em get killed."

"That ain't true, not one word!"

"Maybe it is, maybe it isn't. Don't really matter to me. Just might be a little entertaining to see what happens when you two boys meet."

Arriving at the raider's encampment, Curly ordered Jonathon and Grainger to dismount. Prodded along with jabs from pistol barrels, they were directed through the camp to a large wall tent. Seated at a table in front was a diminutive figure absorbed in the task of dismantling a Colt Navy revolver. Parts of another pistol were scattered about on the table. A Confederate officer's frock coat hung from the back of his ornate chair. The officer was clean-shaven, his hair carefully combed, and he wore an immaculate white linen shirt.

"Hey, Major," said Curley. "Got a couple of birds for you. Say they want to jine up with us." He shoved Grainger forward. "This one claims to be Little Jake's long-lost brother."

Without raising his head, Baxter glanced up. The rows of smallpox scars crisscrossing his forehead reminded Jonathon of a plowed field. His expression was one of extreme suspicion. He busily ran a cleaning rod up and down one pistol barrel while staring intently at the two.

"You say you want to join our little band of brothers?"

"Yessir, Major. We rode all the way from West Tennessee to get here. Served with Colonel Forrest's command."

"Any reason why I should believe you?" Baxter selected several pieces from the table as he began to reassemble one of the Colts.

Grainger swallowed hard. He glanced uneasily around, noting the glares from the men surrounding him and Evans. "Just ask my brother Jake. He's riding with you now. He'll vouch for me."

"The hell I will, you God-damn son of a bitch."

The shrill voice came from behind them. Grainger whirled. His smile of recognition dissolved into surprise when he beheld the look of hatred on his brother's face. "Jake, boy, tell them who I am. Tell them I'm your kin!"

Jake scowled at Grainger. "You're no kin of mine. You ran out on Ma and Pa just when they needed you most. Now they're both dead."

Grainger stared down at the ground, unable at that moment to look his brother in the eye. "I know. Parson Gibbons wrote me about what happened. I'm sorry."

Jake spit. "Sorry don't cut it, Joe. Not two weeks after you run off, the Sorensen bunch came to the farm looking for you. Said you killed their brother and they were gonna hang you. Pa told 'em you weren't there but they didn't believe him. They started shooting. Pa and Ma and me barricaded in the house. We held 'em off for a while. All the time Pa kept saying 'If Joseph was here we'd whip 'em.'"

He scowled. "But you weren't there. Ma took a ball in the back." He pointed to an ugly scar across his forehead. "I got this—knocked me out cold. I woke up down in the root cellar—couldn't hardly breathe cause there was smoke all around. Pa's body was lying there next to me. He'd been gutshot. Must'a drug me down the stair before he died. The house was burned down over us. I buried Pa—but couldn't find enough of Ma to bury."

"The major was raiding over our way. Curly found me passed out by Pa's grave and carried me back to their camp. After I got better we surrounded the Sorensen place—did to them just what they did to us." A wicked grin lit Jake's face. "Not one left."

Baxter set the revolver down and leaned back in the chair. He drummed his fingers on the table for several minutes. The sound only served to intensify Jonathon's unease. Suddenly, Baxter leaned forward. "All right, we'll give you a try. We can use experienced men." Pointing his finger at them, he continued, "But I'll tell you this just once. Don't even think of crossing me. You follow my rules, or you're dead. Rule number one is, you join us, you stay with us. If you don't like that, then get out now."

Jonathon looked at Grainger, who nodded. "I guess we're in."

Baxter smiled. "Good, good. We're not expecting any action for awhile. Find yourself a corner to bivouac. I'll let you know when I've got some work for you."

Grainger turned to Jake. "C'mon with us. You and I need to talk some things out."

Jake snarled. "You go to hell. We've got nothin' to talk about. You just better stay clear of me." Spinning on his heels, he stalked off.

Finding a suitable location to make camp, Jonathon strung a rope between two trees. Stretching a blanket over it, he tied the corners down to create a shelter. Meanwhile, Grainger set about kindling a fire. Filling his large tin cup with water, he set it in the flames.

Jonathon sat down, leaning against a tree. Pulling off one shoe, he contemplated his big toe, protruding through an enormous hole in his sock. Reaching for his haversack, he began rummaging through it for thread and a needle. "You'd best stay clear of that one, he said to Grainger. "He's likely to put a ball right between your shoulder blades, brother or not."

Grainger pulled a wooden spoon and a small cloth sack of ground coffee from his haversack. Emptying the bag into the cup, he stirred the contents as he gazed thoughtfully into the fire. "He's not really my brother, least ways not by blood. My ma died when I was little, and Jake's ma was a widow. She took a shine to me right away. I guess Jake figgered she was being disrespectful to his dead pa, her getting married again so soon after he died. He hated me calling her Ma. Said I didn't have the right. Now Pa, he and Jake got along just fine right from the start. Jake even took our name for his." He wrapped a piece of cloth around the cup handle and gingerly lifted it out of the fire. "That boy never did like me much. We always was fighting over one thing or another." He stood. "I ain't got no sugar for this. Gonna go see if I can find some." He walked off toward the other tents.

Jonathon was still searching through his haversack. The needle was found when it pricked his finger, but there was no sign of the thread. In disgust he finally dumped the haversack's contents onto the ground. Picking through the pile of items, he came across a grease-covered packet of envelopes. It was the letters Winslow had tossed him the day he had been drummed out of the army. He'd forgotten all about them. Untying the slimy string holding them together, he peeled open the first oily envelope. It was from Mary Stewart, dated over six months previous.

"My dearest, dearest Jonathon."

"My love, why haven't you written to me? I have been pining away here in this God-forsaken town waiting for any news from you to assure me that you are safe and well. The only thing that keeps me from going absolutely insane is the hope that one day you will come rescue me from this dreary existence. My lunatic father does nothing but rant and rave about how evil the Confederacy is. No one else here will even talk to me. Everyone else in town gets letters from their soldiers, but not me. Even that terrible Willie Marsh will not write to me. I know his regiment is somewhere in western Virginia.

Jonathon scowled. *Now why did she have to mention that son of a bitch?*

The letter went on with seemingly endless platitudes about how she loved him and wanted him to come back. Evans wadded the paper and tossed it into the fire. *What a bunch of crap.*

He sat back, watching the paper quickly curl, then blaze up. *Oh, I'll come back. When the time's right I'll have some fun with you and then take care of that bastard Marsh.*

Chapter 33

William huffed and puffed as the First Georgia double-quicked through a stand of trees toward the crashing sound of musketry. The late afternoon August sun beat down on them as they worked their way through the underbrush. Thick white smoke filtered through the trees like fog. Fragments of branches and bark rained down on the column as lead missiles tore through the limbs just above their heads. First Sergeant Franklin laughed. "They're shootin' high, fellas! The Yanks never could shoot right!"

Reining up in front of Lieutenant Fitzpatrick, Colonel Merrow pointed at the tree line. "Form line of battle in line of battle here, Lieutenant, then move forward. We're going to reinforce that regiment ahead." He motioned across the open field toward a line of troops hotly engaged. William could just catch a glimpse of blue uniforms beyond the firing line.

Fitzpatrick whirled, shouting. "Company! On the right, by file, into line!" William and the other sergeants loudly parroted the command. The soldiers quickly executed the maneuver from their marching column of fours into two long lines. "First Georgia! Forward, March!"

The regiment surged forward. Soldiers on the firing line turned to see the Georgians moving toward them. Many raised their hats and cheered. "Hurry up, boys, we're getting' low on ammunition!" William and the men quickly moved into position beside the other gray and butternut-clad troops. One man wiped black soot from his mouth, then spat. "Them damn black-hatted fellas have been standing there shootin' at us just as fast as we shoot at them. They don't scare worth a damn!" William glanced down the slope in front of their position to a road on which a line of Union soldiers stood firing fast and furiously.

Merrow's voice thundered above the din. "Battalion, load and come to the ready!" Furiously the soldiers pulled cartridges from their boxes. As he frantically rammed his charge home, William saw the glint of sunlight reflecting from leveling musket barrels. "Shit!" The curse leapt from his mouth as he heard the command, "Aim!" float across the space separating them from the enemy.

"FIRE!" Flame and smoke erupted in a thunderous explosion. Agonized cries rose as soldiers to William's right and left were hit. Still clutching his flag, Color Sergeant Hoskins went down, blood and brain matter pouring from a gaping hole in his forehead. The man to his right jumped forward, raising the fallen banner.

"Aim!" Colonel Merrow waved his saber as he bellowed commands.

"FIRE!" It was the Georgian's turn to unleash their deadly leaden hail. Now William could hear the blue figures scream and fall.

"Load and fire at will!" William reloaded and fired over and over again. He began to lose count of how many times he had fired his gun as the crescendo of musketry rose and fell. The barrel was becoming so hot that he could barely hold onto the weapon. Raising it for another shot, he was just about to pull the trigger when he was knocked sideways. Hit in the side, the soldier beside him had spun around, slamming into him. William's musket boomed as they collapsed together, the lead ball splintering an overhead branch.

Dropping his weapon, Henry leapt to his friend's side. "Willie! Did you take one?"

William struggled to roll the wounded soldier off him. "Naw, I'm okay, but Morris here is bad hit. Help get him off of me."

Grabbing Morris by the arms, Henry pulled him off William's legs. Using his musket as a prop, William got to his feet. "Thanks, Henry." He looked around, quickly selecting two men. "Blanchard! You and Schaefer get Morris back to the surgeon." The two soldiers lifted the wounded man between them, half carrying, half dragging him to the rear. Satisfied that Morris was taken care of, William reloaded and resumed firing.

The battle raged on as the sun made agonizingly slow progress toward the horizon. Neither side would give ground as the two lines continued to pour a murderous fire into each other. Finally, the sun fell below the skyline. With the onset of darkness, the volume of fire mercifully began to fade, eventually ceasing. William and the soldiers on either side sank to the ground in exhaustion. The fight had seemed to go on for an eternity. William could not believe that his regiment had only arrived two hours before.

From the road down the slope came the unmistakable noise of the Federal line being pulled slowly back. Relief flooded over William. *Thank God. Maybe they've had enough and be gone in the morning.*

Gradually, another sound began to be heard across the field; the moaning and wailing of wounded men begging for help. "Water, please get me some water." "Please, God, will someone not be merciful and shoot me!" Wanting to help, the pity William felt was overwhelmed by his fatigue. He fell asleep where he lay, the cries ringing in his ears.

The rising sun brought William awake. Slowly he sat up, rubbing his dust-filled eyes. He picked up his kepi, glancing at it casually at first, then more closely. Something looked out of place. He squinted, then his eyes grew wide. There was a hole through the crown. The bullet had plowed through less than an inch from his scalp. He began to inspect his gear. Taking off his jacket, he found another hole through the armpit. He shivered. *My God, how did I survive?*

Jackson's Corps remained in place, the general inviting an attack from Pope's Federals. And attack Jackson he did, sending brigade after brigade at the Confederate position. Today's fight was turning out as hot as the day before. Some units ran so low on ammunition, they resorted to throwing rocks at the Federals. Just when it seemed that Jackson's position was about to buckle, the feared Rebel Yell was heard off to the south. It was Longstreet, hitting Pope squarely on his flank. The Union lines wheeled to meet this new threat, then were struck in flank again as Jackson ordered his corps forward. It was too much for the Yankees. Many units broke and ran, just as they had one year before from this same field. Pope's army withdrew back to the safety of the Washington defenses.

The following day Sergeant Franklin ordered William to pick out a squad of men and report for burial detail. Getting their shovels and picks from the quartermaster, they trudged out across the battlefield to the position their regiment had held. A ghastly scene of dead horses, mangled bodies and blown apart wagons and caissons spread before them. A number of the bodies had bloated to the point of bursting in the sweltering sun. The unbearable stench overwhelmed the men, especially the newer recruits. Gagging, they doubled over and vomited.

William leaned on his shovel as he gazed out over the field, reflecting on the changes time had wrought within him. *Don't bother me to see 'em shot or blasted to pieces any more, but I'll be damned if I'll ever get used to the smell.* He began to gag as an evil whiff passed his nostrils. Pulling a square of cloth from his pocket, he dowsed it with water from his canteen and tied it around his face, covering his nose and mouth. "All right, boys, let's get to work," he said.

Once their revolting task was completed, William and his detail headed for a nearby stream. Stripping down, they bathed and rinsed their clothing to rid themselves of the horrid stink of death.

Back in camp, William draped his wet uniform across the ridge of the dog shelter he shared with Henry. Picking up a discarded board from the top of a hardtack box, he sat down cross-legged in front of the tent. From his knapsack, he pulled out several sheets of paper emblazoned with a United States flag and the motto "The Union Forever—Death to all Traitors!" He chuckled as he began to write:

camp near centerville virginia
august 31, 1862

dear mother

I take pen in hand to write a few more words to tell you I am still well don't mind the yankee flag on this paper we got supplied with good riting paper and ink thanks to the Yanks I will tell you how in a minute

we have just gone into camp but it seems though we've been fightin almost every day for the last month yesterday we were in another big battle we were fighting near manassas junction it is the same place that the big battle was fought at a year ago

we was really wrong about genril lee back at cheat mountain we all called him granny because we thought he was scared to fight but ever since I got back to the army I've been in one big fight after another the genril is a wonder it's like he knows just what the yankee genrils are thinking cause he hits them front and back and even when we get beat back he hits em again right after he took over the army back in june he kept attacking the yank army for a whole week straight after that no one called him granny again

about three weeks ago genril lee ordered genril jackson to march north to see what the Yanks were doing we had a little brush with them near a place called cedar mountain and we beat em good then we headed for centerville when we got there we found the yankees supply depo lordy you should have seen the good stuff there hams and oysters and lots of boxes of hardtack thats where I got this riting paper we got all the yank genrils truck too his name is pope and someone said that some of his papers said his headquarters were in the saddle that started a joke goin round that popes headquarters is where his hindquarters should be I havent et so much at one time since the war started got me a new pair of pants and shoes too we filled our sacks so full we couldnt hardly pick them up there was a lot of whisky too but jackson ordered us to smash open the barrels and dump them out henry and I laughed ourselves silly to watch some of the boys down on their hands and knees trying to lap up the whisky dont worry mother I didnt drink none you wont need to send another box for awhile because I am fixed up first rate thanks to mr genril pope and the federal army

after we left the depo we took up a position near manassas jackson waited til the feds got right in front of us and opened up we had a hot little fight with a bunch of Yanks that looked like they were wearin pilgrim hats they looked funny but they shore fought good the next day genril pope attacked us again but he got a big surprise genril longstreet hit the Yanks hard on the flank and started them running good thing he attacked when he did cause some of the boys were down to throwing rocks

I have not gotten a letter from mary for over three weeks is she all right her last letter was really short she just kept complaining about how she doesn't have anything to do maybe you could invite her over to the cabin some time I know you dont like her that much but when this war is over and I come back I intend to ask her to marry me so I want the two of you to get along if you do see her tell her I was asking about her in my letters and that I think about her all the time

your affectionate son
william

Rereading the letter a couple of times to make sure he had not forgotten anything, he folded the paper, then stuffed it into a gaily-colored Union patriotic envelope. "I'll post this tomorrow," he mumbled to no one in particular as he slid the letter into his knapsack.

Chapter 34

Crouching low, the boy peered through the thick brush at the magnificent buck. *Pa'll be proud if'n I can bag you, big fella. We'll eat for a month.*

Moving with painful slowness, he slid his Pennsylvania rifle across the rotten log serving for cover. Sighting carefully down the long barrel, he slowly drew back the cock. The click of the hammer caught the deer's attention, its head snapping upright in alarm. The boy froze, praying that the buck wouldn't run. The deer's head darted to and fro. After a moment, the animal fixed its gaze directly at the boy. Staring at the youth for a bare second, the buck spun away.

"Dammit!" The boy yanked the trigger. The rifle cracked. Caught behind the ear by the ball, the buck collapsed, its momentum sending it hurtling over the edge of the ravine.

Elated, the boy scrambled down the embankment. Reaching the buck's side, he began to circle it, his face lighting up in wonder at the size of the animal. Coming around to the deer's head, he drew his knife, then began to tug on its antlers. Something smooth and white caught his eye, half hidden under the deer's neck. He crouched down to get a better look.

Suddenly he backpedaled, his eyes wide in horror as he stumbled over roots and vines trying to get away from the buck's head. Gawking at him from beneath the antlers were the two vacant eye sockets of a grinning, bleached human skull.

Lucinda sat in her porch rocker, grateful for the occasional cooling breeze. She had sought refuge outside from the stifling interior of the cabin. It seemed as though this had been the hottest summer in memory. She looked out toward the garden where Melissa was busily clearing weeds out from between the rows of vegetables. She frowned. "Melissa, you should have your bonnet on, to keep the sun off your head."

Melissa got up from her knees. Placing her hands on her back, she stretched to remove the stiffness. "I'm fine, Mama. That bonnet is too hot on my neck." She kicked up some dust with her toe. "We've got a pretty good crop of carrots, but I don't think the cabbage is going to do too well." A noise caught her attention. She turned to see a buckboard coming up the lane, followed by a rider. "Look, Mama, it's Mr. McCay and Sheriff Lane."

Lucinda stepped down from the porch to greet the visitors. "Hello, Jedidiah. Sheriff, how nice to see you. What brings you out this way on such a warm day?"

Lane dismounted and tied his horse to a porch rail, then took off his hat. "Afternoon, Miz Marsh. 'Fraid we're here on some unpleasant business."

McCay stepped down from the buckboard. He put his hand on Lucinda's shoulder. "Why don't we have a seat on the porch."

Alarm welled up inside Lucinda as her eyes shifted rapidly between the two men. "What's the matter? Has something happened to William? He's been hurt, hasn't he?"

Jedidiah took Lucinda by the arm, leading her up onto the porch. "Last we heard, William is fine. He's not why we've come."

Melissa came running toward them. "What's wrong, Mama?" Lucinda glanced at her and shook her head.

Sheriff Lane drew an object from his coat pocket. "Robert Little's boy was out hunting the other day. Came across a pile of bones down in the bottom of a ravine. We believe they very well could be your husband's remains."

Melissa gasped. Lucinda's face went white. Putting her hand to her chest, she dropped into her rocker. McCay crouched beside her, his hand on her arm. "Are you all right?"

She swallowed hard a couple of times. "I—I think so. Just give me a minute." She turned to Lane. "What . . . why do you think its Aaron?"

The sheriff produced a pocket watch, its case caked with rust. "We found this next to the bones, Mrs. Marsh. It has "A Marsh" inscribed on it. And it looks to have your likeness inside. Sorry the lid's bent. Took a little prying to get it open."

Lucinda gasped as she recognized the contents. Even through the thin layer of mold she could make out the tiny painted portrait. "That—that's the image Aaron had done just after we were married." She felt dizzy. "Melissa, dear, would you please get me some water?" She turned to Sheriff Lane. "Do you have any idea what happened?"

Removing his hat, Lane said, "The skull had a bullet hole in the side. Near as we can figger Mr. Marsh must'a got killed by a road agent. He either fell in the ravine when he got shot or the killer pushed his body down there to keep it from being seen." He nodded to

McCay. "Well, I guess that fairly well ties it up, Jed. Mrs. Marsh has given a pretty good identification."

McCay stood. "So you're not going to do anything more to find out who killed him?"

"I'll be asking some questions, but it probably won't do any good. Been too long. No evidence left to tie this to anyone." He turned to Lucinda. "Sorry 'bout this, ma'am. When I get back to town I'll get with the undertaker to make the arrangements."

"Thank you, Sheriff. I really do appreciate you coming here to tell me."

Donning his hat, Lane tapped the brim. "Thank you, ma'am. Least 'ways now you won't be wondering 'bout him anymore." He mounted his horse. "See you back in town, Jed."

Melissa returned to the porch carrying a cup of water. Lucinda accepted it gratefully. Emptying the contents, she gave the cup back to Melissa. "Thank you, dear. Would you please get a bucket full from the well? I need to wash the dishes."

Melissa looked at her with worried eyes. "Mama, are you all right?"

Lucinda smiled. "I'm fine, dear. Now go along."

Without looking up at Jedidiah, Lucinda took hold of his arm. He cupped his hand over hers. "Are you sure you're all right?" he asked.

She stroked his arm. "Oh, Jed, I want to cry. I think I should cry, but I just can't. I cried for so long after he disappeared. After all this time I knew he was probably dead, but I just never could bring myself to really believe it. I didn't want to believe it. I love him . . . loved him so."

Rising from her chair, Lucinda smiled at McCay. "Thank you, for coming out with the sheriff, Jedidiah. It made the news a little easier to bear." A frown crossed her brow. "There's something else bothering me. That letter I got a few days ago from William? He's saying he's going to ask Mary Stewart to marry him. He wants me to ask her here for a visit so we can 'get to know each other better.' I just don't know what to do. She is such a horrid girl. I've heard such things about her. I can imagine what you must hear around town."

Jedidiah nodded. "I do hear a few things. Most of it not good. It's no secret that she's been dallying with that Parker boy. He's even been seen going in and out of her house. Mrs. Anderson came by one morning all flustered and excited. Said she had just seen him coming out the back door of her house—he was busy tucking his shirt into his pants."

Lucinda wrung her hands. "That's just what I mean. How can I in good conscious welcome that girl into my house?"

Jedidiah brought Lucinda and Melissa to town for the funeral. It was a small affair, attended by just a few of the townspeople. Not many folks were left that had known Aaron. Isaac Stewart appeared with Mary, who showed obvious boredom with the proceedings.

After the service concluded, both Melissa and Lucinda each laid a single rose on Aaron's grave. Putting her arm around her daughter, Lucinda read the inscription on the tombstone. "Aaron Marsh—born New Hampshire, August 16, 1813—died May 23, 1847".

Mr. Stewart came up to her. "Please accept my sincere condolences, Mrs. Marsh. Aaron was a good man. I pray that this service will bring comfort and closure to you and your family. Also, I earnestly hope that your son will emerge safely from this war. Even though I disagree with the cause for which he fights with all my being, I respect William as an honorable man."

Lucinda took Stewart's outstretched hand. "Thank you, Isaac. I was so sorry to hear that you had been dismissed as schoolmaster."

A flash of anger passed over Stewart's eyes. "Strictly politics, my dear lady. The town leaders found my Unionist beliefs highly offensive. Ah, well. I have managed to find employ with a teamster who does not seem to mind my views. Unfortunately, this job will take me away from home for sometimes lengthy periods. I would deem it a great favor if you would look in on my daughter from time to time."

Lucinda glanced over to see Mary conversing gaily with some of the village boys. She remembered William's request. "Of course, Isaac. Perhaps she would like to come out to the farm for a visit."

Stewart smiled. "That would be grand. I am certain that you would exert a wonderful influence on her. I will talk to her about it right away. Good day to you, Mrs. Marsh." Shaking her hand, he headed over to where Mary was waiting.

Jedidiah McCay put his hand on Lucinda's shoulder. He glanced at Melissa. "Lissa, would you wait for us in the buckboard. I have something I would like to say to your mother."

Melissa looked at her Lucinda, who nodded.

Waiting until Melissa was seated in the buckboard, McCay took Lucinda by the hands. "You know how I feel. Now I think it's time for you to move on with your life. And I want to be a part of that. I love you, and I want you to be my wife."

234

She gazed at him, tears forming in her eyes. "It's too soon, Jedidiah."

Distress crossed his face. "But . . . ."

Lucinda placed her fingers gently across his lips. "Please don't say anything more. Don't you understand? I know it's been fifteen years since he disappeared. I thought that I was over him, but now—I just need some time to get my thoughts together. This has brought all the feelings flooding back. Please, please, just give me some time."

McCay felt ashamed and embarrassed. "I'm sorry, Lucinda. I should have waited. I'll give you all the time you need."

She hugged him. "You're a good man. Any woman would be lucky to have you. I know I'm not being fair to you, but I have to work this out by myself." She kissed him on the cheek. "Would you please take us home now?"

Later that evening, after Melissa had climbed to her bed in the loft, Lucinda sat for awhile in front of the fireplace. She glanced at the fireplace mantle. Candlelight caused a flickering reflection on the old tintype of Aaron. Retrieving the image from the place it had occupied for so long, she closed her eyes as she pressed it to her breast. Picking up the candle lantern, she retreated to her bedroom.

Setting the lamp on a small table, she knelt down next to a battered old trunk. She sighed as she ran her hands over the dry leather covering. Opening the case, she began to remove the contents, carefully sorting them into tidy piles. One stack was neatly folded old clothing of Aaron's, another was letters and other documents. From the clothing pile she picked out two white homespun shirts. *I should be able to resize these to fit William.* She stopped for a moment, staring at the candle flame. *I should have done this years ago. But I just couldn't. I couldn't bring myself to believe he wouldn't come back.*

From the stack of papers she drew out a faded letter from Aaron's brother Benjamin. In it were congratulations on Aaron and Lucinda's marriage, and a blessing for long life and many children. *I have to write to him. He'll want to know that his brother has finally been found and laid to rest. And Thomas needs to know about his father.*

Setting Aaron's picture on the table, she blew out the candle. As she slept, she dreamed that Aaron came to her. "I'm all right," he was saying. "Let me go. Live your life and be happy." Then he turned and faded away.

Lucinda awoke to bright sunshine lighting up the brown parchment of the window. Laying there, staring at the ceiling, she replayed the dream in her mind. A feeling of release flowed over her.

The dream's meaning was crystal clear. Aaron had freed her. Oh, she would always love him, but emotional ties that had bound her to his memory had evaporated. Her thoughts turned to Jedidiah McCay.

Jedidiah is such a sweet man. I know he truly does care for me. I've been alone for so long. He's right, it's time to move on. But, I want to have all my children around me when I get married. If I were to accept his proposal, he would have to understand that. Would he still want to marry me, if he has to wait until William comes home? And what about Thomas?

She sat up on the side of the bed. *I'm going to do it. Jedidiah would make a good husband and a good father for Melissa. I don't want to be alone any more.*

Lifting the picture of Aaron, she ran her fingers over the brass frame. *Oh, thank you, my darling. Thank you for giving me your blessing.* Crossing to the old trunk, she raised the lid, carefully placing the tintype inside. *I shall always remember and be grateful.*

Chapter 35

Thomas lifted the bushel basket up to James on the wagon. Pulling a handkerchief from his pocket, he mopped his brow while surveying the tall stalks of corn. "Just five more rows, and we'll have this field done."

James emptied the contents of the basket into the wagon. "Thank God. C'mon, let's take a break." He hopped down beside Thomas. "My throat's dry as the road."

They walked over to a stand of oak trees on the edge of the cornfield. Thomas pulled a jug of water from a small stream. Reclining in the shade of the trees, they passed the jug back and forth. James took a swig, then splashed some into his hand. He patted down the back of his neck. "So what did Stephanie say?"

"She's dead set against it." Thomas reached for the jug and took a long swallow. "Says I must be crazy to even consider enlisting. Said she'd never forgive me if I were to go and do such a fool thing."

"Guess that's pretty definite."

"Course, I don't get to see her a whole lot these days. Every time I go into town I have to watch out for her uncle, and that damn Mattson dogs my every step. You'd think I was spying for Jeff Davis or something."

"He hates Southern boys in general, and you in particular."

"You're right about that." Thomas swatted at a horse fly buzzing around his head. "Problem is, even when I do get to see her, all she talks about is her uncle getting elected to Congress."

"She busy working on his campaign?"

"Yeah, and she drives me almost to distraction. I never met a girl before who talks so much about politics." Thomas chuckled. "Course she said once that the real reason she's trying so hard to get him elected is so when he goes to Washington we'll be able to see more of each other."

Stark took another swig, then corked the jug. "You go and enlist, you won't be seeing her at all."

Thomas stood, brushing leaves from his trouser bottom. "That's what she said." He lowered the jug back into the stream. "Funny, isn't it? Here we are, two Southern boys talking about joining the Union

Army. Sometimes I can't figure out why I'm even thinking about doing such a thing."

"Same reason as me. We don't belong in the South any more than we really belong here. We're both against secession. And as for slavery, hell, you've done more against that since you been up here than some of the worst abolitionists, what with all your trips to Canada with your uncle."

"There's one thing that really scares me about joining up. Willie's in the Confederate Army. What would I do if we should meet on some battlefield? How could I ever think of shooting my own brother? Just the thought of that is unbearable."

James picked up the basket. "Just because you become a soldier doesn't mean you lose your humanity." He grinned. "I'll tell you how to handle that. You get him in your sights, why all you have to do is swing a little and shoot the bastard beside him."

"That's not funny."

"Hey, just joking. Anyways, consider this. There's hundreds of thousands of soldiers on both sides scattered over some thirty-five states, right? The chance of you and your brother facing each other is probably one in a million . . . or more."

A smile spread across Thomas's face. "You know, I hadn't thought about it that way. Thanks. That makes me feel a lot better."

"Glad to be of service. Now, let's get back to work or we'll never get done."

It took just a couple more hours for Thomas and James to complete harvesting the cornfield. Retrieving the jug, they started the wagon up the lane toward the farm buildings. As they entered the barnyard, Pastor Marsh came flying out the farmhouse door waving a piece of paper. "Thomas, come here quick. I just got a letter from your mother. It's about your father."

Thomas handed the reins to James. "Here, tie them up for me, would ya?" He jumped down from the wagon and ran up to the porch. "About Pa? How can that be? He disappeared when I was just a kid."

Marsh handed the letter to Thomas. "Here, read this," he said. "Your mother wrote that someone found his body. Go on, read the letter."

Thomas took the paper from his uncle. He scanned it for a moment, then began to read aloud:

Dahlonega Georgia
September 17, 1862

My dearest Benjamin,

*I write to you today with news about my husband,
your brother Aaron. His remains were recently found
in a wooded area near town. It appears that on the
night he disappeared he was waylaid by thieves and
killed. The sheriff says that he was shot in the head.
He was identified because his pocketwatch containing
my portrait was found with his body. Somehow he
kept the murderers from finding it.*

A strange feeling swept over Thomas. Without taking his eyes off
the letter, he searched with one hand for a chair. He reread the
paragraph as he sat down. After a moment, he looked up at Marsh.
"My God, Uncle Benjamin, this is incredible."

The preacher nodded. "Go on, keep reading."

*We have had a funeral, and his remains were buried
in the town cemetery. Oh, Benjamin, I believe I know
just how you are feeling at this moment, reading these
words. Aaron was such a wonderful man. I still find it
hard to believe that he is truly gone, even after all these
years. And yet, I know that he is still with me. The
night of the funeral, he came to me in a dream. Do you
know what he said, dear brother Benjamin? He told
me to go on with my life. Is that not just like my dear
Aaron?*

*And so I now have more news to tell. Mr. Jedidiah
McCay, who owns the mercantile in town, has asked
me to marry him. I have known Mr. McCay for many
years. He has always been kind to me, and has been
strong for me when I needed someone to confide in.
He has wanted to marry me for some time now, but
until poor Aaron was found and laid to rest I did not
feel free to do so. Now Aaron has given me his
blessing, and I have told Mr. McCay that I will marry
him on the condition that we must wait until William
comes home from this horrible war. I do so want to
have my family around me at such an important event.
Do you think it might be possible that Thomas might
be able to come? How is he? Your last letter said*

something about his meeting a nice girl. I have heard nothing from him other than the few words in your letters. I miss him so as I do William. Please tell him that I hope he is well, and that I would be so happy to have just one letter from him.

William's last letter is full of news of the big battle in Virginia near Manassas. I thank God that he has so far been spared, and pray that the war will end soon and he will be able to come home. Melissa is also well. She is growing into quite the lady. Stephen Merrow comes to see her quite often. He is a good boy, and is very respectful of her. It would not surprise me in a few years to see them married.

That is all the news for now. I hope that knowing your brother's fate will help give you peace. I shall always miss him, and shall always carry him in my heart. But now I know I will be happy married to Mr. McCay. I would be grateful for your blessing on our union.

Your affectionate sister
Lucinda

Thomas looked at his uncle. "What do you think about all this?"

Marsh stroked his chin. "I confess to feeling a certain amount of relief that my brother has been found, and that he can finally rest in peace. I'm just sorry it has taken so long to discover what happened to him."

"What about Mother getting married again so soon?"

"I say God bless her. You can't really say it's too soon. She's been without a companion for so many years. I just wish I could be there to officiate for her."

Thomas handed the letter back to his uncle. "I guess you're right. I don't remember Father very well. I even have trouble picturing what he looked like."

Folding the letter, the preacher slipped it into his coat pocket. "That's understandable. We shall all remember him in our prayers at supper tonight. At least we know that Willie is all right. He's with Lee's army now. She talks about him being in a big battle near Manassas. Must be Second Bull Run, back end of August."

"The letter is dated mid-September," said Rebecca, "I'm surprised it got through the lines so quickly. She wrote this on the same day as

240

that ghastly battle in Maryland. I wonder if Willie was there. What was the name of that place?"

Marsh thought for a moment. "They called it Antietam, after a little creek that runs through the battlefield near a small village named Sharpsburg. The papers mentioned that Jackson's men were engaged, so I'm sure William was involved at some point. I pray he came through unscathed."

Thomas shuddered as he recalled an article from the local newspaper that had recently been reprinted from the *New York Times*. It described Matthew Brady's photographic exhibit of the Battle of Antietam, relating in gory detail his pictures showing dead soldiers strewn across the battlefield. A mental image of his brother's shattered body passed through Thomas's mind. *If I enlist, I could be his killer.* He shook his head. *No, no, James is right. There's no way I would ever encounter him.*

The preacher cleared his throat. "Nephew, I think it's time that you wrote your mother a letter."

Thomas sank back into his chair and sighed. "I know I should. I just haven't wanted to worry her with all my problems."

"My boy, you've done a wonderful job of turning your life around. I have been so pleased to see the progress that you have made from the dark times you were going through. Lucinda doesn't need to know about all the bad times, but I do think she would like to hear about how well you are doing."

"You're right, Uncle Benjamin. I'll write a letter tonight after supper."

Marsh reached over to slap his nephew on the shoulder. "Good man. You write it and I'll see that it gets posted first thing tomorrow."

After supper, Thomas retreated to his room. Lighting an oil lamp, he pulled a sheet of paper from his desk, along with a pen and inkwell. Pondering a few moments, he began to write:

Lymington, New Hampshire
October 10, 1862

Dearest Mother
I take pen in hand to write a few lines that I hope will find you well. I am very sorry that I have not written for such a long time. I do not know what Uncle Benjamin has written about me, but let me just

say that I have had several unfortunate adventures over the last couple of years. Those days are behind me now and I anticipate much better times ahead.

I read your last letter to Uncle Benjamin with much excitement. I am glad that father has finally been laid to rest. I know this must lift a great burden from you. I am so happy that you have decided to remarry. I remember Mr. McCay as a kind, warm-hearted person. I am certain that he will bring you much happiness. I would very much like to attend your wedding, but until the war is over it would be impossible for me to travel down to Georgia.

Yes, I have met a wonderful girl. Her name is Stephanie Carroll. You would like her very much, and I hope someday soon you will be able to meet her.

I hope Willie has remained well. We have just heard about the battle in Maryland that the papers call Antietam. The paper is full of casualty lists. I hope that Willie was not involved, but if he was there, I pray that he came through it uninjured. I have been giving great thought about enlisting myself—

Lifting the pen, he reread the last sentence, then drew a line through it. *Can't say that right now. Have to rewrite this. Better not mention anything about me enlisting. Just get her more worried.* Taking out a new sheet of paper, he rewrote the letter, leaving out the offending sentence.

I will try to do better about writing to you, and will be grateful to hear from you as often as you can write to me. I will be very interested to hear about how your wedding plans are coming along. Give my love to Melissa, and when you next write to Willie, please let him know that I am thinking of him.

Your loving son,
Thomas

Chapter 36

Major Edmond Baxter emerged from his enormous wall tent, stretching as he gulped in a mouthful of cold morning air. Shivering slightly, he glanced about the camp while he buttoned up his lacy shirt. As usual, he was the first one in the encampment to awaken. A cacophony of snores rose around him as the guerrillas slumbered.

Brushing his damp hair back on his head, he sat in the intricately carved chair in front of the tent. He smiled as he gently caressed the gilded armrests. *The throne of a man who would be king.* Looking out over the hodgepodge of tents and blankets, he scowled slightly. *And what fools this king must surround himself with.*

An overwhelmingly sweet scent rose from his body. He had doused himself in lavender water following his bath, something he did constantly to hide the stink of his unwashed men. Behind his back they gossiped that he smelled like a French whore. He was obsessed with staying clean, often bathing morning and night. His shirts were all of bright white linen, and he always seemed to be wearing a freshly laundered one. He once had a slave whipped for accidentally dropping his coat in the dirt.

Baxter's young servant scurried about setting an elaborate breakfast on the table. As Baxter ate, he stood nervously beside the chair, ready to instantly comply with any order his master might give.

"That was very good, Hercules. Just one thing though. The bath water this morning was rather tepid."

Hercules shrunk back as if expecting to be struck. "Sorry, boss, I'm real sorry. It'll be better tonight, I promise."

Baxter glowered at him for a few moments. "We'll let it go this morning. You'll not need to worry about tonight's bath. In fact, you can begin striking the camp. We'll be moving out today."

Hercules' expression turned to relief. "Yessir, boss, I'll get your gear ready. I got your boots polished extra bright last night."

"Very good. Right now, though, I want you to go find Curly. When you get back, see to my uniform. There's a rather ugly-looking spot on the sleeve."

A few moments later Curly walked up the small rise to Baxter's tent, Hercules trailing behind. The major was having difficulty pulling on one of his boots. "Come help me with this, Hercules." The servant squatted in front of Baxter, manipulating the boot until it finally slid on.

Not completely awake, Curly yawned, then reached down to scratch his crotch. "You wanted to see me, Major?"

Baxter snorted with disgust as he reached for his other boot. *Fools and savages.* "We shall ride today. Our larder is shrinking, and funds are becoming thin. Harvests should be well underway so we should have good pickings."

Curly perked up with excitement. "Great. Where we heading for?"

"Time to move our operations elsewhere. The armies are concentrating east of here, near Fredericksburg. So we shall head north and west into Maryland away from them. Both pro-Southern and Union towns there, so the boys need to carry both uniforms."

Jonathon sat up, yawning and scratching his chest. Through blurry eyes he could see Grainger squatting by a fire boiling coffee in his tin cup. Wrapping his coarse wool blanket tight around him, he picked up his shoes and shuffled over to the fire. The heat from the flames felt good. "Winter's coming early this year," he said, "It's only the first week of November and the frosts are getting heavier every night."

Grainger let out a low grunt, but said nothing. Gingerly lifting his tin cup from the fire, he poured some sugar into it from a small cloth bag. Sitting back, he slowly stirred the coffee while staring into the flames with a far-away look.

After several minutes watching his tent mate twirl the spoon around in his cup, Jonathon spoke up. "You gonna drink that? Or you gonna keep stirring until the spoon melts?"

Grainger continued to stir his coffee. "Leave me be. I ain't in a real good mood right now."

"What's the matter?"

"Don't want to talk about it."

Jonathon coughed. "Well, shit, then. Keep shut up for all I care. I'll find someone else who wants to talk. Maybe I can find out who was doing the shooting last night."

Grainger threw the cup into the fire and abruptly stood, his face dark as a thundercloud. "That shot was aimed at me! Someone tried to bushwhack me last night. And we both know who it probably was."

Jonathon was stunned. "What you talking about? You mean Jake?"

Grainger began to pace back and forth. "I was out in the woods taking a piss. Thought I heard someone moving around, but it was too dark to see anything. I had just started back when I saw a muzzle flash and heard a big boom. Whoever it was shot high, cause I heard the ball whiz through the branches over my head. I dropped down and pulled my gun, but whoever it was lit out through the trees. I pulled off a shot but didn't hit anything. When I got back to camp I went right over to Jake's tent. He was sitting by the fire cleaning that Sharps rifle of his. Just sitting there laughing and carrying on with a couple of other fellas like nothing had happened."

Picking up a stick, he poked at the cup in the fire. "I asked him where he'd been. One of the fellas sitting there said 'Why, he's been right here with us all evening.' Jake asked why I wanted to know. When I said someone had taken a potshot at me, he said that it was too bad that they missed. Then he got real serious—swung that big Sharps around so it was pointing right at my belly. Said I oughta watch my backside more carefully."

Jonathon adjusted his blanket. "I'll tell you something, friend. Sooner or later it's going to be just you and him, and it ain't gonna be pretty. One of you is going to end up killing the other. Maybe it wasn't such a good idea coming here. Maybe we ought to think about moving on."

Grainger finally was able to knock the blackened cup out of the fire. "Probably wasn't. I didn't realize he hated me that much. But I got nowhere else to go, so I figger I'll make the best of it. You got to admit we're living a lot better here than we ever did in the army."

Jonathon picked up one of his shoes. Slipping his hand inside, a finger emerged through a large crack at the toe. "Right now we ain't doing so great. We're almost out of food, and I can't patch these old shoes many more times before they fall apart. We haven't been out on a raid in almost a month. I couldn't find any boots that fit in the last town we hit."

Just then Curly walked up. "Pack up your traps, boys. We're moving out."

Jonathon pulled on one of the shoes. "Where to?"

"Wherever the boss tells us. Right now he's saying Maryland. So get your stuff together and get ready to go."

Once camp was broken, the raiders headed northwest out of the Wilderness. Two days later, the column crossed the Potomac River into Maryland, entering the state far to the west. Baxter wanted to give the area around Sharpsburg as wide a berth as possible, because there were still Union soldiers quartered close by guarding the hospitals set up after the Battle of Antietam. Besides, Baxter knew there would be slim pickings there anyway—the armies had scoured the land clean for miles around. Also, Jeb Stuart had been raiding up between Hagerstown and Frederick in October. At the very least, the towns would still be up in arms. The farms and villages in the thin western part of the state would provide more promising booty.

"Baxter's out of his mind." Grainger muttered. "Moving north just as winter's fixing to settle in. We should be going south."

Jonathon nodded in agreement. "All I can say is he better find us someplace warm to hole up in."

After a couple more hours, the column was halted on the crest of a heavily wooded ridge. The road they had been following continued down the slope to a small village. Following his usual plan, Baxter sent two men dressed as civilians into the town. Their task was to case the village to detect where valuables might be kept, and to determine how much and what kind of resistance they might encounter. They would also attempt to discover the townspeople's sympathies, North or South. If they found a Union town, then the raiders would remain in their Confederate uniforms. If the town were Southern leaning, however, they would switch into the Federal jackets each man carried. The blame for the raid would then fall on the Union Army.

Jonathon sat down under a tree, then pulled off one of his shoes, examining the cracked leather and holes in the sole. "Hope there's a shoemaker in that town. These have about had it."

The guerrillas lounged out of sight in the tree line waiting for the scouts' return. About twenty minutes later they came pounding up the hill. "Looks to be a Union town. No soldiers anywhere. Couldn't see many men around at all. Bank's right in the middle."

Baxter grinned. "All right, boys, looks like good pickin's here. Saddle up!"

With a whoop the men rose, leaping onto their horses. Charging out of the trees, they rode down on the unsuspecting town. Part of the group split away, swinging around to enter from the opposite side. The raiders quickly rounded up the townspeople, forcing them out into the middle of the street. Baxter rode forward to address the crowd. "Who's in charge of this place?"

A tall, thin man wearing a nondescript brown frock coat stepped forward through the crowd. "I am Mayor Watson. Who are you, sir? What command is this?"

"Morton's Partisan Rangers, Confederate States Army, at your service. Detached from General Stuart's cavalry. We are conducting a series of raids in retaliation for the despicable acts perpetrated on the people of the sovereign state of Virginia by your vile Yankee army. Your town is to be ransomed, sir."

"Ransomed? What does that mean?"

"It means, sir, that you will deliver one hundred thousand dollars in gold or greenbacks to me immediately, else I shall order your town put to the torch."

"Oh, please, sir, please don't do that. We have nowhere near that kind of money. Besides, we're good Southerners. We've sent many good men to fight with General Lee."

Baxter winked at his men, then turned to face the mayor again. "The only 'good men' are Southern men, and if all the 'good men' are gone, then that must mean all that's left are Union men. Guess that means we'll have to burn you out!"

The mayor went white. "For God's sake, please don't. We have mostly women and children here. They've no place to go if you take their homes."

Unnoticed by the crowd, a small boy worked his way through until he stood in front of Baxter's horse. Reaching down, he scooped up a handful of horse feces from a pile in the street. He flung it at Baxter as hard as he could. The foul brown mass splattered on the major's leg.

Baxter gaped at his soiled pants with horror. "Now look what you've gone and done. Got shit all over my clean trousers! God-damn son-of-a-bitch!" Cocking his pistol, he aimed for the boy's head.

A man charged out from the crowd, pulling the youngster behind him. "Ain't no call to shoot the boy."

Baxter aimed the pistol at the man's chest. "You his pa?"

"That I am," said the man with a tone of defiance.

"Then you should have taught your child some manners. Very well, I will not shoot the boy." He pulled the trigger. The ball slammed into the man's chest, sending him flying backwards. Pinned under the body, the boy began to cry as he struggled to free himself. Baxter raised the muzzle to his lips, blowing the smoke away. "The father shall pay for the sins of the son."

A woman in the crowd screamed. Pushing her way through the shocked people, she ran to the body. Kneeling down beside it, she looked up at Baxter and shook her fist at him. "Damn you! Damn you to hell! You've killed my husband!" She took the boy's arms, pulling him from underneath. She then lay down beside her husband's body, burying her head in his shirt, weeping. The boy knelt next to her, tears streaming down his dirty cheeks.

Unmoved, Baxter turned to his men. "All right, boys, let's get down to business. Curly! Get that wagon over by the livery hitched and bring it around so we can fill it up. C'mon, boys, let's clean out this town!"

Within the space of two hours, most buildings in the town were on fire, the bank had been emptied, the stores looted of their merchandise. Jonathon spotted a shop with the image of a boot painted in the window. Shoes! Dashing through the door, he came upon a scene of total chaos. Footwear of all kinds was scattered across the floor, and flames were shooting out from a back room. Frantically he began searching through the piles, trying on different shoes and boots, trying to make a match. Tongues of fire began to lick at the ceiling. After several frenzied minutes he finally put together a pair of boots that fit.

Grainger's panicked voice boomed through the door. "Evans! What the hell you doin'! We got to get out of here!"

"Don't lose your drawers!" Evans ran outside to see the guerrillas rushing to their horses. Grainger had his foot in the stirrup when Jonathon reached him. "What goes?"

"Yank cavalry headin' this way fast!"

As Grainger swung into his saddle, a signboard over his head exploded, showering him with splinters. Ducking down, he scanned the buildings around him. "Where'd that shot come from?"

Jonathon was busy trying to reign in his spooked horse. "Don't know, and we don't have time to find out. Let's get out of here!"

Peering from his perch high up in a church steeple, Jake ratcheted the lever on his Sharps carbine. He slid another cartridge into the chamber as he watched the two race out of town. *Damn! Got to aim lower next time.*

Chapter 37

William cradled his musket into his shoulder. Blowing into his hands to warm them, he shivered; not only because of the icy December wind gusts swirling through the trees, but also at the spectacle of a sea of blue uniforms across the low plain. One column after another emerged from the shattered town of Fredericksburg, wheeling into line of battle. It reminded William of a huge snake coiling itself in preparation for striking.

First Sergeant Franklin whistled. "Boy, don't them bluebellies look pretty out there." He turned to William, his expression one of scorn. "Looks like they're going to come right at us. Stupid, stupid."

The remark puzzled William. "What do you mean, stupid?"

"Just look out there. They've got to cross almost a half-mile of open ground to get here, and all uphill. When we start shooting, we'll mow 'em down." Franklin pointed toward the left. "Those boys up on the heights have it even better. They've got that stone wall to shoot from. Going to be simply murder. The Yanks' should've attacked us days ago while we were still moving into line here. Now it's too late. What a waste."

"You sound sorry for them."

"In a way, I am. They've had the sorriest excuses for commanders ever since this war started. They've got some real good officers in that army, but Lincoln sure seems to have a talent for picking the worst to command. Ol' Marse Robert has marched rings around 'em. 'Course, that's all the better for us. I sure do think—."

A loud roar from the right of Jackson's line caught everyone by surprise. Hurtling through the Federal ranks, a solid shot knocked blue figures in all directions. William and his comrades strained to see where the cannonball originated. Henry pointed. "Look at that, will ya! Some idiot's out there with only two guns!"

Scanning the field off to the right, William could not help but gape at a lonely pair of artillery pieces, completely out in the open several yards in front of "Stonewall's" position and exposed to Federal fire. The gunners were working their pieces feverishly. All the while, a boyish appearing officer sat behind them on his horse, peering through a pair of field glasses at the Yankee ranks.

Sergeant Franklin snatched off his hat and slapped it against his leg. "I know who that is. That's Major Pelham, from Stuart's horse artillery. I met him right after Sharpsburg. Colonel Merrow sent me over to Stonewall's headquarters with a requisition. Stuart and Jackson were in a meeting—Pelham was waiting out front of the tent. He stuck his hand out and introduced himself. He's only a kid—just nineteen. Wished me luck." He whistled. "That crazy fool is taking on the whole Yank army by himself."

Cheers rose from the Confederate lines as Pelham's two guns kept up the lop-sided fight. From the Federal lines, battery after battery pivoted toward the exposed group. Each time the Union artillery was about to get the range, Pelham would limber up his cannon and shift to another location. Quickly going into battery again, the gunners resumed lobbing shells at the blue mass. The macabre dance continued until Pelham's ammunition was expended, at which point he retired to a rising chorus of Rebel Yells. He had lost one gun and several men, but the gallant youth had stalled the Federal advance for two hours.

"Crazy, brave fool," said Sergeant Franklin. "If the ladies didn't love that kid before, they will now."

The Federal batteries dueling with Pelham now turned their attention back to Jackson's line. Confederate guns held their fire, much to the consternation of William and his compatriots. Henry was beside himself. "Why the hell don't our guns shoot back?"

Franklin motioned for Henry to keep down. "Calm down, corporal. Jackson's either saving his ammunition, or he's trying to sucker them Yanks in. Probably both."

Having endured the cannonade for almost an hour, it seemed to William that the Federal barrage was beginning to slacken. Franklin confirmed it. "They're reducing their fire." He glanced at William. "Get ready. They'll be coming at us now, madder than hornets."

Franklin was right. The long blue lines were moving. As if on parade, the Federals advanced deliberately across the plain toward the woods sheltering Jackson's Corps. At last, the Confederate batteries were allowed to open fire. Scores of Union soldiers went down as shells tore through their ranks. They stopped, hesitated, then started forward again. To William, it seemed as though there was no way possible for them to continue, but on they came.

Sergeant Franklin cried out in alarm. "My God, they're coming right up into that swamp. There's no troops there!" In the center of the wooded area was a patch of boggy ground. The ground was so bad that regiments had been posted on either side and behind, but not across it.

Too late, the danger of leaving a gap in the line became obvious. The Union troops hit the weak spot, driving deep within and enabling them to fire down the flanks of the lines on either side. The First Georgia fought with desperation to hold back the Yankee tide. Lieutenant Fitzpatrick ran back and forth, yelling, cajoling, even slapping his men across the rump with the flat of his sword blade as he tried frantically to keep the troops in position. "Don't let them push us back! Keep up your fire!" But it was no use. Receiving fire from front and flank, man after man going down, the regiment was fast approaching its breaking point. Panicked soldiers began to melt away from the firing line, running toward the rear.

Colonel Merrow rode in among the milling throng. "Form up! Form your ranks, men! If we must retreat, in God's name don't let them see you run. Form up and we will retire in good order."

William and Sergeant Franklin began grabbing at the men around them. "Form up! Form up!" yelled Franklin. "You heard the colonel. We'll retreat, but we won't run!"

Henry blocked two terrified men with his musket. "Back in line, there! We'll go when the colonel says so."

A minie ball whined overhead, sending Merrow's hat spinning from his head. He leaned down to Fitzpatrick. "All right, Lieutenant, time to go. Have your men retreat, but slowly, firing as they go."

Fitzpatrick passed the orders on to his sergeants. What was left of the company retired in intervals, half the men firing while the other half fell back to load.

Loud cheering erupted from behind. "It's old Jube!" "Early's division is here to help!" Reinforcements were pushing into the breach, stopping the Federals in their tracks with rapid volleys. Now the advantage of weight was on the Confederate side. Slowly at first, then with more speed, the Union attackers were driven from the bog. As the Yankees drew back toward the town and river, Jackson's gunners opened up them again.

The First Georgia and other regiments resumed their original positions. Some men were immediately detailed to find and care for the wounded. Others were put to work digging in and throwing up breastworks, in case the Federals attacked again. As they worked, they could hear a rising crash of musketry and cannon fire off to their left. Henry wiped the back of his neck. "Sounds like Longstreet's giving 'em what for."

Lieutenant Fitzpatrick and Sergeant Franklin came striding up to the group. "Stop the work, men, and fall in. Jackson is going to counterattack. At twilight."

Henry's face betrayed his shock as he looked at William. "That man would attack heaven if he thought he could get in that way. It's suicide. Those Yank guns will chew us up."

Waving down Fitzpatrick, William said, "Lieutenant, sir, look what happened to the Yanks when they came across that field to us. You know the same thing will happen to us if we attack."

The Irishman laid his hand on William's shoulder. "I know, lad. But orders is orders. The general thinks we can push those bastards back into the river. Now get back to ranks and get ready. Keep your men off the paths. The artillery is going ahead of the line to soften them up."

As if on cue, several limbers came flying past, dragging their lethal cargo. About a hundred yards in front of the infantry, they pulled up, quickly going into battery. Before the guns were ready, though, Federal cannon opened up. Franklin swore. "Damn! They were supposed to surprise the Yanks, but they've been spotted."

William could see the scared look on Henry's face. "Jackson wants us to advance through *that*? We won't get fifty feet."

Clearly outmatched, the Confederate gunners nonetheless commenced returning the hot fire. Bursting from the tree line, a mounted courier galloped out to the artillery position. Handing a paper to the officer in charge, he wheeled his horse just as a shell burst beneath him, sending horse and rider flying. The officer threw down the paper, quickly barking orders. In an instant, the guns were limbered up again. They quickly withdrew to safety behind Jackson's troops.

An aide rode up, spoke to Fitzpatrick, then sped off down the line. The lieutenant came over to where the nervous soldiers stood waiting in ranks. "Stand the men down, Sergeant," he said to Franklin. "The attack has been called off." An audible sigh of relief rose from the company as they broke ranks.

Night finally put an end to the fighting. Northern and Southern soldiers alike attempted to get what sleep they could, but the constant screaming and moaning of wounded and dying men littering the field made slumber nigh unto impossible.

Throughout the next day sporadic gunfire was the norm as each side remained tensed. No attacks materialized, and as night fell once again over the bloody field, orders were received for the First Georgia to pull back for rest and to replenish its ammunition.

Just as Sergeant Franklin gave the order to break ranks, Henry pointed up to the darkening sky, a look of wonder on his face. "Hey, Willie, will you look at that!"

William turned to look upward. To the north, shimmering ribbons of light wove across the sky.

William was amazed by the spectacle. "What is that?"

"It's the northern lights," said Fitzpatrick, a touch of awe in his voice. "I've seen them before, but never this far south."

Colonel Merrow rode up to the group. "Look heavenwards, men. Look. It's a sign, an omen. God is truly on our side. He has given us a great victory, and now lights up the evening sky to show his approval. What more proof do you need, gentlemen, than this sign that God believes our cause to be just?"

The next morning after roll call, Lieutenant Fitzpatrick called for William. "Willie, boy, I need you to trot up to the quartermaster and draw ammunition for the company. Take a detail and get as much as they will let you have. Burnside may try to come across at us again, and the boys' cartridge boxes are just about empty."

Selecting five men, William proceeded toward the army's rear area. The quartermaster was inside a wagon busily writing in a notebook. Saluting, William said, "Need some cartridges, sir."

The officer didn't look up from his note taking. "What regiment?"

"First Georgia, sir."

"Well, you'll have to wait." The officer motioned with his pencil. "These wagons just came in. I have to finish this inventory before I can disperse any ammunition. Find you a fire to keep warm by. I'll call you when I'm ready."

William and his detachment searched around in a nearby forest for dry wood. Building a small fire, they unrolled their blankets, lying down to rest. William pulled out a piece of paper and began to write:

outside fredericksburg virginia
december 15 1862

dearest mother

I take pen in hand to write again the regiment is now quartered outside the town of fredericksburg we have just had a big battle with the yank army here but you will be happy to know that I have come out all right the yanks crossed the river on bridges made from

253

*planks laid over canvas boats their engineers are brave
fellows they were building the bridges while under fire
from our skirmishers the yanks tried to stop the
shooting by firing their big cannon on the town but it
didn't work our army was on the hills outside of town
the yanks finally got across the river and spent the
night in fredericksburg the next day they came out of
town and attacked us before they could step off major
pelham started shooting with just two cannon and
stopped them cold it was a sight to see with all the
yank guns trying to knock out two cannon they got one
but the other kept shooting til the major ran out of
ammunition then the yanks came at us*

*I will tell you mother it was a hot fight the yanks
kept coming and coming genril jacksons command was
on the right side of the line in a wooded place the
yanks got in among us but we were able to beat them
back over on the left side our boys were on a hill
behind a stone wall they shot down every yank before
they got close to the wall I felt sorry for the yanks
because their genrils were so stupid ordering them to
keep charging like that it was just murder they never
had a chance that night I couldn't sleep listening to all
the awful wailing and moaning coming from out on
that field we heard that a south carolina sargent up on
the hill had gone out with canteens to give the yanks a
drink a couple of the boys and I thought that was a
good idea so we went out to I held one mans head up
and gave him a drink after he swallowed it he looked at
me and said bless you then he died right while I was
holding him I remember thinking right then that
yanks really warnt bad fellas just old black hearted
lincoln wouldn't leave us alone and keep sending brave
men to get killed but I sure changed my mind when
the yanks pulled back across the river and we went into
the town they stole just about everything and what
they couldnt steal they wrecked there was broken
furniture and dishes all across the streets and places
where they had burned piles of books and other stuff
some of the folks that lived there said the yanks had
taken everything they owned*

well ma another christmas is coming and I am still far away from home I wish this war was over and I could come back home you please write soon please tell mary to write I havent heard anything from her in over two months when she does write she don't say much please send some new stockings and if you can spare them some needles and thread so I can fix up my trousers

your loving son
william

Chapter 38

Jedidiah McCay threw a handful of kindling into the pot-bellied stove before returning to his stool at the counter. The raw, gray day was keeping people out of his store, so McCay was taking advantage of the lack of customers to bring his ledger up to date. He looked up as the door opened; a cold wind whistled through as two people entered. A smile crossed his face as he recognized the ladies. "Why, Lucinda, what brings you into town on such a terrible January day?"

Lucinda and Melissa came up to the bench. "We needed a few things, and I wanted to see if any new casualty lists had come out. It's been almost a month since that terrible battle at Fredericksburg, and I haven't heard anything from William."

McCay reached up into his postal pigeonholes. "No new lists. But I think I do have something that will make you feel better." He handed her a worn envelope.

"From Willie?" Lucinda snatched the letter from his hand. "Oh, Jedidah, I'm sorry. That was rude, taking it from you like that."

The storekeeper studied his palm, a mock expression of pain on his face. "No harm done. Still got all my fingers." He grinned at her, then pointed at the letter. "Guess that proves he's all right."

Lucinda tore open the letter, wanting to get into it quickly but fearful that she would damage it in her haste. She read William's account of the battle first to herself, then aloud to Melissa and Jedidiah. Her eyes misted as she read of his wish for the war to be over and to come home.

Coming from behind the counter, McCay stepped behind Lucinda and wrapped both arms around her. She grasped his arm, grateful for his tender support. "Don't cry, Mama," said Melissa. "I know he'll be all right. I've got two pair of stockings knit for him. We'll send him a box right away. Mr. McCay, I'd like to buy some thread and needles to send. Do you have any coffee?"

"Got thread but not sure about needles." McCay gave Lucinda a quick hug. From a shelf, he pulled down a small packet. "Let's see. Ah, I still have a couple he can have. As for coffee, I'm afraid that's something I haven't been able to get hold of any for the past couple of months. Supplies of all kinds are getting in short supply. I've got some chicory you can take."

Lucinda pulled out her purse. "That will do just fine, Jedidiah. How much do we owe you for those things?"

McCay shook his head. "Consider it my contribution to the comfort of a lonely soldier. Besides, after a little bit you'll have part interest in this store anyways. Least wise, I hope it won't be much longer."

Lucinda wrapped her hands around Jedidiah's neck. "At least let me give you this in payment," she said as she gently pulling his head down towards hers. As they kissed, Melissa giggled.

The door opened. Isaac Stewart entered, shivering from the cold. Ice crystals sparkled on his coat. Jedidiah and Lucinda quickly broke their embrace, both slightly pink with embarrassment. Stewart did not seem to notice as he shuffled to the stove. Stretching out his hands toward the warmth, he rubbed them slowly to drive out the numbness.

"Getting worse out there by the minute, McCay. Ice starting to fall. I pretty near slipped on your steps."

Lucinda picked up her packages. "Then we should be getting on home."

Stewart shook his head. "Ice is building up fast on everything, Ma'am. Not safe out there for walking, let alone traveling. Especially with darkness setting in soon. You'd never make it home."

"Oh, dear, then what are we to do?"

Isaac removed his hat, sweeping it across his chest. "Mrs. Marsh, I would deem it a great honor if you would accept the shelter of my home this evening."

"That is very kind of you, Mr. Stewart, but I wouldn't think of imposing on you and Mary."

"Nonsense. It would be wonderful to have guests. We have had little chance for good conversation." Stewart pointed out the window. "And it would be much too dangerous for you to attempt to return home in weather like this."

McCay put a hand on Lucinda's shoulder. "He's right. You wouldn't get a mile. I think you should go with Mr. Stewart."

"But the animals. Who will feed them?"

"They'll be fine for one night," said McCay. "I tell you what. I'll come get you first thing in the morning. We'll all ride back to the farm together. Then I can help take care of your animals."

Melissa took her mother's arm, whispering in her ear. "Mother, I don't want to go there. I hate Mary."

258

Lucinda patted Melissa's hand. "We don't really have a choice, darling. One night shouldn't be so bad." She turned back toward Isaac. "Very well, Mr. Stewart. Melissa and I will accept your gracious generosity."

Stewart beamed. "Excellent, excellent. Jedidiah, would you please send for someone to take care of their buggy? Oh, before I forget . . . I stopped by to see if you have any mail."

"Nothing's come in since Monday." McCay shut the ledger. "Might as well close up. No one else will be coming out in this weather." He gave Lucinda a fond embrace. "I'll see to your buggy tonight, and I'll drop by Stewart's house first thing in the morning to pick you up."

"Don't worry, McCay. I'll take good care of them." Isaac motioned toward the door. "Ladies, please do be careful when you step outside. The ice is treacherous."

Stewart escorted Lucinda and Melissa with great care down the slippery streets to his house. The warmth that enveloped them as they entered felt wonderful.

Mary came rushing down the stairs as Stewart helped the ladies with their coats. "I heard voices, father. Who is it?" Seeing Lucinda, she reached out to give her a light hug. "Why, Mrs. Marsh. Melissa. What a pleasant surprise. Please, make yourself comfortable in the parlor. Uh, Father, can I talk to you for a moment?"

She prodded Isaac around the corner into a hallway. The gaiety exhibited for Lucinda quickly dissolved. "What are they doing here? You didn't tell me we were having company."

Stewart hung his coat on a peg. "This was not planned, my dear. The storm is preventing Mrs. Marsh and her daughter from returning home this evening, so I offered the hospitality of our house."

"But I'm not prepared to entertain." Mary's tone radiated exasperation. "Surely there's room at the hotel."

"And make those two ladies go back out in this weather? Certainly not! They are my friends, and our guests, and you will behave in a civil manner while they are here." Seizing Mary's arm, he leaned into her face. "Do you understand me?"

Mary swallowed hard to keep from crying out from the pain of Stewart's vice-like grip. "Y—y—yes, father, I understand."

Isaac shoved her away. "Good. Now why don't you prepare some refreshment for our guests? And for their sake, if not for mine, please try to be a proper young lady."

Gently rubbing her arm, Mary glared at her father for a moment. Stung by the animosity in her eyes, Stewart turned away, returning to the parlor.

Lucinda and Melissa were seated next to the fireplace. "I hope you ladies are comfortable," said Stewart.

Lucinda was rubbing her daughter's hands. "Yes, Isaac, thank you. Melissa, sweetheart, you're half frozen."

Stewart tossed a log into the fireplace. "That should help. Would you like a wrap, my dear?"

"Thank you, no, Mr. Stewart. I'm fine. You have such a lovely house."

"Getting a bit threadbare, I'm afraid. Not much money coming in right now. The freight company isn't very busy right now. Everything's getting so expensive, and those damnable Confederate dollars are fast becoming worthless. The blockade is more effective than those rascals up in Richmond would like to let on. The evils of secession are coming home to haunt us."

Trying to conceal her embarrassment, Lucinda stared into the flames. Noticing her distant look, Stewart said, "I am so sorry. I promise to make no more pronouncements."

Lucinda looked up at him and smiled. "That's quite all right, Isaac. I know you have strong feelings about what's happening."

"Yes, but I should not force my charming guests to listen to a sermon on my opinions. Let's talk about something much more pleasant. Have you and Jedidiah set a wedding date?"

"Actually, no, not yet. I want so much for William to be here, so I've been hoping against hope that this war won't last much longer, and he'll be able to come home." Her chest heaved with melancholy. "Jedidiah keeps pushing for me to change my mind. He wants to get married right away. But I'm just not ready yet."

"I understand. It's only natural that you would want all your family around you. Once Lincoln finds the right general, the Union Army will force the Rebels to capitulate. Then it won't be very long before William and Thomas can return home." He stopped. "Oh, my, I'm doing it again. My apologies."

Mary entered the parlor, carrying a silver tray holding cups and a kettle. "Would you like some coffee?" She poured a cup and handed it to Lucinda.

"Yes, thank you." Lucinda took a sip. She looked up in amazement. "Why, this is real coffee."

Mary almost seemed to take affront at Lucinda's remark. "Of course it is. What else would we be serving?"

"I apologize for my surprise. I was expecting chicory or something else. Jedidiah—Mr. McCay told me that he hasn't been able to get any coffee for quite some time."

"That's one advantage of Father's many trips with the shipping company. He's able to bring back some niceties that are hard to come by around here."

Melissa was excited. "We're putting a box together for William, and tried to get some coffee to put in it. Could we borrow some of yours to send to him?"

Isaac took a sip, then set his cup down. "Certainly, my dear, we would be glad to contribute."

"But, Father," said Mary, "We don't have that much left, and as Mrs. Marsh just said, we probably won't get any more for awhile."

One of Lucinda's eyebrows rose ever so slightly. "Why, Mary, I would think you of all people would want to do whatever you could to send a little comfort to William."

"Well, of course I want to do that. You know William means the world to me. It's just that, well, with supplies so scarce, I'm not sure how much longer we'll be able to get more."

The other eyebrow shot up. "That's all right. We'll send him the chicory."

Isaac stood, struggling to hold in the anger boiling within. "Mary, darling, go to the kitchen and bring a bag of coffee." Mary looked away, acting as though she had not heard. He started toward her. "Now, young lady."

Mary rose slowly. "Yes, *Father*. As long as it's for Willie, I'm sure we can spare some." She left the parlor, returning a few moments later with a small cloth bag. "Here. And please be sure to tell Willie where it came from, and that I'm thinking about him. Now, if you will excuse me, I think I shall retire for the evening. Goodnight, Mrs. Marsh. You, too, Melissa."

Stewart remained standing until Mary left the room. "I am so sorry, Lucinda. I just don't understand her anymore."

"It's quite all right. I know you've had your hands full." She stood, motioning to Melissa. "It is getting late. I think we should turn in also. Thank you again for your hospitality."

Stewart took Lucinda's hand. "You are very welcome. Your company is always appreciated. Good night."

As Lucinda prepared for bed, Melissa stared into the mirror, pouting. "Mother, can't we go somewhere else? I don't want to stay here with her."

"I wish we could, darling. But it's too late to go anywhere else. Don't worry. We're only spending one night. Jedidiah will be here in the morning to take us home. Let's get some sleep."

"But what if the storm doesn't let up?"

Lucinda slid under the covers. "If that happens, we will go to the hotel. Now come to bed."

The two visitors awoke to bright sunshine streaming through the window. Dressing, they descended the stairs to find Isaac waiting in the parlor with a pot full of coffee and cups enough for all. Taking a seat, Lucinda peered around. "Where's Mary?" she asked.

"Oh, she'll probably sleep late, as usual. Then she'll rush out to Lord knows where. I don't ask where she is going." A look of resignation crossed his face. "These days, I'm not sure I want to know what she's doing." Lucinda and Melissa exchanged a quick glance before accepting steaming cups.

Just then there was a rap on the door. McCay stamped his feet, then stepped into the foyer. "Much better this morning. The ice is already starting to melt away. Got your buggy out front. Your supplies are stowed, and I've got my horse tied on back. Shouldn't have any trouble getting out to the farm. You ladies ready?"

Lucinda gave him a peck on the cheek. "Yes, Jed. Melissa, would you please get our coats?" She held her hands out to Isaac. "Thank you ever so much for your hospitality. If there is anything that I can ever do for you, please don't hesitate to ask."

Taking her hands, Stewart nodded his head. "It was entirely my pleasure," he said.

Arriving at the farm, McCay pulled up in front of the porch. He helped Lucinda and Melissa down from the buggy. "Careful, still a little ice around. Lucinda, it's probably freezing in there. Why don't you start a fire while I unload your goods." Once Jedidiah finished bringing in the supplies, he proceeded to stable the horses.

Melissa was pouring hot water from a kettle into a washtub when McCay returned to the cabin. "I was going to do these dishes when we got back yesterday afternoon," she said.

Jedidiah looked around. "Where's your mother?"

"She's in her bedroom changing. We didn't have fresh clothes to put on this morning. She hates not having a clean set every day." Melissa picked up the tub, struggling with the weight.

"Here, let me." McCay took the tub from Melissa's hands, setting it on the table. Taking a seat, he watched as she submerged dishes in the water. "Haven't seen much of young Merrow around," he asked. "You and he still friends?"

"Course we are. Stephen comes over here as often as he can. But with his father and brother away in the army, he's got a lot of work to do over at Greenfield."

McCay leaned forward. "May I ask you something?"

Melissa continued to scrub intently on a platter. "Surely. What is it?"

"Has your mother said anything more about planning our wedding?"

Melissa stopped wiping for a moment as she stared at the plate. Giving McCay a quick glance, she resumed her washing. "Not a lot. I don't think you should press her on it, either."

Surprised, Jedidiah asked, "Why do you say that?"

"I don't know. She—she keeps saying she's not ready. I know she wants Willie and Thomas back here first. She's just not sure."

"What do you mean, 'not sure'?"

"I don't think she really knows what she wants. Whenever I've asked her about it, she just smiles and says we'll talk about it later."

McCay's face clouded. "You think she's 'not sure' about me?"

Melissa studied her reflection in the plate she had just washed. "I don't know. Really, I'm not the one to ask."

Emerging from the bedroom, Lucinda picked up her work apron. "My, what plots have you two been busy hatching?"

Jedidiah stood. "Melissa, would you excuse us for a bit. Your mother and I need to talk."

Drying her hands, Melissa reached for her shawl. "I'll see that the animals are all right."

The worried expression her daughter wore troubled Lucinda as she took her seat in her rocking chair by the fire. "What did you want to talk about, Jedidiah?"

Straddling the chair opposite hers, McCay leaned forward. "There's something that I need to know for certain." A moment's hesitation, then, "Do you love me?"

Startled, Lucinda raised her hand to her heart. "Why, of course. What a silly thing to ask."

"It's not so silly. Lately it seems like you're having second thoughts about marrying me."

"Whatever gave you that notion? You know that's not true."

"All right, then. Let's set a date for the wedding."

"Oh, Jed, you know we need to wait a while longer. I know Thomas probably won't be able to be here but it would be so grand if William could come home on leave."

Jedidiah leaned back in his chair. "His reenlistment was for the war. That means he stays with the army until the fighting is over. Look how long it's dragged on already. There's no end in sight."

"But the army has won so many battles. Surely the war won't last much longer."

McCay threw up his hands. "General Lee has prevailed, but the western armies are not doing very well. The North outnumbers us three to one. They have more heavy industry than we do. They can recover from defeats much faster than we can. This next year will probably decide what happens. If Lee or Bragg can't destroy their armies, then our cause will fail. If that happens, the hardships we face now will seem like a trifle compared to what the Yanks will do to us."

"You make it sound as though . . . as though we were going to lose."

"Unless something changes drastically for the better, and soon, I'm afraid that's just what is going to happen." He leaned forward again. "If the worst does come, I want to have you near so that I can protect you. You and Melissa."

Lucinda put her hand on his cheek. "You are such a sweet, caring man."

Jedidiah reached up, gently but firmly taking her hand, carrying it down so to grasp it with his other hand. "So answer me honestly. Do you want to get married or not?"

"Of course I do. I just want as much of my family around me as I can have. It's important to me. Can't you understand that?"

"Yes, I understand. I want William here, too. But it could be months or even years before he can come home again."

"Please, Jed. Please be patient with me. Our time will come."

"Are you sure? I'm beginning to have doubts that you really want to get married."

Lucinda tugged her hands from Jedidiah's grip. "What? How can you say such a thing? You're not being fair."

"*I'm* not being fair?" McCay jumped to his feet. "Lucinda, I want to marry you. I've wanted to for a long time. But you keep stringing me along, not willing to commit to a date. Is that it? Are you not willing to make a commitment? Or are you still pining for Aaron?"

It was several seconds before Lucinda broke the tense silence, her voice barely audible.. "I think maybe you should leave, Jedidiah." She closed her eyes, not able to look at him. "Maybe we both need time to think things through."

"Time? I don't need more time." Jedidiah picked up his coat, then walked over to the door. Opening it, he stood for a moment gazing at her. "But I guess you do. Very well, Lucinda. I'll leave you be. I've waited for you this long. I guess I can wait a while longer. But you've got to make up your mind."

The door closed. Opening her eyes, she turned to the fireplace, watching but not really seeing the flames leaping in the hearth. Shocked by the unexpected turn of events, she leaned forward, covering her face with her hands as she began to sob.

Chapter 39

HO! FOR THE ARTILLERY!
VOLUNTEERS NEEDED!

1st NEW HAMPSHIRE LIGHT ARTILLERY
BATTERY F
Serving In the Field with the Glorious
Army of the Potomac!

Now is the time to heed your country's call!
The command has been in active service since the beginning of the
Rebellion.

$150 BOUNTY
To be paid at time of enlistment!

Thomas scrutinized the recruiting broadside. Smaller print described how the unit had covered itself with glory on battlefields throughout Virginia. The line about the bounty was particularly interesting. *That bounty money would sure help out Uncle Benjamin.*

From behind boomed a gruff voice. "Well, if it ain't our local Rebel!"

Offended, Thomas slowly and deliberately wheeled, ready for confrontation. A few paces away stood a soldier, his face lit by a wide grin. Raising his hand, he said, "Now hold on, Thomas. You ain't goin' to hit an old friend now, are you?"

Thomas looked close at the man's face, then laughed. "Why, Bill Stokes, you old jackass! When did you get back in town?"

"Been home for three weeks. Helping Lieutenant Ferrell with recruiting."

"I never would have recognized you in that outfit. Oh, my, just look at those stripes. Now why would the army ever make you a sergeant?"

Stokes held up his arm, rubbing the chevrons with obvious pride. "Why, I'm a most valued man in the battery." He pointed at the poster. "You thinking 'bout enlisting?"

Thomas rubbed his chin. "Maybe someday."

"We could use you, as long as—."

"As long as what?"

The sergeant frowned. "Well . . . um . . . Oh, hell. How're you doing with staying . . . dry?"

Annoyed, Thomas hesitated a moment before answering. "Haven't had a drink in over a year, other than an occasional beer. I'm as sober as the next man."

"Sorry, Thomas. Had to ask." Stokes took off his hat. "Like I started to say, we could certainly use a good man. Haven't had many takers, even with the bounty. We have to head back to the army in a few days. Spring campaign going to start soon."

Thomas let out a loud breath. "I've been pondering on it for quite awhile. But I'm not sure this is the right time. Several things to consider. Besides, I don't know anything about artillery."

Stokes laughed. "Not to worry. We can teach you all that. Seriously, I'd like to you to consider joining up with us. We've got a real good bunch. Everyone watches out for each other."

"Sounds interesting," said Thomas, "but I can't commit right now. Too many irons in the fire."

"Well, if you change your mind, come see me." Stokes slapped his hat back on, then extended his hand to Thomas. "We'll be here 'til the end of the week."

"I'll keep that in mind." Thomas replied as he shook Stokes's hand. "If I don't see you before you go, good luck. Take care of yourself."

After supper, Thomas and his uncle sat in the parlor discussing the war. "I've heard that many officers have resigned their commissions," said the preacher. "Lincoln's proclamation has angered many in the army. They say they enlisted to preserve the Union, not to free slaves."

Thomas nodded. "There will be a few that will leave, but I believe the vast majority will stay the course. Many of them did enlist with the idea of freeing slaves."

"That's true. I know one thing. The Confederacy will never get recognition now from England. Those folks abhor slavery. There were many Britons who were enraged about Parliament granting belligerent rights to the South. Now that Lincoln has raised this struggle to a higher plane, they will most likely reconsider any formal acceptance of the existence of the Confederate States."

Lighting his pipe, Marsh puffed out a large smoke ring, then continued. "I think there will be many others who will enlist now. And at some point, Lincoln is going to have to accept ex-slaves and freedmen into the army."

"That would infuriate the South."

"What of it? Just think of the thousands of black men who would leap at the chance to serve. With their tremendous numbers we would overwhelm the Southern armies. Alas, I'm afraid it will be some time yet before Congress will be persuaded to let negro enlistment come to pass. In the meantime, more and more men will be called to do their duty." Marsh took another pull on his pipe as he looked intently at his nephew. "I know you've been thinking about enlisting."

Thomas sank back in his chair. "The thought is always in my mind. It's overwhelming sometimes. I feel as though the greatest event in my lifetime is leaving me behind. But it's so confusing. Here I am, Southern born, and considering joining the army that is invading my birthplace."

"You may have been born in the South, but I would say that you've taken Northern ideals to heart."

"I'm not so sure."

"My boy, look at your convictions. You're against slavery, are you not?"

"Of course."

"And you feel that secession is wrong, correct?"

"Yes."

"Those two answers tell the tale. You believe in what the Union Army is fighting for. Look at President Lincoln. He was born in Kentucky. His wife's family owns slaves. Yet he is leading the nation toward reunification and abolition."

Thomas knew his uncle was right. Yet the fact that his brother was fighting for the South gnawed at him. "I hear what you say. I still have doubts, though. I've got to work those out before I could enlist with a clear conscious."

"I respect that. What's more, I applaud you for it. If more people had reasoned things out before they jumped, this war would never have begun."

The preacher shifted in his chair. "I don't know if this will help with your decision, but there is something I want you to know. Your aunt and I have discussed the possibility of your enlisting. It is our wish that you do what you think is best for yourself. If you decide to join the army, you have our blessing."

"Thank you, sir. I appreciate that. I did run into Bill Stokes in town today. You remember Bill—worked at the apothecary before he signed up. He's a sergeant of artillery now—asked me to join his unit."

"So what did you tell him?"

"I said that I couldn't right now. Too many things going on here."

"Such as courting a certain young lady?"

Thomas could not suppress a smile. "Yeah, that could have something to do with it."

"What about her uncle?"

"It's easier with him gone. I've been able to see a lot more of her since he won the election and went off to Washington."

"So how does he feel about the two of you . . . being seen together?"

"I'm not certain, to be honest. I've avoided him as much as possible since the shooting incident. But I'm sure he hasn't forgotten. I've had the uneasy feeling that he's been using Constable Mattson to keep an eye on me." An involuntary shiver convulsed through Thomas's body. "I can't seem to go anywhere in town without that fellow watching me. It's as though he's just waiting for any little opportunity to get me back in that jail of his. The man hates me, for no other reason but because I'm from the South. I wouldn't put it past him to manufacture some bogus charge."

Marsh took another pull on his pipe, then blew another smoke ring. "Be careful of that man, Thomas. He's been known to bend the law to suit his own needs. Or for his benefactors. It amazes me sometimes that he hasn't been turned out of office. But there are many in this community who applaud his heavy-handed tactics. Some people would give up most of their rights to have even a little security."

The next day, Thomas knocked at the Carroll home. The housekeeper answered the door. "Good day, Mr. Marsh. Please come in. Miss Stephanie is expecting you."

Thomas handed her his coat. "Thank you, Harriet. In the parlor, as usual?"

Though trying to maintain a deadpan appearance, Harriet's eyes betrayed a twinkle as she hung the coat on a peg. "Of course, sir."

Stephanie was sipping tea as Thomas entered the room. "Your housekeeper believes we're keeping closer company than we really do."

"What makes you think so?"

"Every time I've come by lately, she greets me with a rather mysterious smile. Like she imagines she knows something about the two of us. You been telling her stories?"

"Why, Mr. Marsh. Whatever would I be telling her? It's not like you and I have been . . . intimate." She set the cup down, then turned and patted the settee seat. "Of course, we could remedy that." She giggled.

Thomas sat down beside her. "You are such a wicked woman, my dear." He gazed at her. "But you shouldn't say such things. You know how much I want you."

She took his hand. "I know. I want you, too. Sometimes it's more than I can bear. But we both know we can't. Not yet. Not until Uncle Charles learns to accept that we love each other."

"Fat chance of that ever happening."

"Miracles do happen, my love."

Thomas shook his head. "He'll never get past the fact of my being born in Georgia. And, of course, there's the little problem of me having shot him."

"That was an accident. One that he brought on himself. And where one is born does not make them either good or bad."

Thomas grimaced. "Tell that to the townspeople. You'd think I had cholera, the way I'm avoided. Hardly anyone ever says two words to me. Before the war, there were only a handful of people in town that tolerated me. Even fewer now. Just by chance, I did run into one person today who didn't act like I was beneath contempt."

"Who's that?"

"Bill Stokes. He was one of the few friends I had. Now he's in the army. In town to do some recruiting."

"Recruiting?" Stephanie's expression suddenly displayed alarm.

"Yeah. We talked for a bit. He wanted to sign me up for his unit."

"And just what did you say?" A sharp edge had crept into her voice.

Thomas took a moment before he answered. "I wished him luck. Actually, I told him that I had too many commitments right now. He told me he'd be in town a few more days, if I changed my mind."

Stephanie slipped her hand from his. "Honestly, Thomas, I don't understand you. We've talked about this before."

"Now, wait. I just said that I couldn't right now."

"But you want to. I can see it in your face. You know I don't want you to go. You don't have to. You're from Georgia. Your brother is in the Confederate Army. And *you* want to enlist in the Union Army."

"I realize all those facts. But you know I never believed secession was right. And you know of my work with the anti-slavery group. Before Antietam, I didn't consider the possibility of enlisting. I wouldn't have joined up just to preserve the Union, even believing secession was wrong. But Lincoln's Emancipation Proclamation has changed things. Now there is a new purpose to the war. Like Uncle Benjamin says, now we have a chance to end slavery for all time."

"I think your uncle has been pushing you. He's always been a fanatical abolitionist. He can't go into the army himself, and he has no son to send, so he wants you to be his surrogate to go fight for his principles."

Rising, Thomas crossed over to the fireplace. "If I go, it's because I want to, not because of his wishes."

"Oh, really? He has more influence over you than you realize."

"Please, let's not argue about this." Keeping his back to her, he pretended to inspect a porcelain eagle sitting on the mantle. "I haven't made up my mind yet."

Stephanie stood. "I don't want to argue." She walked over to him. "I just don't want to lose you. So many men have died already in this awful war." He turned to her. She wrapped her arms around his neck. "I love you. Don't you know that?"

Thomas caressed her cheek. "Yes, I do. I love you, too."

Her eyes began to mist. "You intend to enlist, don't you."

"I can't lie to you. I probably will. Not right away, but soon. I feel I have to." He leaned to her. Their lips met in a long and passionate kiss.

Parting, they gazed into each other's eyes for several moments. "Mr. Marsh," said Stephanie softly.

"Yes?"

She fingered one of his shirt buttons. "I would very much like to apply that remedy I spoke of earlier." A quick movement undid the button.

Thomas's cheeks began to burn. "I—uh—oh, my goodness. Steph, darling, we shouldn't do this."

Stephanie took his hand. "Yes, we should."

"But—what you said just a few minutes ago about waiting."

Taking his hand and raising it to her breast, she said, "Just now, when we kissed, I realized something. You are going to go, whether or not I want you to. You may never come back. If that were to happen, I would never forgive myself for not taking every chance to love you in every way." Backing up slightly, she tugged at his hand. "It's time for us." She led him out of the parlor and up the stairs.

Harriet was passing through the entrance hall when the click of a closing door caught her attention. Glancing up the stairs, she smiled, then continued on toward the kitchen.

The peace officer stopped on his beat to rewrap his shawl. Finally satisfied with the way it covered his neck, he reached down to pick up his lantern and continue his walk. Further up the street, a sudden flicker of light caught his attention. He could just make out someone standing in the darkness next to a tree. Pulling a pistol, he hastened toward the shadowy figure. "You, there! What are you doing? Don't move!"

From the gloom came a hiss. "Shut up, damn you. You'll rouse the whole neighborhood."

Raising his lamp, the officer nearly dropped his revolver upon recognizing the man before him. "Beg pardon, Constable. Didn't realize it was you."

Mattson took a strong drag from his cigar. "All right. Just get out of here with that lantern. I'm working on a confidential investigation."

The policeman nodded, then continued on up the street. Leaning against the tree, Mattson drew his coat tight as he intently watched the moving figures silhouetted behind the windows of Charles Carroll's house.

Chapter 40

Shortly after sunrise the next morning, while Thomas and Stephanie slumbered in each other's arms, Harriet was downstairs donning her hat and shawl as she prepared for her weekly trip to the general store. Browsing the market shelves, her eyes fastened on a stack of tinned peaches. *That would be something nice. I can mix those up in a cobbler.* Reaching for a can, she was suddenly aware of a presence behind her. A tap on her shoulder almost caused her to drop her basket. Anxiety mounting, she slowly turned.

"Miss Arnold?" It was Constable Mattson.

"Yes," she replied with a whispered squeak.

"I would like you to come with me to my office."

Now truly frightened, Harriet retreated a step. "But why? I haven't done anything."

"I didn't say you had, now did I, my dear? I'm conducting an investigation, and I need to ask you a few questions."

"I don't know anything. I'm just a house servant," she said, trying to move past the constable. "I have to get back to my chores."

Mattson grasped her arm, stopping her. "Your chores can wait. You're coming with me right now." Tightening his grip, he forced her toward the door.

Less than ten minutes later, she was seated in Mattson's office, her apprehension growing as he sat staring at her across his wide desk. After what seemed like an eternity, he finally spoke. "You're the housekeeper at Congressman Carroll's house, aren't you?"

"Yes, sir."

"So you see pretty much everything that goes on there?"

"I guess so."

"All right, then. I'm going to ask you some questions, and I want straight answers. If I don't get them, I'll see to it that Carroll discharges you. You'll not be able to find work anywhere in this county. Do I make myself clear, Miss Arnold?"

Terror shone in the housekeeper's eyes. "Yes, sir. Perfectly clear, sir."

Standing, he came around the desk toward her. "Very good. Now, have you seen Thomas Marsh in Mr. Carroll's house?"

"Yes, sir."

"Does he come there often?"

"Yes, sir. 'Bout once or twice a week."

"Does he stay the night?"

Harriet swallowed hard. Her eyes moved around the room.

"Look at me, Miss Arnold!" She turned her head back toward Mattson. "I asked you a question!" he said. "Does he stay the night?"

"Not every time."

Mattson circled the chair. "Ah, so some of the time he does stay all night, isn't that true?"

"Y—yes, sir."

"Does he go to her room?"

"Oh, please, Mr. Constable, please! Miss Stephanie is a good girl."

Mattson stopped in front of her. Leaning forward, his face inches from hers, he glared into her eyes. "Answer the question! *Does he go to her room?*"

The housekeeper was so frightened now that she could not control her sobs. Tears streamed down her cheeks as she answered. "J—just once. Last night."

The constable stood, turning his back to Harriet so she would not see his smirk. "Very well, Miss Arnold. That will be enough. You can go now." As she rose, he grabbed her by the arm. "Understand this. If you say anything to Miss Carroll about this little interview, I will follow through on my threat. Do you understand?"

"Yes, sir, I understand. I won't say a word."

"Good. Now get out of here."

Harriet fled out the door. Mattson watched through the window as she ran up the street, then sat down at his desk. Pulling out a sheet of paper, he began to write:

> *Congressman Charles Carroll, esq.*
> *Washington City*
>
> *My dear sir,*
>
> *I wish to inform you that your fears concerning our mutual Southern friend have been corroborated. My sources have confirmed Mr. Marsh has been spending time in your house in dalliance with your niece. I am prepared, on your say so, to take steps that would end this unfortunate incident. I am certain that the proper charges could be found which would put our mutual*

friend away for such time that would enable your niece to forget his existence. I await your instructions.

I am, sir, your obedient servant.
Alvin Mattson, Town Constable

Folding the message, Mattson strolled over to the telegraph station. The operator waved to him as he came in the door. "How's it goin', Alvin?"

"As well as could be expected, Eli. Need to get a wire off, quick. To Washington."

"Washington, you say? Must be important."

"Extremely important." The constable pulled out the paper. "Here." He handed it to Eli.

The operator scanned the message, then looked up at Mattson with an expression of concern. "This is pretty indelicate. You sure you want to send this to the congressman?"

"Very sure." Mattson leaned across the counter. "And I would appreciate it if you didn't breathe a word of this to anyone."

Eli sat down at his telegraph. "Alvin, you know better than that. I don't spill nothin' about anyone's wires. Don't worry, I'll keep mum. But this is shameful stuff." The operator began clacking away on the key.

Less than a week later, Stephanie adjusted her bonnet, then inspected herself in the foyer mirror. Harriet Arnold was busy dusting in the parlor. Stephanie peeked around the corner. "I'm going down to the market, Harriet. Do you need anything?"

"No, ma'am," replied the housekeeper, her voice betraying a slight quiver.

Suddenly concerned, Stephanie entered the parlor. "Are you all right, Harriet? You've been so quiet the last few days."

Harriet did not look up. "I'm . . . fine. Just fine."

The tone of her housekeeper's voice worried Stephanie. "I'm not so certain. Why don't you take the rest of the afternoon off and rest. There's nothing that really needs doing around here."

"Yes, ma'am." Harriet set the duster down. "Thank you, ma'am. I do believe I'll just go lie down for awhile."

Concerned, Stephanie watched her as she slowly climbed the stairs to her room. *What is wrong with that woman? I think we'll have a nice long talk later.*

277

Stepping outside to her waiting carriage, she was pleased to note that the stableman had placed a board on the ground to protect her from melting snow and mud. She looked up. A few wispy clouds floated lazily across a deep blue sky. The warmth of the sun felt good on her face. *I am so glad that winter is coming to an end.* Stepping into the carriage, she pointed the horse toward the street.

Passing the jail, she noticed a familiar boy peering in the window. Reining her horse to a stop, she called out to him. "What are you looking for, Jeremy?"

"Got a wire for the constable. Looks like he's not around. I tried the door. It's locked. Maybe I should just slip this underneath." He held up an envelope.

Struck by a disquieting sense of dread, Stephanie beckoned to Jeremy. "Let me see it."

He stepped down from the walkway, handing the wire to her. She held the envelope up to the light. "Who's it from?"

"Some bigwig in Washington. Congressman Carroll, I think it said."

Stephanie caught her breath. "Why, Jeremy, that's my uncle. You remember Uncle Charles, don't you? Tell you what, let me keep this. I'll be sure the constable gets it. I see him around all the time."

"I don't know 'bout that. I was supposed to give that direct to Mr. Mattson."

"Oh, don't worry." Stephanie slid the paper into her pocketbook, from which she drew two shiny coins. "I'll give him the message. Here, this is a tip for you. Why don't you go buy some candy?"

Jeremy grabbed the money out of her hand. "Gee, thanks, Ma'am." He dashed off down the street.

Glancing about to make certain that they had not been seen, Stephanie tore open the envelope. Her apprehension rising, she read the message:

My dear Constable Mattson,

I wish to thank you for your continued reports concerning my niece. Your last wire was most disturbing. It would seem that Stephanie is taking advantage of my absence to dally with that rebel scoundrel. These liaisons must be stopped. I desire that you might find some way to separate these two. I do not wish to know the details. I wish this to be accomplished as swiftly as possible. Please advise when success is achieved.

Yours,
Charles Carroll, etc.,
Congress of the United States

Oh, my God. She reread the words several times, not believing what she was seeing. It was now obvious that her uncle's hatred of Thomas was more than she had ever imagined. *I've got to warn him.*

Lashing the horse, she directed the buggy down the road toward the Marsh farm, its wheels spinning a shower of snow and mud.

James Stark was leading a horse from the barn when Stephanie came careening into the yard. "Heavens, Miss Carroll, you look an absolute fright. What is the matter?"

Stephanie jumped out of the buggy, running up to Stark. "Oh, James, where is Thomas? I have to warn him."

"He's in the barn. Warn him about what?"

Without answering, she hurried past him toward the barn door. "Thomas! Thomas, please where are you?"

Thomas emerged, wiping his hands with a towel. "Steph! What's wrong?"

She tried to explain, but could only stammer out a few words. "Uncle Charles—danger—arrest you."

Thomas put his arms around her. "Arrest me? Who? Mattson?"

Stark came up beside them. "She's frantic. Come on, let's get her up to the house."

Thomas and James helped her to a seat in the parlor. Rebecca brought her a cup of strong tea, which she accepted gratefully. Pastor Marsh sat in his big chair while the others took seats around the excited girl. "Now what's this all about? What's troubling you?"

Stephanie emptied the cup before answering. "I'm so sorry for being rude, barging in here like this. But I had to warn him." She reached out to Thomas, who grasped her hand gently.

"Warn me about what?" he said with mounting concern.

She swallowed hard. "My uncle and the constable are conspiring to have you locked away. And it's because of me."

Pastor Marsh leaned forward. "What do you mean, my child?"

Stephanie produced the wire. "Here, read this." She handed it to Thomas. "I intercepted this today."

Thomas read the message, then passed it to his uncle. "I told you he was planning something."

Marsh scanned the wire, then looked up at Stephanie. "You say Mattson hasn't seen this yet?"

"No. He wasn't at his office when the delivery boy brought it by. I convinced Jeremy to give it me. So he doesn't know about it."

James spoke up. "Unless the boy says something to Mattson. Even if he doesn't, if Carroll doesn't get an answer back fairly soon, he'll send another message." He glanced at Thomas. "Either way, it won't be long before he's after you faster'n a hound after a fox."

Thomas was staring at the floor. Slowly he raised his head. "Then I have to leave now. Get away from here. Else Mattson will make trouble for all of you."

Rebecca's face betrayed her alarm. "But where would you go?"

Thomas shrugged. "I have no idea. This came on too sudden."

"I have a thought," said Marsh. "Didn't you say your friend— Stokes—was leaving for the army in a few days?"

"Yeah, he's going out on the train tomorrow morning. Why?"

Marsh leaned back. "If you enlist, and go with Stokes, Mattson won't be able to touch you."

A tense silence filled the air for several moments before Thomas rose to his feet. "You're right, Uncle Benjamin. It's the only way. I'll go to see him."

Stephanie took his arm. "You can't go to town now. It's too dangerous. What if Jeremy does talk to the constable?"

"She's got a point, Thomas," said his uncle. Marsh thought for a moment. "Stephanie, you stay here this evening. In the morning, you'll take Thomas right to the station. If you can get him there just before the train leaves, there's a good chance he'll be long gone before Mattson gets any more messages from Carroll."

James let out a whoop and clapped Thomas on the shoulder. "Tomorrow we'll all go in with you."

Marsh turned to him. "No. If we all come into town together, it might draw too much attention. We'll say our good-byes in the morning before he leaves. Thomas, you'd better get your things together."

Well before sunrise, James had the buggy hitched and ready to go. On the porch, Thomas gave Rebecca a hug, then shook his uncle's hand. "Thank you all for everything. You have been so kind to me, and have stood by me every time I fell. You'll never know how much you've meant."

Marsh draped his hand over Thomas's shoulder. "Good luck, my boy. I know you will come back to us, safe and sound. The Lord's blessing be upon you." He stepped back. "Now, go on. You can't afford to be late for this train."

Thomas helped Stephanie into the carriage, then turned to shake James' hand. "I'm going to miss you, friend. I'm glad you'll be here to help Uncle Benjamin with the farm."

James gave Thomas's hand a hard squeeze. "Glad to do it. Who knows, maybe you'll see me in the army before very long. Can't let you have all the fun."

Thomas climbed into the seat next to Stephanie. Giving a final wave to his aunt and uncle, he turned the horse toward the road.

Bill Stokes looked at his watch. "Train leaves in just about fifteen minutes, sir," he said to a seated officer reading a paper.

He was lazily glancing about the platform when a familiar voice caught his attention. "Hey, Bill, don't leave without me."

He looked down the platform. "Why, I don't believe it. Thomas!"

Stephanie and Thomas were striding toward him. "I've decided to take you up on your invitation," said Thomas.

"Well, I'm delighted—but a bit puzzled. Why the change of mind so soon? And who is this beautiful creature on your arm?"

Stephanie blushed. After introducing her, Thomas explained the circumstances of his coming. Stokes turned to the officer. "Lieutenant, did you hear all that?"

The lieutenant rose. "I did." He tipped his hat to Stephanie. "Your servant, Ma'am. First Lieutenant Ferrell." Then he reached out to shake hands with Thomas. "Seems like you need refuge. The place you're going to is not the safest place to disappear into. Are you absolutely certain this is the right thing to do?"

"Don't figure I have a real choice at this point."

"I see what you mean. Are you set to travel?"

"Got a bag packed with all my traps. I'm ready to go now."

"Excellent!" Undoing the straps on a well-worn leather case, Lieutenant Ferrell withdrew several sheets of paper. "Just need to have you sign enlistment papers, then take the oath." He motioned to the man inside the ticket window. "Let me borrow an inkwell and pen for a moment."

Thomas signed the forms where directed by Ferrell. The lieutenant folded the pages, then returned them carefully into his case. "Now, sir, I need to give you the oath. Raise your right hand."

Thomas lifted his hand, repeating the pledge to preserve and defend the Constitution of the United States. Once he had completed the oath, Stokes clapped him on the back. "Congratulations, Private Marsh. You are now a member of the grand old Army of the Potomac."

Lieutenant Ferrell shook Thomas's hand. "Glad to have you, Marsh. Now, quick, say your good-byes to this lovely lady. The train will be leaving any minute now and we've got to get on board."

"Just a minute, Marsh."

The four turned to see Constable Mattson striding onto the platform, his hand resting on the butt of a holstered pistol. "Lieutenant, this man is under arrest."

"What are the charges?" said Ferrell.

"None of your concern, soldier. This is a civil matter. I'd appreciate it if you'd stay out of it."

Stokes stepped forward, stealthily unsnapping his holster. "Hold up, mister. You got a warrant for him?"

Mattson made a show of caressing the pistol stock. "Got a judge working on one now."

The lieutenant spoke up. "Oh, so you don't have a warrant with you at this moment?"

"Had to get here before this fellow got away. Don't worry, I'll have it by the time we get back to the jail. Now step back and don't interfere." He reached out to take Thomas' arm.

"I don't think so," said Stokes, pulling his revolver and leveling the weapon at Mattson. "I think you're the one who'd better back off." He glanced at Ferrell, who nodded.

The lieutenant drew his own pistol. "This man is now a soldier in the United States Army, Mister Policeman, or whatever you are. You are trying to take him without possessing a proper warrant. You can send your request through military channels once you have that warrant, but for now you have no legal standing. So I suggest you withdraw before I have *you* arrested for interfering with military personnel." Glancing at Thomas, he motioned toward the cars with his gun. "Quick, man, kiss the girl, then get on that train."

Down the platform the conductor was yelling for all passengers to board. Black smoke billowed from the engine's stack as the engineer blew the whistle. Stephanie threw her arms around Thomas. "You take care of yourself. And don't you dare get hurt. If you do I'll never speak to you again!"

Stokes and Ferrell grinned widely at each other as Thomas and Stephanie kissed. The lieutenant reached out, tapping Thomas on the shoulder. "All right, boy, let her go and get on board." He holstered his revolver. "Sergeant, make sure our friend here stays put until the train leaves." He turned to Stephanie. "Good day to you, Ma'am. Don't worry, we'll take good care of him." Taking up his case, he stepped up into the rail car.

Stokes motioned to Thomas. "Go on. I'll be right there."

Thomas gave Stephanie another quick kiss. "I'll write, just as soon as I can. Say goodbye to Uncle Benjamin and Aunt Rebecca. Tell the preacher that I'll send him the bounty money once I get it." Picking up his bag, he disappeared into the car.

Stephanie ran along the side of the train, desperately trying to see in through the windows. Spotting Thomas inside, she reached up to rap on the glass. Thomas raised the sash, reaching down to take her hand. "I'll be fine. Don't worry."

The sergeant waved his pistol at Mattson. "Now why don't you just pull that gun out real slow. Use your fingers." Mattson's expression was akin to someone who had just consumed a rotten egg. Carefully, he grasped the pistol butt with his thumb and forefinger, drawing it from the holster. Stokes gestured with his revolver. "Now toss it over in those bushes."

The train began to move as the constable flung his pistol. His own gun still pointed at Mattson's belly, the sergeant hopped up on the rail car's steps. "Thanky, sir. Better luck next time."

Snorting in disgust, Mattson headed for the landing steps to retrieve his gun from the underbrush. Stephanie followed alongside the car as far as the end of the platform. As the train left the station behind, she gave a faint wave. *Be safe, my love.*

Chapter 41

Dahlonega, Georgia
May 22, 1863

My Dearest William,

It is with a grateful heart that I write to you, secure in the knowledge that you have come unharmed through yet another battle. We as well as the rest of the country grieve with you at the loss of our great leader General Jackson at Chancellorsville. I have said many prayers for his wife and infant child. How can our nation prevail when such men are taken from us?

Melissa and I were gratified to learn from your last letter that you received the box with only a few things missing. I wish you had gotten the bag of coffee. There is no more to be had in the entire county.

In answer to your question about Mary, I have had little contact with her since the night we stayed at her house in late winter. At the time I invited her to put a letter in with the box. She said that she didn't have time to write one just then, but would send you one soon. I have no reason to believe that she has not tried to write to you. The mail is very slow these days and sometimes letters do disappear. I have seen her occasionally in town but she has always been occupied, so I have not been able to ask her if she has written.

Melissa is beside herself with fear. Young Stephen Merrow has enlisted in the army and she is frantic.

Yes, my dear son, Mister McCay and I still plan to wed. He has been somewhat impatient but he has agreed to wait for a while longer until you might be able to come home. It would be so grand to have you here to share our moment of happiness. You have been away from home so long. Might it not be possible that the army would grant you a leave to come home?

Colonel Merrow is such a good man. I am sure that if you asked he would let you come. Mister McCay and I will start making our plans the moment that we know that you are on your way.

Your Loving Mother

"Sergeant Marsh."

William looked up from the letter to see Gerald Fitzpatrick brushing dust from his sleeves as he approached. Recently promoted to captain, Fitzpatrick now commanded Company H.

"Yes, sir?"

"Time to get the men up and moving." He slapped the front of his tunic, raising a cloud of fine particles. "Damnable stuff. Gets into everything. Didn't think Pennsylvania could be this hot and dry."

William stuffed the pages into his haversack as he rose. "We've marched quite a ways all ready this morning. How far we going?"

"The general wants to make Wrightsville by noon, so we've got to get moving. Bridge there we have to take."

Less than ten minutes later, the brigade was trudging up the road. As they shuffled along in the late June warmth, Henry chattered on about every topic imaginable, from fresh cherries in the trees to the dust in the road. Feeling drowsy in the heat and not interested in conversation, William tried to ignore him.

Vexed with his friend's silence, Henry poked him on the arm. William glowered. "What'd you do that for?"

"Just wanted to see if you were awake. You haven't said two words since we got going. You been reading that letter again?"

"And just what makes you think that?"

"That scowl. Every time you've pulled that letter out to read, your face gets all screwed. . . up. Ah—ah—atchoo!" Henry's hand shot to his nose, but too late to stifle an enormous sneeze. "God-damn dust."

Shrugging, William replied, "Yeah, you're right. Ma wants me to come home to be there when she and Mr. McCay get married. Says I should ask the colonel for leave."

Henry wiped his dripping nose on his jacket sleeve, then let out a snicker. "Don't think there's any possibility of that right now."

"Yeah." William tugged on his blanket to adjust its position. "Ma says she hasn't talked to Mary. What's worse, I haven't gotten any mail from her in months. Something must be wrong. I need to send her another letter."

286

"You should've written before we left Virginia. It's a little late now. I don't think the folks here in Pennsylvania will post one for you."

"I know. I started a letter the day we left, but Franklin said I might as well put it up. He must have already known we were getting ready to pull out, but he wasn't going to let on. I just wish I knew what was going on back home. Has your ma said anything in her letters?"

"Ah—atchoo!" Henry again drew his sleeve across his nose. "All she talked about in her last letter was about that stupid brother of mine enlisting. First she goes on about how proud she is of him, then she practically cries onto the paper about being afraid she'll never see her husband and sons again. Next she wrote some drivel about the Ladies Aid Society and how she can't get any coffee or sugar. Never says anything about the people in town."

William yawned. "I can't sleep thinking about it. Keeps me awake all night."

"It's that dream of yours that keeps me up," said Henry with a note of exasperation. "Seems like you've been crying out just about every night lately."

"I have the nightmare all the time now. Last night was a really bad one. This time there were lightning bolts all around. You were in it again—got clobbered by one, right between your eyes. Another hit and my hand disappeared."

Henry shuddered. "You still see that dark rider?"

"Yeah, that part was just the same."

"So how were you able to shoot him with one hand gone?" Henry grinned.

William didn't think the remark was at all funny. "Hell, I don't know. It was a dream. Anything can happen in a dream. I'd give almost anything to be able to have one peaceful night."

"Well, if you do it again tonight, try not to yell so loud. Hard enough to get a good night's sleep as it is."

Part of Robert E. Lee's second invasion of Union territory, the First Georgia had been marching northward for most of the past week. Entering Pennsylvania, William and his comrades marveled at fields full of tall, green stalks of corn. Orders were strict regarding foraging, but it was hard for famished soldiers, coming from the war blasted fields and homesteads of Virginia, not to 'requisition' fat cattle and hogs from the local landowners. Officers would pay for the purloined stock with Confederate paper currency, which didn't sit well with angry farmers.

The Army of Northern Virginia was spread across a broad front as it drove into Pennsylvania. General Jubal Early's division was heading northeast toward the area around York. Shortly after it crossed the state line two days earlier, General John B. Gordon's Georgia Brigade dispersed a squadron of militia with little effort from a small village. Early demanded supplies and money from the town's officials, but was able to come up with only a few rail car loads of rations, a quantity of horseshoes and enough liquor to get one of his other brigades quite drunk.

Continuing on to York, General Early ordered the town to relinquish $100,000, along with two thousand pairs of shoes. When town officials were able to come up with only 1,500 pairs and a little over a quarter of the cash, Early declared himself satisfied. He had the footwear issued to those soldiers who needed them most, then used the money to purchase cattle. Sergeant Franklin was amused, commenting that the local farmers had no problem selling their cows for Union greenbacks, even though it was stolen money.

The column was halted behind a small rise. General Gordon, Colonel Merrow and several other officers stood atop the hill, looking toward the town through their field glasses. After several minutes of pointing and other gestures, the gathering broke up. Merrow strode down toward where Sergeant Franklin was holding his horse. Mounting, he spoke briefly to Captain Fitzpatrick, who then returned to his company. "There's militia guarding the bridge," said the captain, "but no artillery. We need to push them out of the way and get across as quickly as possible. The general has learned about an approach to the town through a ravine just on the other side of this hill. He wants no noise that might alert the Yanks."

Even with the soldiers doing their best to be quiet, something had alarmed the militiamen. William's regiment emerged from the ravine to face muskets sighting on them from entrenchments straddling approaches to the bridge. Blue-clad soldiers were busy piling boards in the center of the bridge in preparation for setting it afire.

Forming line of battle, the Georgians moved forward. William was surprised that militia would be able to keep up such a heavy fire while the Confederates advanced on them. Suddenly a plume of smoke rose from the center of the span. The militiamen fired one last volley, then scampered across the bridge.

Colonel Merrow rode up to Fitzpatrick. He pointed at the bridge. "Captain, take your men and get that fire out. Hurry! I'll get another company to suppress the yank's fire. Get moving!"

Fitzpatrick yelled at his men. "Company H! Forward at the double quick!" The soldiers dashed toward the bridge as bullets whistled from the far riverbank. Several men set to work using bayoneted muskets to stab at the pile of burning boards, trying to lift them over the side into the river. Others slapped at the flames with their blankets. Additional troops lined the bank on either side of the blazing structure, returning the fire from across the river. Showers of sparks began to spiral skyward, fanned by a rising breeze. Despite their efforts, Fitzpatrick was forced to admit that his men were losing control of the fire. The supports were now blazing, threatening the structure with failure. Recognizing the futility of their task, the captain ordered his men off the bridge. Retreating, the troops had barely exited the span when the far end collapsed, burning timbers hissing as they plunged into the foaming river. Exhausted, soot-blackened soldiers sank to the ground.

William doused his kerchief with water from his canteen. As he began to wash the ashes from the back of his neck, a cry of "Fire! Fire!" rose from behind. He glanced around. Burning embers from the bridge had landed in a nearby lumberyard. Sawdust and small wood scraps had caught, and soon the neat stacks of boards were ablaze. The sawmill's old, dry timbers quickly became an inferno, and tongues of flame reached out toward nearby buildings. Men from the town quickly formed a line filling buckets from the river, then lifting them up to be poured on the fire.

The Georgians stared at the scene. A frantic woman screamed at them. "Help us! Please, for God's sake, help us!"

Colonel Merrow took off his hat, waving it toward the town. "Soldiers! We must help these people. Stack your arms and break ranks!"

Piling their muskets and accouterments, the men rushed to assist the townspeople. Merrow rode back and forth, directing the troops as if in the midst of battle. Confederate soldiers worked side by side with Northern townsfolk against the conflagration. This time their efforts met with success. Though several buildings were damaged, the town was saved from destruction.

As the last few flames were beaten out, soldiers and townspeople glanced uneasily at each other. Unsure of what to say, they separated, the townspeople gathering off to one side, and the troops returning to their ranks. After a few moments, a red-faced man stepped from the crowd, his white lace shirt pitted with burn holes. Walking up to Colonel Merrow, he offered his hand. "Sir, I am Mayor Holt. I would like to extend my thanks for the gallant actions of your men in saving our town."

Merrow grasped the mayor's hand. "You are quite welcome, mayor. Glad to do it."

"I must admit I was surprised that you helped us. I mean, we've been hearing about how the Rebel Army planned to lay waste to our country."

Taken slightly aback, Merrow replied, "Sir, you misjudge us. Our wish is not to wage war against civilians. General Lee has ordered that no private property is to be damaged."

In an instant, the mayor's expression darkened. "Well, sir, that may be. But an invading army does cause much disruption, just from its presence." He waved toward the burned bridge and lumberyard. "Just as has happened here."

The colonel raised himself in his saddle as straight and tall as possible. "We regret that you have been inconvenienced. War is a hard thing. What you are experiencing is just a taste of the cruel injustices your army has visited on the people of Virginia and other Southerners. You should consider yourself fortunate that this is General Lee's army. Were we to behave like your grand army did at Fredericksburg, your houses and barns would now be burnt out shells, and your possessions scattered across the land."

The mayor stepped back, anger clouding his face. "I repeat my thanks for your assistance. But I have to say, if your people had not started this war, there would have been no need for such actions to be taken. Good day, sir." Spinning on his heels, he strode back to where the townsfolk were still gathered. "Return to your homes," he called out, "and stay there. Don't do anything that might provoke any retribution."

Merrow watched with resignation as the mayor stalked off. Gesturing to Fitzpatrick, he gave orders for the company to bivouac outside of town. "I think it best to keep some distance between us and the populace. Put your pickets out along the riverbank, and assign some men to guard the roads leading out of town."

It was still dark the following morning when the regiment was roused by rolling drums. William rubbed his eyes sleepily while the soldiers fell into ranks. Soon they were on the march again. Noting the direction of the rising sun, he called out to Franklin. "What's going on, Sarge? I thought we were headed for Harrisburg, but we've turned south again."

"Not sure just what's happened, but the word is the army has to concentrate. Probably means the Yanks are close by."

"So where are we going?"

"That little town near the Maryland line that we stopped at a few days ago. Gettysburg, I think the captain called it."

Musketry roared ahead as William's regiment worked its way through a stand of trees. The sight that greeted him as the troops emerged from the forest was staggering. Across a low plain was a small, wooded knoll that was blue with Union uniforms. The ground rose beyond the knoll toward the buildings of a small town. The air was alive with minie balls and cannon bursts.

Colonel Merrow brandished his saber. "When we attack, boys, go forward with a yell. Charge, bayonet! Forward!" The soldiers started forward at a trot, then once across a narrow creek, they broke into a run. Screaming their dreaded "Rebel Yell", they surged toward the Federal line. Loading while on the run, William fired his musket over and over. The attack caught the Yankees off balance. The Union soldiers fired a few ragged volleys at the Confederates closing in on them, then broke, streaming in confusion toward the town.

William was reloading when an aide rode up to the front of the regiment. "First Georgia, halt! Reform your line and hold your position here."

Captain Fitzpatrick saluted. "Why are we stopping, Lieutenant? We're driving 'em good."

"Orders from General Early. Your brigade has gotten itself tangled together during the charge. The general wants you to halt to reorganize. Hays' brigade will continue the attack. Wait here for further orders." The aide saluted, then spurred his horse.

Fitzpatrick motioned for First Sergeant Franklin. "Form the company up here, sergeant. Have the men check their ammunition. Send back to check for our wounded and have someone fill canteens from that stream."

The roar of battle was diminishing somewhat as the Federals were pushed through the town toward the heights beyond. Reforming the company, Sergeant Franklin had William sound the roll. He was pleased to hear from everyone on his muster list. Franklin then directed the company to fall out to rest from their exertions.

The respite was all too short, however. Another aide came riding up, bearing new orders. Fitzpatrick motioned for Franklin and William. "Fall the boys in again. Seems that General Smith has reported a strong enemy force being seen up the York Turnpike. General Gordon's been ordered out in support. Get 'em up."

Henry shook his head with disgust when William repeated the order. "Figgers. Every time I finally get comfortable and start to catch a few seconds of sleep, we're ordered to march again. T'aint fair, I tell you."

Gordon's regiments soon came up on General William Smith's brigade. Colonel Merrow placed the First Georgia to the right of the brigade line, making contact with Smith's left regiments. Captain Fitzpatrick's Company H was ordered out in front of the brigade as skirmishers. If there were Yanks coming down the road, his soldiers would be the first to make contact. The men were posted in squads of four—two men on watch while the other two rested.

William made a quick tour of the line to make certain that every man was ready, canteens were full and every musket was loaded. He reported back to the captain that the company was posted. "Very well," said Fitzpatrick. "Have Sergeant Franklin take charge for now. You go ahead and get some sleep. You look like you could use it."

William saluted. "Thank you, sir." He was bone-tired. Finding a small clump of trees near the center of the skirmish line, he unrolled his blanket and flopped down. Drifting off to sleep, a wonderful feeling of contentment enveloped him. He had never experienced such a sensation of peace. For the first time in several months, William spent a night free from the tormenting dream.

Chapter 42

Thomas listened to the rumble of distant cannon fire as he carefully placed ammunition into the limber chest. The previous day, July 1st, had gone badly for the Army of the Potomac. The Confederates had seemed to come at them from all directions. Badly mauled, the First and Eleventh Corps had taken up defensive positions on the heights south of Gettysburg. During the night, the rest of the army had come up, extending the line down a low ridge. The Artillery Reserve, of which the First New Hampshire was a part, had arrived earlier this morning, and was now encamped behind General Sickles's Third Corps.

His thoughts drifted back over the past few months. So much had happened since he had left Lymington in such haste. Arriving at Fort Constitution, near Portsmouth, he had endured the good-natured ribbing of the veterans. "Fresh fish", he had been called. He spent the next several weeks being drilled in the art of the artilleryman, learning the differences between shell and canister, fuse and primer, rammer and sponge. He endured countless hours on the "school of the piece," mastering the various positions involved in serving the gun. Lieutenant Ferrell and Sergeant Stokes marveled at the ease with which he learned the intricacies of aiming and firing. During his first live practice, he impressed his instructors by sighting the gun and hitting the target dead on with his first shot.

Thomas subconsciously fingered the coil of thin brass wire attached to the side of his kepi. On the train he had asked Bill Stokes about the one fastened to his hat. "That's the mark of a veteran," Stokes had declared with pride. "It's the wire from a friction primer. You see the elephant, you earn the right to wear it. Kind of a tradition in our battery." Thomas had arrived in Virginia for service with his battery just before the debacle at Chancellorsville. Battery A had acquitted itself well in the battle, and Thomas had earned his hat decoration.

Thoughts of Stephanie crept into his mind. Thomas glanced around, embarrassed, hoping no one would notice the immediate physical sensation. He leaned closer into the side of the chest, unconsciously smiling as he mentally replayed their first night together.

"Got that chest full yet, Marsh?"

Thomas almost dropped the lid on his hand as the question brought him back to the present. "Yes, sir. All set. About equal with Hotchkiss and Schenkle shells, with fuses. Enough powder charges for each, with spares."

Lieutenant Ferrell scratched his cheek. "Very good, Private. Any idea where Sergeant Stokes is?"

Thomas pointed. "Over at the guns, sir. Checking the fittings on the pieces, I think."

"All right. Get yourself ready. Lee's been pretty quiet this morning, but it won't last. Make sure the horses are fed and watered, but keep them in their traces. I've got a feeling we could be called up any time."

Thomas saluted. After checking the limber chest one more time to be certain it was securely fastened, he walked over to where the farriers were working on the horses' hooves. "Lieutenant said to keep them hitched. He's got one of his feelings. You know what that means."

The man grimaced, then nodded. The battery had a superstition that whenever Lieutenant Ferrell started talking about a "feeling," action was certain to be imminent. The farrier began to gather his tools. "No big surprise, what with Bobby Lee just across the way."

Thomas retrieved his haversack from the edge of the limber, then sat down, leaning against a large rock. Pulling out an envelope, he raised it to his nose. Though faint, he could still smell the scent of lavender on the paper. Her image once again invaded his mind, causing another intense reaction. Carefully crossing his legs, he looked around, then pulled the letter from the envelope.

Lymington, New Hampshire
May 24, 1863

My dearest,

> *I cannot tell you how much I have missed you since you departed that horrible day. I yearn for the touch of your hand in mine. Soon, my love, I hope that you and I shall be together again.*
>
> *Auntie has returned from Washington. She says that she was homesick but from little slips in conversation I suspect that Uncle Charles ordered her home to keep an eye on me. I am so furious with him for having that*

hateful constable spy on us. Speaking of Mattson, my sources tell me that he is under investigation by the town selectmen. Supposedly he arrested a boy in town on some kind of trumped up charge. The boy turned out to be the nephew of one of the selectmen, who then ordered an inquiry into the constable's abuse of the powers of his office. Someone has even leveled an accusation of embezzlement of town funds. How delicious.

All is well at your uncle's farm. He has remarked several times to me how proud he is of you. James is a big help, but I think he wants to move on. Without you there, he feels that he has no real friends. It would not surprise me if he leaves once the fall harvest is done. I do not know where he would go, but he has mentioned a desire to see the west.

My darling, each day is an eternity as I wait here for you. I know that your duties do not give you much time to write, but please do write as often as you possibly can. I have kept your letters. I cannot bear to part with them. Please, please, keep yourself safe from harm, and come back to me.

Yours in everlasting affection,
Stephanie

"You're going to wear out that letter." Thomas looked up to see Sergeant Stokes grinning at him. "Course if I was to get letters from such a lovely girl, I'd probably spend all my time daydreaming about her, too," he said as he plunked down next to Thomas.

Thomas folded the letter and returned it to his haversack. "What about all your lady friends you had back home? With all the female company you used to have, seems like you'd be getting letters all the time."

"Alas, 'tis true. I barely have time for all my duties between reading all the sweet missives that come my way."

Lieutenant Ferrell rode up. "Sergeant Stokes, we've been ordered up in support of the Eleventh Corps on the hills north of here. Get 'em up."

"Yes, sir!" Jumping to his feet, Stokes motioned to the waiting men. "Battery to move forward, Gentlemen. Follow the lieutenant."

Ferrell waved, then spurred his horse. The four limbers lurched forward as the drivers lashed their teams. The cannoneers double-quicked along behind, doing their best to keep up with the guns as they careened up along the ridge. As they passed by a small white-washed frame house, a sour-faced, bearded officer stood on the porch, watching them intently as they hurried by. An army headquarters guidon flapped in the breeze. Thomas was unimpressed. *So that's General Meade. Lee will probably whip him, too.*

The battery was halted near a red brick arched gateway at the entrance to an old cemetery. As they waited, Sergeant Stokes began to howl with laughter. "Will you look at that, now." He pointed at a sign.

Thomas and the rest of his detachment immediately began to laugh. The crudely painted sign read: *Any person discharging a firearm in this vicinity is subject to arrest.* "I sure hope the jail is big enough for us," Thomas said, tears running down his cheeks.

Lieutenant Ferrell pointed to a line of guns being hooked up to their horse teams. "We're to relieve that Ohio battery. As soon as they limber up, move your pieces into the same positions. Watch where you place your guns. The other battery left holes where their trails dug in pretty deep. They must've been shooting high."

The four cannon were quickly positioned, and the artillerymen scampered to their designated positions. "Shell, one thousand yards, three second fuse!" called out Ferrell. Thomas lifted the heavy copper-plated lid of the chest. Selecting a time fuse, he cut it to the proper length for a 1,000-yard flight, then screwed it into the nose of the heavy, cast-iron shell. He handed the shot and a matching powder charge to a waiting soldier, who placed the items into a large leather pouch. Quickly walking up to the left side of the piece, the soldier held the pouch open so that another cannoneer was able to reach in to receive the round. This man inserted it, charge first, into the gun's bore. A fourth soldier rammed the shot home, while still another covered the gun's vent hole to prevent the possibility of sparks flaring, which could set off the charge prematurely. Lastly, another man inserted a primer into the vent, then attached a long lanyard to it. "Gun ready, sir," he called out.

Lieutenant Ferrell was standing in his stirrups, surveying the enemy positions with his field glasses. Lowering the binoculars, he glanced at his guns to make sure all were ready. "Fire by battery! Ready!"

The men on either side of the cannon leaned outward. The soldier holding the lanyard tensed, ready to unleash the power of his black monster.

"Fire!"

Four lanyards were simultaneously yanked. The fieldpieces roared and bucked, rolling backwards from the force of the discharge. Immediately, the cannoneers grasped the wheels and trails, manhandling the guns back into position. Ferrell intently followed the path of each shell as it screamed toward the Rebel lines. Satisfied that they had the range, he gave the order to his gunners to continue firing at will. Again and again the men repeated the exercise, sending one shell after another at the Confederates.

Chapter 43

Sergeant Franklin, William and Henry peered southward through the shimmering haze. The sound of fierce combat came rumbling from far off in the distance. Dense clouds of white smoke hovered on the southern horizon. "Will 'ya listen to all that shooting," said William. Sounds like quite a fight going on."

Henry slapped at a mosquito. "Yeah, and here we sit, picking our toenails, getting eaten alive by the bugs. There aren't any Yanks out here." He swatted his neck. "Exceptin' maybe an army of bluebelly mosquitoes."

Franklin adjusted his hat to cast more shade on his sunburned neck. "Well, it's for sure we're not going to see any fighting sitting here." He stood, picking up his haversack. "I'm off to do a little visiting with some fella's I know over in the 60th. The cap'n gave me permission, as long as I don't stay too long."

William looked up to see Colonel Merrow striding toward the group. "A-ten-SHUN!" The soldiers immediately leapt to their feet.

Merrow waved. "As you were, men, as you were." Walking up to Henry, he stuck out his hand. "How are you, son?"

Henry glanced at William, a quizzical look on his face, then took his father's proffered hand. "Doin' tolerable, sir."

"Splendid." He turned to William. "And how are you faring, my boy?"

"Doing okay."

"Marvelous." Merrow gazed off toward the south. "Some of the lads are having quite a brawl this afternoon."

"Yes, sir," said Henry. "Wish we were down there helping out."

William was startled as a melancholy expression spread over the colonel's face. Merrow gazed at Henry for long seconds. "Don't be in such a rush. You'll have plenty of chances to do your duty." He clapped his son on the shoulder. "Not that you haven't made me very proud of you already. Because . . . I am proud of you. I want you to know that." He swung to look at William. "I hear how well you take care of your men, Sergeant. Keep up the good work." His gaze fixed intently into William's eyes. "Promise to watch out for Henry, especially."

Puzzled by the remark, William nodded. Colonel Merrow smiled, then turned back to Henry, who looked equally perplexed. "Have to go now, son. Take care of yourself." Mounting his horse, he waved to Henry, then rode off.

William watched Merrow disappear down the road, then turned to his friend. "That was a little strange."

Henry scratched his head. "Yeah. He's never talked to me like that before. Not sure what to make of it."

The day wore on. Still formed on their skirmish line in advance of the brigade, the men of Company H sought shelter where they could from the blazing summer sun. Listening to the rising and falling sounds of battle in the distance, they chafed at their inactivity. It struck William as odd that two brigades should just be sitting next to the road while the rest of the army was engaged. He glanced toward where the other regiments were posted. Large columns of dust were rising into the air. "Hey, Henry, look at that."

Henry stood. "What?"

"Looks like the brigade's getting ready to move." A movement on the road caught his attention. Colonel Merrow was galloping toward them. "Yep, betcha we're going into action. Here comes your pa."

Merrow reined up before Captain Fitzpatrick, who quickly stood and saluted. The colonel returned the salute. "Captain, the brigade has been ordered back. We are to support an attack on the heights south of the town."

"Very well, sir, I'll have the company recalled."

"No need for that, Captain. I've already started the rest of the regiment. You stay put for now—keep your company posted on the skirmish line. The brigade will be long gone before you can get your men back into line."

"If you say so, sir, but I can have the company assembled quickly. I would prefer to stay with the regiment."

Colonel Merrow dismounted. Gently laying his hand on Fitzpatrick's shoulder, he said, "I know you would, Gerald. I have to admit to you that I have a selfish reason for keeping you here. I don't want Henry in this fight."

Fitzpatrick could see anguish in his commander's eyes. "What's wrong, sir? I've never seen you look so disturbed."

Merrow's voice lowered, barely above a whisper. "Don't say anything to my son about this, but I've had a premonition about him. I can't explain it fully, but every fiber of my being is telling me that if

Henry fights any more in this battle, I'll never see him alive again." He shook his head. "I know it seems foolish, but I can't get away from it."

The Irishman offered his hand. "Don't worry, Colonel darling. I'll see that your boy stays out of trouble. Don't think we'll be seeing any action around here, anyway. There's no sign of Federals out to our front."

Colonel Merrow took his friend's hand, grasping it tightly. "Thank you, Gerald. I don't know what I—his mother would do if she lost him."

As the colonel rode away, Sergeant Franklin came running up. "Captain Fitzpatrick, sir! While I was visiting over in the 60th they got the order to assemble. The brigade is moving."

Fitzpatrick sat back down in his chair. "I know, Sergeant."

The lack of response mystified Franklin. "Beggin' the Captain's pardon, sir, but shouldn't I assemble the men?"

"No, Sergeant, we're staying here."

"But why?"

"Orders, Sergeant. That will be all."

"But—."

"I said that will be all, Sergeant."

Franklin saluted. "Yes, sir."

William and Henry were buckling on their accoutrements as the sergeant approached. "Take 'em off, boys. We're not going with the rest of the brigade.

William was dumbfounded. "I don't understand, Sarge. Why not?"

"Don't know. Not for us to question orders, Marsh. Someone higher up has their reasons."

Henry hung his cartridge box on a stack of muskets. "Don't like this, not one bit. We should be going with the rest of the regiment."

Sergeant Franklin pulled a pipe from his haversack. "Seems queer to me, too, but orders is orders."

Late that afternoon, William and his comrades listened anxiously to the rising sounds of battle over the far hills, certain that it was from the attack involving their regiment. The lack of news about their comrade's fate was troubling.

Shortly after midnight, he heard a challenge from one of the pickets. "Who goes there?"

"Major Leslie," came the reply. "I'm looking for the officer in command."

"Over there, sir," William heard the guard reply. A few moments later, the officer stepped from the gloom into the firelight. William stood and saluted.

The major saluted back. "Who's in command of this company, Sergeant?"

"That would be Captain Fitzpatrick. He's sleeping over under that tree."

"Well, wake him. I have orders for him."

William walked over to where Fitzpatrick lay snoring. Leaning down, he put his hand on the Irishman's shoulder, shaking gently. "Sorry to wake you, Captain, but there's some officer here. Says he's got orders for you."

Fitzpatrick coughed. He grimaced as he stood. "Getting too old for this nonsense. All right, Marsh, let's see what this 'officer' wants." Buttoning his tunic, he strode over to the major and saluted. "How may I be of service, sir?"

Leslie returned the salute. "General Smith's compliments, Captain. Form your company. We're moving out and you are to come with us."

Frowning, Fitzpatrick replied, "Major, this company is part of General Gordon's Brigade. Surely it would be better for us to return to them."

"Your orders are to accompany this brigade. We are to reinforce General Johnson's division, but one of our regiments has been detached for service with General Stuart's cavalry. We need your muskets."

"This is damned irregular, sir. We're not part of your command. We should return to General Gordon."

"General Ewell wants every gun he can get to support Johnson's attack. You're coming along. Form your company, sir."

Fitzpatrick rose up stiffly before saluting. "Yes, *sir*, though I do this under protest."

"Your protest is noted. Be ready to move in five minutes."

General Edward Johnson's division had been hitting the Federal right on Culp's Hill since late the prior evening. Some of Johnson's regiments had taken a portion of enemy entrenchments before the fighting ended after dark. Several brigades from Early's division, including General Smith's, had been ordered to Johnson's support. With fresh troops at hand, the general prepared to renew his assault early in the morning. Before his preparations were complete, however, the Federals began their own attack, beginning with a pre-dawn artillery barrage. As Smith's brigade arrived, it was positioned on the far left of Johnson's division.

William shivered in the early morning dampness. "This just don't feel right," he said to Henry. "We should've gone back with our own regiment."

Henry munched on a piece of hardtack. "One fight's as good as another. Me, I can't stand this waiting around."

William studied his friend for a moment. "You're awfully eager this morning."

Henry took a swig from his canteen, then laughed. "Eat, drink and be merry, goes the old saying. For tomorrow you may die." He pulled a greasy chunk of salt pork from his haversack. "I just feel good right now. No aches or pains. Not even a worry about this battle."

"You're making me nervous. Just don't do something foolish and get yourself shot."

"Not me, friend. I intend to live forever."

Fitzpatrick drew his pocket watch. It was just after 7:00 a.m. The fighting had been almost continuous on the hills around them. Stuffing the timepiece back into his vest pocket, he noticed several officers riding toward him. As they reined up before him, Fitzpatrick could see general's stars on one man's collar. The officer saluted. "Captain, I am General Smith. I would like to compliment you and your men. Your company marches superbly."

"Thank you, sir. We appreciate that."

"Having you here presents us with a unique opportunity. I would like you to hold your company in readiness here between General Steuart's brigade and mine. You will act as a sort of 'flying company,' ready to dash to where needed."

"I'm not sure I understand."

"Simply this, Captain. If my brigade is to move forward, or is attacked, you will protect my right flank. On the other hand, if General Steuart advances, your company will guard his left flank."

Fitzpatrick drew himself up. "General, I would like to remind you that we are part of General Gordon's brigade. This company should not even be here. We should be allowed to return to our own regiment."

Smith's face clouded. "You are here and you will stay here, Captain. Unless you have a problem following the orders of a superior officer."

"I will follow your orders, sir. But as I told your aide earlier, I do so under protest."

"Your protest will be noted in my report, sir. As will your uncooperative attitude. Now, you will place your company at the angle where my brigade and that of General Steuart come together. You will hold your company ready for action as needed. That, *sir*, is an order."

Fitzpatrick saluted. "Yes, sir. As you order."

General Smith pulled on his reins, yanking his horse's head around. Fitzpatrick watched him ride away, then turned to Sergeant Franklin. "That man is going to get us all killed."

For the next couple of hours, William waited with the rest of his company while the roar of combat rose and fell. The day was barely started, but for William, it was though time had stopped. The anxiety of knowing that they could be called forward at any moment caused his stomach to churn. He felt helpless, caught up in events over which he had absolutely no control.

Only Henry seemed to have no fear. Indeed, he constantly griped about having to sit and wait. He wanted to get into the fight. The waiting continued to gnaw at William. Observing a staff officer gallop up to Captain Fitzpatrick, he let out loud sigh of relief. "I think you're finally going to get that fight you've been wanting," he said to Henry.

Dismounting, the officer addressed Fitzpatrick: "General Smith's compliments, sir. General Steuart will be moving to attack while we stay here to protect his flank. The general requests that you deploy your company as skirmishers on the flank of Steuart's left company, and advance with their line."

Fitzpatrick returned the salute, then motioned to Franklin. "All right, Sergeant, you heard that officer. Company forward in skirmish order."

"Yes, sir." Franklin looked out across the field to their front at the visible Federal breastworks. "It's going to be near impossible to get across that open space. The Yankees are going to murder us."

"I know, Sergeant. Do the best you can." Fitzpatrick drew his sword. *I'm sorry, Colonel. I tried.*

The advance sounded. A fierce look of determination shone on the face of each man in Company H as they stepped off. The line had barely begun its forward movement when a perfect storm of lead missiles tore through the ranks. Every few seconds, a man would scream and drop. William instinctively leaned forward as he marched, as though walking into a fierce rainstorm. Fitzpatrick waved his saber. "Forward, men! For the glory of the regiment, forward!" The captain had advance barely three steps when a minie ball knocked the sword from the Irishman's hand. Moments later, another tore through his throat. Fitzpatrick remained standing for a only a moment. Looking wildly around, he dropped.

William glanced around for Franklin. Spotting the sergeant a few yards away, he hollered. "Sarge! The captain's down!"

Sergeant Franklin fired his musket, then began to turn. At that moment, a bullet smashed into his chest, hurling him backwards.

Terror rose in William's throat. The entire company was being cut down around him. Out of the corner of his eye he saw Henry coming up. Reaching out, he grabbed his friend by the arm, pulling him toward a large boulder. "Henry, c'mon! We've got to get to cover. Get behind that rock!"

Henry resisted. "What about the rest of the company?"

"There is no more company. They're all dead! C'mon and take cover before we get killed!"

The two crouched down behind the boulder. Minie balls whined as they ricocheted off the edges of the protecting stone. William glanced back across the field behind them. It was littered with dead and dying men. His heart sank. *How the hell are we going to get out of here in one piece?*

Henry peered over the top of the rock. Alarmed, William jabbed his friend with his musket. "Get your head down, you idiot!"

Henry glanced toward William. "I'm just trying to get a fix on who's shootin' at us. Can't see too well." Turning back to once more look over the stone, Henry saw a puff of smoke. The next second his forehead exploded.

"HENRY!" The scream burst from William's mouth. Without thinking, he jumped up to catch his friend. Another shot tore through the palm of his outstretched left hand. The ball's force spun him around. Dropping next to Henry's body, he lay in shock, unable to move or even think.

After several minutes, William began to feel excruciating pain. He held his hand up, staring at it. The ball had smashed through the small bones of his palm. Blood poured from the wound. With his good hand, he managed to retrieve a bandana from his jacket pocket. Wetting it with water from his canteen, he wrapped the cloth tightly around his wound, staunching the flow. Lights were flashing all around his eyes. The loss of blood had weakened him. He tried taking a drink, but rising nausea caused him to vomit. The world around him spun, then faded into darkness.

Chapter 44

Thomas yawned as he shifted further under the limber. The shadow had moved, exposing him to the scorching rays of the sun. No one in the battery was able to get much sleep the night before. Late the previous evening, the Rebels attacked the east side of the hill. The New Hampshire gunners watched anxiously as another division appeared on their front, forming as if to attack. The Confederates began to advance, but then mysteriously stopped and pulled back. Their presence kept the battery on alert throughout the evening. Then just before daybreak, Union artillery on the larger hill to the east opened. Sounds of fierce fighting continued until late morning.

As Thomas attempted to doze, he heard someone yelling his name. *Damn it, now what?* Opening his eyes, he looked up to see Stokes approaching. "Oh, go away, Bill. Let me sleep."

"Cap'n Edgell told Lieutenant Ferrell who told me to find someone to take a message over to General Ripley's headquarters." Stokes tossed a leather-wrapped packet at Thomas. "Here 'tis. You need to get goin' and to bring back an answer right quick. He wants permission to retire to fill our chests."

"Why? We didn't fire that much yesterday."

"He's got that feeling again—been watching the Rebs bring up a lot of guns out west of here. Say's the word is they're going to hit us on this line sometime today. Probably try to soften us up with artillery first. Anyways, he wants the chests as full as he can get 'em."

"What'd you pick me for? I was finally catching a few winks."

"Because, my boy, you're available right at the moment. Now get yourself a mount and get down the ridge."

Grumbling, Thomas got to his feet and slipped the packet into his haversack. Picking out a horse, he began the ride southwards towards the artillery reserve camp.

An eerie quiet hung over the battlefield. The fierce fighting from this morning on the Union right had petered out a couple of hours ago. Only an occasional exchange of musket fire in the distance broke the unsettling calm. Passing General Meade's headquarters, he noticed several officers eating lunch.

Dismounting at the Artillery Reserve headquarters tent, he spoke to a lieutenant seated in front. "Private Marsh, sir, First New Hampshire Battery. Got a message from Captain Edgell."

After reading the message, the officer looked up at Thomas. "Wait here, Private. I'll give this to the general." Disappearing into the tent, he emerged a few moments later bearing a folded piece of paper. "Here's your reply. Tell the captain he is to hold his position. We'll send a wagon shortly to resupply your battery as well as the others on your line."

Thomas stepped back and saluted. "Yes, sir." Just as he turned to leave, two muffled booms caught his attention. The officers seated under the awning looked up from their meal. A sudden explosion up on the infantry line brought them to their feet. Seconds later, an enormous roar erupted from over the ridge.

A lieutenant came racing up, reining in his horse in front of the tent just as General Ripley emerged. "General, sir, the Rebs are bombarding the line. They must have close to a hundred guns out there."

Thomas flinched as a shell passed overhead. The projectile buried itself in the ground behind the tent as he and the officers dove for cover. He waited anxiously for the explosion, but after several dreadful seconds he realized that it was a dud. Slowly he and the others climbed back to their feet. "Thank the Lord for those miserable Reb fuses!" exclaimed one in relief. "Otherwise we'd a been goners for sure!"

General Ripley called out to Thomas. "Soldier, you'd better get back to your battery. This is going to get serious fast."

Without pausing to salute again, Thomas leapt onto his horse. A continuous roll of thunder filled the air as the Confederates poured shot and shell at the Union line. He glanced up the ridge in the direction from which he had come. Explosions rent the ground and shattered the air. *Can't go that way.* He reined the horse to the right. Maybe if he got down to the rear of the ridge he could avoid the shells.

It didn't work. Everywhere he turned, it was as though the Rebel gunners were zeroed in on him. The explosions drove him further off course. Finally, he reined up behind a wagon. *Damn it, I'd have been safer if I'd stayed on the higher ground. Bet the trails of those Rebel guns are digging in. With all the smoke, they probably can't see that they're shooting high.*

Another shell-burst several feet away sent a red-hot fragment slicing through his reins. Before he could react, one more shell smashed its way through the wagon, sending splinters flying in all directions.

One shard buried itself in the horse's flank. The animal bellowed in terror and pain, bucking and jumping as if possessed by a demon. With no reins for control, it was all Thomas could do to keep his seat in the saddle. Yet another explosion just behind the horse caused the terrified beast to stampede, ignoring all of Thomas's efforts to stop or calm it.

The crazed horse plunged through brush and over rock walls as it hurtled along. Thomas desperately tried to hold on, his arms wrapped tightly around the animal's neck. He contemplated escape by leaping off, but quickly dismissed that idea. *I'd probably hit a rock and break my neck.* As he saw it, his only option was to hold on until the horse tired.

Emerging from a clump of bushes, he saw that the horse was coming up behind a line of infantry. Heads turned abruptly as the soldiers heard hoof beats approaching them. Panicked men scattered as the beast bore down on them. Cries of "He's running away!" and "Deserter!" reached his ears as the horse and its unwilling passenger plunged through their line. "Shoot the bastard!" cried an officer. Minie balls whizzed past him.

A foot of rein was still attached to the horse's bridle. Wrapping one hand in the mane, Thomas reached out with the other, frantically trying to snag the flapping piece of leather. The horse was galloping toward a forest. *If I don't get control of this animal soon, I'm going to end up plastered against a tree.* Stretching as far as he could, the section of rein was still just beyond his reach. They were almost to the trees. The broken rein flapped barely an inch from Thomas's fingers. Throwing himself forward one more time, he made another grab. Barely supported on the horse's neck, he felt the leather strap in his fingers. His hand gripped the rein just as the horse leapt into the tree line.

With all the strength he could muster, Thomas yanked the rein back, forcing the horse's head down. The animal began to move in a broad circle as Thomas fought to slow it. The animal's lathered flanks were shivering with exhaustion. Finally, the horse shuddered to a halt, its legs shaking. Drained from his effort, Thomas slumped on the horse's neck. He had been hanging on so tightly that it was several seconds before he could relax his grip enough to allow him to slide off.

Reaching into his cloth haversack, he drew out an old gingham shirt, which he proceeded to tear into several long ribbons. Braiding the strips into a crude rope, he looped it through the bridle, forming a makeshift set of reins. Tying the horse to a tree, he sank to the ground in fatigue.

The bombardment continued beyond the hills. After resting a few minutes, Thomas peered from the woods towards the Federal infantry works. *Shit. If I try to go back out there, those boys will shoot me for a deserter.* He slapped his leg in anger.

Returning to the horse, he gently examined the wound on the animal's rump. A shard of wood protruded about six inches. "Easy, boy, easy," he said as he took hold of the splinter. The horse let out a small whinny as he gingerly withdrew the fragment from the gash, but was too exhausted to react further. *Got to try to find some water.* Mounting, he gazed around. *Guess I'll see what's down this way. Maybe I can work my way down to another part of the line. If I don't run into a Reb picket.*

Making his way through the woods, he came upon a small stream. Dismounting, he cupped water from the brook and drank greedily. Untying a bandana from around his neck, Thomas wet it in the stream, then tenderly cleaned the wound. Patting the animal's neck, he said, "Not a bad cut, old boy. It'll heal up fine."

Remounting, he guided the horse into the middle of the stream. It drank noisily as he looked around, trying to get his bearings. As he gazed off into the trees, a sudden noise from behind brought him up with a start. Recognizing the sound instantly, he stiffened in the saddle. It was the distinctive click of a musket being cocked.

Chapter 45

A dim, hazy light filtered through William's closed eyelids. Slowly opening his eyes, he blinked from the bright afternoon sun. For a moment, he couldn't tell whether the rumble he heard was in his head or not. As consciousness returned, he realized that a tremendous artillery barrage was taking place off to the west. The constant reverberation of cannon fire aggravated the pounding in his head. He felt as though the explosions were emanating from the ground beneath him.

His eyes fell on Henry's corpse. The boy's eyes stared vacantly heavenward, an expression of surprise frozen on his face. Flies buzzed over the dried blood clumped around the gaping hole in his forehead.

William shuddered. Excruciating pain blazing up his arm reminded him of his own wound. The kerchief he had tied around his hand had loosened; crusted blood rasped on his mangled palm. He began to struggle to his knees, but as soon as his head rose above the protecting rock, a shot rang out from across the field. The ball ricocheted off the stone just inches from his face. He dropped to the ground, his breath coming out in short bursts. The agony from his wound was intensifying by the minute. He glanced around in despair. *I've got to get out of here.*

William picked up his canteen, giving it a shake. Empty. Looking around, he spied Henry's canteen. Using his good hand to maneuver, he crawled around his friend's body. He picked up the tin container. *Please.* Shaking it gently, he was gratified to hear liquid sloshing inside. Raising the spout to his lips, he took a swig of warm, stale water. He shook the canteen again. Just a little bit left.

Slowly peeling the grimy, stiff bandana from around his wound, he was appalled to see pieces of bone protruding from the mangled, black mass that had once been his hand. Reaching out, he unstrapped Henry's haversack and dumped the contents on the ground. Picking out a greasy length of cloth, he doused it with the remaining water, then wrapped it tightly around his palm and fingers while trying to ignore the sharp pain.

William gazed around. The only gray uniforms in sight were on the bodies scattered about. Apparently the Confederates had retreated while he was unconscious. He shook his head, trying to clear his mind. *Think, man, think. Got to get back to my lines. Don't want to end up in some prison camp.* He pondered his situation for several moments. *Okay, let's see just how bad off I am.*

Taking up Henry's musket, he placed his friend's hat on the muzzle and raised it up one side of the rock. Within seconds, a shot sent the kepi flying. He set his own hat over the gun's bore. This time, he poked it out the other side of the stone. He held it for several seconds. When no shot was fired, he began to wave it around. Still nothing. *Good. They can't see it from that angle. Looks like that's my best way out.* Slipping his arm through the musket strap so as to drag it, he took one last look at the lifeless form that had been his best friend. *So long, Henry. I will miss you.*

Using rocks, bushes, and sometimes bodies for cover, he worked his way across the field. Painfully maneuvering his way along, he stopped every few feet to gauge his progress. It was evident from the littered meadow that the Confederates had retreated toward his left. But that way was too exposed. William realized he would never be able to cross there without being seen from the Union entrenchments. Surveying the field before him, he spied a small thicket off to the right, bordered by what looked like a shallow ravine just a stone's throw away. If he could make it into that gully, he just might be able to reach the trees undetected. All he had to do was traverse about thirty feet of open ground that held no cover. *It's farther in the wrong direction. But I've got no choice.*

Inching along, he crawled toward the ditch, expecting at any second to hear the crack of a musket. Twenty feet to go. *I can't make it. It hurts too much.* Fifteen feet. *Damn it. I will get there.* Ten feet. *God, I wish I had a drink.*

A musket was fired from the Union breastworks. The bullet hit just a few feet from William, spraying him with dirt. Several more shots were fired. With a final burst of effort, he dove into the ravine. Finally protected from gunfire, he rested for a few moments before starting to crawl toward the thicket. It took several agonizing minutes before he managed to reach the tree line. Scrambling behind a gnarled old oak, he listened as several Minie balls thudded into the opposite side of the trunk.

Gasping for air, William rolled onto his back, worn out by the exertion. His chest was heaving so hard he thought he might break a rib.

The shooting had stopped. Turning over onto his elbows, William peered out from the thicket across the field, squinting at the rock from behind which he had escaped. He could just make out Henry's corpse. Tears began to make tracks through the dust covering his cheeks. *How do I tell the colonel? He asked me to look out for you.*

Beset by a sudden wave of lightheadedness, William felt as though he might pass out again. Rolling once more onto his back, he lay staring up through the tree branches. His throat burned from thirst. *I can't stay here. I've got to find some water. Gotta be some water around here someplace.* Forcing himself to rise, William lifted the musket by the strap. He looked up at the sun filtering down through the leaves. *Don't even know what time it is. Probably mid-afternoon. If the sun's up there, then northeast should be that way. If I go in that direction I should find a Confederate unit.* Stumbling along in his weakened state, he hoped he was moving toward friendly lines.

Pushing his way through the dense underbrush, William moved cautiously forward. The rumble of artillery from across the hills reminded him of summer thunder. Another noise, the welcome sound of a gurgling brook, came to him through the bushes. Water! His throat felt as dry as the dusty field he had left behind.

Cautiously approaching the creek, he was brought up short by a different noise. Someone was there. Grasping his musket tightly, he crept forward. There in the middle of the stream was a Federal soldier watering his horse. He seemed drowsy, or maybe just lost in thought. *Thank you, Lord. That horse will help me get back to the company.*

Anxious not to be heard, William crept through the underbrush, coming up behind the horseman. *Now just stay there a few more moments.* Spasms of pain tore at his hand as William brought the musket up, using his left arm to support the stock. He pulled back the hammer. At the sound of the loud click, the Federal stiffened.

"Get off the horse, Yank." William's voice was raspy as he gave the command. The soldier did not move. "GET OFF THE HORSE!" William's finger tightened on the trigger.

Suddenly, the Yankee put spurs to the horse, wheeled and bore straight for William. Startled, he heard the boom of the musket before realizing he had fired. Instead of hitting the rider, the minie ball plowed into the horse's leg, bone smashing from the impact. The Federal tried to leap clear, but could not pull his boot from the stirrup in time before the hurtling mass of horse and rider crashed to earth.

Whinnying pitifully, the crippled animal managed to stagger to its feet and stumble away into the forest. The soldier lay still on the ground as William slowly approached. The chinstrap had held his cap on his head, and the hat now covered his face. Without really thinking, William reached down to pull the hat away—and then froze.

A horrifying chill swept over him, for suddenly William felt as though he was enveloped by the nightmare once more. But this wasn't a dream. This was all too real. He knew he had to look at the face, but was terrified at the thought of what he would find. He felt as though he might faint again. Slowly, he forced himself to lift the cap.

Shock and anguish racked William's body as he beheld the features of the fallen Yankee. Falling to his knees, he began to wail, "Please, no. Please God, no!" Tears flooding down his cheeks began to spatter on the face of . . . his brother Thomas.

Chapter 46

Trembling, William knelt next to his brother's prostrate form, unable to do anything other than stare. After several terrible moments, Thomas's eyelids fluttered, and a low moan escaped from his lips. Joy welled up in William's chest as he realized that his brother was alive. Ignoring the pain in his hand, he dashed to the creek. Hurriedly filling his canteen, he scrambled back to Thomas's side. Gently supporting his brother's head, William put the spout to his mouth.

Thomas groaned, then coughed as the water slid down his throat. Slowly opening one eye, he peered up at the rough-looking figure holding his head. Coughing once more, he said, "Well, Reb, you haven't killed me yet. Looks like I'm your prisoner, though."

Beside himself with joy and relief, William cried out. "Thomas, don't you know me? It's me, William. It's your brother!"

Thomas opened the other eye, blinking to focus his vision. His eyes flew wide open as he recognized William. "Lord a'mighty, Willie. It *is* you! What the hell are you doing here?" Jumping up, he embraced his brother in a bear hug. William flinched, then gave a small cry of pain. Drawing back, Thomas noticed the bloody rag wrapping William's hand. "My God, Willie, what happened to you?"

"Yank ball got me. Same time that Henry bought it."

"Henry?" You don't mean Henry Merrow?"

"Yeah. We've been pards together through this whole war."

"Oh, my God." Thomas shook his head. "Not good old Henry."

"We've lost a lot of boys from back home. I'm the only one left from our company. Remember Sam Hoskins, the big fellow that was always teasing you at school? He caught one at Second Manassas."

Gripped by an overwhelming feeling of sorrow, Thomas gazed skyward for several moments. "This war has destroyed so much." Reaching out, he gently grasped William by the arm. "Let me take a look at that hand. Come over by the creek."

Thomas helped his brother to the bank of the creek, setting him down at the base of a tree. Trying to use great care, he undid the cloth, examining the wound. "Lord, what a mess. You've got to get to a surgeon, quick."

William winced. "Not bloody likely out here. I'm not even sure where our lines are."

Removing his bandana, Thomas moistened it in the stream, then attempted to clean William's hand. "That's my problem, too. I was trying to get back to my battery just when your artillery opened up. My horse spooked and ran away with me. Some of our own men shot at me—probably thought I was deserting."

William studied Thomas's uniform. "So, brother, how'd you end up wearing blue?"

"Long story. Let's just say I was in trouble, and the army was as good a place as any to get away from it."

"Ma thinks you're still up north. She was talking in her last letter 'bout how she hadn't heard from you."

"Better she doesn't know I'm in the army. Just worry too much. 'Specially if she knew I was in the Union army."

William flinched when Thomas tore a scab. "Ouch, watch it. Hell, Thomas, It wouldn't matter to her one bit."

"I doubt that. When'd you last hear from her?"

"Got a letter a few weeks ago. Just before we marched north."

"So how's she doing? And how's Melissa?"

"Both doing 'bout as well as could be expected. Supplies are short, and Confederate money isn't worth a damn. She's going to get married again. To Mr. McCay. You know, the fellow that owns the Mercantile."

"I heard, just before I had to leave. Mother sent Uncle Benjamin a letter. Said that someone found Pa's body. I was happy to hear it. Ma's grieved for a long time."

"It would've been easier on her if you'd have come home."

The sharpness of William's remark startled Thomas. "I couldn't come home. There was too much going on. Most of it bad."

"Ma kept saying over and over how much she missed you. You never wrote. That hurt her a lot."

Thomas stared at the ground. "I was in trouble, Willie. Big trouble. I caused Uncle Benjamin and Aunt Rebecca a lot of pain. For a long while I wasn't a fit person to be around."

"She wouldn't have cared. Uncle Benjamin would try to be cheerful in his letters but she knew something was going on. From the little things he wrote."

Thomas finished cleansing William's wound. Re-wetting the bandana, he tied it tightly around the hand. "We can argue forever about what should have been. Right now we need to get you taken care of. You need a doctor. I think I can get you back to my lines. Then a surgeon could treat you."

"No way, brother. I don't want to end up in some prison camp."

"But you'll get blood poisoning if you don't get that taken care of soon."

"I'll take my chances. Besides, I figure we're as close to my army as we are yours. I can make it back. You'd best get going before you get caught."

Thomas placed his hand on William's forehead. "You've got a pretty good fever. You'll probably pass out before you get five steps."

"I said I can make it." Bracing against the tree, William struggled to his feet. Thomas reached out to help, but William waved his good hand in refusal. He stood swaying for several moments, his knees shaking. Dizziness and nausea swept over him.

Thomas leapt to catch William before he fell. "Like hell you can make it. Here, put your arm around my neck. I'll try to get you closer to one of your regiments."

William was too wobbly to protest further. He wrapped his good arm around his brother's shoulders. Thomas grasped William's arm, supporting him. "Let's try this way."

"Wait, let me get my musket."

"Forget the musket. Too much weight." Thomas grinned. "You're a lot bigger than I remember, brother."

The two siblings stumbled along through the woods. Coming up to the edge of a small clearing, Thomas peered out. "Too hard going through this underbrush. Don't see anyone out there. We'll try taking a little easier path." Shifting William on his arm, he stepped out from the cover of the trees.

"Hold it right there, Yank."

Thomas turned his head to see two muskets leveled at him. *Shit.*

William held up his bandaged hand. "Wait, fellas, don't shoot."

The taller of the two rebels, a corporal, lowered his weapon slightly. "Don't worry, Sarge, this Yank ain't going to take you anywhere. Okay, bluebelly, let that fellow down real nice and gentle like."

Thomas slowly lowered William to the ground, then raised his hands. "This man is my brother. I was trying to get him back to your army for medical help."

The corporal guffawed. "Yeah, sure. And I bet you're a deserter, and want to jine up with us, too."

William coughed. "He's telling the truth. We are brothers. We found each other after my company got wiped out, and he cleaned my wounds. Please, boys, let him go. He knew he might get captured but he helped me get back here anyhow."

The corporal's expression softened, just a bit. After a few moments of contemplation, however, his face hardened again. "That may be, but brother or not, he's still coming along with us."

The shorter soldier brought his musket down. "Oh, come on, Corp. Let's let him go. It ain't right to take a man's brother prisoner right in front of him. Besides, we'll have enough trouble getting this sergeant back."

A few more nervous moments passed, then the corporal let down the hammer of his firearm. "Oh, hell, you're probably right. Okay, Yank, this is your lucky day. You skedaddle out of here before I stop feeling so generous."

Thomas lowered his hands. "Obliged, Corporal." He knelt down next to William, laying his hand on his brother's shoulder. "You take care of yourself, Willie. Don't forget—you never saw me, right?"

William grasped Thomas' hand. "Please, let me just tell her you're all right."

Thomas gazed directly into his brother's eyes. "If you tell her that, then she'll ask you more questions. No, I've made up my mind. Don't tell mother that you saw me. She doesn't need to know I'm in the army, and I'd just as soon she didn't. She'd worry too much."

"But, Thomas, she has a right to know where you are. She's making Mr. McCay wait to get married until I come home. She'd be really glad to know you're all right. It wouldn't matter which army you're in. Let me tell her. It'd sure make her feel better."

Thomas shook his head. "No, brother. Please do this for me. As far as I'm concerned, she's better off not knowing anything. Let her think I'm still in New Hampshire. When my hitch is up, I'll come home. I promise. But right now I'm counting on you to take care of her and Melissa. Please, William. Do this for me."

His impatience growing, the corporal scowled. "Get going, Yank, before I change my mind."

Thomas glanced at him. "I'm going. Just want to say goodbye." He turned back to William. The two brothers embraced, then Thomas stood. "It was good to see you again, Willie. Take care of yourself."

"You, too," said William.

Thomas tipped his kepi to the two Rebels. "So long, fellas. It was a pleasure." He gave William a wink, then began to stroll toward the trees. Before he had taken more than a few steps, however, a high-pitched voice brought him to a stop.

"Halt! You there, I say. Halt!"

William and the other soldiers spun their gaze to see a dust-covered Confederate officer striding toward them. He carried a sword in one hand and in the other a revolver, aimed directly at Thomas. "Stop, Yank, or I'll drop you where you stand!" His expression reminded William of a hunted animal. He waved the sword toward William and the other two soldiers. "Why the devil are you letting this Yankee get away?" The shrill tone of his voice resonated with fear.

Thomas lifted his hands above his head, then turned with great deliberation. William called out to the officer. "Wait, Lieutenant, don't shoot. That's my brother!"

The lieutenant glanced at William. "Your brother? He's the enemy. Damned Yankees. Killed all my men. Damn them all!" Tears ran down his cheeks. "Damned butchers. Should kill them all." He aimed the revolver at Thomas. "Should kill you now!"

William struggled to rise. "For God's sake, Lieutenant, no!"

Moving with caution, the corporal walked toward the officer, placing himself between the lieutenant and Thomas. He raised his hand. "Now look here, lieutenant. Ain't no call to shoot anyone who's not shooting at you. This here Yank brought the sergeant to us. They both say they're brothers, and I believe them."

The lieutenant glared at the corporal for several minutes, sweat beads dripping from his chin. William was afraid that he might shoot the man. Finally, he lowered the revolver. "All right, all right, I'll not shoot him. But he's a Yank, and by thunder, he's not going to get away!"

Backing away so as not to put the lieutenant behind him, the corporal came over to William. Leaning down, he whispered, "This officer ain't all there in the head, Sarge. If we don't keep your brother as a prisoner, he'll probably get shot."

William looked at Thomas, who nodded to show he understood. "Thanks, Corporal. You're right. That looey is a nut case. I appreciate your trying. By the way, what's your name?"

The corporal stood. "Name's Madison. From Alabama. Other fella's Ross."

"I'm William Marsh. My brother's name is Thomas. Keep a close watch on him, will you?"

Straightening up, Madison winked. "Sure will, Sarge." He turned back to the lieutenant. "All right, then, we'll take him along as a prisoner." He motioned to Ross. "C'mon, Bud, you help the Sarge. I'll keep an eye on the Yank."

"No, Corporal. You two take the sergeant and find a surgeon. I'll take charge of the prisoner."

Alarmed, William again tried to rise. The officer swung his pistol. Madison put his hand on William's shoulder. "Best not try, Sarge. He's crazy enough to shoot." He scratched his chin as he faced the officer. "Um, Lieutenant, maybe we should all go back together. Might be safer that way."

"Nonsense. I'm perfectly capable of guarding this man. The sergeant needs medical attention right away. You get going." Before the corporal could protest further, he said, "That's an order, soldier!"

Corporal Madison shrugged, then waved to Ross. He reached down, grasping William's arm. "All right, Sarge, I guess we'd best be moving."

With the corporal's help, William struggled to his feet. "For God's sake, Madison, don't let that lunatic take my brother. Please. You've got to stop him."

"Can't help it, Sarge. He's an officer. You know we can't do anything—if we tried, we could be arrested."

"No! I won't let him." Grabbing Madison's bayonet from its scabbard, he lunged toward the lieutenant. Wild eyed, the officer stepped back, cocking the pistol as he brought it up. Lacking strength, William only got a few feet before he sank to the ground.

Thomas rushed to his brother's side. "Willie! Quit this right now. It won't do you any good to get yourself shot again. I'll be all right. Go on with those two and get yourself taken care of."

"But, Thomas—."

"No buts, younger brother. You go on, get well, then get yourself back to Georgia." He stood. "And remember. You promised not to say anything." Pivoting, he faced the lieutenant, raising his hands again. "Your prisoner, sir."

His face lit with a strange grin, the officer pointed off to the right. "That way, Yank. And don't try anything."

The corporal watched intently as the lieutenant and his prisoner disappeared over a small hill, then turned to William. "All right, Sergeant, let's see about getting you to a surgeon." Propping him up between them, they carried him across the clearing.

The lieutenant prodded Thomas with the saber. "Move, damn you. You're my saving grace."

Seeing Thomas's puzzled expression, the officer laughed. "Don't know what I'm talking about, do you? You're going to save my honor." He swallowed hard. "You Yanks were murdering us. Balls hitting from all directions. I couldn't stand it."

"So you ran."

Another prod of the saber. "Yes, Yank, I ran. I can still hear the howls of my wounded men, begging me to help them. But I didn't. I ran."

"So what do you need me for?"

"Don't you see. If I bring back a prisoner, my commander will forget all about my 'hasty retreat'. Why, I'll probably even get a field promotion."

The two picked their way over the blasted battlefield. At length, they came upon a Rebel picket post. Challenged, the lieutenant announced to the soldier that he was bringing in a prisoner, and demanded escort to the officer in command.

They were taken to a small barn appropriated as regimental headquarters. A sergeant was busy writing at a field desk just outside the door. "This lieutenant needs to see the major. Caught himself a Yank."

"Just a minute, Lieutenant," said the sergeant as he finished writing.

The lieutenant slapped the desk with his saber. "Now, Sergeant! I don't like to be kept waiting."

The sergeant eyed the officer with a scornful look. He deliberately raised his hand to salute. "Yes, *sir,* Lieutenant Boyd, *sir!* Definitely don't want to keep the lieutenant waiting." His voiced lowered to a whisper as he turned to the door. "No, sir, not someone who skedaddled and left his men to get slaughtered."

A few moments later, several officers emerged from the barn, led by a dust-covered major. "Lieutenant Boyd. I was hoping you wouldn't come back," he said. "It would have been better if you hadn't."

Boyd saluted. "I don't quite understand, sir."

The major pulled a gauntlet from his belt and slapped it on his thigh. "You don't understand? You ran away, you bastard."

"Sir, I resent your maligning my honor. I was stunned by a shell burst during the attack. When I regained my senses, I found that I was separated from my company. While trying to find my way back I came upon this Yankee trying to kill one of our men. After a fierce struggle, I was able to subdue him. I wanted to kill him, but realized he might be valuable for information."

Thomas had trouble restraining himself as he listened to the lie. *If I could only get my hands on you for two seconds. I'd make you pay.*

The major slapped the gauntlet again. "You, sir, are a God-damned liar. Honor? You left whatever honor you might have possessed back there with your dead men!"

Nearing exhaustion from the day's events, as well as emotional strain, Thomas felt what little strength he had left draining from him. He wanted desperately to sit. Periodically, he would begin to sink toward the ground, only to be pricked by the guard's bayonet. Even with the seriousness of his situation, however, he could not suppress a weak smile of enjoyment as he observed the lieutenant's discomfort.

The major scowled for a moment, then motioned to the sergeant. "Take care of the prisoner. Then put this officer under arrest."

Incredulous, Boyd stumbled backward. "But, sir! What about my prisoner? Doesn't that count for something?"

"You desert your troops in the face of the enemy, and think that bringing in some Yank private will make us ignore your guilt? You defy me, sir. Sergeant! Follow your orders!"

"With pleasure, sir." The sergeant grasped Boyd by the arm. "Now, *sir*, if you would kindly unbuckle your belt. Corporal Blakeley, please be so good as to relieve the lieutenant of his arms." He pointed to Thomas. "Then take that Yank and put him with the other prisoners."

As Thomas was led away, he glanced back to see Boyd struggling to free himself from the grasp of two rather large soldiers, screaming at the top of his lungs about "fairness" and "honor."

PART FOUR

"It is only those who have neither fired a shot nor heard the shrieks and groans of the wounded who cry aloud for blood, more vengeance, more desolation. War is hell." – General William Tecumseh Sherman

Chapter 47

The world spun as William struggled to return to consciousness. Nothing looked familiar. Where was he? His hand hurt like blazes.

"Sergeant? Can you hear me?"

The words seemed to come to him through a fog. He fought to keep down the vomit that rose in his throat. The figure of a man in a white coat loomed above him. There were strange markings on the coat. As his eyes finally began to clear, William could see the coat was splattered with blood.

The man placed his hand over William's forehead. "Still got quite a fever."

William's throat was parched. "Please, could I have some water?"

The man turned his head. "Orderly! Fetch a cup of water here!" He leaned down toward William's face. "I'm Doctor Pratt. How are you feeling, son?"

William blinked. "Don't know. Shaky. My hand feels like it's on fire. My fingers are tingling."

Pratt put his hand on William's shoulder. "I'm sorry, son. Your hand was full of gangrene. Don't you remember? We had to take it off. You fainted during the operation."

As William's mind began to clear he began to recall. Two soldiers had laid him out on a table slick with blood. The doctor had said they didn't have anything to ease the pain except whiskey. After he had downed several gulps of the fiery liquid, someone put a musket ball between his teeth. The two men then held him down while the doctor began to saw at his wrist. Vomit rose again as the horrible memory surged up.

Time had seemed to stand still for him. He could not believe that two weeks had passed since his best friend had been killed and he had encountered his brother on the battlefield. The two soldiers they had come upon were from the Second Virginia, part of General Thomas Jackson's old brigade. When they discovered that William had served under Jackson in the Shenandoah Valley, they harangued him with a lively banter about their experiences with Stonewall while they carried him to their regiment's encampment. There, he was loaded into a wagon enroute to the army's field hospital. His wound was dressed quickly, but there was little time to do more as the Army of Northern Virginia began its retreat southward toward Richmond.

Heavy rains fell as the column headed south. William was dimly aware of the groans of the men packed into the wagon with him. One man constantly pleaded for someone to shoot him and put him out of his misery. Upon reaching Richmond, William was taken to Chimborazo Hospital. Long wards built of rough-sawn whitewashed boards covered a hill near the capitol building. It was there that the doctors discovered the gangrene which cost him his hand.

Several days later, an officer entered the ward. He motioned to a surgeon coming up the aisle toward him. "Excuse me."

The man wiped his hands on his apron. "I'm Doctor Pratt. Can I help you, Colonel?"

"I'm looking for two men. They got separated from my regiment at Gettysburg and may be wounded. I've been looking all over for them."

"Do you have their names?"

"Corporal Henry Merrow and Sergeant William Marsh."

Pratt stepped over to a desk just inside the door. Opening a large book, he used his finger to trace through the entries. "Hmm. Don't recollect anyone named Merrow, but Marsh, that sounds familiar. Let's see. Ah, here it is. Sergeant Marsh, First Georgia Infantry. Amputated left hand."

The officer gasped. "His hand? Oh, Lord. How is he?"

"He's one of the lucky ones, I'm afraid. He's expected to recover fully, and will go home. There are so many that will never live to see their loved ones again." The doctor pointed. "He's down there on the right—third from the end."

"Hello, Sergeant." William peered up at the figure standing at the foot of his bed. Recognizing Colonel Merrow, William attempted to sit up. Merrow rushed to his side. "Don't try to get up, Son. You're not strong enough." The colonel retrieved a chair from across the room, bringing it next to the bed. He glanced at William's arm. "I'm sorry about your hand. Glad it wasn't worse. At least you'll be going home soon."

William held up the bandaged stump. "Yeah. The doctor says I should be strong enough to travel in a few weeks."

"That's fine, fine. It took me a while to find you. All I could get was bits and pieces of information. Finally ran across an officer from Smith's brigade who told me your company had been ordered off with them. Said their wounded were all here. I took a chance I might find

Henry, but he's not here." Merrow shifted, leaning closer to the bed. "You were with him. Do you have any idea what happened to him?"

William swallowed hard. "He's—he's dead, sir."

Merrow's face went white as he slumped in the chair. "Oh, my God."

William thought the colonel might faint. Picking up the cup of water on the small table by his bed, he offered it to Merrow.

The colonel put his hand up. "No, thank you William. I'm all right." He straightened in the chair. "Tell me what happened to Henry."

"Well, Captain Fitzpatrick argued when we were ordered to go with General Smith's brigade—said we should be going back to our own regiment. But the general wouldn't listen. He made us go. We marched past the big hills where a whole lot of fighting was going on. The general posted us between his brigade and another outfit. Then he ordered us out as skirmishers to support the other brigade's attack. We had to go down a small hill, then across an open area. The Yanks were dug in good. We didn't get half way before everyone in the company got hit, except me and Henry. We hunkered down behind a rock— couldn't go forward or back. Henry was trying to shoot back when he caught one. He never knew what hit him. I tried to catch him but I got hit and passed out."

Merrow gulped down a sob. "I thank God he didn't suffer. What happened to his body?"

"There was no way I could get him out of there. I must have been out for a couple of hours. When I woke up, all our boys were gone. I barely made it down the hill without getting hit again. The Yanks had control of the area. I hope they gave him a decent burial."

"Not likely. Probably just dug a trench and dumped him in with the other casualties. The Yanks were more likely to tend to their own dead then our boys."

"I'm really sorry about him, sir. He was a brave boy. I lost a good friend out there."

Merrow shifted uncomfortably in his chair. "William, what happened to you was my fault. It was my order that your company stay with Smith's brigade. I had a premonition of Henry's death. When General Early ordered Gordon up to support the attack on the hills south of the town, I figured that Henry would be safe if he was left behind."

A tear made its way slowly down the colonel's cheek. "As it turned out, our brigade was halted before reaching the heights. We didn't engage the enemy again during the rest of the battle." Merrow's voice began to choke. "If your company had stayed with the regiment, Henry would still be alive. It's my fault. I sent my boy to his death. Poor Gerald. All those good men. All dead. Because of me." The colonel buried his face in his hands, weeping.

William wanted to reach out to Merrow, but was afraid to touch him. "Please, Colonel. It's not your fault. There was no way you could know what was going to happen. You did the best you could to protect Henry. He was so proud of you."

Merrow lifted his head, looking at William with swollen eyes. He reached into his tunic, drawing a linen handkerchief from a pocket. "Thank you, William," he said as he wiped his eyes. "I appreciate that. And I'm grateful that Henry had such a good friend." He rose from the chair. "I'm glad that you will be going home soon. This war is over for you. Is there anything I can do for you?"

"Yes, sir, there is."

"Certainly, my boy, anything."

"You remember my brother, Thomas?"

Merrow thought for a moment. "Yes. He went north before the war, as I recall."

"That's right. That day—at Gettysburg—after I was wounded, Thomas and I kind of happened on each other. He's in the Union Army. I almost killed him by accident. Well, he's the one who carried me back to our lines. We met a couple of soldiers who were going to let him go, but this scared shitless lieutenant came up and took him prisoner. I tried to explain to him that Thomas was my brother but he wouldn't listen—just kept shakin' and saying all kinds of crazy things. Then he took him. I haven't seen him since. I've heard all kinds of rumors about the prisoners that were brought back with us, but I haven't been able to find out anything. Could you maybe see where he was taken?"

The colonel frowned. "Do you know his regiment?"

"He was with a New Hampshire battery. That's all I know."

"I'll see what I can do. Don't get your hopes up too much, though. Yank prisoners are scattered all over the place. He could be at Belle Isle. I'll do my best."

William reached out with his good hand. "Thank you, sir. I'd be most grateful."

Merrow took William's hand. "I'm glad I can help. Now, would you do me a favor in return?"

"For sure, Colonel. Anything."

"I will be writing to Henry's mother, to let her know what has happened. I'm going to send her a wire to advise her of our sad news, but I want to follow with a more detailed letter. I'll have it sent here to you. When you return home, would you be so kind as to have it delivered to her? I would be eternally grateful."

"Of course, sir. I would be honored."

William and Merrow continued to grasp each other's hand for several more seconds, then the colonel stepped back. "I have to be going now. Have a safe journey home, William. Take care of yourself and your family. Give my regards to your mother and sister."

"Thank you, Colonel. I will. Keep yourself safe."

Merrow gazed at William. "Safety is no longer a concern of mine, Sergeant. Not until I redeem myself to my son and those men who died with him. Goodbye." Pivoting quickly, he strode out of the ward.

William watched the colonel exit the ward. *Redeem himself? Now what did he mean by that?* After a few moments, he laid back, supporting his head with his good hand. He stared at the rafters. *I'm really going home. Home for good. I can't hardly believe it. Oh, Lord, what will Mary think when she finds out I've lost my hand. It shouldn't matter. If she really cares for me, she won't even notice.*

He scowled. *Yes, she will. She won't want to have anything to do with me now. I won't be good for anything. How am I going to do the farm work with only one hand? I won't be able to chop wood, or milk the cow, or anything.*

Another thought made him brighten. *Maybe Mr. McCay would give me a job in his store. Yeah, I could do that. I still have one good hand. It'll be hard, but I can do it. I'll show everyone that I can. Especially Mary. After all, I'm a soldier who's done his duty for the Confederacy. She has to see that. Now she can't refuse to marry me.*

Several days later, Dr. Pratt approached William's cot. Feeling William's forehead, he grimaced. "Your fever has gotten higher, son. Looks like you're going to be staying with us a while longer than planned." He handed William a packet. "Here, this came for you today."

William opened the package, drawing out two letters. One was addressed to Mrs. Merrow. William's eyes grew wide as he saw that the second envelope was addressed to him from the colonel. Holding it in his teeth, he ripped the cover open, then began to read:

My dear William

I hope this finds you healing well. Enclosed is the letter to my wife that you promised to take to her. Thank you again for doing this for me.

I have located your brother. As I suspected, he is being held at the prison on Belle Isle. I have not been able to communicate with him but did talk briefly with the prison commandant. From what I could ascertain, he is in reasonably good health.

I hope this information is reassuring. Take care of yourself. I shall be returning to the brigade within the next few days. I am certain that after a period of refit and rest the army will be ready to take the field once again. Though we have suffered a setback, our will is strong, and I am certain that God will provide us with final victory.

God bless you, William. May He grant you a speedy recovery.

Yours,
Colonel Bartholomew Merrow

Chapter 48

Jonathon and Grainger shifted uncomfortably as they stood at one end of the semicircle of men. A nervous, snorting horse pawed at the center. On the animal's back, hands bound behind, sat a ragged, sun-burned bearded man. "Baxter, you're a God-damned son of a bitch!" he shrieked. "Boys! Don't let him murder me! I was comin' back. Honest, I was. You all know this ain't right!"

Dressed in full uniform, Baxter sprawled in his ornate chair, one boot resting on a wooden crate. Hercules cowered behind the seat, peeking through the gold-painted scrolls of the chair back. The major lazily spun the cylinder on one of his Colt revolvers. Pointing the pistol at the bound man, he snarled, "You were warned, Morgan." He swung the barrel in an arc over the gathering. "You all were. I made it quite clear to all of you that I would not tolerate desertion. Anyone caught trying would be put to death."

Morgan strained against the knots around his wrists. "I told you, Major, I wasn't running away. I was just going to try to find some food and whiskey. I was comin' back."

Baxter repeatedly cocked the revolver. "So you keep saying. The problem is, I don't believe you." He pointed at the men again. "Most of them don't believe you. An example must be made. You've been tried and found guilty."

"Tried! That warn't no trial. I never had a chance."

Baxter rose to his feet. "Enough of this! You are guilty of desertion and for that you will hang." He motioned to Curly, who held the horse's bridle. Curly nodded, then yanked on the reins. The horse lurched forward, leaving Morgan dangling, his feet jerking erratically. The motion soon ceased; the body swinging gently in the slight breeze.

Scowling, Baxter looked out over the group. "Now you men mark me. This is the fate of deserters. I have warned you before—I'll not tolerate it." He glared about for a few moments, then turned and entered his tent, followed rapidly by Hercules.

The spectacle had a chilling effect on the raiders. What conversation occurred was low-key with hushed voices. Jonathon and Grainger returned to their campfire. Neither spoke for quite a while.

Jonathon scratched figures and lines in the dirt with a stick for long minutes before venturing a comment. "Wasn't right, Morgan getting strung up like that. He was coming back. I talked to him just before he went out. Said he was gonna try to find something to eat, and as soon as he did, he'd bring some back for us."

"Well, why didn't you say something?"

Jonathon tossed the stick into the fire. "I wasn't asked. Besides, Baxter was set on having a hanging. Morgan just gave him an excuse to show that he was still in charge. He wouldn't have listened to me even if I'd said what I knew."

Reaching for a coffeepot, Grainger poured hot liquid into his tin cup. "Baxter sure does seem to be getting crazier all the time. I haven't had a good meal since we moved south again. Pickin's been mighty slim. Things was better in Pennsylvania."

"Yeah, but the Feds made things too hot after Lee got his butt kicked at Gettysburg. Then Baxter got it in his head he'd just follow Longstreet's corps down here to Tennessee. You're right about the pickin's. Don't seem to be much left, even places the Yanks haven't touched yet. There's fighting all over the place. Bragg's army beat the Yanks at Chickamauga and bottled them up in Chattanooga, but his army's not much better off than the Feds. His soldiers keep requisitioning supplies faster than we can steal them. And the fields are bare cause all the men's off in the army, and just about all the slaves have run off."

Lowering his voice, Evans continued: "We need to just cut out on our own. Getting' too dangerous with this bunch. We're not too far from Georgia here. Soon's I get the chance I'm heading back to Dahlonega to take care of business that's been waiting too long."

Grainger took a sip from his cup. "What, that Marsh fellow? He's still in the army, isn't he? How you going to do anything to him?"

"He's still got kin in Dahlonega," Evans replied. "Mother and sister. There's a girl back there, too."

"Well, don't be too hasty. Got to watch for the right time. Look what happened to Morgan. Besides, I've got unfinished business with Jake." His face darkened with hatred. "That bastard needs killing—before he kills me. It's a wonder I'm still whole."

Jonathon nodded. "I said you should'a put a bullet in him a long time ago."

"I know it. Just haven't been able to do much about it. That bunch he stays with hangs pretty close to him all the time. If I was to just out and shoot him they'd be on me like a fleas on a dog." He pointed at

Jonathon. "They'd be after you, too. But I think I've figgered out a way to catch him alone.

"He's always got someone with him."

"Not always. I've been watching him careful since we landed here. He heads out into the woods every night to take a piss before bedding down. I was listening one night when he got up to go. One of his buddies said he'd go with him, that he shouldn't go alone. Jake got mad, said that the guy should know by now that he didn't want anyone with him, that he don't want no one around when he takes a leak. He goes to the same place every night. I'm going out there tonight and settle this."

"You gonna do him?"

"If I don't, sooner or later he's going to get lucky. I'm sick and tired of worrying every second 'bout when he'll try for me again."

"Those fellas he hangs around with will be coming after you."

Grainger stood. Drawing his Bowie knife from its sheath, he ran his thumb along the razor sharp blade. "Not if brother Jake just up'n disappears. They'll never know what happened to him." He glanced up at the moon, rising full and bright over the mountains. "Better get along. With all the carousing, Jake will be needing to find his spot soon. I'll be waiting for him."

"Skin him good, pard."

Sheathing the knife, Grainger gave Jonathon a mock salute, then started off into the woods. Moonlight filtering through the trees made it easier for him to find his way, but he knew the brightness would also cause difficulty hiding from his quarry. Finding the looked-for location, he cast about for a good hiding spot. A clump of bushes next to a large tree looked perfect. He would be able to see anyone coming from the camp without being detected. He sat down behind the bushes, then drew a small flask from his jacket pocket. Taking a long swallow of whiskey, he settled down to await his target.

Grainger watched and waited, anxiety increasing as time continued to pass with no sign of Jake. The flask lay on the ground, long since emptied. He began to feel drowsy as the whiskey took its affect. *Where the hell is that little shit? Did I miss him?*

Something moving through the brush caught his attention. Peering through the bushes, he could just pick out the shape of a man coming toward him. Spying a pistol in his adversary's hand, Grainger's hand brushed the grip of his own revolver. Sweat began to bead on his forehead.

Suddenly Jake halted, bringing his pistol up as he glanced about the small clearing. Fearful he had been discovered, Grainger crouched further down behind the bush.

After several minutes, Jake seemed satisfied that there was no danger. Holstering the revolver, he unbuckled and laid the gun belt over a downed tree. He proceeded to pull off his suspenders, then dropped his trousers and squatted down next to the log.

Drawing his revolver, Grainger stepped out from behind the bushes. "Hello, Jake."

Surprised, Jake nearly tripped on his lowered trousers. Catching himself, he reached for his gun belt.

Grainger cocked the pistol. At the loud click, Jake froze, fingers inches from the butt of his gun. "I'd back off a little, if'n I was you, boy," said Grainger.

Curling his fingers, Jake drew back his hand. "You ain't gonna shoot me, Joe. A shot will bring my pards on the run. They'll turn you into buzzard meat."

"Hadn't planned on shooting you." Grainger drew the Bowie. "Thought I'd just slice you up into little pieces."

Jake motioned toward the pants around his ankles. "You plan to kill me half-naked? How about letting me pull up my drawers, for God's sake?"

"Go ahead."

Jake kept his eyes on Grainger as he slowly reached down for his trousers. He fumbled with one pants leg, trying to make it appear as though his suspenders were caught on his foot. Stealthily he palmed a small dagger from his boot. Staying sideways from Grainger to keep the knife from view, he rose, pulling the suspenders over his shoulders.

"Looks like you've got the drop on me, Joe," Jake said, "Guess this ends it. Too bad my aim wasn't better. Can't believe I missed you with all those shots."

"You never was any good at shootin', Jake. Pa tried to teach you. I'd be willing to bet you never even got a shot off when old man Sorensen attacked the farm."

"You bastard! We all fought hard—even Ma. She got killed because of you. I never could figure why she liked you so much. Even when she was dying, she kept calling your name. *Your* name! She was my mother, not yours. It wasn't right. It's your fault—." Jake whirled, flinging the dagger as he dove behind the log.

The whiskey in Grainger's system slowed his reflexes. Seeing the flash of the blade in moonlight, he tried to turn away but could not move fast enough. The dagger buried itself in his abdomen. Grainger doubled over, sinking to his knees as the pistol slid from his grip. Shaking violently, he grasped Jake's knife, wrenching it out. Cupping his hand over the wound, he tried without success to staunch the flow of blood.

Jake peered over the log. Seeing Grainger prostrate, he moved cautiously toward him. Kicking the revolver away, he stood over the wounded man and laughed. "Well, dear Brother, looks like things have changed. Bottom rail on top, as the slaves say." He leaned down to pick up his dagger, not noticing the Bowie still clenched in Grainger's fist.

Grainger slashed out, opening a long gash on Jake's arm. Screeching from the pain, Jake recoiled. Raising his arm, he examined the cut. "God-damn you, Joe. I was going to finish you off, but now you can just lay there and bleed to death. I hope you take a good long time to die."

Jonathon sat staring into the campfire, wondering how much longer before Grainger would return. He glanced toward the tree where Morgan's body dangled. Baxter had ordered the dead man be left hanging as a reminder to anyone else contemplating desertion. *Somehow, I'm going to get out of here. Then I'm going to find Marsh. No matter where he is. I've waited long enough.*

A rustling in the bushes caught his attention. Expecting Grainger, he was astounded to see an ashen-faced Jake stumble out of the trees, the arm of his shirt stained red.

Yanking out his pistol, he jumped up and ran into the woods, calling out. "Grainger? You okay? Grainger!" *Damn it, where is he?*

A weak voice drew his attention. "Over here." Stumbling toward the sound, Jonathon came upon his friend, leaning against the base of a tree. Getting down on his knees, he bent over his companion.

Grainger looked up at Jonathon through slitted eyes. He coughed, blood spraying from his mouth. "Jake's killed me, Evans. I'm a goner for sure."

"Hold on, pal. Let me look." Jonathon ripped open Grainger's jacket, then his red stained shirt. Blood oozed from the deep laceration in his belly. Jonathon looked into Grainger's eyes. "Ain't no good, pard. He stuck you in the gut. Ain't nothing can be done."

Struggling to his elbows, Grainger reached up, grabbing hold of Jonathon's cross belt. He was gasping for breath now, his voice just a low croak. "You was right, pard. I should'a killed that son of a bitch months ago. Now he's done me. Kill him for me. Kill him. Kill—."

335

A gurgle rose from Grainger's throat. Releasing his grip on Jonathon's belt, he sank to the ground, his eyes rolling up into their sockets.

Jonathon stared at the body. Shifting slightly, he began to go through Grainger's pockets. Finding only a few coins, he snorted in disgust. *Damn it, not much here. But you won't need them anymore.* Retrieving Grainger's bloody Bowie knife, he wiped the blade on the slain man's shirt.

Evans studied the knife as moonlight danced across the silvery surface. *Don't worry, pard. It'll be a pleasure killing that little bastard.*

Shortly after returning to the camp, Jonathon found himself being summoned to Baxter's tent. The major was in ill humor. "I've been told your friend got himself killed. Tell me what happened."

"Don't know too much. He said he was going to settle things between him and his bother Jake. Went off into the woods to lay for him but he got the worst of it."

Baxter dabbed at the sweat on his forehead with a handkerchief. "Too bad for him. Well, it's for the best. The feud between these two has been too much of a distraction." He glowered at Jonathon. "You'd best forget any thoughts of revenge. Jake's friends will likely leave you be, if you don't try to pull something."

"Not me, sir," said Jonathon, "I don't need no trouble."

"Good."

Heading back for his tent, Jonathon glanced again at Morgan's dangling corpse. *Nope, I don't need trouble. Just lay low, mind my own business. And keep an eye out. First good chance I get, I'm gone from here.*

He fingered the hilt of the Bowie knife. *But I won't leave without finishing good ol' Jake.*

Chapter 49

"Come on, Melissa! We'll be late." Lucinda hastily tied the bow on her bonnet, then made a quick inspection of the room to make sure she hadn't forgotten anything.

Melissa raced out of the bedroom, buttoning her jacket. "I'm coming, Mother. Is Mr. McCay here yet?"

Lucinda opened the door. "He's been waiting outside for the past five minutes. Hurry up!" Grabbing her shawl, she dashed out the door.

Jedidiah McCay stood patiently next to the buckboard. He smiled as Lucinda rushed down the steps. "You'd best not be in such a tear, my dear, or you'll trip and end up in the mud. Then you'd be a sight for William."

Laughing, Lucinda climbed into the seat. "I don't think he would mind. All that matters is that he's coming home."

"Is that horrible Mary Stewart coming to Atlanta?" asked Melissa.

Jedidiah snapped his whip over the horse's ears. The carriage leapt forward. He looked over his shoulder to Melissa. "Hard to say. She was in the store yesterday—I asked her if she was coming. She said she would try, but didn't know if she could." He pulled an envelope from his coat pocket. "Told me to give him this."

Melissa giggled. "Mary's been in the store quite a bit lately, hasn't she?"

Lucinda turned to her daughter. "Now what's that supposed to mean?"

"Just seems like she's been flirting with all the older men in town." She pointed toward Jedidiah. "I've even been told that she's been eyeing Mr. McCay."

Lucinda couldn't resist a good-natured ribbing. "Why, Jedidiah. What's all this?"

His sudden look of embarrassment startled her. "Nothing to it," he said. Nothing at all." He turned to look straight ahead. "She just comes by often to get supplies for the school."

She put her hand on his shoulder. "I'm just teasing, darling. I hope you know that."

McCay patted her hand. "I know. Sorry if I'm a little testy. Got a lot on my mind."

"Anything you want to talk about?"

"Not right now. But we will."

Lucinda settled back in the seat. She pulled two pieces of stained paper from her purse. The first was a letter from William, the second a telegraph. Settling back into the carriage seat, she reread William's letter for what seemed like the hundredth time:

Richmond, Virginia
October 3, 1863

Dearest Mother

I am writing this from the hospital in Richmond. Really I am not writing as I am having a nurse here write it for me. I was hit in the hand by a ball at Gettysburg and have been in hospital ever since the army got back to Virginia. Mother don't you worry about me for I am as well as can be expected. The reason that the nurse is writing is because I'm still really sick. Also my left hand was all messed up and the surgeon had to take it off.

Lucinda cringed, just as when she first read the passage.

I am sorry I have not written to you before this but I have been real sick. The doctors said I was really bad off but am now on the mend. Now I have some really good news. I am coming home. My soldiering days are over and the army is sending me home. I don't know just when but the nurse here says not too long. The doctor says he will send you a telegraph when it is time for me to go.

Your loving son,
William

Lucinda now switched to the telegraph:

Mrs. Lucinda Marsh
Dahlonega, Lumpkin County, Georgia
October 12, 1863

Dear Mrs. Marsh,

This is to advise that your son, Sergeant William Marsh, will be departing Richmond on Monday the 15th of October inst. by train and will arrive in Atlanta on or about the following Friday. I am pleased to advise that his wounds are healing well, but caution that he will need several weeks of rest and recuperation, as he is recovering from a bout of pneumonia.

I am, Yours
Colonel Horatio Pratt, Staff Surgeon
Chimborazo Hospital
Richmond, Virginia.

Lucinda closed her eyes and clutched both pieces of paper to her breast. *Thank you, Lord. Thank you for bringing my boy home to me.*

Following an anxious night in the Atlanta Hotel, Lucinda, Melissa and Jedidiah barely touched their breakfast. The train was approaching the station as the trio rolled up in the buggy. Melissa squealed. "We're just in time! Here it comes!" Rushing onto the platform, Lucinda anxiously scanned the cars for signs of her son.

For several minutes, a steady flow of passengers streamed from the cars. But there was no sign of William. Lucinda was becoming frantic. *Oh, my dear. Did he miss the train? Or did something happen to him on the way?* She watched as a few more people disembarked. Still no William. Her grip on McCay's arm tightened. "Jedidiah? Where could he be?"

A conductor stepped out of one of the cars, glancing around as if trying to locate someone. Spotting Lucinda, he hastened over to her. "Afternoon, Ma'am. I 'spect you must be Mrs. Marsh. Got your boy on board. He's awful weak. Don't think he can make it off by himself. Would appreciate a hand with him."

McCay stepped forward. "I'll help."

The conductor nodded in appreciation, and the two men entered the railroad car. Lucinda kept her fingers over her mouth as she anxiously waited for them to return.

After several moments, McCay and the conductor reappeared, supporting William from either side. As they negotiated the steps,

Lucinda and Melissa rushed over to them. Seeing them approach, a weak smile lit up William's face. "Ma. 'Lissa." He reached out to his mother. "Told you I'd make it back."

McCay shook the conductor's hand, thanking him as he turned to go back to the train. Lucinda fought to keep back tears as her eyes surveyed her son. His ragged clothes, pale skin and swollen eyes shocked her, but she tried not to show her anguish over his condition. "My darling William. You're home. Thank the Lord for bringing you home to me."

Mother and son embraced for several minutes. As gently as she could, she cradled his bandaged arm. "Oh, my poor dear."

"I'm . . . all right, Ma. Could've been a lot worse." Gloom descended over his face. "Look what happened to Henry and the others. It's a miracle that I got away."

Melissa hugged her brother. "It's our little miracle, Willie—I mean William."

"We need to get him to the hotel," said Jedidiah. He motioned toward the carriage. "Let me help you over." Wrapping his arm around William's waist, McCay supported the trembling soldier with an arm around his shoulders and neck. Reaching the carriage, he helped William to climb inside. "Just a short ride back to the hotel, my boy. A night's rest will do you good before we head back to Dahlonega."

As the others climbed into the buggy, William glanced around. "Where's Mary. Didn't she come to see me?"

McCay settled into his seat. "Nope. Probably busy at the schoolhouse."

"What's she doing there?"

"After the town council fired her father, they couldn't find anyone to take over as schoolmaster. When Stewart left town to join the Union army, Mary was left all alone, without an income. The council took pity on her and hired her to teach. Figured that as the former schoolmaster's daughter, she would be as qualified as anyone to take on the job." He pulled out the envelope. "Here, she wanted me to give this to you."

Momentarily forgetting his missing hand in his excitement, William tried to tear open the letter. Gently, Lucinda reached out, taking it from him. "Here, let me do that for you."

Opening the envelope, she withdrew a folded piece of paper and handed it to him. Despair at his disability gave way to preoccupation as he began to read:

My dear, dear William

> *I am so glad you have come home. I was so very sorry to hear about your wounding, and am grateful that you survived your horrible ordeal. I want very much to see you but have not been able to find the time with my duties as schoolmistress. My father's traitorous act of joining the Yankees has left me with the burden of keeping up the house by myself. There are several people in this town who will not associate with me because of him. Thank goodness for your mother's fiancé Jedidiah. Sometimes he is the only one who will talk to me. I see him often at his store. We've had some wonderful conversations.*

Melissa gave William a playful poke. "So what does she have to say? Something depressing, I'll bet."

William looked up from the note. "Mary says that Mr. McCay is the only one in town that talks to her."

"That's strange." Lucinda glanced at McCay. He was hunched down in the seat, staring at the horse's head. "Jedidiah, I didn't think that you even liked her. That's the second time I've heard you and Mary mentioned at the same time." She giggled. "If I didn't know you better, I'd worry about something scandalous happening."

McCay cracked the whip, causing the horse to speed up. "I don't like her. But then I don't have to like everyone I do business with. That's all it is. Business. Nothing else."

Momentarily puzzled by Jedidiah's sulkiness, Lucinda decided it was best to ignore it. "Does Mary have anything else to say, William?"

"Just that she'll come see me once she has the time." He folded the letter as the carriage reached the hotel.

Due to William's condition, the trip back to Dahlonega took an extra day. "It's sure good to see the old place again," he said as the buggy pulled up in front of the cabin.

McCay helped William into the house, taking him to the back bedroom at Lucinda's request. He protested about taking her bed but she cut him off with a "shoosh," saying that it would be his room until he was better.

While Lucinda and Melissa rushed about finding clean clothing for William, and heating water to bathe him, McCay sat out on the porch in Lucinda's rocker. Back and forth he rocked as he mulled over what he wanted to say. *May not be a good time. May be the best time. I just don't know. But if I leave here without asking, I'm going to bust.* His rocking increased with his agitation. *But he's home now. I have the right to ask. Damn it, I'm going to ask.*

Lucinda stepped out onto the porch, wiping the perspiration from her forehead. McCay stopped rocking and stood. "How is he?"

"Oh, Jedidiah. He's so weak. I don't know how he survived the journey."

"Well, he's young yet. He'll do okay now, with all the nursing he's going to get."

Melissa emerged, having changed into a work dress. "I'm going to the barn to milk the cow. I think some fresh milk would be good for him."

McCay watched her disappear into the barn, then turned to Lucinda. "We need to talk. There's something I've got to say."

"What about, darling?"

"It's been quite a while now since you said you would marry me. I know how important it was for you to wait until William came home. Well, now he's home. I think it's time we picked a date for the marriage."

"Oh, Jedidiah. We can't just yet. William is home, yes. But he's still got a lot of healing to do. Surely you know we have to wait until he's gotten well again."

McCay stared at her in silence for several moments, his expression darkening.

"Jedidiah, what's the matter?"

"Maybe we should just forget the whole thing."

The anger in the words surprised her. "What do you mean?"

"I'm beginning to think that you really don't want to get married."

"Why, how can you say such a thing?"

"Because you keep finding excuses not to. Every time I ask you about setting a date for the wedding, you find some reason to say wait. Well, I don't want to wait any more."

"I don't understand why you're being like this. I've explained why we need to wait. And it's only for a little while longer. Until William is well again."

"William is well enough. Besides, you'll still be able to care for him after we're married. It's not like we're leaving town."

"You know that after the wedding I'll have extra chores. I'll still have the farm, but then there's the store, too."

"I'm perfectly able to take care of the store. I've done it all these years by myself, haven't I? Or are you saying that you can do a better job?"

"Oh, for heaven's sake, Jedidiah. That's not what I meant at all."

"What you meant was, that you'd rather stay here on your farm and nurse your son. Without me around."

Grasping an arm of the rocker, Lucinda hesitated before replying. "That's not fair. You're asking me to choose between him and you."

"God in Heaven, Lucinda. I'm not asking that at all, damn it."

"Mr. McCay! I'll not tolerate cursing in my presence."

"Very well, then, Mrs. Marsh. You shan't have to worry about my swearing around you anymore." McCay jumped down from the porch, snatching the horse's reins from around the post. He leapt into the buggy. "Make up your mind, Lucinda. I can't wait forever." The whip cracked, and the carriage plunged down the road.

Shaking with anger, Lucinda shook her fist at the dissipating dust cloud. "I'll get married when I decide the time is right, Mr. Jedidiah McCay! And not a moment before." Slamming through the door, she dropped into her chair by the fireplace, crossing her arms as she stared toward the rafters.

"Ma?"

Lucinda glanced up to see William peering from behind the bedroom door. "Darling, you shouldn't be out of bed. You've got to build up your strength."

William shuffled over to a chair beside his mother. "Ma, I'm all right. I heard you and Mr. McCay arguing."

"Don't worry about that. We've disagreed about when to get married for quite a while."

"Then you still plan to marry him?"

"Oh, of course." Lucinda rolled her eyes." He's just impatient."

"He's right about one thing. It's ridiculous for you two to wait any longer. You should have gotten married a long time ago."

"But, William, it's been important to me that I have my family together. I didn't know how long it would be before you came home. But now you're here. I know it won't be long until you're well enough. Then you'll be able stand up with us. I want you to give me away."

William gulped, then smiled. "You honor me, Mother. I'll do my best for you, even though I'm not the eldest son."

"Of course, it would be grand if Thomas could be here. And I'm sure that Jedidiah probably thinks that I'll use his absence as another excuse for delaying the wedding further. I know that he can't be here. I haven't heard from him in so long. The only word I get is from your Uncle Benjamin." Lucinda suddenly noticed her son's deep-set look of concern. "Why, William, what's the matter?"

William was struggling with his conscience. *I made a promise not to tell. But it's not fair to Ma. She'll be so worried if I tell her. But Thomas doesn't want her to know.* He glanced at his mother. Her look of concern melted his arguments. *Damn it, I know I promised you, brother, but she's got to know.*

He reached out, slipping his hand around Lucinda's. "Ma, there's something I need to tell you. It's about Thomas."

"Thomas? Good gracious, what?"

"He's in the Union Army. Artillery."

Lucinda gazed toward the ceiling for several moments without responding. Then she looked back at her son with a weak smile. "I already know that, William. Your uncle was able to get a couple of letters through the lines. He told me about how Thomas was forced to join the army to avoid some trouble."

"How long has it been since you heard from Uncle Benjamin?"

She thought for a moment. "It's been awhile. The last letter I got from him was dated mid-June."

"Then there's more that you don't know about."

"What do you mean?"

"Well, we kind of bumped into each other at Gettysburg." William gripped his mother's hand tighter. "No, that's not really true. After I got wounded, I shot at a Yankee to get his horse. It turned out to be Thomas."

Lucinda's eyes flew open. Seeing her distress, William held up his hand. "No, Ma, I didn't hit him. Just the horse. He was all right."

Lucinda put her hand across her chest. "Heavens, William, you just gave me a fright. But what did you mean when you said he 'was' all right?"

"He helped me get back toward our lines. We ran into a couple of soldiers who wanted to take him prisoner, but just when I had them convinced to let him go, some crazy mad lieutenant comes up and takes him. I tried to stop him but the other soldiers held me back. There wasn't anything more I could do"

"Oh, my Lord. We must write the government to see if they can find out where he was taken."

"I already know. Colonel Merrow found out for me. Thomas is in Belle Isle Prison Camp. It's on an island below Richmond."

Lucinda shot out of the chair. "Then I have to go to Richmond. At once. He needs me."

"No, Ma, you can't"

"And why not?"

"For one thing, he doesn't want you to know where he is. I'm breaking a promise I made to him, telling you this. He'd never forgive me if he found out."

"That doesn't matter. Those prison camps are terrible places. He could die there. I *must* go."

"Ma, no! You have no idea what it's like in Richmond. Every evil that you can think of has taken up residence there. It's no place for you. You wouldn't be able to get near Thomas, anyways. You'd just be one more worry for him. Besides, what about Melissa? You can't leave her here alone. You know I won't be much good for awhile."

Lucinda ran her fingers along the mantle. "I know you're right. But the thought of him stuck in that prison camp. Maybe sick. Maybe even dying. For all we know, he could be dead already. And there's nothing I can do about it."

"Thomas can take care of himself. He's strong, and he's smart. He'll survive. He'll probably get exchanged and sent home."

"Do you really think so?"

"Makes sense. Food and supplies are awfully short these days in Virginia. Seems to me that it would be easier to parole the prisoners and send them away. Less to have to deal with."

"You're probably right. Thank you for being so reassuring. I know so little about what's going on in the country these days. It helps to know that you believe he's all right."

William turned away. *I wish I truly believed it.*

Chapter 50

Mary Stewart breezed through the door of the Mercantile. Gliding up toward the counter where Jedidiah McCay was busy writing in his ledger, she tapped to get his attention. "Good afternoon, Mr. McCay. How are you this fine sunny, fall day?"

McCay peered over the top of his glasses at her. "Well as can be expected. Can I help you with something?"

"My, you're in a bit of a surly mood today. I just stopped by to find out if William got home all right."

Jedidiah turned a page in the book, then continued writing. "Took him and his family home last night."

"How's he doing? I mean, how is his wound?"

"He's going to stay laid up for awhile. Why the questions? Didn't think that you were still all that interested in him."

"He's a dear sweet boy, and I hope we're still friends after him being away all this time. Of course I'm interested in what happens to him. Why wouldn't I be?"

McCay glanced up again. "Just the way you keep carrying on with that idiot Parker. And don't think I haven't noticed your flirting with me."

"Why, Mr. McCay. There is absolutely nothing going on between me and Parker." She bent over the counter. "I wasn't sure you even noticed me. Besides, there's no harm with a little flirtation. It's not like you're married yet."

"May not be any marriage." McCay mumbled the words, not really intending for Mary to hear them.

"Jedidiah—uh, Mr. McCay? What do you mean, no marriage?"

"Nothing to fret your pretty head about. I'd rather not talk about it."

Mary blinked. "Do you really think I'm pretty?"

McCay looked straight into her face for several minutes before replying in a softened voice. "Yes, I think you're very attractive. What I can't figure out is why you chase after scoundrels. You could have the pick of any man in the county."

She leaned further toward McCay, a mischievous sparkle growing in her eyes. "Actually, Jedidiah, it's always been you that I really want.

It's too bad you're already taken." Taking an apple from a barrel in front of the counter, she stepped back. Pretending to examine the fruit for bruises, she peeked at McCay from the corner of her eye.

Taken aback by Mary's boldness, Jedidiah cleared his throat, then turned his attention back to his ledger. "I am flattered, Miss Stewart, but you shouldn't be making comments like that. It might be misconstrued."

Mary laughed. "Really, Jedidiah, you must know by now that I don't care a whit for what other people think. You're a very handsome man. Mrs. Marsh should be careful. If she doesn't come to her senses soon and marry you, I'll come after you myself. And I usually get what I want."

For a split second, McCay's mind filled with lurid thoughts of the two of them entwined. He shifted position as the image caused a physical reaction. Embarrassed, he averted his eyes. *How the devil could I think about her like that? Lucinda's the only one for me.* "I'd rather you didn't talk like that. Lucinda and I may not agree on everything, but she's a wonderful woman. I will be honored to be her husband. Now, if you don't need anything, I have work to do."

Mary took a bite of the apple, then set it on the counter in front of McCay. "Ta-ta, then, Jedidiah. I have a few things to do at the schoolhouse. Thanks for the lovely chat." She ran her fingers lightly over her breast. "If you ever need someone to . . . well, talk to, keep me in mind."

Jedidiah's eyes followed Mary's figure as she sashayed out the door. *Lord help me. I wish she'd stay away from here. Too much temptation for a lonely person.*

Mary spent the rest of that afternoon cleaning the schoolhouse, setting out materials for Monday's lessons. Almost done, she glanced up at the clock. Remembering that Parker had said he would be by her house at seven, she hurried to finish, then sped down the street to her home.

Following an hour of frantic lovemaking, Parker rushed out with hardly a word. Lying alone and frustrated, Mary tried but could not will herself to sleep. Every creak and groan of the old house seemed to resonate in the still of the night. Erotic thoughts involving Jedidiah McCay ran through her mind as she tossed and turned under the big fabric canopy.

Hearing the big grandfather clock downstairs chime the hour of eleven, she finally surrendered to the fact that sleep would not come. Rising, she slipped on her robe, then descended the stair and stepped through the front door. Taking a seat out on the front porch, she rocked slowly as she breathed in the cool autumn night air. She felt a sense of wicked adventure, sitting outside with just a robe to cover her.

Thinking back on her evening's dalliance with Parker, she was unable to stifle a small shudder. *I don't know why I keep letting that oaf paw at me.* A mental picture of William flashed through her thoughts. She smiled as she remembered the nights they spent together while he was home on leave. She began to drift.

A distant crash of glass roused her. She glanced down the street toward the Mercantile. Though it was difficult to see in the darkness, she caught a fleeting glimpse of a figure running from the front door. She waited for several moments, certain that the noise would raise an alarm. But the town remained quiet. No one had heard.

Curiosity overcoming her fears, she crept down the street, nervously glancing about lest someone see her in her scanty covering. Stealing up the steps, she discovered the door standing open with one pane of glass broken. She peered in. It was hard to see anything in the dark room. A low moan caught her attention. Picking her way through the gloom, she came around the end of the counter to find Jedidiah McCay crumpled on the floor.

"Mr. McCay!"

Stooping, she helped the storekeeper to a sitting position. Reaching up to his head, he gingerly touched a nasty gash. "Mr. McCay! My goodness, what happened to you?" she said.

Taking his hand from over the wound, McCay stared at the blood covering it. He mumbled a few words that were barely loud enough to hear. "Thief—broke in—I caught. Hit me with something—." He tried to rise, but had no strength to do so.

Mary grasped his arm. "Here, let me help you." With her assistance, McCay struggled to his feet. Groggy from the blow to his head, he had to grab onto the counter to keep from falling again. Still holding his arm, Mary raised it over her shoulders, propping him up. "Come on, we've got to get you to bed."

Barely able to support him, she managed to half carry, half push McCay up the stairs to his room. Taking him to the bed, she propped him against the headboard, then lit a lamp. Looking around, she spied a bottle of bourbon on a sideboard. Quickly she poured some into a tumbler. Sitting next to him, she held the glass up to his lips. "Here, drink this."

McCay gagged as the liquid burned his throat. He shook his head, trying desperately to clear his thoughts, but could not quiet the fire that blazed in his brain.

Mary extended her hand, tenderly stroking his cheek. "You poor dear, you've had it bad tonight."

A scowl crossed his face. "Bad end to an all round bad day."

"What do you mean?"

He winced. "Big fight with Lucinda."

Mary's curiosity was piqued. "Oh. So that's why you were so upset earlier. What did you two argue about?"

McCay pushed her hand from his cheek, then stared off into space. "Don't want to talk about it." A wave of dizziness passed over him. He felt as though he might fall again.

Seeing Jedidiah sway, Mary reached out, gently drawing him toward her. Weak and unable to resist, he leaned against her shoulder. She began to lightly rub his forehead. "Maybe it would make you feel better if you told me about the argument."

The soft touch of her hand was soothing. He felt as though he could drift away. "I want us to be married, but she keeps coming up with reasons to wait."

"Why does she do that?"

"I don't know. Maybe she just doesn't want to get married at all." He let out a weak moan. "Your hand is so soft."

Mary could hardly contain the excitement rising within her. Moving her hand to Jedidiah's chest, she began to gently stroke. After a few moments, his head rose from her shoulder. Her heart began to pound as he stared at her with an almost childlike look of gratitude.

Inching forward, she brought her face close to his, expecting him to suddenly back away. But he did not move. She lightly touched her lips to his, then drew back, waiting for his reaction. They stared at each other for several more seconds. Mary leaned forward again, this time kissing him with more firmness. His hand moved up to her shoulder, pulling her body tightly against his.

Jedidiah's eyes slowly opened as sunlight streamed through the window. His head felt as though a red-hot poker had been pushed through it. The room seemed to be out of balance. He closed his eyes and shook his head, then reached out to steady himself as he started to sit up. His hand brushed something strange and soft. *What the devil?* Through bleary eyes he could make out something under the blanket next to him. His hand trembled slightly as he lifted the cover. His eyes flew wide open. *Oh, my God!*

Mary opened her eyes, stretched, then smiled. "Good morning."

Jedidiah leapt from the bed. He stood staring at Mary for a moment, then realization dawned that he was stark naked. Yanking the blanket from the bed, he wrapped himself. Mary giggled. She lay uncovered, totally nude. Spinning awkwardly, Jedidiah turned from her.

"What's the matter, dearest?"

"Ah—what—how—did you get here?"

"Don't you remember? Last night, when you were hit on the head?"

"What? Oh, yes." Fighting to remember what had occurred, he sat down in a chair, his head pounding. "Mary, what we did—that wasn't supposed to happen." He began to rub his hands together as though trying to cleanse them of soil.

Mary sat up on the edge of the bed. "Jedidiah, you act as if we had done something wrong."

McCay looked at her, his face pained. "Wrong? Of course we did something wrong, Mary. Don't you see? I love Lucinda. We're going to get married."

"That's not what you told me last night. You said you two had argued. You called off the wedding. You told me you loved me."

"I don't remember any of it. Nothing." Picking up her robe from the floor, he flung it at her. "Come on, Mary, you've got to leave. Now."

Mary pressed the garment to her chest. "Why are you being so cruel to me? I would think you'd be grateful. After all, you were in really bad shape last night."

The wound in McCay's head was throbbing. "I am grateful for you coming to my aid. But what came after—it should never have happened."

"You didn't seem to mind last night."

"Well, I mind now! For heaven's sake, girl. Please clothe yourself!"

Mary stood, wrapping the robe about herself. "Very well, if you insist. But I was more comfortable the way I was."

Unlatching the door of a closet, Jedidiah pulled out a shirt and trousers. Hurriedly dressing, he said, "I don't care how comfortable you are. You've got to leave." Grabbing Mary by the arm, he propelled her toward the door. "Come on, I've got to get you out of here."

Opening the door, he glanced back and forth. *Good, no one here.* "This way, down the back stairs."

Mary resisted the shoving. "Heavens, Jedidiah. You'd think we were criminals or something."

Reaching the bottom of the stairs, McCay peeked around the corner. Still not seeing anyone, he began to drag Mary across to a small alley.

"Jedidiah!"

Recognizing the voice, McCay stopped in his tracks. *Oh, no. This has got to be a nightmare. Surely I'll wake up soon and this won't be happening.*

Mary waved her hand. "Why, Mrs. Marsh. Melissa. How good to see you. How are you this fine morning?"

McCay slowly turned to see Lucinda, her hand cupped over her mouth. Melissa stood next to her mother, shock obvious on her face. He smiled weakly. "Lucinda. What are you doing here so early?"

Trying mightily to recover her composure, Lucinda clutched her purse. "Might I ask what is going on here, Mr. McCay?"

"Going on? Going on? Why, nothing. Miss Stewart was—well, she—."

Mary stepped out in front of McCay. "Poor Mr. McCay was robbed last night. The thief hit him on the head. He was hurt pretty bad—I was just helping him."

Lucinda was examining Mary's robe. "If you were helping him last night, my dear, then why are you coming down his back stairs this morning?" she said, her voice thick with indignation.

McCay tried to speak but Mary kept on. "The poor dear needed a lot of care. For most of the night. Isn't that right, Mr. McCay?"

Jedidiah gave a weak nod. "Lucinda, darling. Please. This is not what it seems to be."

Lucinda took her daughter's arm. "Come, Melissa, we're going home. Mr. McCay, I think it would be better if we did not see each other for a while. Probably a very good while." She gave Mary a withering glance. "As for you, Miss Stewart, I intend to talk to William about what kind of girl he has been courting. And I'm sure the town council would like to hear more about the kind of 'lady' that is teaching our children."

Fury clouded Mary's face as she stormed toward Lucinda. Shoving her finger under the older woman's nose, she said, "Don't you dare threaten me. You don't have any claim to Jedidiah. You've made it pretty obvious that you have no intention of ever marrying him. Don't you even think of talking to the council about me, either. If you do, I'll find a way to get even. I promise you that."

Now it was McCay's turn to be angered. Grabbing Mary by the arm, he threw her out into the street. "Get yourself on home, you wretched little creature. I'm sorry I ever let you into my store. Get out of my sight."

Picking herself up from the dirt, Mary adjusted her robe with a flourish. "You're a bastard, Jedidiah McCay. You and Lucinda deserve each other!"

As Mary stalked off, Lucinda and Jedidiah turned to face one another. "I am so sorry about this," he said.

"I'm sorry too," said Lucinda. "I still need some time to myself."

McCay rubbed his shoe on a plank. "Please, Lucinda, let me explain what happened. I'll do anything to make amends."

Lucinda shook her head. "No, Mr. McCay, not now. I don't feel like discussing this at the moment. I need to think a few things through. Goodbye."

Jedidiah felt his heart sink as Lucinda and Melissa turned to walk away. Returning to the store, he picked up a small glass lamp, stared at it for a few moments, then threw it across the room. It shattered on the pot-bellied stove. He could not hold back a cry of despair. "Damn you, Mary Stewart! Damn you to hell!"

Chapter 51

Misty rain fell on the somber group clustered around the gravesite. Stephanie Carroll stood beside her Aunt Mildred, protecting her with a large black umbrella. The elderly lady mumbled continuously, her voice barely audible. Stephanie had stopped trying to understand what the grieving woman was saying. Glancing over to Thomas's friend James Stark, who had taken position behind them, she smiled weakly. She was grateful that he had offered to stay close, ready to assist if necessary, as her aunt's fainting spells were becoming alarmingly frequent.

Pastor Marsh stood beside the tombstone, head uncovered, his silver hair curling from the drizzle. "My friends, let us not mourn this man's passing from us. Rather, let us celebrate his life as a public servant—judge, statesman and United States Congressman. Let us remember the service he provided to his community, his state and his country." He raised his eyes heavenward. "Let us also remember his family. May they find solace in these words from the Book of Matthew—'Blessed are the poor in spirit, for theirs is the kingdom of heaven. Blessed are those who mourn, for they shall be comforted.'" Lowering his gaze to the assembly, he closed his worn, leather-bound bible. "God bless you all. I thank you all for coming."

Stephanie squeezed Mildred's arm. "It's time to go, Auntie."

Mrs. Carroll's expression was blank. The lack of recognition in her eyes was painful to Stephanie. James stepped up beside her, gently taking her arm. "Let me help you, ma'am."

Stephanie glanced at him with gratitude. He smiled back. Together, they helped the elderly lady through the mud to their waiting carriage. James motioned to Stephanie. "Why don't you get in first, then I'll help your aunt in."

Stephanie nodded. Climbing into the buggy, she reached out, grasping her aunt's trembling arm as she guided her into a seat. James provided support as the elderly woman stepped up into the carriage. Leaning back, the driver handed Stephanie a towel. "Thank you, sir," she said gratefully as she patted the moisture from her aunt's face and hands.

Satisfied that Mrs. Carroll was safely aboard, Stark circled around to Stephanie's side. She offered her hand, which he grasped gently. "James, thank you again for staying with us," she said. "I don't know what I would have done if Auntie had collapsed during the service."

"Entirely my pleasure, Miss Stephanie. I am at your service whenever you might need me." He held her hand for several more moments, gazing into her face. "Whenever." Stepping back, he bowed, then wheeled to leave. She watched as he untied his horse and mounted. *What a perfect gentleman. Thomas is fortunate to have a friend like James.*

Proceeding to dry herself, she heard her name being called. She looked up to see Pastor Marsh splashing toward her through the wet grass.

Stephanie reached out with the towel. "My goodness, Pastor, you need to go get under cover. You're soaked, and you'll catch your death."

Lifting his hat, Marsh dabbed the moisture from his forehead and cheeks. "These are the Lord's tears, my dear. He weeps for your uncle, as he does all his departed children across this torn land."

"That was a wonderful eulogy. I know Aunt Mildred appreciated it."

Marsh glanced at Mrs. Carroll, who sat motionless, staring straight ahead with a vacant expression. "How is the dear lady?" he asked, his voice hushed. "Has she shown any sign of improvement?"

Stephanie grasped the carriage door. "Not much, if any. Her mental health has never been all that good. Uncle Charles's death was too much a shock to her system. I fear she may never be completely lucid again."

"Such a tragedy, your uncle collapsing in Congress like that."

"He had built himself up to such a frenzy giving that speech. It was too much for his heart."

Marsh nodded. "The man certainly had a passion for his causes. His beliefs were unshakeable, be they right or wrong."

"That is so true, Pastor. Despite what he tried to do to Thomas, I will miss him very much." She leaned toward Marsh. "Have you heard anything more about him—Thomas, that is?"

"The only information I've gotten since he disappeared at Gettysburg is a rumor that he might be in a prison camp somewhere. But I haven't been able to confirm that."

"They're not still saying he deserted, are they?"

"Sergeant Stokes wrote that he doesn't believe it. He said Thomas had been sent for resupply just before the Rebel bombardment, and the last time anyone saw him, he was galloping toward enemy positions. Said some of the men in the outfit always thought he was wearing the wrong uniform, being from Georgia. It's all a lot of rot. Thomas may have done some stupid things in the past, but desertion? I'll never believe that. I've written to a friend of mine at the War Department in Washington. I pray he'll be able to find out something."

"I hope so."

"One thing's for certain. With your uncle's passing, and with Mattson's dismissal as constable, it would be safe for Thomas to return home." Wiping his face again, he handed the towel to the carriage driver. "Take these ladies home right away before they catch their death." Turning back to Stephanie, he placed his hand over hers. "Please send word if you need anything. Anything at all." Stepping back, he waved to the driver, who whipped the horse's reins.

A week had passed when Stephanie answered a knock at the door to find Marsh standing on the porch. "Why, Pastor, what a pleasant surprise. Come in, come in. What can I do for you?"

Marsh handed his coat and hat to Harriet, then took a seat in the parlor. "I received a letter in today's post from my friend in Washington. He has news of Thomas. I hurried to town because I knew you would want to hear as soon as possible."

"News about Thomas? What is it? Is he all right?"

Marsh pulled an envelope from his vest pocket. "Here, why don't you read it?"

Stephanie sat next to the preacher, her hands shaking as she began to read:

Washington City
October 20, 1863

My dear Benjamin,

It was so very good to hear from you again, old friend. I am glad that all in your household are faring well.

After receiving your missive, I have endeavored to locate your nephew. I am afraid I must be the bearer of unhappy news. First, I have confirmed that he is being held as a prisoner of war in Belle Isle Prison in Virginia, just outside of Richmond. Reports are that the prisoners there are subjected to inadequate provisions and lack of shelter.

I fear my second bit of news is worse. There has been testimony by several soldiers that he was observed riding at full gallop toward enemy lines, just as the rebel's immense bombardment of our army's center began on July Third at the battle in Pennsylvania. He was fired upon, but was apparently not hit. When and if he returns from Virginia he will most likely face charges of cowardice and desertion in the face of the enemy. I have read several reports of how many of our soldiers, veterans all, took flight due to being unnerved by the tremendous barrage that afternoon.

In looking over his service records, I see no indication that would lead me to believe that Private Marsh would desert to the enemy. The fact that he is being held as a prisoner of war would tend to indicate that there were extenuating circumstances of which we have no knowledge at this time. The officers in his battery have vouched for his character, and to a man, say that they do not believe he is capable of desertion.

I will investigate the possibility of prisoner exchange, but I would advise against pinning too many hopes on it. The exchange process is, at best, a sporadic and unreliable process. When the happy day of your nephew's release does occur, I would like to tender my services as defense counsel for him.

I am, yours &
Major Julius Simpson
General Staff, War Department

Her eyes reddening, Stephanie looked up at Marsh. "Oh, Pastor, he's alive! I've been so afraid."

"I know you have, my child. That's why I rushed here as soon as I read the letter."

"But how could they think of charging him with desertion? Hasn't he suffered—will suffer enough in that horrible place?"

"I think it would be best to save that worry for after he's released. Right now our prayers should be directed toward his safety during his imprisonment, and for his speedy liberation."

Stephanie scanned the words again. Tears streaked her cheek as she reread the line "*Reports are that the prisoners there are subjected to inadequate provisions and lack of shelter.*" Her jaw tightened with determination. "I want to go to Richmond."

The preacher was startled. "Richmond? That's impossible."

"Why? There must be a way. I have to find a way to help him."

"You'd never get through the lines. Besides, what of your Aunt? Mildred needs you here, more than ever."

"I'll find someone to take care of her. Harriet can do it."

"Stephanie, my dear, think about what you're saying. Harriet is a wonderful housekeeper, but you know she's not up to seeing to all of Mildred's needs. There is no one in this county better qualified to care for her than you. You would never forgive yourself if something happened to her while you were gone."

"But—what of Thomas? He could die in that prison."

"That is in God's hands. We will pray for his deliverance. I will write back to Julius. He may be able to do something. He mentioned the possibility of exchange." Marsh wrapped his hands around Stephanie's. "But you cannot go. I think you know that."

Anger, frustration and helplessness all boiled within Stephanie. "It's just that I feel so—so powerless. There's nothing I can do to help him."

"Pray for him, my dear. With all the love you feel in your heart. I am sure that our Lord will hear you." Stephanie closed her eyes, moisture squeezing from between her lids. Reopening them after several minutes, she looked at the preacher and smiled. "Yes. You're right, of course. It was a silly idea." She handed the letter back to Marsh.

He raised his hand. "Keep it," he said. "It may continue to give you comfort, as a token of his existence. I want you to have it."

The preacher rose from the chair. "I must get back. As much help as James is, he can't finish the harvest by himself." Catching Harriet's attention, he motioned for his coat and hat. "You've made the right decision, my dear. It's time for you to give back to your aunt the love and care she and your uncle gave you all these years."

"That's true. After my parents died all those years ago, he and Aunt Mildred took me in. They treated me like their own child. I owe them a lot."

Stephanie followed Marsh out onto the porch. "You don't know how much I appreciate your coming, Pastor. Every bit of news I can get about Thomas makes me feel closer to him."

Marsh leaned down, kissing her forehead. "I know he cares for you deeply, my dear. Have faith. Our prayers and your love will bring him home."

"I'm certain of it. Oh, would you please thank James again for me? He was so kind to help with Auntie at the funeral."

"I will. He originally told us that he planned to leave after the fall harvest, but for some reason has changed his mind. I'm glad. With Thomas gone, he's been of great assistance here on the farm." Putting his hat on, he patted Stephanie's shoulder. "I'll let you know just as soon as I hear anything else."

Stephanie leaned against a post as she watched Pastor Marsh ride away. *Oh, Thomas. What's happened to you? What will happen to us?*

Chapter 52

William sat next to the fireplace, fidgeting in his chair while watching his mother wash clothes. Lucinda glanced at him occasionally, wishing he could settle down. She understood his restlessness, confined to the cabin since his return.

He tossed a hunk of wood into the fire. "I can't figure why Mr. McCay doesn't come around anymore. He's been kind of stand-offish whenever I've seen him. 'Lissa just changes the subject whenever I say anything about him. And you haven't mentioned him hardly at all since right after I got home. What's going on? When are you two going to get married?"

Lucinda did not look up from her washing. "I'd rather not discuss that subject right now."

"You never want to talk about it. Something's gone wrong between you two, hasn't it?"

"Please, William. I'd really rather not speak about it." Lucinda scrubbed furiously at a stain on a shirt. "It's really none of your business."

His mother's sharp tone was surprising, and also vaguely irritating. Standing, he reached for his tattered jacket and kepi. "Ma, I'm going into town."

Startled, Lucinda looked up. "You're still terribly weak, darling. I don't think that's a good idea."

"Got to get out. Been cooped up too long." He carefully pulled the coat over the stump of his wrist. "Going to see Mary. I haven't heard hardly anything from her since I got back, and I can't stand it anymore."

Lucinda had gone totally motionless, her hands still immersed in the wash water. After several long moments, she reached for a towel, drying her hands as she walked over to her rocker by the fireplace. She motioned to another chair. "Come and sit down, William. There's something you should know."

Puzzled, William sat. "What do you mean?"

"Jedidiah and I are not—well, we aren't going to get married."

"Why? What's the matter?"

"Do you remember the argument Mr. McCay and I had the evening you came home?"

"Yes."

"And do you remember the next day, after Melissa and I came back from going into town? You asked me why we were so upset, wanting to know what happened."

"You wouldn't tell me."

"We went to the Mercantile to pick up a few things. What I really wanted to do was to apologize to Jedidiah. After you and I talked about Thomas that night, I couldn't sleep, thinking about what was said. I finally realized that he was right. I was afraid to make changes in my life right now. But I had to admit to myself that it was time to make a decision—that I couldn't put my life and the lives of those I love on hold any longer. So when we went to town, I was going to tell Jedidiah that I was ready to set a date for the wedding."

"So what happened? Why didn't you?"

"Melissa and I waited outside the front of the store for quite a while, but there was no sign of him. We were just turning to leave when—oh, my." A sob burst from Lucinda's throat.

William leaned forward, laying his hand on his mother's knee. "What, Ma? What happened?"

Lucinda wiped her moist cheek with the dishtowel. "Jedidiah was coming down the back stairs—with Mary Stewart."

William's eyes flew wide open. *"Who?"*

"She was wearing—Oh, dear Lord—she only had a robe on."

William's stomach began to boil. "I don't believe it."

"Oh, William, it's true. My heart was broken, thinking that Jedidiah had been carrying on with some other woman. And with Mary, of all people."

The churning in his belly grew as William rose, stumbling to the fireplace. He felt chilled, even standing in front of the flames. The world suddenly seemed disjointed, out of place. "Can't be, Ma. It just can't." He turned to look at his mother, moisture clouding his eyes. "I love her, Ma."

Standing, Lucinda wrapped her arm around her son. "I know you do. That's what makes it so hard to tell you all this. But you have to know. She threatened me. She said that if I told anyone, either you or the town council, she'd get even. The expression on her face frightened me, William. It was a crazy, vicious look. I was really afraid of what she would do."

Melissa entered the cabin carrying a milk pail. An immediate sense of apprehension struck her as she saw her mother and brother standing by the fireplace. "What's going on? What's happened?"

William turned slightly, glancing at her. He looked at his mother's crimson face, then patted her hand. "I've got to go to town. This needs settling."

Lucinda clutched at his jacket sleeve. "No, William, please don't."

"Got to, Ma." Gently lifting her hand from his arm, he headed out the door past Melissa.

Lucinda stretched her hand out toward her daughter. "Stop him, Melissa. Don't let him go."

"Why, Ma? What's he going to do?"

"I told him about Jedidiah and Mary." Melissa gasped. Lucinda collapsed into her chair. "He's gone to confront her. Stop him, 'Lissa, please stop him."

Melissa spun and ran out toward the barn. William was struggling to lift his saddle onto the horse.

Melissa grasped the saddle. "Don't go, Willie. Ma can't take it if you get hurt again."

Beads of sweat were evident on William's forehead. "I've got to do this, 'Lissa. Please, help me cinch this up."

Melissa gripped the saddle tightly, not moving as she stared into her brother's eyes. The pain she witnessed tore at her heart.

William gazed at her for a moment. "Please, Melissa. Let me go," he said, his voice barely audible.

Seconds passed while they stood, looking at each other.

"Damn it, Willie." Pushing her brother out of the way, she centered the saddle on the horse's back, then reached underneath to fasten the cinch strap. Unused to hearing his sister curse, William stepped back as she finished tying the strap off, then reached for the reins. "Go on, go get your heart broken," she said angrily as she handed the reins to William. "She's no good, Willie. She never has been."

William swung onto the horse, then leaned down to wipe Melissa's cheek. "I know you and Ma are trying to protect me. But this is something I have to do for myself. I'll be all right." Bracing himself with his stump, he turned the horse's head toward the road.

The early December morning was crisp and clear. He breathed in the sharp, clean air as he rode. The pressure in his chest was almost gone, and he felt a renewed strength in his body. *Good to get outside again. Even though it's for a bad reason.*

William reined up in front of the Mercantile. Lost in thought, he reached with his missing hand as he began to dismount. Thrown off balance by the mistake, he fell backwards, landing with a thump under the horse. He sat there for several moments, trying to recover his wits. A few people watched and murmured, but no one offered any assistance. Rising to one knee, he grasped the horse's cinch. As he pulled himself to his feet, he heard a laugh behind him.

"Look at the poor little crippled soldier boy. Never could stay on his horse."

Memories of a long-ago beating flooded to the surface as William recognized the voice. Hiram Parker. One of Jonathon Evans's ruffians. William kept his back to him.

"Leave me be, Parker. You and I've got nothing to talk about."

Parker spat, then guffawed. "S'pose you're going to see your precious Mary? The town tramp?"

William spun, his face ablaze with fury.

A wide grin split Parker's face. "Ooh, look at this. Got a rise out of you, didn't I?" He spat again. "Hell, there's no secret about it. 'Course, she hasn't been as much fun since she did it with McCay."

An explosion went off in William's brain. Without thinking, he lashed out at Parker, who easily dodged the awkward jab. Parker laughed, then swung with his fist, catching William in his gut. Caught off guard, he staggered back, the wind knocked out of him. Parker followed, aiming at William's chin with a hard right, sending him flying against the rump of his horse. He sagged to the ground, his strength depleted.

Parker stood for several minutes studying his opponent while he massaged his knuckles. Drawing a knife from his belt, he knelt down over William. "Mebbe I should just chop off that other hand. Then you won't be so much trouble." Gasps rose from the crowd as several people stepped back, but no one seemed willing to intervene.

Jedidiah McCay burst from the Mercantile door, a shotgun in his hands. He leveled the piece. "Drop that blade right now, Parker, or I'll cut you in half!"

Hesitating for only a second, Parker released the knife, letting it fall to the ground. Standing, he backed away as McCay came down the steps. "Get going, you little bastard," said McCay. "Get out of here before I give you both barrels."

As Parker beat a hasty retreat, McCay stooped down, taking William by the arm. "Let me give you a hand, son." He helped William to his feet. "Come on in. You've got a cut under your chin. Let me wash it up."

Up in McCay's rooms, William sat while Jedidiah wet a cloth, then dabbed at the blood on his jaw. "Mind telling me what that was all about?" asked McCay.

William stared straight ahead, unsure what to say.

McCay rinsed out the cloth in the basin, then handed it back to William. "Somehow I think it's got something to do with Mary Stewart."

William patted the cut. "Ma told me what happened."

Jedidiah leaned against a wall. "I figured she would. I want you to know I never intended for that to happen."

"How could you?"

"I've been trying to understand myself, but I still don't know for certain. Hell, William, I don't even remember much of what happened. I was upset that night. Mad at your mother, yes. Frustrated because it seemed like she was never going to commit to a wedding date. Kept coming up with more excuses to put it off. I was lonely, too. I was just sitting in a chair that night, angry at the world. Heard a noise down in the store. Went downstairs to check. Next thing I knew I was on the floor."

He pointed to the partially healed gash on his temple. "Someone hit me on the head—just about knocked me out. A few minutes later, Mary came in. Everything was spinning. She helped me up here— cleaned the blood off my head. I felt confused, not knowing what was going on. She kept looking at me. I felt like I was going to drown in those brown eyes. Then she kissed me . . . and the next thing I remember was waking up the next morning with her in bed beside me. I felt dirty, and so ashamed. All I could think about was how I had betrayed your mother. I told Mary that, but she just laughed at me. I tell you, William, I wanted to strangle her right then. I tried to get her out of here before anyone could find out, but—."

"But Ma and Melissa were outside."

"That's right. God help me, William, I am so ashamed for what I did. Please believe me when I tell you that I love your mother. There is no one else. Certainly not Mary Stewart. I despise that girl for what she's done to me."

William sat silent for awhile. Rising, he tossed the cloth into the basin. "Got to go talk to her."

"I don't know if that's a very good idea."

"Maybe not, but I've got to hear it from her. Got to set things straight. To find out whether she's got any feelings for me. Or if she ever did."

"She's dangerous, William. She'll only hurt you again. She hurts everyone who comes in contact with her."

"That may be." He stepped to the head of the stairs. "Thanks for cleaning me up. I know you didn't mean to let things get out of hand. I'll talk to Ma. She still loves you. Maybe I can make her see it wasn't your fault."

"Thank you for understanding. I'm grateful. Tell her that I love her, and that I'll do anything to earn her forgiveness." He put out his hand.

William grasped Jedidiah's hand, nodded, then headed down the stairs.

Several minutes later, William stood on the Stewart house porch, pounding on the door. Opening it just a crack, Mary peered out at him. "Oh! Willie—uh—hello—uh—wait just a minute 'til I get decent." She closed the door with a bang. Muffled sounds, like frantic voices, filtered through the door. Several minutes later, Mary reopened it. "Come in, come in, Willie darling."

William's eyes followed her as she led him into the parlor, watching her intently as she straightened her dress. Stopping by the mantle, she turned, gave a quick glance past William, then back to him.

"Let me look at you. You've changed, Willie. You look—well, paler than I remember." Her eyes repeatedly returned to his stump. "How have you been?"

He sat down on the sofa. Looking down, he noticed a wastebasket with several wadded pieces of paper. Something about them looked familiar. "Tolerable. I've wanted to see you ever since I got back. Why didn't you answer my messages?"

Mary feigned surprise. "Messages? What messages?"

"I sent notes to you. By anyone who stopped by the farm. Lots of them."

"My goodness. I don't know what happened. I didn't get a single one."

William reached down into the wastebasket, plucking out a wrinkled piece of paper. His handwriting was visible on it. "Then what's this?"

"Why, Willie, I can't imagine how that got there." She unconsciously glanced toward the closet again.

366

"Probably all the other notes ended up that way, too."

"And just what do you mean by that?"

"I mean that you're a liar. You've been lying to me all along, haven't you?"

The shocked expression on Mary's face was genuine this time. "Who do you think you are, calling me that?"

"All these years I thought you cared for me. I've been a fool. You only care for yourself, you little whore. You torment everyone around you. You've ruined my mother's happiness with what you did with Mr. McCay."

Mary's cheeks were becoming crimson. "Your mother? It's your mother who's ruined my life. I've been discharged as schoolmistress. And it's your fault. You and your mother. You two are the real liars. You've been spreading falsehoods all around town about me."

"What lies? They're not lies. Mother told me about you and Jedidiah."

"Just what did she tell you?"

"About how she caught you two together."

"Why, Willie, do you believe that I would do such a thing?"

He stared at her, as though he was seeing her for the first time. Her expression of disdain was repulsive. "Yes, I do. You've been acting like a trollop for years. And I was an idiot for not seeing it before now. You never cared for me." He pointed at the portrait of Julia Stewart. "You're just like your mother!"

Her rage growing, Mary slapped him across the face. "Bastard! Don't you dare mention her." Spinning around, she suppressed a sob, not wanting him to know how agonizing it was to listen to his words.

The force of the accusations surprised her. How could he say such things to her? Her emotions were running wild. Part of her wanted to say she was sorry, to find a way to make up to him. She *did* care for him. The nights they spent together during his furlough flashed in her mind. Oh, to have him hold her like he did then. But he wasn't being fair. After all, he'd been gone for years. What did he expect of her? To do absolutely nothing while he was away? That's it. It wasn't her fault, it was his. Leaving her to cope with her stupid, Yankee-loving father. She had a right to some fun, didn't she? Even if it was with a dullard like Parker. Willie had no right to accuse her like this. That's it. It was all his fault. He came here to hurt her. Well, she'd fix him. He was the one who was going to hurt.

Mary turned back to face William. "You know something, my darling, dear Willie? I actually did have feelings for you. At one time.

But you left me here to waste away in this god-forsaken place while you went off to war. Who are you to accuse me? I'll bet that you left a string of girls behind."

"I did not! You're the only one I ever spent the night with. I loved you. I had hoped that one day, we would get married."

Mary laughed. "Married! Oh, what utter drivel. You know, Willie, you are such a pathetic, naïve little boy. Let me set you straight about something. Yes, I wanted Jedidiah McCay. He was so upright, so proper. The only real man left here in town, and I wanted him for myself. It was a perfect opportunity. He was weak, not in control. We were in bed together."

A snort. "But he passed out on me! I spent the whole night pushing and prodding him, trying to get him to wake up long enough to make love to me, but he just lay there like a stone."

"So you lied to Ma, about his saying he loved you?"

"Oh, for heaven's sake, I made that up."

William rubbed the cut on his chin. "What about Parker?"

"Parker? What's he got to do with anything."

"Just that he was bragging about the two of you."

Another glance toward the closet. "That fool? I keep that numbskull on a leash for when I need someone to service my needs. That's all he's good for."

A loud noise from across the room caught their attention. "What was that?" asked William.

Mary frowned. "Just something falling over in the closet, probably. Doesn't matter."

William rose. "Goodbye, Mary. I still love you. But I can never forgive you what you've done." He pointed toward the closet. "Tell Parker—or whoever else you're hiding in there—that he's welcome to you."

Mary watched in stunned silence as William passed out the front door. Angry and confused, she felt paralyzed. She couldn't believe that he had actually walked out on her.

A few moments later, the closet door opened with a crash. Parker came tumbling out, tangled in several coats. Mary looked at him with disgust. "You idiot. I told you to be quiet. He figured out you were in there."

Throwing off the coats, Parker stormed over to Mary. "Who the hell cares, you little bitch. What did you call me? Numbskull? What the hell does that mean?"

Mary turned away from him. "It means you're stupid. Now get out of here." She gave a wave of dismissal. "By the back door, so no one sees you."

Parker grabbed her by the arms. "Stupid, am I? I ought to wring your pretty little neck!" Forcing her back against the wall next to the fireplace, he clamped one hand around her throat.

Struggling to free herself, Mary reached out toward the mantle, grasping at an ornate vase. Swinging as hard as she could, she smashed the pottery against the side of Parker's head. Dazed, he staggered backward, blood streaming from a nasty cut.

Dashing over to a sideboard, she pulled out a huge single-shot pistol. Steadying himself against the parlor door, Parker watched wild-eyed as Mary leveled the gun, and strode toward him. She shoved the muzzle underneath his jaw. "Get out of my house, you God-damned bastard! If I ever catch you around here again, I'll blow your head off." She pulled the pistol back just enough to allow Parker to slip past her. He staggered toward the street door. Mary waved the gun. "No, damn you. Out the back so no one can see you."

Drawing a handkerchief, Parker pressed it on his wound as he stumbled toward the kitchen and the rear door. As he slid through, he turned, muttering. "We ain't done yet, little miss high-and-mighty. You're the second one who's pulled a gun on me today. I won't forget that. You ain't seen the last of me."

Mary cocked the pistol. "Get out of here. Just leave me alone!" Frightened now, Parker took off at a run. She watched him disappear around a corner, then slammed the kitchen door so hard one of the glass panes shattered.

Laying the pistol on the table, she sat, her hand massaging her bruised throat. She began to tremble, slightly at first, then with increasing violence. Tears flooded down her cheeks. *It's not fair, it's not fair. They're all bastards—all of them. Willie, Parker, McCay, Lucinda. They've left me nothing—nothing. I'll get even—they can count on that.*

Chapter 53

"Where the hell did they come from?" Baxter peered through his field glasses at the butternut-clad horsemen charging down the hill, blue-crossed battle flag whipping in the winter air. He grabbed Curly by the arm and pointed. "Confederate cavalry! They're on us!"

Baxter and his guerrillas had moved their operations into eastern Tennessee, taking advantage of General Longstreet's advance on Knoxville. With strong Union sentiment in the region, they conducted most of their raids wearing Confederate gray. Today, however, they were clothed in Yankee blue. Scouts had detected Union cavalry raiders in the area, so on this day Baxter decided to impersonate Federal troops. The latest foray had yielded sparse results, however. Gathered near the edge of a small woodlot, the guerrillas were violently arguing over the division of the meager spoils when the Rebels came boiling over a nearby rise.

Taken completely by surprise, the raiders scrambled to catch their horses and mount. A volley of shots toppled several before they landed in their saddles. Within seconds, the cavalrymen were in among the guerillas, cutting them down with buckshot and pistol balls.

Firing his two heavy pistols, Curly glanced over his shoulder to Major Baxter. "Boss, we got to get out—!" Curly's warning was cut short by a shotgun blast that shredded his chest. Red speckles spattered Baxter's uniform. Letting loose a string of expletives, the major dashed toward a clump of poplars, behind which Hercules was holding his horse.

Paralyzed with fright, the servant was either unable or unwilling to release the reins. Lashing out, Baxter slammed his revolver barrel against Hercules's cheek, knocking him to the ground. As he leapt into the saddle, he spotted a Confederate officer charging after him. Spurring his horse toward the tree line, he fired a shot at the approaching horseman, swearing furiously as the ball missed.

Bounding through the forest, he continually glanced back over his shoulder at the soldier chasing him. Whether his horse was more rested than his pursuer's, or stronger, he quickly outdistanced them. After several minutes, he lost sight of the officer. Smiling, he faced ahead just in time to realize that his path was taking him on a direct course to the edge of a ravine. Wrenching back on the reins, he barely managed to pull up his horse before plunging over the precipice. As he peered down at the bog, a bullet whined past his ear. Spinning around, he was amazed to behold his pursuer galloping toward him, pistol raised to fire again. Before he could cock his polished Colt, a pistol ball caught him in the throat. Tumbling from the saddle, he careened over the edge of the gulch.

The surviving guerrillas were scattering in all directions, desperate to escape the slaughter. Having caught a wounded horse, and with no notion of which way to go, Hercules had followed the fleeing Baxter. He broke through the edge of the forest just in time to witness the major's demise. Pulling up behind a cedar brake, he remained hidden until the Confederate departed.

Even though gunfire continued to echo through the trees, Hercules dismounted and crept to the edge of the ravine. Knowing that danger was all around, he still could not resist the urge to peer down into the mud-pit. The Major's corpse lay face down in the slime, filthy brown mud slowly enveloping the once immaculate uniform. A grin spread across Hercules' face. He chuckled, then burst out laughing. "Ain't gonna shine them boots no more now, boss."

Convulsed in uncontrollable laughter, Hercules seemed totally unaware of the danger still around. His racket caught the attention of another of the pursuing soldiers, who brought it to an abrupt end by firing a shot that lifted a chunk of the slave's scalp. His body tumbled into the pit, coming to rest on top of Baxter.

Jonathon Evans had managed to emerge from the melee unscathed, and was now galloping through the woods. The sound of gunfire faded behind him. Confident that he had escaped, he pulled the reins to slow his horse. As he moved along at a slow trot, he caught a glimpse of movement through the trees not far away. There was something familiar; something that raised the hair on the back of his neck. Pulling his pistol, he crouched down in his saddle, trying to identify the stranger. Through a clear spot in the brush, he finally was able to see who it was. Jerking himself upright in the saddle, he let out a bellow. "Jake!"

Reining up his horse at the sound of his name, Jake turned back to see who had yelled at him. "What the hell do you want, Evans?"

Jonathon leveled his pistol. "Put your hands out where I can see 'em, Jake. You and I've got unfinished business, boy."

Jake lifted his hands a few inches. "Just what the hell are you talking about, Evans?" He scowled. "I ain't too all-fired happy about you drawing down on me."

"Made a promise. Haven't kept too many promises in my life, but this one I've got to keep."

"Promise, huh? Someone must be pretty trusting."

Jonathon cocked the revolver. "Yup. Promised Grainger I'd kill you first chance I got. Looks like now's as good a time as any."

Yanking the reins, Jake spun his horse around, charging Evans while pulling his Sharps rifle from its leather boot. Startled by the suddenness of Jake's attack, Jonathon's shot went wide of the mark. Before he could cock the pistol again, Jake galloped to his side, shoving the carbine's muzzle into his chest. Jake grinned. "Shoe's on the other foot now, bud. Looks like you've screwed up on this promise. Drop the piece."

Evans allowed the revolver to slide from his fingers. Jake pushed the barrel hard against Jonathon's sternum. "All right. Now, both hands on the pommel."

Glaring straight into Jake's eyes, Evans slowly lowered his hands, laying them across the front of the saddle. Jake chuckled. "So brother Joe is reaching from the grave. Before I send you along to meet him, I just want to know one thing. Joe was too ornery to have any friends. Why the devil are you tryin' to get even for that son of a bitch?"

"Let's just say we had a lot in common." Jonathon's eyes blurred. "He was the closest thing to a pard I've had."

Jake let out a laugh. "You know, Evans, I almost feel sorry for you." He gave Jonathon another poke, his eyes narrowing. "But not much. Been nice chattin', friend, but I need to move on. Say hello to Joe when you get to Hell."

Jake pulled the trigger. The hammer snapped—but did not fire. Realizing a split-second before Jake did that the rifle had misfired, Jonathon catapulted toward his opponent, knocking him from his saddle.

Crashing to the ground, the two grappled, rolling over and over between the horse's legs. Jake clawed at his opponent's eyes, while Jonathon wrapped his hands around Jake's throat. Out of the corner of his eye Jake spotted the Sharps. Gasping for air under Evans' chokehold, he stretched out with his hand. Wrapping his fingers around the muzzle, he lifted it and swung. Letting go his stranglehold, Jonathon ducked, but not fast enough to avoid a glancing blow to his temple. Stunned, he rolled to the ground next to one of the horses. Shaking his head, he frantically tried to clear it.

Using the gunstock for support, Jake struggled to his feet. Gripping the barrel of the rifle with both hands, he staggered over to where Jonathon fought to regain his senses. Swinging the gun like a club, he aimed for Evan's head.

Before Jake could bring the weapon down, Jonathon jerked to one side, rolling between the horse's legs. Grabbing a stirrup, he pulled himself up as Jake dashed around the animal's rump. Jonathon snatched Grainger's Bowie knife from a sheath tied to the saddle. Jake swung again with the carbine. Fending off the clubbed weapon with his left arm, Evans thrusted, sinking the blade up to the hilt in Jake's stomach.

The two stared at each other for several moments. Jake tried to speak, but the only sound that emerged from his trembling lips was a squeaky hiss. Jonathon released the Bowie. Jake slid to his knees, the rifle clattering to the ground. Evans knelt, looking intently into Jake's face. "Looks like you're going to be the next one into hell today, friend." Reaching out, he yanked the knife from Jake's abdomen. Jake's eyes fluttered for a moment before he let out a faint moan and collapsed.

Wiping the blade, Jonathon returned the Bowie to its sheath, then mounted his horse. He gazed down at Jake's body. *Well, Grainger, you old bastard, I've done for you. Your brother's on his way to meet you.* Gathering the reins, he pointed his horse southwards. *Nothing left for me around here.*

A far off rumble of thunder rolled across the hills. Evans glanced up to see dark clouds building on the horizon. He shivered. The air had a scent of snow to it. *Got to find some place to hole up for the night.* He remembered an abandoned farmstead where the band had sheltered the night before. *Shouldn't be more than a couple of miles away. Maybe I can reach it before the storm breaks.*

Trotting along through the forest, he came upon the trail the raiders had left the previous day. *Good, not much further.* He pulled his Union blouse tighter around his chest. The air was definitely getting colder.

A dull boom echoing through the woods roused Jonathon's curiosity. *That didn't sound like thunder.* Drawing his revolver, he reined his horse down to a slow walk. Another boom. He knew that he was close to the farm clearing. *Damn it. What the hell is going on?*

Dismounting, he crept up beside a large oak, from where he could get a good view of the farm clearing. The gunshots were increasing in intensity. Peering around, he could make out puffs of smoke coming from the cabin windows. *Who the hell's in there and what are they shooting at?*

The distinctive crack of a pistol drew his gaze off to the far side of the clearing. *Got to get a better view.* Keeping low, he maneuvered around the tree. A flash of blue caught his attention. *Yank cavalry! But how many?* From what he could see, and judging from the volume of fire, he guessed there were at least three soldiers blazing away at the cabin.

Jonathon remained crouched next to the oak for several minutes, unsure what to do. White specks of snow were beginning to swirl through the air. He glanced up at the sky and scowled. *Damn it. Probably have a blizzard before too long. What the hell do I do now?* He brushed some flakes from his blue blouse, then glanced at the cabin again. Two muskets were visible, returning fire toward the Federals. *Maybe I can even the odds a little.*

Taking up the horse's reins, he crept through the underbrush until he was behind the cavalrymen. Tying off the horse, he drew his carbine from its boot, then began working his way from tree to tree, coming up behind the soldiers. He swallowed, then stepped out into the open. A big sergeant swung around, his revolver leveled.

Jonathon raised his hand. "Hey, don't shoot! I'm Union."

The sergeant lowered his gun at the sight of the blue coat. "Good way to get yourself killed, sneaking up on someone like that."

"Sorry about that. I was riding by on scout and heard the shooting. What goes here?"

"Got a couple of Johnnies holed up in that cabin yonder. Trying to smoke 'em out."

"That so? What's so important 'bout two Rebs?"

The sergeant pointed skyward. "See that storm coming? We want that place for shelter. Them Johnnies got there first, but we'll get 'em out." He grinned. "Besides, I never waste a chance to kill Rebs."

Jonathon's eyebrows rose. Fighting to keep his rising anger hidden, he said, "I could use a dry place to put up, too. Need some help?"

"Sure." The sergeant pointed off with his pistol. "Go on 'round that way. Try to flank 'em."

The two other Yanks continued popping away. The sergeant looked back at the cabin. "Now we'll skin those damn Rebs."

Cocking the carbine with one hand, Jonathon pulled the revolver with the other. "Actually, I think I'll take a little of your skin first." Leveling the rifle at the sergeant, he pulled the trigger. The force of the bullet sent the sergeant sprawling. The other two cavalrymen spun, firing as they turned. Ducking down, Jonathon shot one, but before he could shoot again, the remaining soldier fired. The ball passed through the muscle of Jonathon's thigh, causing him to lose his grip on the carbine. The Federal cocked his pistol, but before he could fire again, Jonathon shot once more, the bullet slamming into the Yankee's chest.

He felt at the wound on his leg. Hurt like hell. Holstering the revolver, he reached down, ripping a piece from the sergeant's shirt. Pressing the cloth to his wound, he staggered to his horse. A sensation of white-hot needles lanced through his leg. Grasping the saddle, he tried to pull himself up. The pain and growing weakness made it impossible for him to mount. He tore off the Union tunic, tossing it into the bushes, then retrieved his Confederate jacket from the saddlebag. Struggling to pull the coat on, he limped out into the clearing. "Ho the cabin! Don't shoot! I'm Confederate!"

"The hell you say!" came a voice from inside the house.

"It's true. I got the drop on these Yanks. They're all dead. Need some help. I caught one in the leg."

"Damn Yankee! You think we're stupid?"

"I'll prove it. Let me come out into the open. No weapons."

Several moments of silence passed. Jonathon figured they must be arguing about what to do. The voice called out again. "Okay, whoever you are. Show yourself, but don't try no tricks. We've got our guns on you."

Jonathon unbuckled his belt, dropping it to the ground. The torment in his leg was growing unbearable. Trying desperately to stay on his feet, he tottered out of the tree line. Raising his hands, he called out to the cabin. "Well? You satisfied yet?" Overwhelmed by the pain, he sank to the ground.

The cabin door creaked. A quivering musket barrel poked through. "You just hold steady right there." Two ragged apparitions eased through the opening, their rifles leveled at Jonathon. One motioned to the other. "Bert, you go take a look at him while I cover you."

Warily, Bert walked over to Jonathon. He stood over the wounded man for a moment, then poked Jonathon's thigh with his musket. Jonathon winced in pain. Bert grinned, then straightened up. "Hey, Zeke, looks like this feller's tellin' the truth. He's got a pretty good-sized hole in his leg." He pointed toward the bodies. "And there's three dead Yanks over there." He reached down with his hand. "C'mon and let me help you up. We'll get you over to the cabin."

Leaning his musket against a porch post, Zeke walked over to help. Supporting Jonathon between them, Zeke and Bert helped him into the cabin, laying him on a blanket next to a crumbling fireplace. Bert turned back to the door. "I'll go get them Yanks' horses. Might be something to eat in their haversacks."

"My horse is tied up behind them," said Jonathon. "Be grateful if you'd bring it up to the house."

Zeke knelt down next to Jonathon, examining his leg. "You're mighty lucky, friend. Looks like the ball missed the bone." Dabbing a cloth in a bucket of water, he cleaned and bandaged Jonathon's wound. "Lucky for us you turned up when you did."

Bert burst through the door, his arms overflowing with blue cloth. "Got some good Yankee greatcoats here. Just a little blood on 'em. Got some real coffee, too."

"How'd you get them buried so fast?" asked Jonathon.

"Didn't bury them. Left 'em to the buzzards."

Jonathon stared out through a broken window as exhaustion flowed over him. *Buzzards. There were buzzards back then, too. But I buried them. Couldn't leave them to the buzzards.* His mind drifted back—back to a girl kissing him. A girl who then died. She stood before him, her naked body covered with blood, gazing at him with eyes that held no life. Those eyes—even though he tried to look away from them he could not. Eyes accusing him, full of death. His own death. He wanted to scream but his lungs had no air. He shook violently.

"Hey, you okay there?"

He came to, roused by the voice and someone shaking his arm. Bert was kneeling by him, his hand on Jonathon's shoulder.

"We thought you'd gone out of your head. You was saying some pretty strange things. Something 'bout eyes."

Jonathon sat up. His head throbbed. "Nothing. Just a bad dream. How long was I out?"

"Just about an hour or so."

A fire burned in the fireplace. Evans shifted to soak up the soothing warmth. Heavy snow was beginning to fall outside. Before long the men had to move their chairs to avoid white flakes that sifted down through holes in the old roof. Bert pulled a battered pot from the fire. He grinned as he sniffed the hot liquid. "Ain't had any real coffee for better part of three years." Pulling up some tin cups, he filled them from the pot. Opening a small cloth bag, he poured some of the contents into each cup. "Those Yanks even had sugar. Now this here's Heaven."

Jonathon accepted a steaming cup gratefully. The warm liquid felt good going down his throat. The ache in his temples was easing. He leaned back against the wall, sipping slowly. "Where you boys from?"

Zeke set his cup on the table. "Alabama, near Muscle Shoals. Got separated from the army when we got beat over by Knoxville."

"You with Longstreet?"

Bert emptied his cup with a slurp. "Yeah. Been with him since the beginning of the war." Setting the cup on the table, he laid down on his blanket.

"You two must have seen a lot of action."

Zeke's eyes fixed on a hole in the floor. "Too much."

"Any idea where he is now?"

"Hell no, and I don't care. Bert and me have had enough. We're headed home just as fast as we can get there. We found this cabin to ride out the storm—that's when those Yanks jumped us. Guess they had the same idea." He let out a yawn. Rising, he stretched his arms, then scratched his side. "Long day. Guess I'll catch some shut-eye."

Jonathon watched while Zeke unrolled his bedroll in a corner. He also felt sleepiness descending upon him. He tried to fight the drowsiness, afraid that the nightmare would return. Before many minutes went by, the cabin echoed with the sound of snoring.

Jonathon woke stiff, but feeling better. He looked around, scowling. Zeke and Bert were nowhere to be seen. *Now what are those boys up to? Couldn't have gone too far. Their possibles are still here.* Picking up his carbine and accouterments, he hobbled over to the table. Dipping some water out of the bucket, he set to work cleaning his weapons.

After several minutes Bert and Zeke came through the door. "Freezin' out there," said Bert.

Evans moistened a wad of cloth. "Where'd you go?"

"Just out seeing to the horses." Bert tapped Zeke on the shoulder, motioning toward the fireplace. "C'mon over here. I want to talk to you 'bout something."

Bert and Zeke crouched down next to the fire. As he used the ramrod to run a wet wad down the barrel, he glanced over to the two. They were staring at him, but looked away quickly. A prickly sensation went down the back of his neck. *Now what's going on?* Easing his revolver from its holster, he slipped it out of sight beside his leg, positioned so he could grab it fast.

After several minutes, the two soldiers stood and walked toward Jonathon. His hand inched toward the pistol grip.

Zeke spoke. "Look, Evans, me and Bert, well, we was thinkin'. You must be pretty handy with a gun, gettin' the drop on those bluebellies like you did." He glanced at Bert, then back to Jonathon. "We could use another good feller along with us. We're likely to run into a lot more Yanks before we get home."

Jonathon relaxed, pulling his hand back from the gun. "I appreciate your offer, but—." His face darkened as an image of William Marsh pushed to the front of his thoughts. "But, no. I'll just hang around here for awhile 'til I've healed up a bit, then I'm heading back home to Georgia." Drawing the Bowie from its sheath, he ran his thumb along the knife-edge. "Got some accounts to settle there."

Chapter 54

"Hey, Marsh, wake up! Wake up, man! I just heard we're to be paroled!"

Irritated at his sleep being interrupted, Thomas opened his left eye a small bit, peering out at his tent-mate. "Go 'way, Roberts. It's just another rumor. We aren't ever going to get out of this place."

Roberts gave another tug on Thomas's arm. "It's the truth, I tell you. I heard it from a boy from the 23rd Pennsylvania who was talking with a fellow who works at the cook shack. He overheard a guard saying that the lieutenant was supposed to get another batch ready to leave."

"He heard, they heard. It's just gossip. You fresh fish are all the same, believing every rumor that comes down. I don't know how many times I've told you not to believe all the talk you hear in the camp."

"Just because I haven't been here very long doesn't mean I'm stupid. Look, they must be going to let some more go. That five hundred that left right after Christmas didn't make hardly a dent in the population. Those people across the river in Richmond town want to get rid of us. The papers say so. Just the other day O'Brien got one that said that they was scared that we was going to get loose and pillage the city."

Thomas rubbed his eyes. "Okay, don't believe me. Why don't you go out and find someone else to bother."

"Fine, I'll leave. You go right to hell, Marsh. I can find someone else to talk to." Roberts grabbed his blanket and scooted out of the tent.

Thomas stretched. No use trying to get back to sleep. He crept out through the flap, his breath streaming from his nostrils in clouds as he glanced around. Roberts sat beside the tent, pulling his blanket tight around him. Thomas knelt down beside him. "Hey, Roberts, I'm sorry. I'm not too sociable when I first wake up. I'll ask around, see if I can hear anything more about an exchange."

A toothy grin spread across Roberts's face. "You'll see. We won't be here much longer. I can't wait to get home to tell my folks about this place."

Thomas smiled. Thad Roberts couldn't be more than seventeen, full of boyish hope and good humor. Serving with Custer's cavalry in the Shenandoah Valley, he'd been captured by some of Mosby's partisans. Thomas felt an almost parental concern for the youth.

Standing, he rubbed the arms of his tattered artillery jacket to build up some warmth. *If those officers come over from Libby today, maybe I can get a new blouse.* The Federal government had shipped a load of uniforms through the lines to Richmond to be issued to the prisoners. Union officers from Libby Prison would come to the island periodically to pass out the clothing. Not all made it into the prisoners' hands, however. Thomas noted with contempt that several of the Confederate guards were wearing Union blue.

He shivered while surveying his surroundings. Belle Isle was close to the southern bank of the James River. No walls enclosed the prison camp, just a wide ditch inside earthworks. The ditch served as a "dead line." Prisoners would be shot if they attempted to pass over it. On a small hill overlooking the camp, artillery was trained on the compound. There were no buildings, just a few hundred widely differing styles of tents to house the prisoners. Across the wide channel of the river rose the church spires and smokestacks of Richmond, capital of the Confederacy. A couple of times Jefferson Davis and members of his cabinet had visited the island to observe the prisoners.

Thomas considered himself fortunate, actually. Being squeezed with ten other men into a tent with rotten canvas was better than the ones who had no cover at all. Hundreds of men lay out in the cold, spooning together trying to keep warm.

The sound of a commotion caught his attention. A wagon carrying a burly sergeant and two other armed soldiers was entering the compound. Reining up near the center, the sergeant stood up on the wagon seat. Cupping his hands to his mouth, he let out a bellow. "All right, you damn Yankees. Fall in for mail."

Excited men rushed into loose ranks. Passing mail through the lines was near impossible, but some did dribble through. News from home and loved ones was a major cause for celebration.

As he did every time, Thomas joined the crush of men desperate for a letter, though he didn't really believe there would be anything for him. He had often observed men reduced to tears after the last missive was passed out, leaving them empty-handed once more.

The sergeant held up a small wooden crate. "Box here for Thomas Marsh. New Hampshire artillery."

Thomas was incredulous, not believing what he had just heard. A box for *him*. He rushed up to the wagon. "I'm Marsh."

The sergeant shook the box, then handed it down to Thomas. He chuckled. "Don't look like it was packed too good."

One side of the crate was smashed open. Thomas peered inside, then glared at the sergeant. "There's nothing in here. What happened to it?"

The sergeant shrugged. "Can't rightly say, Yank. Someone else must have needed your stuff more than you did."

Feelings of loss and betrayal welled up within Thomas. Leaning back, he lifted the box to throw it at the sergeant. Alarmed, the guards brought their bayoneted muskets to the ready.

Thomas felt a hand on his shoulder. He glanced back. A gray-bearded corporal was staring at him with melancholy eyes. "I'd put that down if I were you, friend. Ain't worth getting shot over."

Thomas lowered the box. He gave the corporal a weak smile. "You're right. Wouldn't want to give them the satisfaction." He reached out, taking the corporal's hand. "Thanks."

"You're welcome. Too many men dying here. No need to commit suicide. Your time will come soon enough." The corporal tightened his grip, then turned and limped away. Thomas watched him go, then headed back toward his tent.

Roberts looked up as Thomas returned. "What did ya get, Marsh? Hope it's something good to eat."

Thomas threw the crate down at Thad's feet. "Didn't get anything. Damn Rebs broke it open and stole it all."

Roberts grinned as he reached for the box. "Not a total loss. We can use the boards for firewood. If we split it up into small pieces, maybe we can make it last a couple of nights."

Thomas could not help grinning. Thad's eternal optimism constantly raised his spirits.

Roberts continued prying off the remains of the lid. "Hey, what's this?" Tacked to the underside of the slat was an envelope. "Hey, Marsh. There's a letter hooked here." He tore the paper from the cover and examined the writing. "Who's 'Miss Stephanie Carroll'?"

Thomas ripped the letter from Roberts' hand, his heart skipping a beat at the sight of familiar handwriting. Diving into the tent, his hands shook as he tore open the envelope.

Lymington, New Hampshire
November 3, 1863

My darling Thomas,

I put pen to paper in the earnest hope that this letter and box will make their way to you. The news that you were taken prisoner was distressing and welcome at the same time. I thought I might die when you were declared missing after Gettysburg. To know that you are alive and not killed has given me great joy, but that is tempered with much sadness, knowing that you are being held captive by the Confederacy. I pray that you shall be exchanged before very long, and return home to me. I long to hold you in my arms.

I hope that the things we are sending reach you intact. Your Aunt Rebecca knitted the socks, and Harriet baked the pies for you. I hope you have some way to open the tins of peaches.

Rolling his eyes, Thomas shifted to try to calm the growling in his belly.

I received a letter from your mother. She is concerned about you of course, and has written letters to President Davis and Governor Brown trying to gain your release. She writes that William has returned home. He has lost his left hand as a result of his wounds and is very weak, but she expects that he will recover.

Startled, Thomas reread the paragraph again. *Oh, my God, Willie lost the hand. And Ma knows about me and where I am, damn it.*

Your uncle and aunt are doing well. James Stark has decided to remain at the farm instead of entering the army. He has been of great help to Pastor Marsh, and he has been a dear to me as well. It has been a comfort to have him to talk to.

Thomas unconsciously raised his eyebrows. *Now what's that supposed to mean?* Guilt washed over him as he immediately regretted his suspicions. James was his best friend, after all. He continued reading.

> *You will be pleased to know that Constable Mattson has been turned out of office. He has left the state for parts unknown. With him gone and with the passing of Uncle Charles it is safe for you to return once you have been released.*

Another surprise. *Charles Carroll dead? When did that happen?* Thomas felt like yelling out, but stifled the response. He felt free. He could go home now.

> *We found out where you are being held through a friend of Pastor Marsh in Washington, a Major Simpson. He has offered to assist you once you are released.*

A frown crossed Thomas' face. *Assist me? With what?* He glanced around the camp. *He must be involved with repatriating prisoners of war or something like that.*

> *My love, you never leave my thoughts, not even for a moment. I pray that the day will come soon when you return to me. I know that it is not considered proper for a young lady to ask this, but I love you too much to be bound by social rules. My dearest, will you do me the honor of allowing me to become your wife?*

Thomas gulped. He reread the sentence several times, not quite believing what he was seeing. Turning his face upwards, he closed his eyes, trying to imagine that Stephanie was standing there before him. In his mind's eye, he reached out to take her hand. *Yes, my darling, oh yes.*

A few days following the receipt of Stephanie's letter, Thad came rushing into the tent, giving Thomas's shoulder a violent shake. Rising onto his elbows, Thomas glared at the boy. "What the hell do you want now? I swear, one of these days I'm going to beat the crap out of you for doing that." In his anger, he failed to notice the seriousness of Thad's expression.

385

Roberts released his grip, pulling back. "Sorry, Marsh, but I figured you'd want to hear this. Just heard a new rumor."

Thomas groaned and rolled his eyes. Roberts held up his hands. "I know, I know, you don't believe in them. But this is different. I've heard it from several sources."

"All right, so what this time? Did the Confederacy surrender?"

"Don't be a smart ass. Something about a new prison camp down in Georgia. The word is that the Rebs are going to send most of us down there to get us away from Richmond. One thing, should be warmer than here."

"Georgia? But that's where—." Thomas swallowed hard. He was about to blurt out that he was from Georgia. He'd felt it wise not to let on to anyone that he had been born down South. "Where abouts?"

"Heard tell they're calling the place Camp Sumter. Somewhere in the middle of the state. Near some little town call Andersonville."

"Andersonville? Never heard of it. Well, can't be any worse than this God-forsaken island. When's this supposed to happen?"

"Don't know yet. Maybe in a few weeks."

Thomas suddenly noticed the dark expression on Thad's face. "What's wrong?"

"I—I thought sure we'd get exchanged by now. If they send us to Georgia, I'll never get home."

Thomas smiled. "Just because they ship us south doesn't mean we won't be exchanged. It's just too crowded here. Hey, you won't have to worry about your feet freezing anymore."

A small bubble of moisture trickled down Thad's cheek. "If they send me to this Camp Sumter, I'm not going home. I'll die there. I just know it."

Thomas had never seen Roberts so discouraged. He wanted to say something else to raise the boy's spirits, but the words just wouldn't come. The sad, disturbed look Thad wore alarmed him. "Go on and get some sleep. Things will be better in the morning."

Thomas watched as Roberts crawled to his side of the tent, pulling his blanket tightly over himself. Thomas lay back, gazing up at the multitude of holes in the canvas ceiling. Stars shone through several of the openings. *Andersonville. I wonder how far that is from Dahlonega. Maybe my family can help me there.* He pulled Stephanie's letter from his pocket. *Closer to home, but farther away from you.*

He pressed the envelope to his lips. *Somehow, I will get back home to you. I swear I will.*

Chapter 55

Climbing down from the carriage, Lucinda took a moment to adjust her coat. Trying the handle of the Mercantile's door, she found it locked. She peeked in the window but saw no movement. A hand-written sign said "Closed Until 2 O'Clock".

Walking around to the side of the building, she began to climb the stairs leading to the rear door. Her heart seemed to pound louder with each step. Reaching the landing, she stood for several minutes before raising her hand to knock. Hesitating again, her knuckles hung an inch from the door. Fighting off an impulse to escape, she took a deep breath, then rapped.

McCay's voice echoed from inside. "Just a minute. Be right there." Shortly, the door swung open. Jedidiah was thunderstruck when he beheld Lucinda standing before him. "Lucinda. Ah . . . Hello."

"Hello, Jedidiah. May I come in?"

He stepped back from the door. With a clumsy flourish, he waved her inside. "Why, certainly. Of course, come in, come in!"

Entering, Lucinda gave the room a quick scan, then immediately felt ashamed at her fleeting suspicion. That was not why she had come. As she removed her bonnet, she turned her head to keep Jedidiah from seeing the scarlet rising in her cheeks. "I wasn't sure you'd be here. I went to the front first and saw your sign."

Jedidiah closed the door. "To tell the truth, I was feeling a little under the weather this morning. Was going to wait 'til later to open up."

"Are you all right? You're not coming down with something, are you?"

"Don't think so. Really, I was being a little bit lazy." He turned to look at her. Several minutes of awkward silence passed as they gazed at each other. Every few moments one would begin to speak, but words would not come.

Lucinda felt as though she would burst. Finally she spoke up. "I . . . I wanted to see you. To apologize."

Surprise flooded Jedidiah's face. "Apologize? What for? I'm the one who hurt you."

"No, I do need to say I'm sorry. Sorry for believing the worst. For not giving you a chance to explain."

Crossing over toward the fireplace, McCay sat down in an old, overstuffed chair. He rubbed his hands together as he gazed down at the floor. "I don't blame you for thinking badly of me. It must have been quite a shock for you to encounter Mary coming down from here in her dressing gown."

"Yes, it was. I was horrified to see her like that. And I did assume the worst." Lucinda laid her bonnet on a dresser. "What you don't know is that William went to talk to her about it. That day when you rescued him from Parker."

"He told me he was going to talk to Mary."

"He did more than talk. He confronted her about all the evil things she's been doing. Do you know what she did then? She laughed at him. Then she told him that you two didn't—well, really do anything."

Jedidiah looked up. "That can't be true. But I don't know—that is to say I don't remember. The whole night is still a blur. I do vaguely remember her kissing me. But the first real memory I have is waking up in bed with Mary lying next to me."

"William told me about the kiss. He also said that Mary confessed that she tried, but that you wouldn't wake up."

McCay looked at Lucinda, astounded. "I—I'm not sure what you mean."

"You must have passed out from that bang on the head. Mary told William that she tried to rouse you all night but couldn't. When you finally did wake up, it was morning and nothing had happened. It made her so angry that she decided she would get even by making you *think* the two of you made love."

Jedidiah's face darkened. "Why, that little bitch. She made me believe that we were intimate. I've been so ashamed for . . . nothing." He looked up at Lucinda. "Well, almost nothing. I do remember kissing her. But I didn't mean to—I didn't know what I was doing."

"I know that. And I can't say that I'm happy about what happened. But I do understand. Mary was out for another conquest. She took advantage of you." Lucinda began to unbutton her coat. "I came here to say I'm sorry. For thinking that you were deceiving me. I'm sorry for jumping to the wrong conclusion."

"It was entirely understandable. After all, she was here in my room, in my bed. I was weak. I should never have let any of that happen."

Lucinda brushed his cheek with her fingers. "You were hurt. You weren't in your right mind. If you had been, she never would have gotten that close."

"I didn't mean to, Lucinda."

"Please, stop apologizing to me. I do understand. I'm the one who needs to say I'm sorry for not trusting you."

McCay cupped her hands in his. "Thank you for coming and telling me these things. I've been miserable, thinking I'd lost you."

"Don't worry, darling. We won't let anyone come between us with falsehoods again." She began to refasten her coat. "But I probably should go. You need to open the store."

Jedidiah held up his hand. "Please. Don't go. Until you stopped by, I was not really in the mood to face the world. You have certainly brightened my day." Jedidiah motioned to a closet. "Why don't you put up your coat and stay a little while."

Lucinda smiled. "I'd like to. We have some catching up to do." She lifted the latch on the closet, then hung her coat inside. Closing the door, she swung the latch into its slot. As she turned away, the door popped open. Puzzled, she threw the latch again and waited for a few seconds. Satisfied the catch was holding this time, she began to turn away. Just then the door sprung open once more.

Watching Lucinda's struggles, Jedidiah could not help chuckling. After seeing her try for a third and fourth time to secure the door, he exploded in laughter.

"Just what is so funny, Jedidiah McCay?"

"I'm sorry, my dear." Walking over, he reached for the catch. "There's a certain way you have to close it." He chuckled again. "You've got to do it just right, or the door won't lock correctly." Pulling the door open, he shoved the handle back into the latch. "Looks like it's locked, doesn't it?"

Lucinda nodded. "Try to open it." Lucinda took the handle and gave it a slight tug. The door popped open. "See? Now watch carefully. If you don't put this in right, the latch won't hold." He closed the door again, latching it one more time. This time, he gave the latch an extra shove, driving it further down into the slot with a loud click. "Now try it." Lucinda pulled on the door handle once more. This time it did not budge.

"How long has it been like that?"

"Oh, years. Sometimes it'll swing open on its own, other times it'll stay closed. Won't be locked, though, unless you hear the click."

"Why don't you fix it?"

Seeing her quizzical look as she stared at the knob, Jedidiah laughed again. "You know, it never occurred to me to get that fixed. Just got used to it being that way."

"Well, my darling, after we're married I'll help you remember all these little chores."

"Oh, I'm certain you will. You'll probably make me paint the store, too."

"That's a good idea. It certainly could use freshening."

"Well, maybe once this war is over, I can get some paint in."

Lucinda's expression turned sad. "Once the war is over. Oh, Jedidiah, it can't go on much longer, can it?"

"I don't think so. The Army of Tennessee hasn't won a major battle since Chickamauga, and they were badly beaten at Chattanooga. The Yankees are massing for a big push south. But I hear General Johnston is in command now. He's been working hard to whip them into shape. Word is they just gave the Federals a bloody nose at Rocky Face Ridge."

"Do you think the Union Army will reach us here?"

"Hard to say, but the big prize for them will be Atlanta. Nearly every railroad in Georgia funnels through there. If the Yanks take the city, they'll not only stop supplies from reaching us, but also Lee's army in Virginia. It could mean losing the war."

Lucinda stepped closer to him. "Then I don't want to wait anymore."

"What do you mean?"

"I want us to get married. Within the next month."

McCay stared at her for a moment. He grasped her by the arms, pulling her toward him. "Do you really mean that?"

Lucinda smiled, reaching out to caress his cheek. "Yes, my love, I do mean it. I've been so foolish. You've been right all along. We can't wait any longer to see what the future will bring. We may not have a future if the Union army reaches here. We have to live for today."

"I can go out and get a preacher right now. We could get married today."

"Not today, my darling. I do need a little time to prepare."

"But—."

Lucinda pressed her fingers to his lips. "Don't worry, my darling. I'm not having second thoughts. It's just that I want to have a proper wedding . . . in a church, with family and friends. And I want to make a new wedding gown. When Aaron and I got married all those years ago, I didn't have a gown. Just an old gingham dress. A judge married us, and the only people there were my father and a couple of people the judge dragged off the street to be witnesses. I don't want to get really fancy, but this time, I'd like to have as close to a proper wedding as I can."

"I understand, my dear. Go ahead, make your dress. You can take anything from the store you need. Why don't we plan to get married one month from today? Would that give you enough time?"

Lucinda wrapped her arms around Jedidiah's neck. "Yes, darling, that would be perfect. By the end of March I should be able to finish a dress that will make you so proud."

Jedidiah pulled her closer. "It's so wonderful to see you smile again. I've missed you so much." They gazed into each other's eyes for several moments, then he leaned forward, pressing his lips to hers. For several long minutes they kissed with growing intensity.

Lucinda pulled back, smiling. She glanced toward the bed. "Is that where the evil deed was done."

Suddenly uncomfortable, Jedidiah blushed. "Yes, I'm afraid it is."

The edges of Lucinda's mouth began to curl upward. "And you're sure now that nothing happened."

McCay was puzzled. "We've already gone over that. You know that nothing happened. You just told me that. What are you getting at?"

Lucinda began to play with his top shirt button. "I was just thinking that—." With a quick yank she tore off the button. "That maybe we could try that little scenario ourselves."

Incredulous, Jedidiah could not suppress a broad smile. "Why, Mrs. Marsh. Just what are you proposing?"

Fingering for the next button, she suddenly tore that one off also. "You did say you weren't going to open the store this morning, didn't you?"

"I think the good people of this town will allow me a morning off," he said, reaching for her bodice.

Chapter 56

"All right, Yank, get a move on." Thomas felt a prick of sharp steel in his back. Spinning around to confront his tormentor, he found himself staring into the black void of a musket's muzzle. The point of the attached bayonet hovered barely an inch from his nose. "Don't try nothin', or I'll drop you where you stand."

Thomas glared at the guard for a moment before retaking his place with other prisoners making their way up the train platform. Being penned up for the past five days in a cattle car had left him more ill tempered than any time since his capture. He glanced up at the station sign. AUGUSTA. A myriad of emotions welled up within him as the name seemed to bob around his memory. He had returned to Georgia for the first time in over a decade. He breathed a silent laugh. *What a way to come home.*

Entering the rear car, he worked his way through the crush of bodies to the opposite side. Leaning against the rough board wall, he steadied himself as the train lurched into motion. Thad Roberts, his companion from the camp, sat on the floor, absent-mindedly scooping up handfuls from a layer of old straw, letting it filter through his fingers and fall back to the floor. He performed the mindless ritual repeatedly.

Listening to the click-clack of the wheels on the iron rails, Thomas closed his eyes, his thoughts floating back over the past few weeks. Back to the day great excitement gripped the Belle Isle camp.

Several groups of men had been assembled and marched away, causing rumors to fly among the remaining prisoners. Gossip about exchanges and a return home heartened some. Mostly, though, the speculation centered on being moved to a new camp in Georgia. Some were terrified by the prospect, but more than a few held the opinion that nothing could be as bad as where they were. Thomas heard the names of Camp Sumter and Andersonville repeated. The names held little meaning for him.

By the third day, it was Thomas and Thad's turn for relocation. Formed up into squads, they were marched by way of a planked-over railroad bridge into Richmond. Herded into an old tobacco warehouse, Thomas spent the next two weeks watching the comings and goings in the Confederate capital. Down the street a short distance was another brick warehouse which housed captured Union officers. A placard with letters of peeling paint proclaimed "LIBBY & SON. SHIP CHANDLERS & GROCERS". Over a hundred Federal officers had escaped from there earlier in the month, causing great alarm in the city.

Near the end of February, panic gripped Richmond once again, fueled by rumors of a raid in force by Union cavalry. Thomas and his fellow prisoners watched with glee as companies of militia and batteries of artillery rushed up and down streets past their prison. The next day their joy turned to consternation as they watched processions of new Federal captives being marched by. They were crushed to learn that one purpose of the failed raid was to liberate the prisoner of war camps.

This new threat added to public demands that the prisoners be removed from Richmond. A few days into March, Thomas and about two hundred men were ordered out into the street late at night. Shivering in the frosty air, they were formed into ranks, then marched under heavy guard to the railroad depot. Soldiers from a company of Alabama infantry stood atop the cars, watching intently for any signs of escape attempts. Herded into boxcars, they soon began to clatter southward. Crossing the James River over a high trestle, the men peered down at Belle Isle. Thomas was not sorry to put that hateful place behind him.

The old locomotive wheezed and puffed as it strained to pull its sad cargo. Late the next afternoon they had reached Raleigh, North Carolina, where they were taken off and marched to another train to continue the journey. This was only the first of several transfers from one train to another. From Raleigh they traveled to Charlotte, then to Columbia, South Carolina.

A chronic lack of supplies and maintenance after four years of war had left the Southern rail system in shambles. The prisoners had to endure long hours confined to the cars, either waiting on side tracks for other trains to pass, or for repairs to either the train or tracks. By the time the captives reached Augusta, they had endured nearly a week enroute.

Rousing from his daydreams, Thomas opened his eyes, squinting as the early afternoon sun filtered through the car's side, spotlighting his face. He tapped Thad on the shoulder. "You got anything left to eat?"

Standing, Roberts dug in his pockets. "Just a little of this moldy pone. It's not much, but you can have it if you want."

Thomas reached for the crumbling yellow lump of cornmeal. He gave it a sniff, then took a bite. The sour, musty taste caused him to gag. Barely able to keep from vomiting, he spit the mass out. "God damn it, I'm sick of this! Oh, for some decent food!"

Overcome with frustration, Thomas stamped his foot—and was startled when the floor gave way with a loud *crack*. He and Thad stared at each other for a moment, then both knelt down. Wiping the rank straw from the floor, they found that the plank underneath had given way. Immediately they began to work at the board, but before many minutes had passed, their fingers were bleeding and full of splinters. Thomas looked up at the curious faces watching them work. "Hey, any of you got something we can use to carve on this board?"

After a few moments of shrugs and mumbling, one man spoke up. "I got an idea. Here." Pulling off his worn shoe, he turned it over to reveal a metal horseshoe-like appliance tacked onto the heel. Prying it off, he handed it to Thomas. "See if this heel plate will work."

Accepting the implement with thanks, Thomas set back to work hacking at the board. Before very long, he had enlarged the opening to about a foot across. "Hold this," he said, handing the tool to Thad. Taking off his jacket and kepi, Thomas stuck his head down through the hole. A hail of cinders and pebbles showered him as he tried to inspect the underside of the car. Yanking himself back up, he shook his head. He grabbed Thad's arm, yanking it in exultation. "We can do it! The space between the axles and ties is plenty wide enough."

"Wide enough for what? What are you talking about?"

"Look, we make this hole big enough for a man to slip through. After dark, we'll start lowering ourselves down. There's a couple of rods to use for handholds. We just drop down between the rails and let the axles go over us. In the darkness the guards will never notice us. We keep still until the train is out of sight, then we can get up and run for it."

Thad frowned. "But what about the moon? It was almost full last night. It'll still be bright tonight. The guards will still be able to see us."

"We'll have to take that gamble. Maybe it'll be cloudy. But this may be our only chance to get away before we arrive at the new prison. I'm going to risk it. How about you?"

Thad looked at Thomas for several seconds, then nodded. A murmur of agreement passed through the other prisoners. "Okay, then," said Thomas, pulling his jacket back on. "We'll try tonight. Now let's make this hole bigger."

A loud bang was followed by a shriek from the locomotive's whistle. An earsplitting squeal of metal on metal echoed along the track as the engineer applied his brakes. The prisoners struggled to keep their footing as the train shuddered to a halt. Loud cursing went up as inertia piled the men toward the front of the car. It took several minutes for the captives to untangle themselves.

A quick inspection revealed no injuries, other than a few bruises. One of the men peered out through a crack in a wall board. "Hey, they're taking everyone out of the other cars." He turned to Thomas, pointing at the hole. "You've got to hide that fast."

Thomas tore off his jacket, flinging it over the hole. Scraping up a pile of the old straw, he spread it over the coat. He glanced at Thad. "If nobody looks too close, that should keep it hidden."

The bolt was thrown and the door rolled open. A sergeant stood outside, motioning with his musket. "Everyone out. Over in that field yonder. Don't even think of trying anything."

"What happened?" asked Thomas as he jumped down.

The sergeant let out a snort. "It ain't really none of your business, but something came up off the track and jammed up in one of the wheels. Going to take a while to fix it. If it was up to me, you'd stay put. But they got to empty the broke car, so the cap'n said to take you all out."

The prisoners were herded out into an old cornfield. As they sat down among the stubble, a captain came around the front of the locomotive, striding over to the group. He stood for a moment, surveying the prisoners before he spoke. "Okay, you men all know the rules. Stay on the ground. Anyone stands up before we say so gets shot." The sound of several muskets being cocked served to emphasize the point.

Lying down in the dirt, Thomas felt the poke of a corn stalk in his back. Digging up several pieces of stubble, he managed to clear a small space to recline in. Rolling onto his back, he gazed up at the clouds passing across the mid-afternoon sky. *Would really help if it would rain tonight.* He shivered, missing his jacket as a chill breeze passed by.

Thomas had just about dozed off when Thad began to shake him violently. Squinting to see what his companion pointing at, Thomas rolled over to see a guard peering into their boxcar. Swallowing a gasp, he watched with rising panic as the soldier climbed inside. He felt faint. *Oh, God. If he steps on that tunic—.*

Helpless, the prisoners watched as the guard circled the car. Thomas clenched his fists. He looked around at his fellow captives, seeing the expressions of fear rising in their faces.

The sergeant walked over to the car. "C'mon out here, Leyton."

Without a word, Leyton jumped down from the boxcar. The sergeant pointed. "Need a guard by the engine. Get on up there."

An enormous breath escaped from Thomas's chest. He glanced at Thad, who began to grin. Thomas gave a weak smile in return. "That was too close."

One hour passed, then another. The sound of snoring mixed with the clang of hammers. Footsteps crunching among decaying stalks roused Thomas from his snooze. Squinting in the mid-afternoon sun, he could see two of the guards leaning on their muskets a few feet away. Bored, Thomas listened in on their conversation.

"You got a chaw?"

"Yeah, here."

"Be good to finally get home."

"Yeah, I'll be glad to be done with this duty."

"You're right about that. Guarding prisoners is hell. And I'm sick of all these train changes. You'd think we could just put them on one train and run 'em all the way through."

"At least we've only got to do it one more time, at the next station."

"How long 'til we get there?"

"Captain said it's only about three hours down the line. Should make it jes' before sunset."

"Good. Makes it a lot easier moving these Yanks in daylight."

Thomas's eyes shot open. Whipping his head around, he stared at Thad. It was obvious from his friend's expression that he had heard the guard's remark also.

Roberts grabbed Thomas's arm, whispering in a voice breaking in fear. "Did you hear that? We're going to change trains again before dark."

"I heard, I heard."

"What are we going to do? How are we going to get away if it's still light?"

Thomas waved his hand. "Shut up a minute and let me think." He glanced around, making a quick inspection of the guards and the train. He turned back to Thad. "Look, there's only two guards on top of each car. The rest of them stay in the boxcar behind the tender. We're in the last one. While we're moving, the guards are probably looking ahead.

We'll wait a half hour after we get started, then go ahead with the escape."

"But the Rebs will see us! You can't be certain they won't be looking back."

"I know. We need some kind of diversion." He glanced around. "Wait here. I'll be right back."

Keeping low and creeping along so as not to attract attention to himself, he worked his way over to some prisoners sitting a short distance away. "Hey, fellas. I need your help."

The soldiers eyed Thomas with suspicion. An older man with a reddish beard spat. "What kind of help?"

Thomas pointed to the rear of the train. "Back in our car, we've got a board loose. We were going to make a break for it tonight but we've found out we're going to change trains before it gets dark. So we're going to try it before we get to the next stop. We need something to take the guards' attention away from us."

The edges of the man's mouth curled in a scowl. "Why should we stick our necks out? Ain't going to do us no good."

Thomas pulled off his shoe. Retrieving a small roll of paper money, he held it out to Red Beard. "This is all I've got. I hid it from the Rebs to use for buying food. There's no telling how much we'll get fed in Georgia. You're welcome to it."

Red Beard reached for the greenbacks, but before he could take them, Thomas snatched the money back. "Do we have a deal?"

The soldier ran his fingers through his beard. "Well, we could stage a fight, or somethin'. All right, you got a deal." Thomas tossed him the money. "When do you want this to happen?"

"Any of you got a timepiece?"

A short, stocky man pulled a pocket watch from his vest. "I do."

"Good. Wait 'til thirty minutes after the train starts. That'll give us time to get ready. Whatever you do, make it loud. When we hear your commotion, we'll head out." Thomas held out his hand. "Thanks for your help."

Red Beard took his hand. "Hell, it'll be fun to see the Rebs' faces when they find out you're gone. Good luck."

Thomas crawled back to Thad, reaching him just as one of the guards bellowed. "Okay, Yanks. We're ready to go. Back on the train."

"What did they say?" Thad asked anxiously as he stood.

Thomas winked. "Tell you once we're back on board."

Climbing back into the boxcar, Thomas waited until the door was closed and bolted. As the train began to roll, he spoke in a low voice to the prisoners. "Boys, we're going to have to move quick. The Rebs are going to put us onto another train at the next station. We'll get there before dark. So we have to go now. I've talked to some men in one of the other cars. If those fellows do like they promised, we should be hearing a commotion from up ahead in a few minutes. Just as soon as they start, lower yourself down through the hole. There's a couple of steel rods just below the hole that you can grab onto. Use them to lower yourself down onto the tracks. It's going to be awful rough, but it's the only way. As soon as you're clear of the axle, just let go and drop down to the ties. Then lay still until the car gets a ways down the track. Once you're sure you're in the clear, head for the woods and keep going. It'll be best to travel at night. Stay out of sight during the day. Just keep heading north. Good luck to you all."

It seemed as though time had reversed itself as the soldiers waited for the promised distraction. Anxiety grew as long minutes ticked by. Thad wiped sweat from his neck. "Those bastards, they're not going to do it."

"Give it a little more time." Thomas was trying not to let his concern show, but he, too, was beginning to believe they had been let down.

A sound filtering through the wall caught Thomas's attention. He strained to hear as the noise began to rise. Loud, angry voices were coming from the car ahead of them. From above, they could hear footsteps as the guards moved forward.

Thomas was gleeful. "It's working." He gave Thad a long glance, then snatched up his jacket, exposing the opening. Donning his blouse, he sat down next to the hole, his feet dangling through the cavity. "Okay, then, here we go."

The ties flickered by underneath. Throwing Thad a quick salute, Thomas worked his way through the hole. Using a long metal bar fastened under the carriage for a handhold, he lowered himself down between the rails. The large iron wheels rolled along the top of the rails less than a yard away. Lowering his feet, he felt his bones rattling as his boots began to bang along the ties. Swallowing hard, he released his grip on the rod.

Sharp pain lanced through his back as he landed on one of the oak ties. Unable to control his movement, his momentum carried him toward the oncoming rear axle. For a brief, frightening moment, he felt as though he was going to bounce underneath the sharp flange of the wheel. Seconds later, the car passed from overhead, and he tumbled to a stop.

He lay still for several moments, his breath coming in short, explosive bursts. Turning onto his stomach, he lifted his head to look back toward the receding train. Thad was lying a several yards up the track, groaning and holding his knee. Raising himself up, Thomas could see beyond his friend as several more men appeared in the rail bed. He began to rise, watching as another pair of legs appeared under the car. Though hard to see because of the distance, he could make out the man lowering himself, then letting go. He started to turn away, then looked again. With horror, he watched as the soldier rolled onto the rail, the wheels slicing through his legs.

An un-Godly scream made the guards spin. Spotting the fugitives, they opened fire. Several men went down with the first volley. A loud screech tore through the air as the engine's brakes locked. Soldiers began to pour out of the front boxcar. Thomas yelled at Roberts. "Go, Thad! Make for the woods!" The two bounded off into the forest as musket balls tore through the trees above them.

As they crashed through the underbrush, Thad began to fall behind. After about fifteen minutes of frantic running, Thomas heard his friend cry out. Glancing back, he saw Roberts crumpled up on the ground, writhing in agony. Turning back, he rushed to Thad's side.

"My knee. I banged it up when I dropped from the train. It's all swoll up. Can't walk on it anymore."

"We've got keep moving, Thad. They're right on our tail." Thomas grasped Roberts by the arm, pulling him up. "Here, lean on me. I'll help you."

The pair managed only a few steps before Thad gasped in pain. "Please, I've got to stop."

Thomas helped Roberts over to a log. Sitting, Thad began to massage his knee. "Can't do it. You go on, Thomas. Leave me here."

"Boy, you are crazy if you think I'm going to let you get captured again."

Thad stared hard at Thomas. "Look, you and I know that if you try to help me, we'll both get caught. They're gaining on us, aren't they?"

Thomas could not look at Thad. He simply nodded.

"There's no way I'm going to outrun them with this bum knee. You have to leave me behind. And I want you to."

Thomas struggled with his feelings. Knowing he would surely be captured if he didn't keep on the move, the idea of abandoning his friend was abhorrent. Still, he realized that unless he did just that, he had no chance of escape.

"Come on, Thomas," said Thad. "There's no time to argue about this. Can't you see I'm right?"

Thomas kicked a pinecone, then turned back to face Thad. "Okay, I admit it. You're right. We're going to have to separate. Only way to throw them off. Maybe that way one of us will get away. But I'll try to pull them after me. I'll be able to move faster."

Thad stuck out his hand. "Agreed. Been a pleasure knowing you, pard. Hope to see you back up north someday."

Thomas gripped Thad's hand tightly. "Same here. You take care of yourself."

Thomas began to run. After traveling a short distance, he let out a yell. "This way, pard!" Sprinting up a hill, he called out again. *They ought to hear that.* Further and further he ran, every few minutes letting out another yell.

Reaching the crest of another hill, Thomas paused to catch his breath and listen. Oddly, the sound of pursuit seemed to be moving away from him. He stood hunched over, his hands on his knees, his chest heaving from his exertions. Suddenly the thud of a distant gunshot echoed through the trees. Standing upright, he cupped his hand to his ear. Another boom. *Damn, they must've got Thad.* Lowering his head, he murmured a small prayer for his friend.

After several moments, he glanced westward toward the setting sun. Looking around, he tried to get his bearings. *I've got to keep heading north by west.* Taking a deep breath, he set off down the hill. *North by west. That's where home is.*

Several hours later found him pushing through a hedge, emerging onto a narrow cart path. Silvery light filtered down through the bare branches of an old, knarled oak. A large rock lying half buried next to the tree looked like a good place to rest. Sitting on the stone, he glanced up at the rising moon. *Full and bright. That's good and bad. Easier for me to see by but also easier to be seen. Better stay off the roads. I'll have better cover if I move cross country.*

Crossing the path, he plunged into the woods. Before long, the moon disappeared behind high clouds. Figuring that as long as he traveled in a straight line, he should make good progress, even though he was unable to see very well. Several times he tripped over roots or stones. Coming down an embankment, he slipped on wet leaves, landing in a small creek. After stumbling along for what seemed to be hours, he was heartened to see the moon re-emerge once again. The moonlight revealed an open area ahead of him.

Might be another road. Maybe I better follow it a ways. Be a lot easier than traipsing through these woods. Making his way through a stand of pines, he came out onto the road next to a small boulder. He glanced around. Something about this place looked . . . familiar. The tree next to the rock—he had seen it before. The stone—he had sat on it! He slapped his forehead in disgust. *Damn it to hell! I've been going in circles. I'm right back where I started from.*

Leaning against the boulder, exhaustion rippled through his body. He began to sob uncontrollably. *What do I do now? I don't know which way to go. I don't want to die this close to my home.*

A noise from up the path caught his attention. Wiping his eyes with his sleeve, he squinted to see in the faint light. A horse and rider were moving toward him.

Thomas leapt behind the rock. Kneeling down low beside it, he peered out at the horseman. From his uniform, the rider looked to be an officer. The man's head was swaying to and fro, as though he were asleep.

Thomas quickly formed a plan. Several limbs of the oak looked as though they were heavy enough to support his weight. He began to climb, making his way out onto a large limb overhanging the path. Praying that the soldier would not notice him, he swung himself upright, preparing to leap.

Got to time this right. Sweat trickled down his back as the soldier came closer. As the horse plodded under the tree, Thomas swallowed hard and jumped. Crashing into the officer, the two of them plunged to the ground. Both men lay stunned by the impact for several moments.

Groggy, Thomas pulled himself to his feet. Picking up a broken length of tree limb, he staggered toward the soldier. Glancing around with alarm, the man reached for his buttoned holster, but before he could aim his heavy dragoon pistol, Thomas swung, knocking the weapon from his grip. With another swing, Thomas brought the club down on the officer's head. Standing over the man's limp body, he raised the limb high over his head, ready to deliver a killing blow.

He stood for a moment, trembling as his rage began to subside. Lowering the club, he tossed it aside, then knelt down next to the officer. Placing his hand over the man's mouth, he was relieved to feel a strong flow of breath. He proceeded to unbuckle the soldier's belt. *Don't want to kill you, friend. Just need your horse and gun.* Fastening the belt around his waist, he picked up the heavy revolver and slid it into the holster.

The officer's horse was grazing next to the boulder. Moving slowly, Thomas reached for the reins. Nostrils flared, the animal shook his head. "Don't you give me any trouble, fella'. The last horse I rode got me captured." The horse blinked, then lowered his head and resumed feeding.

Tying the reins to a branch, Thomas began to inspect the saddlebags. From inside one he pulled out a piece of salt pork wrapped in greasy paper. He gobbled it down, then took a swig from a canteen hanging from the pommel. Looking in the saddlebag again, he drew out an envelope and a folded piece of paper. Holding the letter up so it was illuminated by the moon, he read aloud: "Lieutenant Geoffrey Olmstead, Twelfth Georgia Infantry." Turning toward the unconscious officer, Thomas gave a mock salute. "Pleased to make your acquaintance, Lieutenant Olmstead. Sorry to mess up your furlough."

Dropping the envelope, he turned his attention to the folded paper. Opening it up, his face glowed with delight as he realized what it was. "A map, by God! Now maybe I can find my way home."

Chapter 57

William finished polishing the final button, then held up his uniform jacket. *Pretty worn, but Ma did a good job patching it.* Reaching for his kepi, he applied a little bootblack to the bill. *That should do it.* Donning the coat, he called out toward the bedroom. "Ma, I'm going out to hitch up the buggy."

Lucinda's voice came through the door. "Do you need help with that?"

Glancing at his stump, William replied, "Nope. I'm good."

Behind the closed bedroom door, Melissa was busy helping Lucinda adjust her wedding dress. "Oh, mother, it's beautiful."

Lucinda gazed at her reflection in a small looking glass hung on the wall. "Thank you, darling. I hope Jedidiah likes it."

"He's going to love it." Melissa giggled. "Of course, he probably won't be looking at the dress that much."

"Oh, you little imp." Lucinda gave her daughter a playful slap on the arm. She looked once more into the mirror. "Well, I guess I'm as ready as I'll ever be." Moving into the cabin's main room, she walked toward her rocker by the fireplace. She stared at the chair for a moment, then reconsidered. "I'd better not sit down. I might not be able to get up again."

Melissa smiled. "You're probably right. Those hoops would get caught." She let out a deep sigh. "I wish Stephen was here. I haven't heard from him for so long."

Standing next to the hearth, Lucinda reached up to the mantel, lifting a tintype of the family taken before Thomas's departure. The four people stared out from the picture with vacant expressions.

As William came in the door, she glanced up at him. "There's only one thing lacking that would make this the perfect day. I do wish your brother could be here with us now. I wonder how he is. There hasn't been a word about him in months."

"Don't worry, Ma. I'm sure he's fine. Remember, Thomas is a lot safer in a prison camp than out on a battlefield somewhere."

"I know. But all those stories about soldiers dying in those places. He could be sick . . . or worse."

William put his arm around his mother's shoulders. "Don't get yourself all worked up thinking bad things, Ma. Not today. Today is a happy day."

Lucinda turned and put her hand on William's cheek. "You are so much like your father. He always knew the right thing to say, too."

William blushed. "You never said that to me before. I wish I could remember him better. I was just a little kid when he left."

"He was mighty proud of you. And your brother. As I am." Her hand went to her face. Realizing it was wet, she looked around. "Oh, dear, I need a handkerchief."

Pulling a piece of white cloth from his jacket pocket, William dabbed at the moisture. "We'd best get a move on. Don't want to keep Mr. McCay waiting too long."

Taking his mother's hand, William escorted her to the waiting surrey. After helping Lucinda and Melissa into the rear, he climbed up into the front seat, collecting the reins in his right hand.

Lucinda leaned forward. "Do you need Melissa to help you drive?"

"Nope. I'll do fine. You two ladies just relax. You're in good hands. Well, at least one good hand." He laughed, then snapped the reins. As the buckboard started, William's thoughts turned with pride to how well he was adapting to the loss of his hand. Fully healed now, he was able to use his stump to hold items in place while he worked with the fingers of his other hand. He felt strength growing in his right arm.

As they trotted down the road toward Dahlonega, Lucinda reveled in the bright spring weather. Closing her eyes, she took in a deep breath. "Just smell that fresh air. Spring is such a wonderful time of year. Look at the beautiful dogwoods blooming." She gave Melissa's hand a squeeze. "I am so happy. Everything is perfect."

Coming into Dahlonega, William maneuvered the carriage to a small church just off the courthouse square. Jumping down, he looped the reins over a post, then rushed to the side of the buggy to assist his mother and sister as they stepped down. Lucinda took his arm, and the family entered the sanctuary.

Jedidiah McCay was engaged in conversation with the pastor. Turning when he heard the large oak door squeak, his face lit up as he watched Lucinda approach up the aisle.

William took his place as best man. Melissa stood beside Lucinda as maid of honor. The preacher smiled, then began. Jedidiah and Lucinda gazed into each other's eyes, barely hearing the words of the sermon. Impatient, the preacher cleared his throat with a loud "harrumph".

His face turning red, Jedidiah whispered an apology. The preacher nodded, then continued. "If anyone has good cause that these two should not be married, let him speak now, or forever hold his peace."

A squeak from the rear of the church caused Melissa to turn her head. Curious, she glanced back over the pews. A stranger was entering the sanctuary. An instant feeling of disgust swept over her as she looked at the matted beard and tattered clothing. Heads began to turn, and a murmur rose from the congregation as the vagabond walked slowly up the aisle.

And yet . . . there was something familiar about this man. The way he moved, his eyes . . . . Melissa gasped, her hand shooting up to her mouth as recognition dawned.

The astonishment on her daughter's face caused Lucinda to turn to see why. The gaunt figure continued to approach. Stopping a few feet from the altar, the man gazed at Lucinda without speaking, his face filling with emotion. Lucinda blinked several times, certain that her eyes were deceiving her.

The apparition raised his hand. "Hello, Mother."

The wedding party stared, unbelieving. Lucinda was the first to move. Rushing toward the man, she began to cry as she wrapped her arms around him. "Thomas! Oh, my dear Thomas."

William slapped his brother on the back. "How the hell did you get here, you old cuss?"

"Long story, Willie. Take a while to tell it." Thomas leaned down, kissing his mother on the cheek. "Looks like I've come in the middle of something important." Giving Lucinda another hug, he stepped back. "You all go on with what you're doing. I'll just sit over here."

After taking several minutes to regain their composure, Lucinda and Jedidiah stepped back to their place in front of the preacher. "Now, friends, if we can continue without further delay," he said, then resumed the wedding ceremony.

Upon being pronounced husband and wife, Jedidiah and Lucinda kissed, then turned to see Thomas standing, loudly applauding.

Climbing into the buggy, the wedding party rode up the street toward the Mercantile. McCay drove while Thomas followed on his horse. As they passed Isaac Stewart's house, William was unable to resist a sideways glance toward the building. A curtain moved in one of the upstairs windows. Blinking, he looked again. No other movement was visible. Memories of a night in that room long ago began to surface. He closed his eyes, trying to suppress the recollection.

Arriving at Jedidiah's store, they climbed the stairs to his rooms. As they entered, McCay disappeared into the next room, to reemerge moments later bearing a platter containing a glass of water, two loaves of bread and a large wedge of cheese with a small knife sticking in it. "Here you go, my boy," he said as he set it down on the table. "I expect that you're starving. Help yourself."

"Thanks. I am pretty hungry. Haven't eaten for a couple of days." Unbuckling his gun belt, Thomas hung it on the high back of one of the table chairs. He covered it with his tattered coat, then sat, pulling the tray close. Carving off a hunk of cheese, he proceeded to devour the food. Swallowing a piece of bread, he looked up to see Lucinda watching him intently, a broad smile on her face. Embarrassed, he lay the knife down. "Sorry, Mother. My table manners are kind of rusty right now. Didn't mean to be rude."

Lucinda smiled. "Please, son, go ahead and eat. Everyone here can see how famished you are."

Washing down the mouthful of bread, Thomas wiped his mouth with his sleeve. "I'm afraid I've interrupted your wedding party. I hope my presence doesn't hurt any plans you have for your honeymoon."

"Oh, shush," said Lucinda. "Jedidiah and I hadn't planned on taking a honeymoon now. We didn't think it appropriate with the war still on. Besides, your being here is the best wedding present in the world. It's been so long since you've been away up north. Finish eating, please. Then I want you to tell us all about what's been happening to you. I especially want to hear about your Miss Carroll."

Thomas sliced off another piece of bread. "Speaking of Stephanie, I need to let her know I'm all right. And Uncle Benjamin and Aunt Rebecca, too."

Jedidiah spoke up. "I'll try to get a message off tomorrow. Somehow we'll let them know up north that you're alive and well."

"Thanks, Mr. McCay. I'd be grateful." Between mouthfuls, Thomas related his experiences of the past few years. The group sat captivated as he told of his encounter with Constable Mattson, and of his life in the Union Army.

Lucinda was amused to note that Thomas became especially animated when talking about Stephanie Carroll. When he described his imprisonment at Belle Isle, she let out a gasp. "Oh, darling, it must have been so terrible there. I almost went out of my mind when I heard you had been captured."

A quizzical look passed over Thomas' face. "Stephanie wrote in a letter that you knew about me. How did you find out I was in prison?"

"Why, when William told me how you rescued him when he was wounded at Gettysburg."

Thomas gave William a glance laced with irritation. "So you told her, did you? After I asked you not to?"

William shrugged. "She already knew part of it. She got a letter from Uncle Benjamin about you joining the army. So I figured it was all right if she knew the rest."

Thomas stared at the tray of food for a few moments. "Well, I guess you did the right thing. Seeing as how Uncle Benjamin had already revealed my little secret." He turned to Lucinda. "I didn't want you to be worried about me. That's why I asked Willie not to tell you. I was afraid that if people around here heard that you had a son in the Union Army that it would cause you trouble."

"No one from around here knows about it," said Jedidiah. "And no one needs to know. Now, I for one would like to hear how you managed to get from Richmond to here."

Thomas resumed his narrative, keeping the family spellbound as he described his escape from the prison train and subsequent journey back to Dahlonega.

"Marvelous, my boy, simply marvelous," said McCay. "You certainly have had quite an adventure. We are all relieved that you managed to survive so many perils." He noticed that the cheese and bread had disappeared. "Would you like something more to eat?"

"No, thank you, sir. That was plenty for now." Standing, he moved over to a seat by the fireplace.

Melissa rose from her chair. Moving over to the table, she picked up the tray and knife. "Here, I'll clean this up." Taking the platter into the next room, she came back with a damp cloth and proceeded to wipe off the table, working her way around it. When she reached the chair on which Thomas's tattered coat was draped, she gave it a push to move it out of her way. The motion tipped the chair over. As it came crashing down, the belt holding the old dragoon pistol clattered to the floor.

Alarmed, Thomas jumped to his feet, sending his own chair flying. "For God's sake, be careful."

Surprised by the sudden anger in her brother's voice, Melissa rushed to retrieve the belt and coat. "I am so sorry, Thomas."

Calming down, Thomas picked up his chair and resumed his seat. "It's okay, 'Lissa. I'm sorry I yelled at you. It's just that that old gun has a hair trigger." He looked at Jedidiah. "Almost shot my foot off with it."

Lifting the coat, Melissa asked, "Where did you get this old thing?"

"Found it hanging in a barn where I hid one night. I didn't think it would be too good for me to be roaming around the countryside wearing a blue jacket, so I borrowed it."

"Borrowed it, you say? And I suppose you intend to return it?"

"Well, no. Leastwise not until I can find a good one."

Jedidiah chuckled. "I think we can take care of that." He pointed at the closet. "I've got an old duster in there. Not much to look at but it's better than that thing."

"I'll get it," said Melissa. Unlatching the closet, she hung the gun belt and tattered jacket on pegs inside. Looking through the clothing hung within, she selected a long, gray coat. She held it out. "Is this the one?"

"Yes, that's it. Try it on, Thomas."

Melissa handed the coat to her brother. Pulling it on, he laughed as it fell loose around his frame. "Little bit baggy right now. Need to put some weight back on."

"Some of Ma's good cooking will take care of that," said William.

"Yep. You and I both know the army doesn't feed you well." He poked his brother. "I'll just have to stay long enough to fatten up again before I go back."

Lucinda sat upright, looking shocked. "What do you mean, go back?"

"Back to the army. Up in Virginia."

"But there's no reason for you to go back. You're here with family. You need to stay."

"I can't stay. I enlisted for three years. I have an obligation."

"What about your obligation to your family?"

"Mother, don't you see? If I don't go back they'll list me as a deserter." The hurt in his mother's eyes pained Thomas. He turned to his brother. "Willie, help me out here. You know what I'm talking about."

William shrugged. "Lots of men deserting from our armies every day. Probably are from your army, too."

A glare. "Willie, come on. Who's side are you on?"

"Strange thing to say, Thomas. You're the one that's been wearing blue."

Thomas rolled his eyes. "Look, brother, I'm not going to get into a political discussion right at this moment. Do you agree with me or not?"

"Sorry." William turned to Lucinda. "He's right, Ma. When you give an oath, well, it's duty."

Tears were beginning to stream down Lucinda's face as she turned to her husband. "Oh, Jedidiah, can you please help me? Both my sons are defying me."

McCay took Lucinda's hand in his. "It's not defiance, darling. You've raised a couple of good, strong men. Thomas is right. He has to go back." He wiped her cheeks with a handkerchief. "It's not just a matter of duty. What about Stephanie? How can he return to her with a desertion charge hanging over him?"

Thomas walked over to Lucinda, laying his hand on her shoulder. "I'm sorry, Mother. Please don't cry. After all, I just got here. I'm not going to leave right away. Why don't we talk about this in few days?"

Lucinda wiped her tears. "All right. We'll talk later. But I'm going to do my best to convince you to stay."

William stood. "It's getting late. I think we should be heading back to the cabin," Grinning, he motioned toward Lucinda and Jedidiah. "And leave these two alone."

"Right you are, Willie," said Thomas. "It'll be nice to see the old home place—." He stopped as a series of loud clangs echoed from outside. "What's that noise?"

Jedidiah leapt to his feet. "It's the fire bell." Rushing over to the window, he tore back the curtains. A bright glow lit up the buildings below. He craned his neck to see up the street. "Oh, my God! It's the Stewart house. It's on fire!"

Chapter 58

Mary Stewart drew back the curtain on her bedroom window, watching the wedding party make its way up the street toward the Mercantile. Of particular interest was a bearded man in a tattered coat, riding behind the carriage. *Who is that with them?* With rising curiosity, she studied the man, trying to figure out why they would invite a tramp like that into their place. She sniffed. *When I get married only the best people will be there. No riff-raff.*

Spotting William looking toward the house, she stepped back, letting the curtain drop. Sitting on the edge of her bed, she crossed her arms, rubbing her hands up and down from elbow to shoulder. She glanced back over the covers. Her mind's eye created an image of her and William making passionate love.

A strange noise filtered up from downstairs. Sounded like someone going through a drawer. The banging got louder. Curious, she lifted an oil lamp from the dresser and crept down the stairs toward the kitchen.

Peering around the corner, she was startled to see the back door swinging open. Frightened now, she set the lamp on the table and softly latched the door. Turning, she let out a gasp. Standing behind her, illuminated in the flickering light of the lamp was Parker, hat clenched in both hands. "What the hell do you want?" she said, setting the lamp on the table. "I thought I told you never to come back here. How did you get in?"

Parker kept flipping his hat over and over. "Just reached in through the broken glass and opened the door. Simple." He grinned. "I've missed you, Mary. Ain't been the same without you."

"You mean you haven't found anyone else to play with. Isn't that it?"

"Oh, come on, Mary. Let's let bygones be bygones. I know you ain't got any for awhile, either. Come on, let's go upstairs."

"Go away!" Yanking open a drawer, Mary was searching for a knife when another voice startled her.

"Looks like I've walked into the middle of something." Jonathon Evans stepped into the light. "Hello, Mary. I hear you've missed me."

Feeling faint, Mary started to tremble.

413

Picking up the lamp, Jonathon began to wander through the house. Mary and Parker followed behind as he entered the parlor. "So where's your old man?"

Mary scowled. "Gone to join the Yankees. I don't know where he is and I don't care."

Evans stopped at a large desk. Setting the lamp on the top shelf, he proceeded to rifle through the drawers. "Stewart always was a bluebelly at heart." Pulling out a small bag of coins, he dropped them into his trouser pocket. He turned to Mary. "Got any more cash around? Need to buy some supplies."

Mary sidled up beside Jonathon, putting her arms around his neck. "Don't worry about that. You can stay here with me as long as you want. I'll get you anything you need." She pressed closer to him. "Anything."

Annoyed, Jonathon pulled her arms away, pushing her back. "I've no intention of staying around this shit-hole of a town any longer than I have to. I just need powder and ball, enough food to fill my saddlebags, and some information. Once I've got that, I'm getting the hell out of here."

"Then take me with you. Please, I'll go anywhere with you."

"Absolutely not. Last thing I need is a woman tagging along."

Stunned by this rejection, she tried to think of ways to bargain with him. What if she had what he wanted? "You said you needed information. Maybe I can help."

"Maybe you can. I need to know where someone is."

"If I find out for you, will you take me with you?

Evans stared at her for a few moments. "Depends."

Grasping for any hope, Mary asked, "Who are you looking for?"

"Why, your friend and mine." His eyes narrowed to slits. "William Marsh. That asshole humiliated me. Forced me out of the militia and got me run out of town. I've never forgotten that."

Parker could not resist the urge to jump in. "Marsh? I can tell you where he is. He's right here . . . in town. His Ma got married today to that storekeeper, McCay."

Mary glared at Parker.

Jonathon's brows shot up. "Let me get this straight. You saying that son of a bitch is here in town?"

Mary fingered Jonathon's lapel. "Yes, he's over at the Mercantile. They've all gone over to McCay's rooms over the store. I saw them myself, not more than two hours ago. The five of them are probably celebrating."

"Five? Who else is there?"

"Willie, his sister, Jedidiah and Lucinda. And some tramp. I don't know who he is. Just showed up. They knew him, though. Seemed real glad to invite him along."

"Marsh and McCay, I can take care of. No problem with the women either. But with a stranger—." He glanced at Parker. "Any idea who this 'tramp' might be?"

Parker nodded. "I know who he is. Saw him go in the church. Recognized him right away, even with the beard. He's Thomas Marsh."

A smile spread across Jonathon's face. "Well, well. The son what turned Yankee. This is getting better all the time. Got the whole clan in one place."

A faint sensation of guilt washed over Mary, but she quickly dismissed it. "What are you going to do?"

"What do you care? I thought you didn't have any particular affection for any of them."

"That entire family is nothing but scum," said Mary. "It would suit me fine if they all dropped off the face of the earth."

"Don't you worry, missy. I'll take care of William Marsh for you. He's going to be dead before the sun comes up. Him and that Yankee boy." Snatching up a paperweight, Jonathon threw it into the fireplace. It shattered, glass shards flying in all directions. "Once I finish that little piece of business, then I'm heading west. Easy pickin's out in California."

Mary rubbed Jonathon's arm. "Then you'll take me with you?"

Jonathon snorted. "Take you with me? Hell, no. I don't intend to drag any liabilities along with me."

"But, you . . . you said you would. If I had the information you needed."

"Didn't say anything of the sort. Besides, Parker was the one who told me where he was."

Mary felt rage boiling up. "Damn you. I've waited for you all these years. You can't throw me away like trash."

"Listen, missy, that's all you ever were. Trash. Just someone to waste a little time between the sheets with."

Balling her hands into fists, she began to beat on Jonathon's chest. "Damn you! Damn you to hell!"

Grabbing her wrists, he pulled her close to him. "You always were a little wildcat. That's what made you so much fun." Pinning her arms behind her, he crushed his mouth down on her lips.

Fighting to liberate herself, Mary wrenched one hand free. She lashed out, slapping him across the face. "You ignorant, filthy bastard. I can't believe how stupid I've been, pining for you all these years. You're no better than a mad dog. Even with only one hand, Willie Marsh is more of a man than you'll ever be."

Still holding one of Mary's arms, Evans gave it a jerk. "Marsh lost a hand?"

Parker spoke up. "He got himself wounded at Gettysburg. The doctors chopped his hand off."

"Interesting. Too bad they didn't chop off something else." He let out a guffaw.

Squeezing Mary's arm tighter, Evans yanked her close as he leered at her. "But before I take care of that little chore, I think a little pleasurin' is in order. Don't you think so, Parker?"

Mary squirmed in Jonathon's grasp, fighting to extricate herself. Laughing, Evans pulled her toward him, leaning down to kiss her once more. Lashing out with her free hand, she raked his face with her nails.

Hurt and enraged, Evans slapped her with the back of his hand. "Damn you, you little slut."

The impact sent Mary reeling. Finding herself freed from his grip, she whirled, rushing over to the sideboard.

"Watch it, Evans!" yelled Parker. She's got a gun in there."

Snatching the old pistol from the cabinet, Mary was in the act of spinning around when Jonathon charged toward her. Grabbing her by the wrists, he struggled with her for control of the weapon. Mary tried desperately to free herself from Jonathon's vise-like grip. The muzzle was almost even with his elbow when the gun went off. The ball whizzed past Parker's head, piercing the portrait of Julia Stewart.

Surprise on Jonathon's face turned quickly to rage. "Little bitch!" Swinging Mary around, he slammed her against the wall. Stunned, the pistol slipped from her fingers. She staggered toward the fireplace. Seizing her by the arm, Jonathon struck her with a back-handed slap. The blow sent Mary careening toward the hearth. Unable to catch herself, she fell, her forehead slamming into the sharp corner of the mantel. She let out a weak cry as she crumpled to the floor.

Jonathon stood panting for several moments, staring where Mary lay like a broken doll. Parker gaped. "Damn it, Evans. You've killed her."

Evans glanced at Parker, then looked back at Mary. Edging up to her, he poked her with the toe of his boot. There was no response. Kneeling down, he put his hand on her shoulder and pulled, rolling her onto her back. Blood seeped out of a deep laceration on her forehead. Her eyes were open, staring at him without seeing. Jonathon recoiled. A cold chill traveled down his spine. It was if her eyes had fixed on him, penetrating deep into his very soul.

Snatching up the lamp, he smashed it against the wall. Flaming oil spread across the floor, eager tendrils of flame searching out combustibles to feed upon. Jonathon stared at the growing blaze for several minutes. Parker let out a bellow. "Come on, Evans, we've got to get out of here!"

The sound of Parker's voice broke Jonathon's stupor. "Yeah— yeah. Let's go." Crashing through the locked front door, the pair fled around the corner and down an alley.

Mary stirred, coughing from the smoke swirling around her. Her eyes opened to behold raging columns of flame surrounding her. Sparks were falling on her dress, singeing multiple holes in the fabric. She slapped at the burns in a futile effort. Above the fireplace, the edges of the portrait began to char and curl as flickering orange fingers devoured the canvas. With horror, she watched as the paint forming Julia Stewart's face began to soften and flow. Mary's eyes widened with terror. Her mother's eyes seemed to glare out at her, the once beautiful smile contorting into an evil sneer. The roar of the flames sounded like laughter.

A scream exploded from Mary's lips. She spun around, searching for an avenue of escape. The inferno boiled all around her. Her lungs burned from the acrid smoke. She began to crawl. *There must be some way out. There has to be.*

Chapter 59

CLANG! CLANG! CLANG!

The bronze bell echoed out through the streets, its cry rousing the townsfolk, calling for help as tongues of fire licked through the windows of Isaac Stewart's home. A bucket brigade was rushed together, and within minutes a chain of men and women commenced pouring pails of water on the flames. Other lines worked to wet down adjacent buildings, in an attempt to protect them from flying cinders.

William ran from person to person, fear and desperation rising within him. "Where's Mary? Have you seen Mary Stewart?"

"Haven't seen anyone."

"Nope."

"Sorry, no."

William spied Sheriff Lane standing by the water pump, directing the rescue efforts. He rushed over. "I can't find Mary anywhere. Do you know where she is?"

Lane yelled at a man on the bucket line. "Damn it, be careful! The water belongs on the fire, not on the ground." He turned to William. "Sorry, boy. Been no sign of her. Haven't had a chance to look for her yet."

William pointed toward the house. "How did it start?"

"Don't know for sure. Jack over there said he saw someone running from the front of the house a few minutes before he noticed the fire. He's the one who rang the bell."

William ran back over to where Thomas stood passing water buckets. "I can't find Mary. No one's seen her anywhere." He seized his brother by the coat, dragging him out of the line. "You've got to help me find her."

Heads turned as a ghastly scream burst from within the blazing house. "Oh, my God!" cried William. "She's still in there!" Frantic, he began to peel off his jacket, cursing his awkwardness with the lack of two hands. Throwing the coat to the ground, he started toward the inferno.

Dropping the pail, Thomas stepped in front of William. "No, Willie! You can't!"

Face contorted with anxiety, William tried to sidestep his brother. "Get out of my way! I've got to get her out of there."

Thomas grabbed William by the arms. "It's too late! You'll only get yourself killed!"

Seeing the brothers struggling, Jedidiah rushed over. Thomas glanced at him. "Help me, Jedidiah. He's trying to go inside."

As McCay and Thomas wrestled to restrain him, William fought to free himself. "But—Mary—she's . . . . Let go, dammit!"

The will to resist drained from William. He glanced from Thomas to McCay, his expression full of torment. "Please, please help me get her out," he whispered.

"It's too late, son," said Jedidiah in a hushed tone. "She's gone."

Feeling the fight go out of William, Thomas and Jedidiah released their grip on him. Tears rolling down his soot-streaked face, he gazed at the blazing structure. He slumped to his knees in the dust, chest heaving as he began to weep. In a voice now barely audible, he continued to plead. "Please, somebody. Please get her out of there."

Flames now engulfed the entire building. Abandoning the water line, the townspeople moved back as intense heat poured out of the conflagration.

Lucinda knelt down beside her grieving son. "Oh, William, I am so sorry." Tenderly, she pulled his head to her breast. Burying his face into her, he sobbed uncontrollably. Mother and son rocked slowly as the fire raged on.

Someone in the crowd yelled out. "There she goes!" With a grinding roar, the upper floor sagged, then crashed down in a blossom of sparks. Bucket crews rushed back into line to extinguish flaming embers carried onto surrounding buildings by the hot wind.

For the next hour the townsfolk worked to beat down and contain the dwindling fire. William sat on the ground next to Lucinda, staring off into space. His emotions spent, he felt nothing but emptiness.

McCay pulled out his pocket watch. "One-fifteen." He glanced toward the remains of Stewart's house. Little was left that was recognizable. He reached down for Lucinda's hand. "Come on. There's nothing more we can do here. Let's go back to the store."

Tired and covered with soot, the family turned away from the glowing pile of rubble. As they made their way back up the street to the Mercantile, William looked back one last time. Flickering scarlet light reflected in his moist eyes.

Mary.

Chapter 60

Jedidiah, Lucinda, Melissa and the brothers dragged through the door of McCay's apartment. Still in a daze, William sat at the end of the table. Jedidiah collapsed into his big chair. Lucinda sat on the bed while Melissa found a seat next to the fireplace. Thomas leaned against a corner.

The ticking of the old schoolhouse clock on the wall grew loud in the silence. Long moments passed before Jedidiah raised himself up. "I for one could use a drink. Anyone else?" Straightening up, Thomas motioned for McCay to remain in his chair. "You stay there, Jedidiah. I'm closest. I'll get it."

"There's a bottle of claret in the cabinet next to the window," said Jedidiah as he resumed his seat. "There's some glasses in there, too."

"Okay." Thomas turned the handle, opening the door. The next second he crumpled to the floor, his temple bloodied from the impact of a gun butt.

Shocked by the sight of Thomas collapsing, the family began to rise, but before they could reach their feet, the door swung wide open. In sauntered Jonathon Evans, a Colt revolver in his hand and a sinister smile on his face. "Evenin' folks. You all just sit right down again before someone else gets hurt." Following him into the room was Parker, also brandishing a pistol.

Groaning, Thomas attempted to rise. Parker lashed out with his boot, catching him in the spine. Thomas fell back to the floor and lay still.

Vaulting from the edge of the bed, Lucinda rushed toward her injured son. "Hold it right there, lady," said Parker as he raised his revolver, leveling it at her.

Brought up short by the sight of the weapon, Lucinda hesitated a moment, then her eyes narrowed in anger and determination. "You can shoot me if you want, but I'm going to take care of my boy." With that, she knelt down next to Thomas, using her skirt to wipe the blood from his head.

Jonathon glanced at them. "Your boy? Can't be Willie . . . ah, this must be Thomas, the long lost brother." Glancing around the room, his gaze settled on William. "Well, well, well, if it isn't my old friend. How're you doin', Willie boy?"

Pushing up from the table, William stood. "Tolerable, Evans. Just tolerable. What are you doing back here?"

"Just came back to get reacquainted. Been a long time."

"Not long enough."

Jonathon stepped toward him, his pistol aimed for William's chest. "My, that's not very hospitable. Not at all. I would've thought you be glad to see me after all this time."

"Not likely." Laying the palm of his good hand on the table top, William leaned forward. "Why are you doing this?"

Jonathon's eyebrows rose in bogus dismay. "Don't you remember?" His expression hardened. "You humiliated me. Got me kicked out of the militia. You made me a laughing-stock. The livery owner fired me. No one else would give me a job. Acted like I was lower than dirt. All because of you."

"You brought that all on yourself. After you and Parker, here, tried to kill me."

"We weren't going to kill you. Just having a little fun, that's all."

"Beating me near to death—that was all in fun?"

"You deserved what you got." Jonathon's fingers brushed the hilt of Grainger's Bowie knife. "Just like you deserve what I'm going to give you now."

A low moan escaped from Thomas's lips. Parker kicked him again. "Keep quiet, asshole."

Furious, Lucinda leapt to her feet. "You leave him alone! He's already hurt bad enough!"

Snatching a handful of Lucinda's hair, Parker dragged her away from Thomas's prostrate body. As she shrieked in pain, he wrapped his arm around her neck, then shoved the muzzle of his revolver into her ear. "Lady, you'd best keep your trap shut."

Enraged, Jedidiah launched out of his chair. "Damn you, let her go! If you hurt her, I'll hunt you down and kill you, so help me!"

"I don't think so, storekeeper." Parker grinned, leveled his pistol at McCay, and fired.

Lucinda screamed, struggling in Parker's grip. "Jedidiah!"

A look of surprise on his face, McCay toppled backward toward the hearth, knocking over a set of fireplace tools. He gazed at his arm in stunned disbelief as a red stain began to spread across his white shirtsleeve.

Evans was livid. "What the hell did you do that for, you jackass?"

"Just getting even. He pulled a gun on me a while back. These folks have always been uppity, treating me like trash."

Kneeling down beside Jedidiah, Melissa inspected his wound while he gazed at her, his eyes glassed over in agony. Ripping a piece of cloth from her petticoat, she began to fashion a tourniquet around his arm. Looking about as she worked, she noticed the fireplace poker lying less than a foot away. She gave a furtive glance toward Evans and Parker. Satisfied that their attention was elsewhere at that moment, she slid the poker under the folds of her dress, then resumed work on Jedidiah's arm.

Recovering from the shock of seeing her husband shot, Lucinda resumed struggling to free herself from Parker's clutches. Holstering his pistol, he drew a knife from his belt. Pressing the tip of the blade against Lucinda's cheek, he snickered. "You'd best be still, Ma'am. I sure wouldn't want to see you get cut." Lucinda gave a small cry of pain as a trickle of blood rolled toward her chin.

Unable to bear any more, Melissa raised the poker and charged at Parker. "You louse! Leave my mother be!"

Shoving his pistol into his belt, Jonathon moved to intercept Melissa as she crossed the room. Grabbing her by the arm, he yanked the poker from her grip. As she resisted, he dragged her to the corner closet. Throwing her inside, he slammed the door shut and threw the latch. "That'll hold you for the time being, missy."

Taking advantage of Evans's distraction, William started around the table. Parker yelled. "Hold it right there, Marsh! Take another step, and I'll cut your Ma!" William halted in mid-step, unsure how to proceed.

Evans turned back toward William, flashing an evil grin as he fingered the handle of the Bowie knife. "Maybe I can get a little pleasurin' from her after I finish with you. Didn't get none from that Stewart bitch."

William's eyes shot wide open as the truth dawned on him. "Mary . . . the fire? YOU started the fire!" Hatred and rage boiled up. Without thinking, he charged at Evans, swinging with his good hand. "You God-damn—!"

Sidestepping, Evans slammed the poker across Williams's forehead. Stunned, he stumbled backward.

Jonathon waved his hand with a beckoning motion. "C'mon, Willie boy."

Swinging again, Evans struck William across the abdomen, doubling him up. Another blow to the shoulder sent him crashing to the floor.

Tossing away the poker, Evans straddled William's legs, standing over him as he fought to regain his senses. Kicking out, Evans brought the tip of his boot up under William's chin. Bright lights flashed inside his eyes as his head snapped back from the blow. Dazed, he lay stretched out on the floor.

Evans stared at William for several minutes, rubbing the hilt of the Bowie knife. Dropping to one knee, he grabbed William by the hair, wrenching his head back. "I made a promise to myself a long time back, boy. Now I aim to keep it."

Jonathon slowly drew the knife from its sheath. "Now, Willie boy, it's payback time." He raised the Bowie. "I'm going to enjoy slicing you into little pieces."

Groggy, unable to respond, William closed his eyes and waited for the end.

BOOM!

Staggered by the sudden blow, Jonathon froze in position for several seconds, a his face a mask of bewilderment. Releasing William's scalp, he raised his hand to wipe his jacket. It came away dyed scarlet. Glancing down, he could see blood oozing from a gaping cavity in the left side of his chest, the red stain spreading across his jacket like a flower. He studied his blood-covered hand for a moment, as if not comprehending. He rose to his feet, stood trembling for a second, then began to rotate. What he saw caused him to stare in shock and disbelief.

Melissa stood in the closet door, Thomas's heavy dragoon pistol clenched tight in both hands. Bluish smoke curled up toward the ceiling. She started shaking violently as she glared back at him, her cheeks streaked with tears welling from her eyes. Dropping the gun, she sank to the floor, sobbing hysterically.

With halting movement, Evans turned back, looking down at William. "Damn you—." The words were barely audible. Slipping from his grasp, the Bowie clattered to the pine floorboards. Knees buckling, he spiraled down, crashing to the floor. The impact dislodged the revolver from his belt. It bounced toward William, who strained to reach it.

Dropping his knife, Parker fumbled for his pistol. As he brought the weapon up, desperation galvanized Lucinda into action. Biting down hard into Parker's hand, she ripped away a deep shred of his flesh. He let out a howl of pain as Lucinda wrenched herself free of his grip and began to claw at his face. He swung the pistol, the barrel glancing off her skull, causing her to cry out. As she fell to the floor, she wrapped her arms around Parker's legs. Off balance, Parker pivoted, firing at William. The ball whizzed by his head, taking a notch out of his earlobe.

Snatching up the Colt, William rolled, cocking it. Before Parker could fire again, he pulled the trigger. The bullet caught Parker in the shoulder, spinning him around. Blood streamed down his arm as he kicked his way out of Lucinda's grasp and fled out the door.

Still dizzy from the blow to his head, William struggled to his feet. Staggering out the door, he peered into the darkness to see where Parker had. The whinny of a horse from nearby caught his attention. Running down the stairs, he turned the corner just in time to see a horse galloping down the street, Parker swaying to and fro as he fought to stay in the saddle. William fired a shot, but missed.

William dashed back up the stairs. Lucinda was crouched down next to McCay, busy redoing the bandage around his arm. Thomas was sitting on the floor, leaning against the wall, while Melissa dabbed at his head wound with a wet cloth, sobbing all the while. Thomas winced, then glanced up at his brother. "Did you get him?"

"No. I got off another shot, but he was wobbling so much I missed him. But he's hurt bad. Look, I need your horse. If I hurry I can catch him."

Lucinda spun around. "No! You can't. Let him go!"

William spun the cylinder on the pistol, checking the number of rounds left. "Ma, I've got to. He helped kill Mary, and I'm going to kill him."

"You're not going to kill anyone, son."

He whirled to see Sheriff Lane coming through the door. "Give me the gun, boy."

William stood motionless, his grip on the pistol tightening. Struggling to his feet, McCay held out his hand. "Give it to him, son. You've done enough for tonight. Let the sheriff take care of it."

Through her tears, Melissa pleaded. "Please, Willie. Don't do this."

William was gripped by uncertainty. "But he's the enemy."

Thomas pulled himself to his feet. "Your war is over, Willie. You've done enough fighting."

William looked from one face to another. A multitude of emotions raged within him. He didn't know what to do.

Lucinda stepped toward him. "William, I almost lost you tonight. I don't want to take another chance." She laid her hand on the revolver. "Now give him the gun."

Trembling, William turned the pistol over to Lane. "Don't you worry, Marsh," said the sheriff. We'll get him. Now you best stay here with your family." He looked over at Evan's body. "I'll send some men up to get him out of here." Glancing at McCay, he said, "And I'll send the doc over, too."

William shuffled over to the bed and sat down. The pain, fear and rage that had been pent up inside him began to subside. He felt as though someone had opened a spigot, draining him. Lucinda walked over, sitting next to him. He turned his head to look at her face. Taking his hand in hers, she gazed into his exhausted eyes. "It's over, son. It's all over."

Chapter 61

It was well after the noon hour by the time William rose from his pallet in the back room of the Mercantile. Stretching as he slowly sat up, he winced at a sharp pain lancing through his temple. Rubbing the spot, he took a slow inventory of the numerous aches throughout his body. With great effort, he pulled on his shirt and trousers. Lacing up his shoes, he walked up to the front of the store, unlatched the door and stepped outside. A sign proclaiming "Closed For Wedding" still swung on the exterior doorknob.

Sitting on the front steps, he peered around the town square. Covering his eye sockets with his hand, he rested his elbows on his knees, praying the headache would go away.

The sound of hoof beats coming to a stop caused him to look up. Shading his eyes from the sun, he saw Thomas staring down at him from the saddle.

Thomas lifted one leg, curling it around the pommel. "Afternoon, Willie. Finally decided to come out into the world?"

"Yeah, just woke up a little while ago."

"I left early to run some errands. Mother and Mr. McCay were awake when I came down, but Melissa was still asleep."

"No wonder. She was hysterical for a long time after shooting Evans."

"That's why Mother insisted she stay upstairs instead of sleeping in the other room down with us. This morning Mother said she kept waking up screaming."

William frowned. "I didn't know that. Haven't been upstairs yet. Hope she's okay." He pointed toward the upper floor. "How was Jedidiah doing when you left?"

"Doc was here this morning. Said he's going to be all right. It'll be a while before that arm heals up, though. But between Ma and 'Lissa he's got the best nurses in the county to take care of him."

"That's for sure." William rubbed his head again. "So where have you been?"

"Down to the telegraph office. Mr. McCay said I should talk to a man named Johnson there. Just trying to see if there was some way to get a message north to Stephanie. She still has no idea where I am."

"Can he do it?"

"Johnson says it won't be easy, but he thinks he can get it through. Says if the lines are still up he can relay a wire through to Lynchburg, Virginia. Fellow he knows there has been taking messages through the lines to Washington. Will probably take a while but he thinks he can get it through." Thomas studied William for a moment, noting the pale tint of his skin. "So how are you doing, little brother?"

"Head hurts. Can't seem to move much without something aching. Evans beat me up pretty good last night."

"All of us. My back feels like that freight train ran over it again." Dismounting, Thomas tied the reins to a pole, then sat down next to William. "Look, I didn't get much of a chance to say I'm sorry . . . about Mary, that is."

"Rather not talk about it." Lowering his head, William stared at the ground.

"All right, but I think I should tell you something. After I left the telegraph office I went to see Sheriff Lane. He's sent riders out looking for Parker, but there's been no sign of him yet. He also had some men searching what's left of the Stewart place. Hasn't found any sign of Mary's body. He figures the fire incinerated her."

William winced. "I said I don't want to hear any more about her."

Thomas put his hands up. "Okay, okay. I apologize. Just thought you should know."

William blinked a couple of times to clear his eyes. He looked up at Thomas. "Hey, I'm sorry. Didn't mean to snap at you. It's just going to take a while to get over a few things."

"I understand," said Thomas, placing his hand on William's shoulder. "We've all been through quite a lot." He sat beside William on the stair. "One thing I've learned, though. Let time do its work. Things will seem better after a while."

"You still planning to leave soon?"

"Not right away. But you know I have to go, Willie. This war still has a ways to run." Thomas motioned toward the stairs. "Mother still doesn't want me to go. But I have to. I figure to wait until Mr. McCay is back on his feet again. He asked me to stay to keep the store going while he's laid up. Course I think it's his way of keeping me around for awhile, to keep Mother happy. But once he's up to taking over again I'm heading out."

"You going right back to the army?"

"No, first I'm heading back to New Hampshire as quick as I can. Stephanie is waiting for me there. She's really something, Willie."

"She must be." Taking a deep breath, William slapped his knee. "I better get moving. Need to go down to the livery and get my horse. Got to go out to the farm to check the animals."

Thomas looked off across the square. "I'd stay away from there for a little bit. The liveryman is hopping mad. His prize mare was stolen sometime last night during all the excitement."

"Any of the other animals taken? What about ours?"

"No, just that one. The sheriff thought Parker took it at first, but he must have had his own horse tied up out back. Least ways that's where Lane found Evans's horse." Thomas pointed at his mount. "Why don't you take my horse? I'm going to be busy getting the store ready to reopen."

William glanced at the animal for a moment, then rose. Unwrapping the reins, he gave the horse a pat on its neck. "Thanks. I may be gone for awhile, though. May just go for a ride. I feel a need to be alone."

"Take all the time you need. I'll tell Mother where you've gone."

William mounted and began to ride up the street. Coming abreast of the remains of the Stewart house, he noticed two little boys busy rooting around in the ashes. Angered, he cantered up to them. "Get out of there, you little bastards!" Straightening up, the boys gawked at him for a moment, then took off running.

He gazed at the rubble and cursed the boys again. *They got no respect. It's like walking on a fresh grave.* Wisps of smoke still rose from a jumble of charred boards that had once been the staircase. Lowering his head, he closed his eyes, whispering a silent prayer. Then he yanked the reins to pull the horse's head around, and started along the street toward the edge of town.

Keeping the horse at a slow trot, he headed up the road toward the farm. Passing the gate to Greenfield, he glanced up toward the big house. The yard was overgrown with weeds, and the front columns were speckled with peeling paint. His thoughts turned to the day he had delivered Colonel Merrow's message to Henry's mother. The black of her mourning dress seemed to reflect in her grief-filled eyes. She had said nothing, just nodded when he handed her the packet. Then she had closed the door in his face.

William entertained a brief thought that he should go up to the house and pay his respects once more. He began to reach out to unlatch the gate, but drew back. *Not now. I can't right now.* He pointed the horse back up the road.

A few yards from the farm's fence line, he reined in. Sitting there, he stared at the cabin. From the barn he could hear the plaintive lowing of the cow. Turning his head, he looked at a once well-worn path that led off into the woods. Now it was thick with scraggly brush. Glancing at the house one more time, he turned the horse down the path.

Working his way through the underbrush, he emerged into a clearing. On a small hill overlooking a creek stood a majestic, ancient oak tree. Dismounting and tying the horse off, he undid a blanket from the back of his saddle.

Climbing the rise toward the oak, he spread out the blanket at its base, then lay down. Staring up through the tree limbs, he could pick out small reddish buds on the branch tips. *Won't be long till the leaves start coming out.* Birds twittered high in the branches. His chest heaved in a sigh. *Springtime. It'll be good to see green on the trees again.*

White clouds rolled across the sky. As they billowed and transformed, he imagined faces looking down at him. Faces of missing friends.

He reflected on how he had changed—how the war had changed him. He felt old. He began to notice a pain in his left hand. Strange how an extremity that no longer existed could hurt. He held his arm up, staring at the stump for several minutes. It felt as though someone was pushing red-hot pins into it. He gave his arm a shake. After a few minutes, the pain began to subside.

Changes. The changes weren't just physical. Something deeper had happened to him. He thought back to the burial detail after Second Manassas. The sights and smells had sickened him then. Now even the carnage he had witnessed at Gettysburg had little effect on him.

He felt so lost. He wished he could go back in time, to make his own changes. Redirect the flow of events to alter their outcome. He thought of Henry Merrow. Good old Henry, who always found something to laugh—and grouse—about. Then there was solid Gerald Fitzpatrick—he was the true backbone of the old company. And Colonel Merrow, who had always looked out for him. Where was he now? Was he still alive?

Evans. How could someone carry that much hate for so long? Where had that scoundrel disappeared to, only to show up on his mother's wedding day? And look what Evans's hatred has done. Even in death, he's going to keep haunting Melissa. Killing a man—going to take a long time to get over that. Especially for someone who's too squeamish to swat a bug. Thank God Ma is so strong. Melissa's going to need her as much as Jedidiah will. And no telling what troubles Thomas has waiting for him.

And Mary. He still could not bring himself to believe she was truly gone. What could he have done differently to make her love him the way he loved her? And he did love her, in spite of the terrible things she had said and done. Maybe if he had gotten to the fire a few minutes earlier. Could he have saved her? And if he had saved her, would that have been enough to open her heart to him? So many questions. Questions that now would never have an answer.

He gazed toward the creek. The gurgling sound of water splashing over the rocks was soothing. In his mind he went back. Back to a happier time. He imagined Melissa splashing around in the water, soaking the dress her mother had stitched for her. His soft laugh changed to a whimper. *She was so innocent back then.*

A sound born on the breeze brought him out of his reverie. Thunder? He scanned the distant hills for the source. The noise came like a dull thud echoing through the mountains. He squinted, as though that would help him hear better. Another thud. He rolled his eyes as he recognized the sound. Artillery, far in the distance. His eyelids closed. *We were all so innocent then.*

AFTERWORD

My first thoughts toward writing this book occurred after a conversation with my Aunt Cecil Costine of Lancaster, New Hampshire. Our family historian, who unfortunately has passed away, Cecil was the first to share with me the tale of two ancestors, brothers, who served on opposite sides during the American Civil War. That conflict has acquired many names over time: The War Between the States, the War of the Rebellion, The War of Northern Aggression, et cetera, et cetera. After learning about the division in my own family, one more name, the Brother's War, developed a much more personal meaning for me, and served as the foundation for this novel.

During the conflict, families both North and South were torn apart, much like the nation itself, as brothers, fathers, uncles and nephews chose opposite sides according to their beliefs and traditions. My own family's story begins with my great-great granduncle, Abel Cummings Marshall, who journeyed from the thick forests of Northern New Hampshire to the mountains of North Georgia to seek his fortune during the Dahlonega Gold Rush. There he met and married Lucinda Hawkins of South Carolina, who bore him four children; two boys and two girls. Abel disappears from all records prior to 1850—whether he died or simply abandoned his family is unknown. The youngest son, Cummings Marshall, traveled north to New Hampshire during the decade prior to the Civil War, while his older brother William Henry Marshall stayed in Dahlonega. William Henry joined the Dahlonega Volunteers, which eventually became Company "H" of Colonel James N. Ramsey's First Georgia Volunteers. When the regiment mustered out of service in March of 1862, William Henry reenlisted in Cobb's Legion of Cavalry, serving until the end of the war. As for his brother, in 1863 Cummings enlisted in the First New Hampshire Heavy Artillery, and was posted to Battery Reno, part of the ring of defensive forts surrounding Washington, D.C. In that fortification, Cummings saw little action, essentially sitting out the war.

My own intense interest in the War Between the States developed at an early age. As a child, I received a Marx Civil War play set as a

Christmas present, and spent many a day fighting desperate battles with the plastic soldiers. Over the years that set disappeared piece by piece through loss or destruction until it suffered complete extinction.

In my twenties I graduated to the "adult" version of battle recreation, joining a reenactment group that eventually became the Seventh Florida Infantry, a reconstitution of a unit that fought with the Confederate Army of Tennessee. Dressing in wool uniforms and carrying a nine-pound musket on my shoulder gave me a taste, albeit a limited one, of the hardships endured by the soldiers of both sides in that terrible conflict.

Though this is very much a work of fiction, I have tried to make the historical events as accurate as possible in the context of the story. Many details of the locales mentioned are accurate—for example, the bricks constructing the Dahlonega Courthouse actually do contain enough gold for them to "sparkle" in the sunlight. The "Old Man of the Mountains" watched the millennia pass from atop Cannon Mountain in New Hampshire's Franconia Notch until 2003, when the forces of nature finally caught up, causing the famous profile to tumble from its perch. Granite Staters, whether current or former, grieved his loss as one would feel the death of a family member.

The real Dahlonega Volunteers marched forth from Lumpkin County to join the First Georgia Volunteers in Macon at the beginning of April, 1861. Incidents that occurred to the company such as departing Dahlonega to the sound of anvils, the late arrival at Camp Oglethorpe in Macon and the resignation of Captain Alfred Harris due to old age are true. The mishap of the soldier tumbling from the top of the train during the trip from Pensacola to Richmond did actually happen, although it was a member of the Quitman Guards, Private Mark Brantley, who was killed instantly.

I have also tried to use authentic quotes where appropriate. The snippet of Governor Brown's speech to the First Georgia, Colonel Ramsey's remarks to the regiment before marching from Richmond to join the Army of the Northwest and Lt. Col. Clarke's admonishment to his men before leading the charge at Laurel Hill, while slightly paraphrased, contain their actual recorded utterances. William Marsh's letter complaining about General Robert E. Lee's failure at Cheat Mountain, while fictitious, does convey the prevailing opinion that Lee's soldierly skills were overrated. The nickname "Granny Lee" was pinned on the general at that time, and it would be months before

Lee's legend as the South's most audacious and beloved commander would begin to take root.

The chronology of events for the First Georgia follows the actual timeline of the regiment until it was mustered out of service in March of 1862. From that date on, my First Georgia is entirely fictional, though I have placed it with other Georgia regiments in General Thomas J. "Stonewall" Jackson's Second Corps of the Army of Northern Virginia. For the August 28, 1862, Battle of Second Manassas, and during Lee's invasion of Pennsylvania in 1863, I have placed Colonel Merrow's regiment with the Evans/Lawton/Gordon Georgia Brigade, though for the Battle of Fredericksburg, I have "detached" the regiment and placed it with other troops at the point of Union General George Gordon Meade's breakthrough. During Second Manassas on August 28, 1862, William's regiment is part of Jackson's "Right Wing" opposing a brigade of Wisconsin and Indiana troops, the famed "Black Hats" who would earn the moniker of the "Iron Brigade" for their stand during the fight. The spectacular stand at Fredericksburg of Major John Pelham, who stalled the Union advance for nearly an hour with only two artillery pieces, did actually occur. Though the conversations during the fire at Wrightsville, Pennsylvania, are fictitious, troops from General Gordon's Georgia Brigade did work side by side with townspeople to contain the blaze which threatened the village.

On July 1, 1863, Gordon's brigade, now part of General Jubal A. Early's Division of General Richard S. Ewell's Second Corps, was involved in the initial Confederate attacks, and was subsequently dispatched to positions along the York Turnpike to intercept a reported advance of Federal cavalry (which turned out to be false). Later, Gordon's men were sent to participate in an attack on Union-held Cemetery Hill, but were halted before commencing their advance. The brigade was not engaged for the rest of the battle. The fights involving Steuart's and Smith's brigades on Culp's Hill on the morning of July 3 did occur, but the use of the Volunteers as a "flying company" is invented.

Though my ancestor Cummings Marshall was actually in the First New Hampshire Heavy Artillery, in the storyline I have chosen to place his fictional counterpart Thomas Marsh in the First New Hampshire Light Artillery, commanded by Captain Frederick M. Edgell, which actually was posted July 2 and 3 on Cemetery Hill, where the battery fired 353 rounds at the enemy. The description of prison camp at Belle Isle, where many Union captives from Gettysburg ended up, comes from official reports and other records. On March 2, 1864, a cavalry raid with the aim of liberating the prisoners failed, but caused an escalation of demands by Richmond citizens that Belle Isle be emptied and the prisoners sent far away. The result was the transportation of the soldiers to the infamous Camp Sumter in Georgia, better known as Andersonville.

Baxter's Guerrillas, on the other hand, is a purely fictional unit. Partisan troops, such as McNeill's Rangers, under Captain John H. McNeill, and later his son, Captain Jesse C. McNeill; and Mosby's Raiders, led by Colonel John Singleton Mosby, did operate within the state of Virginia, but were not known for changing uniforms—rather, Baxter's bushwackers are an amalgamation of several guerrilla groups, such as William T. "Bloody Bill" Anderson's Missouri partisans.

I am extremely indebted to everyone who contributed their time, expertise and patience in the completion of this work. Several people read portions of the manuscript and offered valuable suggestions, including Clarice Hinson, Cynthia Coan, George and Muriel Hamilton, and Linda Stephens. I extend a special thank you to W. Hunter Lesser, author of *Rebels at the Gate: Lee and McClellan on the Front Line of a Nation Divided*, whose help in research for this novel also extended to my non-fiction book about the First Georgia Volunteer Infantry. Others who offered help and insight include Susan Ledford and Dr. David Wiggins. For those whose names I have unintentionally omitted, my apologies, and thanks also for your help and support. Any omissions or errors of fact or opinion are mine alone.

The most important asset a writer can have is a wife who is a friend, supporter, proofreader and all around helpmate. I am fortunate to have all of these and more in my wife Cathy. To her, this work is lovingly dedicated.

GEORGE WINSTON MARTIN

Hendersonville, NC
November, 2012

ABOUT THE AUTHOR

George Winston Martin was born in Northern New Hampshire, resided for thirty years in Florida and now calls Western North Carolina home, along with his wife and twin daughters. He is a graduate of Embry-Riddle Aeronautical University of Daytona Beach, Florida.

Martin participated in American Civil War reenactments for eighteen years as a member of the Seventh Florida Infantry (recreated). One son of his great-great-grandfather's brother was a private in the First Georgia Volunteer Infantry (C.S.A.), while a second son served in the First New Hampshire Heavy Artillery (U.S.A.).

Martin's first book, "*I Will Give Them One More Shot: Ramsey's 1st Regiment Georgia Volunteers,*" was the recipient of the 2012 "Award for Excellence in Research Using the Holdings of An Archives," presented by the Georgia Historical Records Advisory Board (GHRAB).

Made in the USA
Charleston, SC
17 June 2016